Soul Mates

When Romance and Reincarnation Collide

Liz Morrison

Brighton Publishing LLC
435 N. Harris Drive
Mesa, AZ 85203

Soul Mates
When Romance and Reincarnation Collide

Liz Morrison

Brighton Publishing LLC
435 N. Harris Drive
Mesa, AZ 85203
www.BrightonPublishing.com

ISBN 13: 978-1-62183-240-9
ISBN 10: 1-621-83240-6

Copyright © 2014
Printed in the United States of America

First Edition

Cover Design: Tom Rodriguez

All rights reserved. This is a work of fiction. All the characters in this book are fictitious and the creation of the author's imagination. Any resemblance to other characters or to persons living or dead is purely coincidental. No part of this publication may be reproduced or transmitted in any form or by any means, electronic or mechanical, including photocopy, recording, or any information storage retrieval system, without permission in writing from the copyright owner.

Acknowledgements

To Rick, Lindsey, Carley, Holly, and R.J. Morrison. What can I say? You guys are the best; thanks for your support.

To my publisher, Kathie McGuire, and Brighton Publishing for giving me and my book a chance; your support and guidance were invaluable.

To Connie Hayes, an ace with a red pen; thank you for your mad grammar skills and your willingness to read and re-read again (and again).

To my daughter, Lindsey Morrison, and my dad, Don Costanzo, for assisting me in cutting 20,000 words—that's a lot of words! And, Dad, thanks for reading your first historical/contemporary young adult romance novel…more to come.

To my mom, Shirley Costanzo, and her mom, Grandma Dressler; your love of a good romance novel is generational. And, Mom, thanks for being my biggest fan.

To Jack Chadwick, my high school history teacher who inspired my love of history by making it a story I wanted to keep reading—thank you, Mr. Chadwick.

To Becky Neil and the students of the Parkway South HS Book Club, Mary Ann McFarland and the students of the Parkway West HS Book Club, Joni Patton and the Parkway North HS History Club, and Kim Bay and her 8th Grade ELA students at Parkway Central MS; thanks for letting me share my story and my passion for the past with all of you. Your input and support was really appreciated.

To my extended family and my friends (Facebook Friends included); your support in person and online makes me even more excited for my book to be published—I hope you love it.

Finally, a shout out to the people at Google Earth who made it possible for me to see the world from my laptop, to all the people who contributed to preserving the history of World War I on the World Wide Web, and to the St. Louis County Public Library for providing great resources in print.

Dedications

Dedicated to the remembrance of the 8.5 million soldiers killed in action, the 21 million soldiers wounded in action, the 7.7 million soldiers missing in action, and the approximately 10 million civilians who died from the use of total warfare in what U.S. President Woodrow Wilson called "the war to end all wars"; the Great War for Civilization 1914 – 1918 (World War I).

Preface

Life. Death. Rebirth

For the past few months, my life had been a series of questions.

Was it possible a person could be born again? Was it possible some dreams are not dreams at all, but memories of a past life? Was it possible that I, Charlotte Susan Longley of St. Louis, Missouri, could have been given a second life to finish unfinished business from a previous life? Was it possible my unfinished business was intertwined with someone else's unfinished business?

If it was possible, then what was the probability those two lives would come together again? Could they pick up where they left off? Could they start over, based on who they are today?

I knew my study abroad in France would be life-changing.

I had no idea the adventure would lead me to a cemetery—a cemetery where I searched for a tombstone…a tombstone that could very well be mine.

Maybe, I decided, *some questions should be left unanswered.*

Chapter One

CHARLIE

The line of people waiting to pass through security at International Departures snaked around the stanchions. For possibly the hundredth time, I checked to make sure I had my driver's license and passport.

Glancing at my phone, I read the text from Katie and Ryan. They were ahead of me in the security line. At almost six feet tall, Katie looked like a model and was hard to miss in any crowd. I was relieved to see her, but the anxious feeling in my stomach didn't subside.

The whole thing was surreal—we were actually going to France for a semester abroad.

My head hurt. Rubbing my temples, I was overwhelmed by the feeling of sadness and loss that had plagued me for the last year. My mom and dad were afraid to let me go, yet they were afraid not to let me go. Luckily, Ryan and Katie agreed to spend the summer and first semester of our senior year with me in Rouen. They knew something wasn't right with me, and Rouen, France, seemed to be the answer.

The line slowly moved forward as each person handed the TSA agent a passport. One step…two steps…we trudged along. I rubbed my forehead as the pain increased.

The men walked in a line. Many stumbled as they clutched the shoulder of the soldier preceding them. White gauze covered their eyes, indicating some medical treatment had been provided at the front. I noticed the gas masks slung over their shoulders. The soldiers must not have had time to put on their masks before the mustard gas seeped into their trenches.

Clutching my hands, I stared at the heavens. There wasn't much to see, really, as the night sky was thick with smoke from the battle. From my location, I couldn't tell whether the soldiers were British, American, or French. I prayed William was not among their ranks, and yet I prayed I'd see him again. I wonder how God handles conflicting prayers.

"Charlotte," Lilly commanded, "it's time to get to work."

"Miss? Miss?" the TSA agent repeated.

He sounded frustrated. He must have been trying to get my attention for a while.

I don't remember walking to the podium. Sweat trickled down the back of my neck. My head continued to pound.

"Sorry," I said as I handed him my passport, ticket, and driver's license.

"Here you go," he responded as he handed them back. "Are you okay?"

"Yeah," I replied. "I'm just a little nervous, I guess. This is my first international flight."

The zombie-trance thing obviously wasn't appreciated at International Departures.

"Lots of people feel that way," he replied with a smile. "You'd better get moving. People with places to go hate it when the line slows down, even for a pretty girl like you."

"Thanks," I said, returning the smile.

The line moved pretty quickly—no time for another Throwback Thursday moment. Shaking my head, I tried to push the vision…memory—whatever the hell it was—out of my head.

As I approached the conveyor belt and scanner, I saw Ryan putting on his shoes. He shoved his glasses up his nose, pushed the hair out of his eyes, and glanced right at me.

I waved, signaling for him to wait for me. He gave an awkward wave as he slid into his Sperrys. *Ryan's so cute, if a girl is into nerdy, kind-of-preppy guys,* I mused.

"Hey, you're here," I said, as I hugged my friends.

"You know what I like most about Charlie?" Ryan remarked to Katie. "Her grasp of the obvious. It's really pretty amazing."

"Ha, ha," I replied.

Katie linked her arm in mine as we walked down the terminal to our departure gate.

"Don't take this the wrong way, but you look like hell," she told me. Then she added, "Well, as much as you ever look like hell."

"Headache," I replied, "I've got some Advil in my bag. I just need a good dose."

She gave me the look. "You sure you're okay?"

"Yes."

Katie and Ryan both knew about my issues. In fact, they'd started watching some reality show on reincarnation called *The Ghost Inside My Child* or something. Not much into reincarnation.

A few other students approached our group. "Hey, I'm Mike from West High. This is Libby and Holly. Libby goes to Central, and Holly goes to North. I think you guys are staying with us in Rouen."

"I'd like you to meet the medical team who will be working with us at Washington University Base Hospital Twenty-One. The hospital is located on the outskirts of Rouen."

"Charlie."

I could tell by the tone of Katie's voice she'd repeated my name several times.

"Oh, sorry. I have a headache," I said quickly. "I'm Charlie. We go to South." I kind of smiled. "I guess you already knew that."

I rubbed my temples and closed my eyes. Throwback Thursday—it was starting to be debilitating. Maybe going to Rouen was part of the problem...not the solution.

We heard an announcement over the loudspeaker. "Air France Flight 681 is now ready for passenger boarding."

For better or for worse, I was going to Rouen.

WILLIAM

I continued to search the web. Site after site listed endless possibilities for language study, cultural immersion, community service, and working holidays abroad. I could backpack through Europe or become a licensed snowboard instructor in Canada.

The opportunities were endless, but my patience wasn't. *Maybe a gap year isn't for me,* I silently reasoned. *Possibly going straight to university from Eton is the right thing to do.*

Right, then. One last click and then I'd give up.

"University it'll be," I said to myself.

One last scan, and there it was—a semi-intensive language program with an opportunity to teach English to French businessmen in Rouen, France.

How ironic, I thought. *Rouen has been at the forefront of my thoughts for several weeks. Why didn't I think to search by location?*

Rouen had a family connection. My great-great grandfather's younger brother, William James Harrington, had died from a sniper's bullet in November of 1918. He was buried in the St. Sever Cemetery in Rouen.

Rouen—a destination my parents would agree was appropriate for my future.

Picking up my mobile, I dialed home. If my mum supported my gap-year plan, it was a sure thing my dad would support it, too.

"Sophia Harrington."

"Hello, Mum. It's your favorite son."

"Hello, Wills." I could hear the smile in my mother's voice. "Let me guess. You have a brilliant idea for your gap year, and you hope to gain my support before you talk to your dad. Or, you'd like me to talk to your dad after you convince me your idea is brilliant."

"Mummy," I replied with a hint of sarcasm, "I was ringing to check on your health."

"And..." the smiling voice responded.

"Right, then," I replied. "Rouen, France. The experience is a semi-intensive language program with an opportunity to teach English. The fee for the class is waived if I teach French businessmen conversational English. The program includes boarding on site. The added bonus is the ability to research the life and death of my namesake. I'll send you the link, so you can review the opportunity."

I continued, "I have a strange feeling I need to go to Rouen. I feel compelled to go right now. I feel like if I don't go soon, I'll miss something important."

"Wills, are you having the dreams again?" my mum spoke quietly into the phone.

"Yes," I replied. "More intense and more real than I remember. I wake up and have a hard time separating the dreams from reality. I think great-great-Uncle William wants me to discover something about his life or death, and he wants me to go now."

A long pause followed. "Send the link, and I'll review the opportunity with your father. William was his great-uncle, after all."

"I love you, Wills." The smile was back in her voice. "This is a brilliant plan; a perfect way to spend your gap year."

"Thanks, Mum. I'll send you the link. Cheers, then."

My shoulders tensed. I felt as if a momentous event was about to occur, and if I didn't hurry, I was going to miss it.

Dropping my head back, I stared at the ceiling. *Damn dreams,* I fretted.

A loud knock startled me back to the present.

"Hey, Wills," the jovial voice of my best mate Andrew followed the knock.

Andrew entered the room with his usual enthusiasm. I must have appeared especially glum, because he noticed.

"Hey, old chap, what's got you down? The other blokes are wondering where you've been hiding. I was directed to request your presence for a game of football." Sitting on my bed, Andrew waited for my decision.

Though Andrew might think I was bonkers, it was time to discuss my dilemma.

"Andrew, what I'm going to tell you makes me a rather odd fish. You have the dubious honor of being the one person outside of the Harrington family with whom I'm sharing my secret." I paused briefly. "I trust you not to judge."

Andrew lounged on my bed. His eyes were closed and he had his arms behind his head. It was Andrew's listening position, the position he'd assumed since we were first-year boys.

I tossed a book at his head; perfect shot. Andrew sprang up, "Bloody hell! I thought you wanted me to listen."

"Sorry," I laughed. "I need you to read the book jacket."

"Right, then. *Soul Survivor: The Reincarnation of a World War II Fighter Pilot.*"

While Andrew read the book jacket, I waited impatiently for his response. "Well, that's rather interesting," Andrew murmured more to himself than to me, "a book about a little kid who apparently is a reincarnated Yank fighter pilot from World War II."

Andrew gazed at me quizzically, "So you think you're James Leininger. Yes, old chap, you are an odd fish; one sandwich short of a picnic."

"Do you think it's possible?" I asked cautiously.

"That you're James Leininger? Absolutely not," he retorted.

I threw a pair of rolled socks, hitting him in the head. "Reincarnation. Do you think it is possible for a soul to survive? Do you think someone could be reincarnated?"

"Hmm…" he pondered. "It seems possible. Is it probable? I don't know…I guess it could happen. I know it's part of some belief systems, so other blokes think it's possible."

Soul Mates ~ Liz Morrison

I slowly exhaled. Sharing my strange history with Andrew was harder than I'd imagined. I'd hoped to convince him to join me in my gap-year experience. This might be intriguing enough to convince him to ditch his plans and join me in Rouen.

Andrew was propped on the pillow, waiting for me to begin. *Should I show Andrew my sketchbook, or should I begin at the beginning?* I stretched my neck back and contemplated the ceiling again. Beginning at the beginning seemed to be the best course of action.

"Right. I started talking at the age of three. My first words were, 'Where's Charlotte?' According to my mother, this struck her and my dad as odd, because no one in the family was named Charlotte. First, my mum thought I'd heard the name on the telly, but she could find no evidence. She told me I walked around picking flowers, saying, 'Member Charlotte.' They videotaped me talking about Charlotte. I told them Charlotte was my girl.

"They also recorded me singing, '*Bombed last night, and bombed the night before; going to get bombed tonight, if we never get bombed anymore. When we're bombed, we're scared as we can be; can't stop the bombing from old higher Germany.*'"

I glanced at Andrew. His eyes remained closed.

I continued with the story. "I drew lots of pictures—pictures of battles. Mostly the pictures had men apparently stuck on barbed wire, or hiding in ditches. There were pictures of men on horses being slaughtered by men with machine guns. Some pictures looked like a hospital, with rows and rows of beds. Many of the pictures included a girl."

"Was she pretty? Do you have the drawings?" Andrew asked.

"Well, it's hard to tell," I replied somewhat sarcastically, "I was four or five years old. Mostly, it was a head on a stick with lots of brown and yellow hair and really big teeth. Yes, my parents saved all of the drawings. Other questions?"

"I'm sound," Andrew replied.

"As my parents recall, the nightmares began at the same time as the drawings. My tormented screams woke them up in the night. Mostly I shouted, 'Gas! Gas! Gas!' or 'Down! Stay Down!'

"A psychiatrist described my actions as post-traumatic stress syndrome, similar to the experience of soldiers returning from the first Gulf War. The good doctor couldn't explain why a four-year-old had symptoms similar to a battle-scarred veteran. My parents didn't know what to do. At about this time, my family went on holiday to my dad's ancestral home—you know, the one in Brighton?" I paused and waited for a response.

"Yes, I remember."

"My parents shared the story with the family. Grandmum was interested in the story. She believed one of her father's brothers died in the Great War. She also remembered my name, William James Harrington, was the name of his deceased brother.

"Grandmum found an old photo album with a photograph of William James Harrington, my great-great-uncle, who died in Rouen, France, in November of 1918."

"Are you named after the bloke?" queried Andrew.

"That's what my parents say," I replied. "My mum showed me the photograph of William James Harrington, and I abruptly stopped drawing gruesome images from the Great War. I also stopped having nightmares…until now."

"Until now?" Andrew repeated.

"About a month ago, they started again…vivid dreams of a soldier's life in World War I. The dreams have pretty intense battles scenes. It's like playing *Call of Duty,* but with really high-def graphics. When I wake up, it feels like a memory, not a dream. And there's the girl…Charlotte. Whatever this is, it's somehow connected to Rouen."

I paused for a moment, waiting anxiously for Andrew's response.

"Basically, you believe you're reincarnated from the soul of your great-great-uncle, who was in World War I," he summarized.

"It's most likely the story unfolded in Rouen, and there's a fit bird named Charlotte somehow involved."

"Well, you've summed it up quite nicely," I said.

"Hmmm," Andrew stated. "That explains your mum's phone call, checking to see if I was interested in spending my gap year with you in Rouen. I did have my heart set on working a tanker across the Atlantic. Instead, it appears we'll teach French businessmen English and partake in French language immersion classes...oh, and lest I forget...participate in ghost hunting. That's not bad."

We were going to Rouen.

Chapter Two

CHARLIE

Staring into the blackness out of the small window next to where I was resting my head, I wondered how many other planes might be in the sky tonight. I remembered seeing a YouTube video illustrating flight paths—so many patterns of light streaking across the sky. It made me feel insignificant, and yet it also made anything seem possible.

I readjusted the pillow that I'd placed between my head and the window frame and considered pulling down the small shade, but I liked looking into the pure black of the night sky.

My mind wandered as I slowly drifted to sleep. *Are the little windows on airplanes called portals, like the windows on ships?* I asked myself. *I wonder how many ships are sailing below me, across the Atlantic Ocean.*

Why was I thinking about ships? I closed my eyes, pulled my blanket to my chin, and nestled into my pillow.

The smell of the ocean assailed my senses as we waited patiently on deck of St. Paul, an older ship from the White Star Line. Though I didn't share my fear with my companions, I sincerely hoped our ship didn't meet the same fate as Lusitania. And though my companions said nothing, they probably shared my fears.

My double-breasted military-style dark-blue coat covered my blue serge dress, providing protection against the elements. A representative from the Red Cross had issued our uniforms upon boarding St. Paul. I'd immediately changed from my civilian clothes. Though it was mid-May, the breeze on deck was quite chilly. My coat kept me nice and warm. Some of the girls thought the ensemble was unflattering. It gave us a certain measure of protection against the unwanted and unsolicited attention of young men. Personally, I liked my new uniform.

"Charlotte! Charlotte! Come join us!" Lilly shouted, waving me toward a small group of nurses posed for a photograph. I adjusted my blue felt hat to a flattering angle as I stood with the other girls.

I leaned over the rail of the deck and studied the New York City skyline. So many changes had happened to me since April 6th, the day the United States declared war against the Central Powers.

It seemed impossible that only a month earlier, my father arrived home from Washington University's School of Medicine and explained how he'd secured me, a seventeen-year-old, a position as a nurse with a team of doctors and nurses traveling to France, at the request of our British allies.

Just two nights ago, our unit attended a farewell service at St. Louis' Christ Church Cathedral. Then we'd traveled across the country by train, arriving in New York City to travel across the ocean to join our allies. I couldn't believe I, Charlotte Alexandria Rawlings, was part of the war effort. As we prepared for departure, I prayed I was up to the challenge.

The ship steamed away from the shore. I took a deep breath to calm the butterflies in my stomach.

The voyage across the Atlantic would take eight days...eight days of traveling through water known to be infested by German U-boats. I hated fearing a U-boat attack, and I hated not being able to share my fears.

The portholes were screwed shut and covered so no light from the cabin could be seen by the Germans. The blackened and secured portholes made the cabin quite dim and stuffy. The secured portholes provided a poignant reminder of the perils of crossing the U-boat infested Atlantic. Rather than providing comfort, it fed my fears. Glancing around the cabin, I tried to picture St. Paul in her glory days as a passenger ship, steaming swiftly across the Atlantic. It would have been lovely to be a passenger on such a ship.

"Ladies and gentlemen," the captain announced over the jet's PA system, "we are experiencing some turbulence. Please return to your seats and ensure your seat belts are fastened."

Rubbing my eyes, I was startled to see Katie and Ryan. My dream had seemed real…

My dress was stunning, but the looking glass reflected the strain of the past two weeks. Tomorrow we'd travel from Southampton to Le Havre. After two weeks of training, the Brits believed I was ready for my duties in Rouen. I hoped they were correct in their assumption.

"Charlotte," Lilly called from the hallway, "we don't want to be late."

"Lilly, you look absolutely lovely," I told my friend. The dress flattered Lilly's robust figure. Lilly laughed, replying, "You look rather stunning yourself."

We descended the ornate staircase, arms linked, greeting a crowd of grateful Englishmen.

I whispered to Lilly, "As an American girl, being around members of the British upper class is rather daunting. They do, however, seem to take their responsibility to the British Empire very seriously."

"Yes, they do," Lilly replied. "The family with whom we're staying has four sons serving as officers in the British Expeditionary Force. The casualty rate among officers is incredibly high."

"Good evening," I greeted several new acquaintances as we walked into the crowd. I recognized Lady Harrington from last evening's gala. Moving through the crowd, I approached her.

"Good evening, Lady Harrington," I said with a smile. "May I join you?"

"Yes, my dear," she made a space near her on the settee. "Are you ready for your work?" She seemed rather sad—as sad as she'd seemed last night.

"I'm not sure if one is ever ready for this work, but I hope to help in any way I'm able," I replied.

"*My youngest son is in France,*" *she told me.* "*He enlisted at the age of seventeen—too young to join.*"

She shook her head, as if still dismayed that her young son was in the war. "*William was attending Eton College when war was declared. He was fifteen years old, and like so many of his compatriots, he wanted to join immediately. William convinced a recruiting officer to let him join as a junior officer. He'll be eighteen on June twenty-first, just a few weeks from now.*"

She glanced up from her clasped hands. "*I've not received a letter from William in several weeks. I fear he shall not see his eighteenth birthday.*"

I wasn't sure what to say, so I said, "*Lady Harrington, write down your son's name. I promise I'll look for him when I arrive in France.*"

Smiling sadly, she opened her reticule and pulled out a photograph. "*This is my son,*" *she said proudly as she showed me his photograph.*

He was an incredibly handsome young man. What a shame I'd never meet him, *I silently mused.*

She turned over the photograph and wrote his name: William James Harrington.

I examined the photograph, placed it in my small handbag, and said, "*I'll look for your son.*"

Unexpectedly, she embraced me. I was speechless. "*I didn't have the opportunity to give my son a proper goodbye. If you—I mean, when you find William—please embrace him for me.*" *She chuckled softly.* "*I expect he'll enjoy the embrace much more from you than from me.*"

My neck was stiff. I adjusted the pillow and leaned into the side of the plane...

The port of Le Havre was similar to Southampton. Men in uniform were everywhere. The war was certainly on in France.

In the States, signs of war had been few. I wondered if the situation had changed in the three weeks we'd been abroad. Are our streets crowded with young men ready to die for God and country? *I silently asked myself.* I wonder how many of the men we pass on the street will make it home to their sweethearts or wives. Is the conflict worth the lives of so many young men?

People cheered as we walked by. The Yanks were here. I was proud to be one of the first Americans joining the conflict.

"Lilly," I whispered, "where do you think we're going?"

Lilly shared her thoughts in a conspiratorial tone. "Well, I overheard the officers talking as we were escorted to the ambulances. I believe we're going to our base hospital in Rouen."

"Why would they only bring the nurses?" I asked. "If we're going to Rouen, they'll need the entire unit."

Lilly seemed unconcerned. "I love all of these men in uniform. They're so handsome and so helpful," Lilly whispered as a young French officer assisted her into the back of the ambulance.

The officer turned to assist me. In French he said, "Beautiful American nurse, it is my utmost pleasure to be of service to you."

I replied in French, "Flattery will get you nowhere, good sir." Flashing him a brilliant smile, I accepted his assistance into the waiting vehicle.

My good humor disappeared abruptly. The ambulance was clean, but the overwhelming stench of bleach and other disinfectants reminded me the vehicle usually transported wounded men.

This was war, and I was in it.

Ten nurses traveling to Base Hospital Twenty-One joined Lilly and me in the ambulance. The ambulance was very quiet as the reality of the situation affected us all. A British soldier shouted, "Move out!"

The ambulance was so quiet. The rhythm of the moving vehicle lulled some of the girls to sleep. I laid my head back and shut my eyes...

"Charlie! Wake up, Charlie! The flight attendants are serving breakfast," Katie said enthusiastically.

What a dream. It had seemed so real. The Throwback Thursday daydreams, combined with the reality show night dreams, were really messing with my head. *Maybe I should have watched that TV show about the reincarnated kids with Katie and Ryan.* I thought to myself. Then I reconsidered. *Mmm—not so much...a little to otherworldly for me.*

"Are you okay, Charlie?" Katie asked. "You have the Throwback Thursday look. I blame this on our freshman history teacher. You were so boringly normal before we learned about World War I. Maybe you should sue Mr. Mihevc."

"I had kind of a strange dream," I told her. "It wasn't weird or scary; it was just super-real. It feels like a memory. That's the best I can explain, except to say I'm surprised I'm on a plane, rather than a ship. Hey, and don't hate on Mr. Mihevc—he's our favorite teacher."

Turning in her seat, Katie studied my face intently. "Are you nervous?" she inquired.

"I'm nervous and excited," I replied softly. "Definitely more excited than nervous. I feel like I've waited my entire life for this moment. We built this trip up so much, I hope we're not disappointed. Maybe it won't live up to our expectations."

"I know, right," Katie replied. "I wish my expectations weren't so high, but I can't change them now."

"Anyway," Katie continued, "you must've been super tired. You slept the entire flight. What were you dreaming about?"

"The usual," I reported. "You think I'd mix it up and dream about hot guys. Instead, I dream about medical ships and hot dead guys. Well, they're not actually dead when I dream about them. Anyway, this time it was different. It was about traveling to—you'll never guess—Rouen. Dreaming about traveling to Rouen, even if it's in a different time period, makes perfect sense, right?"

Over the PA system a flight attendant announced, "Ladies and gentlemen, we've started our initial descent into the Charles De Gaulle Airport. We'll be arriving in Paris in approximately twenty minutes."

I smiled at Katie and Ryan. Our adventure was about to begin

Chapter Three

WILLIAM

The Booking Office Bar was Andrew's brilliant choice to meet prior to our departure for Rouen. The bar offered direct platform access at St. Pancras International railway station, allowing our parents an opportunity to enjoy an evening out while sending us off on our gap-year adventure.

The location was ideal, as we were traveling by Eurostar from St. Pancras International to Rouen-Rive-Droite. It also permitted our parents to buy our supper.

"The Victorian architecture of the station is quite impressive," my father mused. "The cathedral-like windows lining the walls and the dark wood furnishings are spectacular. I believe the bar is thirty meters long."

"Wills," my mum said as she glanced at her watch, "when will Andrew arrive?"

"Well, his scheduled arrival time was thirty minutes ago," I replied. "If he arrives in the next fifteen minutes, Andrew will be early."

"Andrew is a good lad," she said. "I'm certainly pleased he's accompanying you on your paranormal adventure." She flashed my dad a smile as she tossed her hair over her shoulder and glanced at the entrance again. "It is, however, not a good time to be late. If you boys would like to eat prior to your departure, Andrew needs to arrive soon."

Soul Mates ~ Liz Morrison

"Well, my love, I'll take a lap around the bar and see if Andrew and his family are seated at another table." Dad pushed his chair back and stood up.

Before my dad left the table, my mum exclaimed, "Andrew and company have arrived."

My mum and I stood, greeting Andrew and his family. My dad embraced Andrew's mum and clasped Mr. Graham's outstretched hand.

"Hey, old chap!" Andrew said as he shook my hand. "What's on the menu?"

Andrew dropped his duffel bag and backpack on the floor, took a seat at the table, and perused the menu.

The server approached our table to take our drink orders.

I glanced at my watch and realized we didn't have much time for a bite.

Noticing me checking the time, my dad hailed the waitress back to our table. "Miss," he said, "we'd like to place our order now, as these young chaps have a train to catch."

"Certainly, sir," the waitress replied.

The waitress was quite attentive and the service was incredibly quick.

"Wills...William..."

My mum must have repeated my name several times before I actually heard her, because she spoke in her Why-aren't-you-listening, you-irritating-boy voice.

"Sorry, Mum," I said, looking up from my meal of fish and triple-cooked fries.

"Grandmum sent us a packet of old letters and other items belonging to Harrington. She thought you might find the items useful. The satchel arrived in the post this morning." She pulled a leather satchel from her large tote.

"Take good care of this. It's almost one hundred years old," my mum stated, handing me the satchel. Gingerly I touched the faded, soft brown leather. *What mysteries will be solved or revealed when the contents were examined?* I wondered.

Andrew glanced at his watch and flew out of his chair, knocking it to the ground. My mum and Mrs. Graham grabbed their wine glasses and saved them from a tumble.

"What's the rush, mate?" I asked.

"I hate to draw this meal to an end," he responded, grabbing his backpack and duffle bag, "but our train leaves in ten minutes. Luckily, due to my incredibly thoughtful planning, our train is conveniently located."

I retrieved my backpack and duffle bag from the floor. Grabbing the satchel from the table, I shoved it into my backpack. No time to worry about the past when I was running really late in the present.

Our parents stood up, sharing hugs all around.

"Right, then," I said. "We need to make our way to the train, or we won't be going anywhere." I wanted to avoid an avid display of emotion in public, so I shook my dad's hand vigorously and gave my mum a quick embrace.

Waving to our parents, we walked quickly through the bar toward the platform. The departure times were posted just outside the door, and we quickly scanned in at the check-in barriers.

I glanced at Andrew. He raised an eyebrow. I knew that look—it was a challenge of speed and endurance. "Quite right." We raced to our train.

Breathless, I arrived at the door of the train a good ten seconds ahead of Andrew. Clearly I was the winner of this little competition.

"Well, old chap," I said, as Andrew arrived at the door, "what took you so long?"

"No problem," he gasped. "I'll win next go."

I nudged Andrew with my shoulder as we entered the arched door frame leading into the carriage. "Winner gets window," I declared.

Soul Mates ~ Liz Morrison

We shoved our duffle bags in the compartment and put our backpacks on the floor under our seats. The train pulled away from the platform as we sat down.

"Well, that was a close one," Andrew said with a grin. "Wills, I might grab a bite from the bar-buffet. Missing dessert was quite the tragedy. Do you mind staying with the bags?"

"Not a problem," I replied. "I plan to have a nice rest." Slouching into my seat, I placed my hands behind my head and closed my eyes. My mind began to wander as I dozed...

The queue of young men waiting to enlist in His Majesty's army was quite impressive. Many of the blokes in the queue were those enlisting unwillingly, due to the Military Service Act of 1916. I couldn't understand why a bloke would be unwilling to fight for king and country.

I reviewed the documents in hand. My papers indicated my successful completion of coursework at Eton College. They were my ticket to enlisting. Eighteen was the age most blokes completed their coursework. With any luck, they won't ask for a record of my birth and accept the evidence as presented, *I told myself.* After all, men are being conscripted to His Majesty's service. Why would they refuse a young man who's ready and willing to fight?

I'd considered enlisting under a false name, as many boys did during the early days of the war. But it would be unfair to my family if I died for my country without their knowledge.

In her last letter, my mother shared the unfortunate tale of her maid's son. She believed the boy enlisted at the age of fifteen under a false name. No one had heard from him in over a year. He'd probably died in battle, under a false name, and the family couldn't be notified. My mother described how my father, a member of the House of Lords, had contacted Sir Arthur Markham, a leader in the House of Commons, in the fight to stop the enlistment of boy soldiers. They hoped, her letter concluded, Sir Markham might be able to assist in locating the young man.

I knew my decision to enlist early would hurt my mother, but not knowing what happened to her youngest son if death befell me would be cruel punishment indeed. I wouldn't have my family suffer the fate of uncertainty by enlisting under a false name.

"Next," the recruiting officer called from his desk.

The words of Sir Henry Newbolt's poem Vitai Lampada came to mind as I stepped with feigned confidence toward the recruiting officer. "Play up! Play up! Play the game!" And so I shall.

"Good afternoon, sir."

"Where did you go to school, son?" he asked as he glanced up from his paperwork.

"Eton, sir," I replied.

The recruiting officer recognized my lineage even before I spoke the name of my public school. *If all goes well, I'll be enlisted as a junior officer, I told myself.*

My accent, my credentials, and the size of my chest were the commodities I was banking on to ensure enlistment into His Majesty's ranks.

The officer studied me closely. I was a big lad, standing over six feet tall, with broad shoulders and expansive chest, due to my place on both the rowing and rugby teams.

"Let's see your paperwork, son."

I handed him my records with a sure and steady hand. I waited patiently as he scrutinized the documents.

"You're quite the scholar. His Majesty needs men of intelligence in his ranks. If you pass the physical exam, you'll earn that prestigious honor," the officer stated as he returned my papers.

"Thank you, sir," I replied with heartfelt sincerity. I hoped my exuberance was masked behind my deferential attitude. I'd passed the greatest hurdle to enlistment—the validation of my paperwork.

The rest of the process was quick. I received my uniform and my assignment. I was going to France before my next birthday. Ironic really—I was a seventeen-year-old, pretending to be an eighteen-year-old, who was given the assignment of a nineteen-year-old.

Soul Mates ~ Liz Morrison

I walked briskly from the recruiting station to my home. It seemed best not to share my plans. I'd send a note after my arrival in France, enclosing a photograph of me in my uniform. I hope they're proud, I thought.

"Wills! Wake up!" Andrew said as he shoved my shoulder. "You're absolutely no fun as a traveling companion. However, I did meet several young ladies who wait for us to join them in the dining car."

Andrew was quite the ladies' man. It annoyed him that I wasn't, and it annoyed me that he cared.

"You go with the girls," I told him. "I'm going to listen to some music and relax. I'm really not in the mood for a short-term relationship with some girl on a train."

"A short-term relationship with a girl on train describes exactly the mood I'm in," he responded. "I couldn't have said it better myself. If you're sure you're not interested, I'll have to soldier on alone."

I glanced at my watch. We'd arrive in Paris soon. There, we'd make a change for our connection on a Corail Intercities train. According to the web, the trip from Paris to Rouen would take about one hour and fifteen minutes.

Sighing deeply, I realized that in less than two hours, I'd confront my dreams...or memories. Would it be like a bolt of lightning, or a non-event?

The latest dream was a new addition to my repertoire. The trip was already adding more pieces to the puzzle. The problem was, I didn't know the puzzle I was attempting to solve. It was bloody frustrating.

Had encouraging Andrew to join me been the right choice? I hoped telling Andrew about my strange past and past life hadn't been a mistake.

Since telling Andrew, our friendship seems to be a bit off, I thought. *It's probably just me, concerned my best mate thinks I'm bonkers. He hasn't mentioned it, so he probably hasn't given it a passing thought.*

Soul Mates ~ Liz Morrison

I watched the scenery flash by as I gazed out the window. Paris was quickly approaching, and then we'd be on to Rouen.

I hope reality isn't a nightmare, I thought.

Chapter Four

CHARLIE

The Rouen-Rive-Droite train station was an incredible building. Katie, who's into art and architecture, described the building as Art Nouveau. After our flight to Paris and our train ride from Paris to Rouen, I thought we'd be too tired to admire the architecture, but we were too pumped to be tired.

Our group was smaller in size than the original group from St. Louis. I hadn't realized the entire group wasn't staying in Rouen. So now it was me, Katie, Ryan, Mike, Holly, and Libby. Ms. Booth and the rest of the students traveled to a different language school in southern France. Ms. Booth would travel between the two sites on a monthly basis. The prospect of having no chaperone 24-7 made the trip even more of an adventure.

"Look," Mike said. "There's our ride."

A white van with the name of our school on the side was positioned for pickup. The six of us collected our bags and walked to the van.

"Bonjour!" The driver waved us over to the van.

"Bonjour!" we replied in unison. Glancing at each other, we totally cracked up.

"Sorry," Ryan said in perfect French. "We've had a really long day and we're a little silly." I think he was going for "slaphappy"; I wasn't sure how well slaphappy would translate into French.

Soul Mates ~ Liz Morrison

"What's your work assignment?" Holly asked while we waited.

"I requested an opportunity to work with historic sites connected to World War I," I replied.

Katie replied for Ryan too, "Ryan's doing something business-related, and my project is connected with Monet."

Before Holly could share her project, we boarded the van. Katie read the brochure aloud. "The school is located on the left bank of the River Seine, close to the center of Rouen. Students will live in apartment-like dwellings. In addition to French lessons, the school offers afternoon activities, including visits to museums, theatre evenings, visits to radio or TV stations, restaurant evenings, and sporting activities, such as swimming or skating. In addition, students can join Saturday excursions to amazing places like Paris, Mont Saint Michel, and Monet's garden at Giverny." Katie paused for a breath. "I hope it's as amazing as it sounds." Everyone murmured their agreement.

The tension in the van increased with each passing mile. Reality was sinking in. We were here, and for better or for worse, we were living in Rouen for the next six months.

Gazing out the window, I tried to memorize the sights and sounds. Ryan was glued to his phone, apparently providing his followers with a blow-by-blow account of our trip in 140 characters or less.

Whatever, I thought to myself.

Katie read the guidebook, Mike had fallen asleep, and Holly and Libby were in a deep discussion. I gazed out the window as the driver maneuvered the van along the narrow city streets.

I was disappointed. I'd thought I would feel an immediate affinity with Rouen the moment I arrived at the train station. And—well, nothing.

It was so cool to be here, even if I was disappointed, with no recollection from my dreams. I loved the street names: rue Jeanne

Soul Mates ~ Liz Morrison

d'Arc, rue Méridienne, and rue Léon Blum sounded so...well, French.

The van pulled up in front of a five-story red-brick building—our new home.

I hadn't realized how tired I was until I almost fell out of the van. If the driver hadn't assisted me, I would have done a face plant on the curb in front of our new place.

A handsome, dark-haired guy, probably in his early twenties, was in the welcome center. He glanced up and appeared genuinely happy we—the Americans——had arrived. Ryan, the self-appointed ambassador for the group, shook hands with the welcome guy and introduced us.

All our rooms were pre-paid, so registering at the residence hall was super easy. The welcome guy—I think his name was Peter—explained the rules of the house. I wasn't paying much attention; I was ready to crash.

"Hey, Charlie! Focus, will you?" Ryan said.

"Oh, sorry...I'm a little tired," I said.

"A little?" Ryan joked. "You're ready to fall over, girl. You really need to get some sleep."

"Aren't you guys tired?" I asked. "Seriously, how can you all be so—I don't know—awake?"

Katie glanced at me. "We're in France. How can you not be awake?" she retorted.

We waited for Peter to check us in to the residence hall. Katie registered after me.

"Hey, Charlie," she said. "We're both on the fourth floor, but we're not sharing a room. You're in 402 and I'm in 404."

"*Oui, Mademoiselle.* All of the rooms are single occupancy."

"Looks like the guys are on the third floor," Mike said.

"Well, what are we waiting for?" I said, with forced enthusiasm. "Let's go check out our new home."

25

We grabbed our bags and walked to the elevator. We stepped into the elevator with all our bags and pushed the button for floors three and four.

The stairs were right next to the elevator. Knowing me, I'd use the stairs more than the elevator. I don't really care for elevators.

"Oh, look! Third floor. It's time to say goodbye to the boys. Bye, boys," I said with a grin.

"Not so fast, Charlie," replied Ryan. "When are we meeting for dinner?"

"Let's say in three hours." Katie answered. "Charlie will have time for a nap, and everyone will have time to get settled."

"Okay, we'll meet you ladies downstairs in three hours," Ryan said, stepping out of the elevator.

"Works for me and Charlie," Katie replied. Holly and Libby nodded in agreement. The door closed on the boys, and we completed the ride to the fourth floor.

"I can't believe we have our own little apartments. I thought for sure we'd be sharing," Holly said as we walked down the hall toward our rooms.

I reached my door and turned the key in the lock. Pushing open the door, I entered my new home. Apparently, Katie opened her door at the same time.

"Oh, it's totally cute!" Katie exclaimed.

The room was very compact and very clean. The main room included a futon, bookshelves, and a desk—all very serviceable for a student. There was a small dining table with two chairs, and a little kitchen; maybe a kitchenette. I'd thought for sure we'd share a large, communal shower, like a college dorm, but we had our own bathroom.

Awesome, I thought.

I walked next door. Katie sat at her dining room table. She looked at me and grinned. "I love it," she said. "I feel so independent, and you're right next door. It's like we're living in the same house, just not the same room. Works for me."

"I love it, too," I responded as I walked out of Katie's room into the hallway. "Okay, I'm going to sleep for the next two hours. I want to enjoy our first night in Rouen."

"Sounds like a plan. I'm going to walk around the building and check out the neighborhood. I'm not tired at all," Katie replied.

"Maybe Ryan can go with you. I hate thinking you're alone in a new city with no protection."

"Oh my God, Charlie," Katie said with mock shock. "You sound like my mother."

"Sorry," I apologized. "We probably shouldn't have watched *Taken* as one of our pre-departure movies. After all, our dads aren't some super-cool secret agent dudes who can fly to Rouen and bust up the bad guys. So you have to stick with Ryan as your protector. Please."

Katie grinned. "Okay, Ryan can be my protector for a walk around the block. Go to sleep and don't worry about me."

"Promise?" I persisted.

"Pinky swear," Katie held up her pinky finger.

Katie shut the door, leaving me alone in my new room. I eyed the futon, knowing I could pull it out and convert it into a comfortable bed. A power nap would be perfect.

WILLIAM

I looked around the trenches at my men. My men—what an odd thought, given our present circumstances. Amongst my men, I was unseasoned. Many of the seasoned soldiers waiting quietly in the trench had played the waiting game in numerous trenches across the European theater. The experienced soldiers realized each time they survived an attack they might not be so lucky in the next encounter. The fresh-faced soldiers who accompanied me to the front were nervous with anticipation as the terrors of the unknown invaded their imagination.

Which is worse, I wondered—knowing what's to come, or not knowing what's to come? If I survive this encounter, I decided, I'll be able to formulate my own conclusions.

According to the battle plan, the big show would begin around 0300 hours.

It was interesting, if not somewhat unnerving, to watch the men mentally prepare for battle. Some were deep in thought, while some joked to cheer up their chums. Others made sure letters to their loved ones were secure on their person in preparation for the ultimate sacrifice.

I should take the time to write a letter to my mum, but I don't know what to say, *I told myself.* I'm glad I enlisted under my own name, so if this is the day I die, the army officials will be able to notify my family with a telegraph or form.

Approximately fifty men served in my platoon. As a second lieutenant, I was the lowest commissioned officer in the ranks. Though I tried to ignore the reality, the average life expectancy of a second lieutenant was approximately six weeks. Knowing the life expectancy of those of my rank, I knew my chances of survival were slim.

My greatest fear, however, was not the fear of dying. My greatest fear was not being brave enough.

I considered walking through the men and sharing inspirational words or words of courage. But I was at a loss for words, as I'd never faced battle. Climbing to the top of the trench, I kept my head low, so as not to have it blown off before the battle began.

I gazed at the stars and wondered if this would be the last time I'd see them.

I climbed back down the ladder and almost knocked over one of the lads from Brighton with whom I'd traveled. "Well, sir," he asked, "are you nervous?"

I studied him thoughtfully before I replied. "How are you feeling, Thomas?"

"I've felt better, sir," Thomas replied. Then he flashed me a grin. "We'll give Fritz what-for, sir. He won't know what hit 'im."

Soul Mates ~ Liz Morrison

I chuckled. At the front, the men referred to the Germans as Fritz. It made the enemy less intimidating, I reckoned. "That we will, Thomas; that we will."

I shook his hand. He joined his chums to wait for the signal.

We were prepared for this battle. Prior to our arrival at Messines, we'd seen a scale model of the area to be attacked. We'd been briefed on tactics and the identified objectives of the battle.

The strategy we'd use differed from the training I'd received a few weeks earlier. At training, we learned to wait for a high-ranking officer to blow his whistle at the appointed hour, and the men would file quietly forward behind me, the second lieutenant. The men would negotiate the steep climb out of the trench and walk directly into a barrage of enemy fire. Once clear of the trench, the men were supposed to hold formation around their officers and walk steadily toward the enemy.

In practice, however, according to the blokes who'd actually been in battle, No Man's Land was an inferno of noise and smoke and screams. The officers were usually killed at the onset of the battle, and the men were left to fend for themselves.

My commanding officer tapped me on the soldier. "Lieutenant," *he said,* "gather your men and prepare to evacuate the trench. Good luck."

I glanced at my timepiece. It was 0230. "Gentlemen," *I began,* "we'll silently depart the trenches. When you reach the dead ground in front of our trench, stay low. We don't want to gain the attention of Fritz prior to the explosions. I'll wait at the top of the trench to direct you to your positions."

Looking around the circle, I quietly said, "For king and country."

Securing my weapon, I climbed the ladder to the top. My head cleared the top of the trench. Slithering on my stomach, I occupied the dead ground. The men silently followed, creeping as quickly as possible to cover the ground.

At zero hour, our artillery opened up a terrific barrage of fire against Fritz's front line. Suddenly, a glaring flash of light illuminated the sky and the ground trembled like an earthquake. A rush of hot air from the explosion dropped debris of wood, iron, and earth on our position. Dust smothered us.

The blast was shocking in its intensity. I had no doubt they heard the blast quite distinctly in England.

The first wave of infantry moved forward. I held the men back, waiting for the second explosion. Nothing happened.

Our orders were to move in twenty-five-yard intervals, explosion or not. Following orders, I directed my men forward.

We entered No Man's Land amidst the dust and debris. The men moved purposefully toward the German line. Then the second mine exploded.

The force of the explosion tossed me into the air. Then I plummeted to the ground.

I'd heard when a man is about to die, his life flashes before him. My life must have been rather boring, as the only flash I saw was the fire from the explosion.

Why am I sleeping in a hole? *I wondered.*

I'd never been knocked out cold in my life. Was I out for five minutes or five hours? I wondered. *The air was still thick with smoke. The sound of battle raged around me. It was quite clear I was trapped in a hole in the middle of hell.*

The left side of my face was in severe pain. I couldn't open my left eye. My left hand ached, and my wrist was numb.

Raising my right hand with trepidation, I examined my face. Warm, sticky matter—probably blood and skin—oozed under my fingers. I was fairly certain my face had been damaged, and my eye might be gone.

Blind and disfigured, and only one day on the job, *I told myself.* But not dead—well, at least I'm not dead yet.

I was certainly glad I'd sent the photograph to my mum before having my face blown off.

Soul Mates ~ Liz Morrison

I flexed my muscles to determine the extent of the damage. I must be pretty badly wounded, *I decided. The dust and smoke made seeing the rest of my body impossible.*

My eyes adjusted to the surroundings. The first thing I saw was a severed foot lying an arm's length from my head. The foot stood upright in an army boot, having been blown cleanly from the body. It was a sickening sight.

"My God, they blew off my bloody leg," *I said to myself with shock and dismay.*

Studying the bloody boot, I realized it had belonged to a German.

Well, we blew up one of the bloody Huns, *I thought.* "Hun" *was a bloody brilliant term for the German barbarians.*

I could feel my legs, but I couldn't seem to stand up. I was bloody lucky my leg was still attached to my body. "Damn lucky," *I said quietly.*

The beams of a pocket torch illuminated my hellhole. I couldn't tell whether the man holding the torch was enemy or ally. I decided it didn't matter. If he was a German, he'd shoot me and it would be over. If he was one of my mates, I might ask him to shoot me as a mercy killing, similar to putting down a horse.

My mind wasn't functioning properly. The last thing I wanted to happen was to have the bloke leave me in my current position.

"Here," *I mumbled. Then,* "I'm here," *I said, with more force.*

The man with the torch jumped into the pit and landed near the severed foot.

"You might want to watch yourself, mate," *I said.* "Seems to be body parts with no bodies amidst the debris."

"Lieutenant Harrington, is that you?" *The man shined the torch into my eyes—or rather, into my eye. I recognized the voice.*

"Thomas," *I said,* "how are the men?"

"Sir," Thomas replied, "it's glad I am you're alive. You need to get out of here. Can you walk?"

"Thomas, I need some assistance. I can feel my legs, but I can't remember how to use them. I think if you give me a hand, I should be able to muddle through."

My left arm was closest to Thomas. Without warning, he grasped my left hand and gave me a tug. I almost lost my stomach in response to the pain.

"Thomas, I believe that one might be broken," I gasped. "Let's try this one."

I lifted my right hand toward Thomas, and he pulled me to my feet.

"Sir," Thomas said, "it appears your leg might be damaged, as well."

At his words, I glanced down at my torn trousers and saw the blood and gore for the first time. I took a deep breath and placed my right arm over Thomas's shoulder. "Let's get out of this hellhole."

Thomas grinned. "With pleasure, sir."

Surprisingly, we made it behind the trenches to the advanced dressing station. Thomas bore the brunt of my weight, as I struggled to stay conscious.

Trudging slowly toward the dressing station, I realized Thomas shouldn't be aiding me. British battlefield protocol was such that if a bastard was wounded in battle, his comrades could not come to his aid.

"Thomas, I appreciate your assistance. I believe I can carry on," I told him.

Thomas paused for a moment.

"You see, sir," Thomas explained, "the station is located close to the main road, so's wounded blokes such as yerself can be easily transported by motor ambulance to the main dressing station. If I leave you here by the side of the road, a stretcher bearer will be along in a jiffy to take you into the station."

I fought a losing battle to remain standing. "Thomas, thank you for your assistance; I believe I need to lie down," *I said.*

Blackness and moments of awareness intermixed. Men groaned. I wonder if I was groaning, too. The smell of antiseptics, blood, and sickness was overwhelming. The smell alone should have kept me awake. The blackness was stronger than the stench.

I drifted between consciousness and unconsciousness; life and death. The state of near consciousness may have lasted a few minutes, a few hours, a few days. I had no sense of time or place.

I dreamt of war—a horrible nightmare. Shells exploded all around me as I attempted to find my men. Somehow I'd misplaced a platoon of fifty soldiers. How does an officer misplace fifty soldiers?

Fierce German soldiers surround me, advancing on me with bayonets at the ready. I covered my face, protecting my head from another blow. The death blow ascended; I woke with a start, gasping in pain...

Several things were evident, and I ticked them off in my head. One, I was injured and in pain. Two, I wasn't surrounded by Hun soldiers. Three, I didn't know what had happened to my men. Four, the electric light bulb overhead allowed me to see the surroundings, and it appeared I was in a hospital of sorts. Finally, my uninjured hand was being held by a vision of beauty.

She was simply the most beautiful girl I'd ever seen. Big, blue eyes, straight little nose, incredibly luscious lips, all surrounded by light-brown hair with golden highlights. If God had said, "William, describe your perfect girl," she'd be it. I realized this must be heaven.

The vision gently touched my cheek and smiled into my eyes. She studied me with grave intensity.

"Are you an angel?" *I inquired.*

She laughed and her eyes sparkled. She leaned closer.

She's going to kiss me. It'll be my first kiss, I thought. A kiss by the angel of...I guess, of death.

If she was the angel of death, I was ready.

"Are you William James Harrington?" *she asked.*

"Wake up, mate," Andrew said with exasperation. "You slept the entire trip from Paris to Rouen. You missed the dancing girls, the buffet, and the cocktails. Actually, no dancing girls. I met a couple of blokes from the States who are spending some time in Rouen. I've got their numbers in my mobile."

Rubbing my hands on my face, I tried to erase the memories of the war, but tried to burn the memory of the girl into my brain. She was a stunner. *I can't even chat up a girl properly when I'm dreaming,* I silently chided myself.

"We're almost at the Rouen station," Andrew continued, apparently oblivious to my befuddled state of mind. "Let's get our gear, so we can make a quick exit."

"No problem," I replied. I grabbed my backpack, my duffel bag, and my leather satchel. "Let the adventure begin."

Andrew laughed as he grabbed his belongings. "It already has, and you've slept through it."

I contemplated Andrew's comment as we waited impatiently for the train to arrive at the station. If discovering more about the first William James Harrington was as good as my dreams, it would be quite an adventure.

As we disembarked the train, I felt nothing. I'd thought I would feel some kind of connection to this place, to Rouen.

Chapter Five

CHARLIE

"Lilly," I said, jostling her shoulder. "Lilly, wake up. We're at our hospital."

Lilly woke quickly, unlike me—I usually struggle to wake up. However, I hadn't slept the entire trip, due to the anxious, nauseated feeling in my stomach. What if I'm not up for the job? *I asked myself.* The other nurses have years of experience, and I have none. My father has faith in me and my ability, but he's my father. He's supposed to believe in me. What if I let everyone down? What if I let him down? *I hated being plagued by uncertainty and doubt.*

"Ladies," Lilly said, "be prepared for sights we've never seen; injuries we've never treated. We not only represent ourselves...we also represent the United States of America. We'll heal the wounded, comfort the dying, and make our country proud."

I wanted to burst into a rousing round of applause. The nurses were solemn as they contemplated Lilly's words. Applause was probably not appropriate.

The door of our transport opened. A young British officer said, "Welcome to Number Twelve General Hospital of the British Expeditionary Force."

The officer assisted each nurse out of the transport.

"BEF Number Twelve is situated on a racetrack, the Champs des Courses, at Rouen. The sandy, gravel-covered ground of the racetrack provides the best drainage in Rouen," he continued. "Rouen is in the midst of the rain belt of the Seine Valley."

As the young officer talked, I tried to take in our new home.

The hospital appeared to consist of moss-covered tents. I supposed the moss was for camouflage.

I only noticed two huts. As we walked by the huts, the officer explained that each hut held approximately thirty beds, with an adjacent operating room.

The hospital, he explained, had 1,300 beds. Most of the wounded were treated under the tents or canvas. The permanent buildings of the racetrack were administration buildings. The racing turf remained open.

"*The grounds are excellent for tennis, cricket, and other ball games, as well as for drills and practices,*" *he informed us.*

I wondered when we'd have time to play tennis. After all, there was a war on.

"*The British,*" *he explained,* "*attempt to make the surroundings of all military hospitals as pleasant and attractive as possible.*"

I noticed grass covered the ground between the tents, and flowers were in bloom. For a hospital in the middle of a war-torn country, it really was quite pleasant.

The guide stopped in front of wooden huts located inside the paddock fence. "*This will be your residence at BEF Number Twelve. Please organize your belongings and meet in front of this building in fifteen minutes.*"

"*Lieutenant,*" *Lilly asked,* "*will this also be our residence when the area becomes American Expeditionary Force Base Hospital Twenty-One?*"

The lieutenant really looked at Lilly and the rest of us closely for the first time.

"*Yes, it will, ma'am,*" *he replied.* "*We're quite excited to say the American Expeditionary Force is in Rouen.*"

Lilly glanced at me and raised an eyebrow. I knew that look. It was her We're-in-it-now expression. With Lilly as our head nurse, we were in good hands.

Soul Mates ~ Liz Morrison

"Thank you," Lilly replied. "Please give the nurses thirty minutes to stow their belongings and partake in a few personal matters."

The soldier blushed to his hairline. Lilly did that to people. It wasn't what she said; it was her method of delivery. To the best of her ability, Lilly would take care of us.

We quickly changed into our clean uniforms and met our guide in front of the hut. Our job, he explained, was to get the facility ready for the Yankee doctors.

This work we understood. No one mentioned it, but we were thinking it: How are we going to handle 1,300 beds when our small team was equipped to support 500 wounded men?

Settling in for the night, I asked, "Lilly, do you think wounded will arrive this evening?"

"I don't know, Charlotte. No matter what happens, we're ready to do our job. Go to sleep. Tomorrow is going to be another long day."

Surprisingly—or maybe not so surprisingly, considering I hadn't slept in two days—I fell right to sleep.

No wounded arrived in the middle of the night. We woke to the arrival of our doctors and the enlisted men who'd accompanied us from St. Louis. I put on my uniform and secured my hair in a bun.

The doctors waited for us outside the hut. I wanted to rush out and hug my father, but I restrained myself. He saw me standing with the other nurses and winked. I smiled in return.

The day flew by as we learned the system of BEF Number Twelve. The British policy of not marking the wounded was deemed ineffective by our doctors. We'd know whether their concern was warranted when the wounded arrived.

At dusk we retired. I looked at my fellow nurses and saw they were as exhausted as I. It wasn't physical exhaustion—it was mental.

Retrieving my journal from under my pillow, I found a fresh page and wrote today's date: June 12, 1917. I jotted down a few sentences to remind me of my first day as nurse at Base Hospital Twenty-One.

Before placing the journal under my pillow, I looked at the photograph of William Harrington. "Please God; let William reach his eighteenth birthday. Good night, William," I said softly to his photograph as I placed it in my journal.

Someone hammered on the door and announced, "Incoming wounded."

"Here we go," Lilly said. "Ladies, put on your uniforms and let's get to work."

Rushing to get dressed, I threw my hair into a disheveled bun. Now wasn't the time to worry about a perfect hairstyle.

Lilly quickly looked us over and nodded her head in approval. "Let's go, ladies."

We followed Lilly into the night. The wounded had arrived.

I wasn't prepared for the reality of war wounds.

Walking wounded, wounded on stretchers, and men whose wounds no longer mattered, as they hadn't survived the journey, slowly came off the transport. I stood motionless, trying to determine where I should go and what I should do. Everyone needed our attention—all of them, all at once.

"Nurse! Nurse!" a voice shouted in my general direction. "Nurse, we need your assistance."

I walked purposefully toward the voice and the wounded soldier and prayed I'd be able to help.

I saw the young man lying on the stretcher with blood leaking through his head dressing. I was no longer afraid or unsure—I was a nurse, and I knew my duty.

The young man on the stretcher looked similar to the photograph of William James Harrington. This young man's mother was counting on me to see him through.

I quickly and efficiently removed the bandage covering his head. By the amount of blood he was losing, I knew he needed immediate assistance. *His pulse was strong—with immediate care, this young man would make it through the night.*

I said a prayer as the young man was moved to the operating tent and I moved to the next soldier.

That night was the longest I'd ever spent. I'd never fully recover from my first experience with the wounded...boys with both arms in slings, armless boys, legless boys, boys with bullets through their head...not dead, but disfigured beyond recognition.

"Charlotte," Lilly called as she approached me a little after dawn, "you did good work."

I stared at the grassy field. Two days ago, we'd arrived in Rouen. I tried not to cry as I recollected all the young men—fit and hale one moment; disabled or dead the next. I shook my head and wondered aloud, "Will I be able to do a night like this again?"

Lilly put her arm around me. "Charlotte, you'll be able to do this again."

I wanted to turn into Lilly's arms and sob. Instead, I drew in a deep breath and gave Lilly a somewhat unsteady smile.

"Lilly," *my voice no longer quavered.* "I'm going to check on my first patient. He had a head injury that, with prompt treatment, will only be a mild inconvenience."

"Prepare yourself for the worst, Charlotte," *Lilly said softly.* "Many of the men who arrived last night didn't survive to see another day. Your young man may not have made it through the night."

I nodded, turning toward the hut housing recovering patients. I wish I'd asked his name, I chided myself. It would certainly be helpful information.

I prayed. "Please God, let him live." *I realized, as I continued my walk, that praying about things that may have already come to pass is not fair to God. If he was already dead, praying for him to be alive would be a wasted prayer. So I thanked God for saving those he could, and welcoming those he couldn't.*

I entered the first hut, asking the attendant where soldiers with head injuries could be found. The attendant looked at me with a stunned expression. I must look horrible, *I reflected.*

The attendant stumbled over his words. "Right over there, miss." He pointed to a row of beds on the far side of the hut.

Giving him a bright smile, I said, "Thank you."

He blushed from his neck to his forehead. I was afraid to look at my uniform. Did I rip it in the night? *I wondered.* Is something inappropriate exposed?

I glanced down. Everything appeared to be intact. Maybe he was nervous around women.

Walking up and down the aisle, I carefully examined each face. I didn't see him.

"Please, please, please, help me find him." This was a good prayer—even if he was dead, knowing his fate was better than knowing naught.

I was losing hope. One hour had passed—no luck. I searched several tents, to no avail.

I needed to go to sleep, but I couldn't give up the search. My inner voice said, "Yes, you can, Charlotte. You have a job to do for all the wounded, not just one young man."

My inner voice was right. I needed sleep, so I could begin applying clean dressings in a few hours.

"Charlotte," a voice called from across the tent.

"Hello, Dr. Father," *I walked toward my father, trying to keep myself together.*

"Well, you're a sight for sore eyes," he remarked.

I laughed; I can't believe I actually laughed. "I must be quite the sight," *I replied.* "I scared one man speechless."

"Charlotte, your hair tumbled out of your bun. Even with blood on your apron and blue rings under your eyes, you look like an angel."

Soul Mates ~ Liz Morrison

I squeezed his arm. *"Right, Father—an angel. You're nuts."*

"Why aren't you asleep?" he asked.

"Well, if you must know, I'm looking for someone," I replied. *"The first soldier I assisted. I want to find him"* I said. *"He had a head injury that was mostly bluster, his pulse was strong, and I had the stretcher carrier bring him directly to you in surgery."*

"Hmmm," my father considered the information. *"Let's see, right after the transport arrived, I treated a young man with a blow to the head with a fresh dressing...your work?"*

I nodded.

"In addition to the head wound, the soldier had a broken wrist and a broken clavicle. He had shrapnel and a belt buckle embedded in his leg. He came through surgery quite well. Let's see, he'd be in the hut connected to the operating room," my father concluded. *"Let's take another look."*

I turned toward the hut. *"Not that hut, Charlotte—I performed his surgery in the operating area connected to the hut next door."*

"Dr. Rawlings! Dr. Rawlings!" a voice called from a nearby tent. *"We have a bleeder, sir."*

Squeezing my arm in farewell, he walked quickly to the tent. I continued to the hut. This was the last place I'd be checking. My father had treated the young man...whether I found him or not, he'd live to see another day.

Walking into the tent, I started my slow journey down the first aisle.

Then I saw him. Funny, I'd know him anywhere, and I don't know him at all, *I marveled.*

"Thank you, God," I whispered.

I carefully examined the soldier. Even with a bandage swathing half of his forehead, he was my idea of physical perfection. His hair was chestnut brown with glints of gold, his eyebrows were dark, and he had a chiseled jawline and slight cleft in his chin. He looked so young, lying helpless in the bed.

I gently lifted his right hand...the hand not injured.

Suddenly he opened his eye and stared intently into mine. His deep-set eye was an unusual shade of dark, warm gray.

I couldn't help myself. I used my free hand to gently touch his cheek. Our gazes locked. I realized I knew this man. I'd studied his photograph each night for almost two weeks.

"Are you an angel?" he asked.

I laughed. Bending closer, I whispered, "Are you William James Harrington?"

"Charlie! Charlie! Wake up! Let us in!" Katie and Ryan banged on my door, waking me from an incredibly vivid dream.

"I'm coming," I said as I rolled off the futon and landed with a crash on the floor.

Hearing the crash, Ryan and Katie laughed.

"Oh my God," Katie said. "She must've crashed into something."

"Only Charlie could crash into something in a room with such limited furniture," Ryan responded laughing even harder.

"Har! Har! Har!" I said, opening the door. "And by the way, I didn't bump into anything. I fell off the bed." I laughed too. It was pretty funny.

"What's the big rush? Where have you guys been?" I asked.

"Dumpster diving," Ryan replied, falling to the ground, laughing and holding his sides.

"We brought you a present," Ryan said, tossing a brown satchel at me. I dropped the darn thing. They laughed harder.

"Will you guys please tell me what's so funny?" I pleaded.

"I don't think I can speak," Katie struggled to breathe and not laugh.

Ryan took a deep breath, "Okay, so, Katie and I are walking around the building, just checking out the sites. We locate the stop for public transportation, a couple of cafés, and a great, big dumpster."

At the word "dumpster," Ryan and Katie practically rolled on the floor laughing.

"Katie sees this old briefcase on top of the bin, and she's all like, 'Ryan, we need to get that briefcase for Charlie. You know how much Charlie likes old stuff,'" Ryan mimicked Katie. It was too funny.

"To make a long story short," Katie chimed in, "Ryan climbed up a fence and on top of the dumpster to get the briefcase." Katie started laughing again.

Ryan picked up the story, "Much to my dismay, I fall on my ass, right next to a pile of sh...crap."

"Right next to a pile of crap, yuck." The picture was too much; preppy Ryan landing next to a pile of crap, holding an old, leather bag. I started laughing again. Tears rolled down my cheeks.

Ryan was all dignified. "Yes, next to...what is the more refined word?...manure." He fell over laughing.

"Wow! Just so I could have a dirty, old briefcase from a French dumpster? You guys really are the best friends a girl could have. Ryan, dumpster diving in Rouen is definitely something to tweet about."

"Okay, enough of the questions," Ryan said from his position on the floor. "We're leaving in thirty minutes for the café you located when you researched Rouen."

"I met a Brit on the train from Paris. I think he's staying here, too," Ryan continued. "I'm texting the dude, inviting him to join us. After all, our intense language training begins tomorrow. We might as well enjoy the night. Okay ladies, in the lobby in thirty minutes." Ryan walked out the door.

"How was your nap?" Katie asked.

"Awesome. I'm ready to take on Rouen," I announced.

"I'm getting ready—I'll come and knock," Katie said as she left my room.

Opening my journal, I wrote down everything I remembered about the dream. First and foremost, I was going to find Base Hospital Twenty-One.

Chapter Six

WILLIAM

The living quarters for students at the international language school were better than I'd anticipated. All the linens were provided, and the rooms looked clean. After my latest dreams—or memories—of life in the trenches, the smell of bleach and fresh, white sheets was a welcome addition to the dorm room.

The memories from the dreams on the train were more vivid than my memories of the numerous years I'd spent at Eton.

It was rather disconcerting how the dreams were becoming part of my reality. I'd not shared my fears or dreams with Andrew. He was my best mate, but the bonds of friendship might break if he knew I suffered from shell-shock after a dream.

I wanted to lie on the futon and have a kip, but I was afraid to fall asleep.

I wasn't foolish enough to think the dreams would end, but I wasn't prepared for the vivid recollections of war. The battle of Messines Ridge, the battle I remembered—or more correctly, dreamt of—on the train from Paris to Rouen was considered a victory for us and our allies. However, I—or rather, the first William Harrington—had served as a junior officer in His Majesty's army and was lucky to be alive. Hours after waking from the dream, I felt disoriented, like I'd actually fought in the battle…shell-shocked.

And the girl—well the girl, if my dream had been a memory of the event—she was a nurse; the most beautiful nurse a bloke could hope to meet after being wounded in battle, or any other time.

Now, however, I wondered whether she was important to William, or just a vivid memory of waking up in a field hospital. After all, I'd thought she was an angel. I recalled her voice as she laughed at me. I wasn't smooth with the birds in any lifetime.

"William," Andrew called from down the hall. "Get your lazy arse off the bed. We're meeting some Americans at a café."

"Andrew," I replied, "this is France. Wouldn't it be more appropriate to meet some French women at a café?"

Actually, meeting some Americans sounded like it might be rather fun. I didn't know any Americans, but I'd watched their shows on the telly.

Andrew entered my room with a bloke about our age who looked like a bit of a scholar. I believe the American phrase is a nerd.

The American extended his hand and introduced himself. "I'm Ryan from St. Louis."

I grasped his hand and said, "William."

Americans were an interesting breed. Telling me he was from St. Louis might hold some sort of significance for other people from the States. For me, it meant nothing.

Andrew seemed to like the bloke, so I was sure, over the course of the next several months, I'd learn about St. Louis.

I pulled my jumper over my head and followed Andrew and Ryan down the hall and down the three flights of stairs, leading us into the courtyard of our flat.

"Well, my two best friends and I are here for six months to participate in the intensive language study program and take some general education classes," he told us. "It's for the summer and our first semester of senior year. We met up with some other students from our area who are now part of our group. It'll be great to add some Brits to the mix."

I hadn't known Americans cared about learning other languages.

The streets of Rouen were incredibly narrow. Some of the buildings looked medieval, while others looked incredibly modern.

As we strolled down the streets, I hoped Andrew knew where he was going, or we'd never find our way back to the flat. I had the address in my mobile, just in case we really got lost.

"My friend Charlie found this café when we planned the trip," Ryan explained. "It's been open since the early 1900s. Lots of places around here have probably been open since the early 1900s—probably even longer. Back home, we have buildings from the time period, but not businesses operating in the same place for over one hundred years."

"Charlie's totally into the history of the place. The rest of us are here for the adventure," Ryan continued. "Charlie did all the research and got us interested in traveling to Rouen, actually convincing the French teacher to organize the program in Rouen."

"Well, Wills and your mate Charlie will certainly have much in common. Wills convinced me to spend my gap year in Rouen."

"Right," I replied. *I won't have much in common with the American, unless he's a reincarnated World War I doughboy,* I thought as we continued down the street.

The streets became increasingly familiar. Each step along the cobbled pathway increased my confidence.

I knew the café to which we were heading from a dream. "Are we going to the Couleur Café?" I asked.

"How'd ya know?" Ryan asked in surprise, "Oh, wait—you probably did research, like Charlie. I bet the one-hundred-year-old business triggered something in the brain."

Andrew sent me a questioning look.

I knew exactly where I was, and where we were going. It felt like I'd walked this road numerous times.

In my head, I did an accounting of the buildings, quizzing myself on what was coming up next. When a patisserie I'd anticipated was gone, I felt a strange sense of loss. I knew I'd have to cope with all of this later, but for right now, I was enjoying the anticipation of arriving at our destination.

"Hey, William," Andrew shouted. "Slow down, old chap...this isn't a race. I believe we're taking a friendly stroll to a café with our new friend from the States."

Andrew and Ryan caught up. "Sorry," I said. "This seems oddly familiar, and I got carried away."

"That's what Charlie said," Ryan remarked. "We were strolling down this avenue, and Charlie started walking really fast. It was really bizarre. Anyway, we found the café, and Charlie was totally pumped."

Maybe Charlie was a reincarnated doughboy, I thought. *That would be incredibly freaky...but on the other hand, it would be nice to share memories from the trenches with another bloke who thought he'd been there.*

Then I corrected myself. *No way the bloke from the States is connected to my strange predicament,* I decided. *Wishful thinking.*

"Ryan," I said, "I think I'll like your friend Charlie."

Ryan gave me an oddly disgruntled look. "Everyone likes Charlie," he muttered.

I saw the bright umbrellas outside the café from a block away. I had a sense of homecoming. Embracing the power of the past, I enjoyed the feeling.

It was an odd, bittersweet feeling, like I was returning to a place I loved, but the place wouldn't be the same, because the people who made it special wouldn't be present...like visiting the home of a loved one who'd passed away; you remember all of the great times you shared, yet the memories made their absence more evident.

"Hey!" Ryan waved to a group sitting at a table in the café.

"Did you get lost?" a striking brunette called out to Ryan.

We reached the table and Ryan conducted introductions. "I'd like you to meet William and Andrew, a couple of blokes from the UK."

"Blokes?" the striking brunette inquired sarcastically. "Did you pick that up on the walk? It's true American girls love British accents, but only from Brits."

Soul Mates ~ Liz Morrison

Andrew pulled a chair over to the brunette and extended his hand, "It's a pleasure to meet you, and I have an authentic British accent. I'd argue that you Americans have the accent, but being the bloody-brilliant bloke I am, I never argue with a beautiful girl."

"Hi! I'm Katie," the brunette responded, shaking Andrew's outstretched hand. "We're from the Midwest, and we don't have accents."

I shook hands with the rest of the Yanks.

"Where's Charlie?" Ryan asked as he glanced around the table.

"Charlie's in the café, channeling a past life or something." Mike glanced at Katie.

"Does Charlie often channel past lives?" I asked.

"Just since the trip to Rouen," Kate replied. "It's like Charlie's daily life is one big *déjà vu*. I hope it'll be over soon." She turned her attention back to Andrew.

"I'll be back in a minute," I said. The pull to enter the café was too much to resist.

The sense of nostalgia overwhelmed me. I grasped the handle of the screen door leading into the dimly lit interior of the café. My chest hurt and it was hard to breathe.

"What took you so long?" a soft voice with an American accent asked from across the room. "This painting is amazing. This chipped-off part…I know what should be here. You guys think I'm crazy, but I swear I've been here before." Her hand gently glided over the missing piece in the painting.

I stared at the girl's back. She had long, thick, wavy blonde hair hanging almost to her slender waist. I froze. The hair…the voice…familiar, yet not familiar.

"Sorry?" I replied. *Brilliant!* I groaned inwardly. I was a tongue-tied fool.

She turned from the painting and smiled. "Oh, sorry—I thought you were someone else." She sounded embarrassed.

My head started to swim and I grasped the back of the nearest chair to stop myself from passing out. *Pull yourself together, old man,* I said to myself as I took several deep breaths. *Breathe. The dream girl is going to think you're bloody bonkers.*

Dream girl—right. Now I was having dreams when I was wide awake, in the middle of a French café.

"Oh my gosh," she said. "Are you okay? Here, sit down."

Pulling out one of the chairs at the table, she reached out to help me. At her touch, a shock of electricity shot up my arm. Looking into her eyes, I knew she felt it, too.

"Wow!" she exclaimed. "I've shocked people before, but that was crazy. If you'd been standing up, it would've knocked you over for sure. I didn't realize I had so much static electricity." Her voice changed from confused to in-control.

"I'm going to be a nurse and I've taken some courses at the community college," she continued. "Put your head between your knees and breathe deeply. You're going to be just fine," she said in her sexy American accent.

Her face was beautiful…as beautiful as I remembered. She was simply the most beautiful girl I'd ever seen—big, blue eyes, straight, little nose, incredibly luscious lips, surrounded by light-brown hair with golden highlights. If God had said, "William, describe your perfect girl," I would have described this mysterious American girl. She was very much like the girl in my dreams, only more beautiful and more real.

"Hey! Are you okay?" she asked. "Seriously—you look like you've seen a ghost. I usually don't have this effect on guys."

Finally I spoke. "You don't frighten me. I don't know exactly what happened. I'm certainly glad a future nurse is present to save me from a mysterious ailment."

"Okay, the future nurse thing is a little thick. I wanted you to feel confident in my advice. I am going to be a nurse," she said, a little defensively.

Soul Mates ~ Liz Morrison

I grasped her hand and she stopped talking. *Interesting*, I thought, *the strategy seems oddly familiar.*

"I'm William Harrington, and you are...?" I asked softly.

"Charlie. I'm Charlie," she replied.

She gazed intently at my face. "Your name is familiar to me. Do I know you?"

"Hey, Charlie!" Ryan called from the entrance. "What are you doing?"

Ryan's gaze rested on Charlie and me. I realized I was holding her hand. Frankly, I had no intention of letting go.

"Oh, I see you met my new friend from the UK," he said. "I knew you guys would have a lot in common; I didn't think you'd be holding hands after two minutes of conversation."

Charlie noticed our locked hands and gently pulled her hand out my grasp. It was painful...losing the touch of her skin.

I swear she felt it, too. She gave me a quizzical look and shook her head like she was physically trying to clear her mind, or make sense of what made no sense.

"Ryan, can you ask the waitress for bottled water? William came in and almost passed out. My blinding good looks brought him to his knees—you know—the usual impact I have on unsuspecting guys from England. Of course, he's the only guy from England I've ever met."

"No worries, Charlie," Ryan said as he approached the counter.

Ryan joined us at the table. "Seriously, dude, are you okay? You're totally pale. Nurse Charlie will take good care of you, but she's had, like, two seconds of nurses' training, so I'm not sure how qualified she is to take care of you if you're really sick. Oh man—or maybe it's like the movie *Contagion,* and we're all going to die."

"Thank you, Mr. Drama Queen," Charlie interrupted Ryan's performance. "Leave our British friend alone. William," she said, looking at me with laughter in her eyes, "in my unprofessional opinion, you'll be fine. Let's join the others."

Just like the first time, the electric shock of her touch caused my entire arm to tingle.

"Oh my gosh! I'm so sorry," she apologized again. "I just keep shocking you."

"Hey, Ryan! Come here," Charlie grabbed Ryan's arm.

Ryan looked at Charlie like she was crazy. He seemed to like crazy.

"Nothing," she said.

"Nothing?" Ryan responded.

"I didn't shock you when I touched you," she elaborated. "So, apparently I only shock guys from the UK—good to know."

She'd felt nothing when she touched Ryan. It seemed to verify Charlie and I were connected in a somewhat painful and slightly unnatural manner. I liked the shock feeling, in a kind of masochistic way.

Charlie turned her one-hundred-watt American-girl smile my way and said, "Okay, let's go meet your friend. I'm going to shake his hand and see if I can knock him out of his chair."

"C'mon guys," Ryan said. "We're conducting a scientific experiment. Our hypothesis: Charlie's magnetic personality has a shocking impact on dudes from the UK."

Charlie shoved Ryan toward the door.

Turning toward me, she extended her hand. "Dare ya," she said, holding out her hand for me to grasp.

Never one to resist the opportunity to be shocked by a volt of electricity, I grasped her hand to let her pretend pull me to my feet. The jolt of recognition was there, but this time it was more of a current than a shock. I held on to her hand.

Tilting her head back, she looked up at me and said, "This really is amazing. It's like a current of electricity. I've never felt anything like this before. Kind of weird, don't you think?"

Bloody hell! I thought to myself. *What did she say? Something about amazing.*

"Right," I replied. Now I was truly a blithering idiot.

"Charles, come on," Ryan said from the door. "Aren't you going to try out your theory? Obviously you've shocked one of the Brits. Go try your power on the other one."

Charlie gave me a perplexed look and shrugged. I knew if I died right now, right at that very moment, I'd die a happy man.

"My hand, good sir?" she prodded.

"Sorry?" I replied.

I was holding the aforementioned hand. "Oh, you want me to let go of your hand. I'm not sure that's a good idea. It will be free to shock other unsuspecting males from Britain."

I'm chatting her up, I marveled. *I've never chatted up a girl. Bloody hell!*

"You know, Charlie...may I call you Charlie?" I asked.

She nodded her affirmation.

"Please call me Wills," I said. "I may still be suffering from the effects of your overwhelming beauty and charm. I cannot possibly walk into the courtyard without your assistance. Being as you're a future nurse, and it is part of your nursing code to never leave a patient alone and suffering—if it's not part of the nursing code, it bloody well should be—I'll retain your hand, so you may assist me to our next destination."

Hell! If I was going to chat up this girl, I was going to do it better than anyone had done it before.

Charlie nodded her head and rolled her eyes.

She's so damn cute, I thought.

"Come on, then," she replied, linking her arm through mine and grasping my hand.

"Do you feel safe and secure?" she asked with a hint of sarcasm.

I looked down at our linked arms and hands, and responded with sincerity, "Yes, I do." I winked at her.

"Whatever."

The table was alive with laughter. Andrew, as always, was the center of attention. He's never met a stranger.

"Finally," Ryan said as we approached the table. "I thought you guys might've been abducted by aliens or found a hole in the space-time continuum to transport you back to World War I."

"Hey, Ryan," Charlie said in a disgruntled voice. "You promised."

Clearly there's something here I missed, I thought as I studied Charlie's expression.

"Andrew, allow me to introduce you to Charlie," I said.

"Charlie's a girl. I thought she was a bloke, from our conversation with Ryan," Andrew replied. Andrew eyed Charlie with interest. I've seen that look hundreds of times.

Not this time, and not this girl, I vowed silently.

"Ryan, you made me sound like a guy?" she complained "Thanks, buddy! I owe you one."

Charlie grinned at me and extended her hand to Andrew. Andrew noticed our exchange. I shrugged in return.

Andrew grasped Charlie's hand.

"Nice to meet you, Andrew," Charlie said.

"The pleasure's all mine, Charlie," Andrew replied.

Andrew's charm wasn't business-as-usual; it was bloody irritating. *He can direct his attention to the brunette, and leave Charlie to me,* I fumed inwardly.

Charlie smiled at Andrew, but directed her attention back to Ryan and me. "Well, my hypothesis is incorrect," she announced. "Apparently I only have a shocking effect on boys named Wills from the UK."

Katie looked perplexed. Charlie grinned and said, "I'll tell you later."

I added two more chairs to the table. I wanted to grab Charlie, but that would be bad form. Charlie sat down in the chair between Ryan and me.

"William—or rather, Wills," Katie said as she looked pointedly at Charlie and raised an eyebrow, "is also interested in World War I. According to Andrew, he's quite the expert on the era. They selected Rouen for their gap year based on Wills' interest."

"What the hell is a gap year?" Mike asked.

"They don't have a gap year in the States?" Andrew asked. Then, answering his own question, he said, "Obviously not—if you had a gap year, you wouldn't have asked. The gap year is the year after graduation from year twelve, and before going to university," he explained. "It's an opportunity to find oneself, prior to making a commitment to the future.

"Some of our mates are learning to be snowboard instructors in Canada; others are engaged in global service projects, and others, such as Wills and myself, are earning a little cash while living abroad. It's the time when young Brits are exploring their options."

"No gap year in the States," Katie responded. "We graduate from high school and go to college—well, not everyone goes to college. Some people join the military, others get jobs, and some get married."

The Americans looked at Katie like she was totally bonkers. "Sorry. Not anyone we hang out with. We're more of the go-to-college, find-a-career, and get-married-much-later kind of group," she clarified.

Libby chimed in. "Who knows what you want to do when you're eighteen years old? You go to school for four years and earn a degree when you don't know what you really want. It's a lifetime commitment."

A lifetime commitment with Charlie? I thought. *Count me in.*

Bloody hell! I needed to focus, or everyone was going to think I was daft.

"Hey, it's starting to get dark," Mike said. "Think we should head back?"

As we started walking toward the flat, I managed to ensure I walked with Charlie.

"Oops," Charlie said. Grabbing her arm, I kept her from falling. Once again the jolt of—I don't know…recognition—shot up my arm. Instead of letting go, I slipped her arm through my own.

"It's a British thing," I assured her.

Cocking her head to one side, she shook her head and smiled toward the ground. We walked in what I decided was companionable silence.

"So, Wills," Charlie said softly as she studied the ground. "That shock thing is totally weird. But once I get comfortable, it feels like a…" pausing, she rubbed my arm.

"A lovely, warm current," I filled in.

She glanced at me and smiled. *Bloody, bloody hell!* I thought. *One smile and I can't remember my name. What's my name?*

"Lovely," Charlie repeated the word. "In the States, we'd say 'nice.' I like lovely. A lovely, warm current; works for me," she said as she glanced up to meet my gaze.

Once again, I was speechless.

Chapter Seven

CHARLIE

William Harrington. Wills Harrington. I was speechless.

I just wanted to look at him. His eyes were a dark, warm gray and he had a little cleft in his chin. When he smiled, the strong lines of his cheeks deepened into dimples. He had a great jaw line. His brown hair had golden highlights. And, for some reason, he was interested in me.

I needed a conversation starter. *I don't know what to say,* I fretted. In my head I had thousands of questions, but for some reason, none of them seemed to come out of my mouth.

"Charlie." "Wills." We started speaking at the same time.

"Ladies first," he smiled.

I looked into his eyes—bad idea—and couldn't remember what I was going to ask. The funny thing is, I think he forgot what he wanted to say, too.

We laughed again.

"Let's try this again," he said. "Charlie, what are you going to study at the language school?"

I could handle that question. "I'm doing the intense language program for the first month," I told him. "After I complete the language program, I'm going to work at the Office de tourisme Rouen. I'm hoping to create themed walks or guided tours connected to military history in the area. How about you?"

"Andrew and I will practice our French while teaching local business leaders conversational English," William replied. "Part of the assignment is taking our students to London and other business and economic centers."

"Oh, that sounds really awesome," I said, hoping I didn't sound as disappointed as I felt. *I just met this guy, and he's leaving—just my luck,* I thought.

"I thought it sounded great, until two hours ago," William responded. "Now I believe staying in Rouen and working at the language school is the ideal position for me."

Oh my God! I marveled. *He's totally flirting with me. I don't know how to flirt.*

"Which sites do you want to visit?" Wills asked. "Notre Dame Cathédral, Eglise Jeanne D'Arc, Vieux Marche, Le Gros Horloge?"

I locked my gaze on my hand, which was wrapped around his arm. "I plan on visiting those sites," I proceeded cautiously. "I'm actually more interested in a few sites that don't appear to be high on the list of local attractions. I'm really hoping to go to this racetrack that was converted into a hospital during World War I. I want to travel to a few battlegrounds and explore sites in the Rouen vicinity connected to the war."

I glanced up to look at his face. His friend had said he was interested in World War I, but it could be a pickup strategy—kind of a strange one, but it worked for me.

William stopped midstride and pulled me to a halt. He turned me so I faced him. Placing his hands on my shoulders he looked into my eyes. *His eyes are beautiful,* I thought.

"Charlie, I have a massive favor to ask," he said. "Will you wait for me to return, so I can explore those sites with you?"

I would have promised him anything. "If you really want to go, I'll wait for you," I replied.

"Hey, Charlie," Ryan said, walking toward us. William grabbed my hand and pulled me toward the group.

Soul Mates ~ Liz Morrison

Ryan looked at our clasped hands and lifted his eyebrow in a question. I shrugged in response. I'd never held hands with a guy in public. I'd never wanted to hold anyone's hand in public—or in private, for that matter.

Ryan was obviously disturbed by the whole hand-holding-with-a-guy-I-met-like-two-minutes-ago thing.

"We need to get some groceries and stuff for our rooms. Do you want to stop on the way back to our place?" Ryan asked.

We were almost back to our apartment. The neighborhood was really pretty in the dim evening light. The walk home had seemed much quicker than the walk to the café...or maybe being with William made the walk go by so quickly. Or possibly, because I didn't want the walk to end, it ended all too quickly.

"Sure," I replied. "Great idea."

I turned to William, "Do you want to join us?"

"I'd like to go with you to the grocers, but I don't need to make any purchases," William turned toward Ryan and explained. "Upon our arrival, I was given the assignment to take a group of students to London. I meet them in the morning, and we travel for several weeks."

"So, you're leaving tomorrow?" Ryan asked.

"That, apparently, is the plan," William replied. "It's rather ironic, planning to spend my gap year in Rouen, and my first assignment is to holiday in London."

"Quite ironic," Ryan said.

Ryan seemed really happy about something. Who knew Ryan thought shopping for groceries would be such a thrill?

"Well, it was nice meeting you, William," I said.

"Likewise," William replied.

"I guess I'd better go," I said as I pulled my hand from William's grasp. The hand-holding thing was awkward as we said goodbye.

William wouldn't let go of my hand.

"I think I might need that—it kind of goes with the rest of me," I said as I gave my hand a tug.

"Charlie," William said, "may I ring you?"

I must have looked perplexed.

He tried again. "May I have your number, so I can ring you?" This time he held up his cell.

"Oh, you want my number so you can call me. 'Ring' means 'call'—got it," I replied. I'm pretty sure I blushed. "Why don't you hand me your cell, and I'll put it in?"

Now William looked perplexed.

"Your phone," I clarified for him.

"We call it a mobile," he replied. "So, 'cell' means mobile phone—got it," he added with mock seriousness.

Oh, he's kidding, I thought.

"Sorry for teasing," he said. "You're just so damn cute, I can't seem to help myself. Here's my mobile."

He handed me his phone. "Would you like me to put my number in your mobile? Just in case you need to call me for assistance in translating your English to my English. I'm always one for helping a damsel in distress."

I typed my number into his phone and handed it back. I gave him my phone and he typed in his number.

At least we had some connection; even it was just a number on my cell. Thinking of connections, somehow we completed the entire transaction with our fingers linked.

"Splendid," he said. He typed in something and my phone buzzed. "Read it later."

"Charlie," Katie called, "say goodbye to your English boy. We need to get going."

I looked into his warm, grey eyes and smiled as I tugged on my hand.

Soul Mates ~ Liz Morrison

William lifted my hand, turned it over, and kissed the inside of my wrist.

It was totally old-fashioned and totally hot. I had a feeling this boy could be the downfall of all of my virtuous intentions.

"Good night, Charlie," he said.

"'Night, Wills," I replied.

I pulled my hand from his grasp as I turned and walked away. Three steps later, Wills grabbed my hand. The shock was more powerful; the electric current caused my arm to tingle. The urge to hold onto his hand and not let go overwhelmed me.

"Just checking," Wills said with a grin.

He dropped my hand, then dashed across the street back to our apartment complex. He pounded Andrew on the back as the two of them jogged into the building, engaged in a sort of trip-and-knock-you-over type of male-bonding exchange.

"Okay, Charlie," Katie said, "What was that all about?"

"Seriously, Charlie," Ryan added, "you knew the guy for, like, ten seconds and you're all over him."

"I wasn't all over him," I replied, disgruntled by the accusation.

"He probably thinks you're like the American girls from the movies—easy."

"Ryan," Katie interrupted, "stop being mean. Charlie, you guys look like you belong together. Your body language is like a couple who've been together for years. It's really intriguing."

"You don't know what you're talking about," Ryan responded angrily. "He thinks he can get a quick lay from the American chick. His buddy Andrew was quite explicit in sharing what a player his friend William is. If I didn't like Andrew, I would've punched him in the mouth. Seriously, Charlie, according to Andrew, William uses the 'shock' thing all the time. 'I must know you from another life...we're so connected, blah, blah, blah.'"

"Your British accent sucks," Katie said. "Did Andrew really say William was a player? Honestly, Andrew struck me as a player. William didn't seem like a player. I'm a pretty good judge."

"Charlie is so naive and sweet. She's such an easy target for dudes who get around. She doesn't have a clue how attractive she is, either, which makes her an even easier mark. Seriously, it makes me sick," Ryan continued.

"Hello!" I said. "I'm standing right here. I'm not naïve, and I'm not a bad judge of character."

"Let's get our groceries," Katie said. "We can argue about this in the checkout line."

Grocery shopping was a momentary distraction from Ryan's tirade against William. *I can't figure out why William's friend would totally bash William to Ryan,* I pondered. *Maybe he thought it made William seem manlier, or Andrew cooler.*

If I hadn't been mad at Ryan, grocery shopping would have been fun. The selection was a mix of the familiar and the unfamiliar—sort of like my overall experience in Rouen.

When we stepped outside of the grocery store, day had changed to night. It was pitch-black out, and the street lights projected an eerie glow.

"Ryan, I know you have my back," I said. "I really, really, really appreciate it. However, I don't know why, but I feel like I have a connection to William I can't explain. The electric current—or whatever it is—I felt it, too. So, maybe William has some strange current, making girls feel an electric shock. But, I don't think so." I spoke slowly and thoughtfully. "Katie, you shook hands with William. Did you feel anything?"

Katie shook her head. "Nope, nothing," she said.

Ryan shook his head, "Andrew has no reason to tell me his best friend is a player if he isn't a player. I don't know...maybe he was trying to impress me. I don't think it's impressive to talk about how his friend wants to bang my best friend. It just pissed me off."

Soul Mates ~ Liz Morrison

Katie and I grabbed Ryan's arms. "You are the best friend a girl could have, Ryan, and we love you," Katie said, "but I think we should give him a chance. After all, Charlie will have three weeks or so to determine if he's a player or the real deal, without her virtue being in danger. He's pretty hot, though. It might be worth it, even if he is a player. Nothing wrong with a guy with a little experience."

"Katie," Ryan and I said in unison. We laughed. The tension was gone.

Katie was a virgin, too; she just gave the impression that she was experienced. Katie, Ryan, and I had decided, in maybe the seventh grade, we wouldn't give it up without it being special…with someone who was special.

"You can learn a lot about a guy on Facebook," Katie said. "We can friend him and find out his back story."

She squeezed Ryan's arm. "Ryan, are you feeling better, now that we have plans to research Andrew's story? Don't you think a real player would have numerous photos documenting his conquests? We can check out Andrew's page, too."

"Yes, I am," Ryan agreed, "but, I'm mostly glad the dude is leaving town, so Charlie can get her head on straight. It's probably his bloody-brilliant British accent."

We walked into our new home and waved at the young man working at the reception desk. The lobby area was empty, except for a few people who were lounging in chairs reading. I guess I'd been hoping Wills might still be awake and waiting for me in the lobby.

A girl can dream.

We entered the elevator. I preferred to take the stairs, but we had our grocery bags. It was easier to ride in the elevator.

"G'night ladies," Ryan said as he got off the elevator. "I'll meet you in the lobby at seven a.m."

"Do you want to talk about the William thing?" Katie asked as we stepped off the elevator into our hallway.

"Not tonight," I replied.

We stopped in front of our doors. I set down my groceries, retrieved the key from my purse, and unlocked the door.

"Good night," I said. "See you bright and early. Knock on my door and we can go downstairs together." I slipped into my room and closed the door.

I unloaded the groceries and organized the shelves. After my kitchenette was in order, I organized my clothes, my school supplies, and made my futon into a comfy bed.

My bathroom was small, but big enough for me to lay out my face wash and stuff. The place was starting to look like a home; though it really needed some photos or something to make it more personal. A photo of William would be a nice touch.

Oh—thinking of William, I can't believe I forgot he sent me a text. All the arguing with Ryan distracted me, I guess.

I picked up my cell and read his text. The message was really earth-shattering:

"Hey."

Chapter Eight

WILLIAM

Waiting for Charlie to text me back was killing me. *I leave early tomorrow, and I need to know if she felt a connection, or if she was just being nice.*

She didn't seem the type to tease a bloke; but my limited experience made me a poor judge of girls and their wiles. Who was I kidding? I had no experience in attracting girls. I'd snogged a few, and it was good, but it wasn't great. I just wasn't interested in any of those girls.

Now that I am interested—keenly interested—I don't know how to proceed, I worried.

If Andrew hadn't been acting a bit off, I would have asked him for advice. Andrew had a vast amount of experience, and he was happy to share it. I needed a guidebook or something on how to move forward with this girl. She was my past and my future—I knew it.

My mobile vibrated and I picked it up. It was a message from Charlie:

Hey.

How to respond?

What are you doing?

Charlie replied,

Getting ready for bed. You?

I really wish she hadn't mentioned getting ready for bed. I wondered what she was—or wasn't—wearing. Luckily, she couldn't see me or read my mind.

Packing, I replied. I wish I was remaining in Rouen.

Me, too, Charlie confirmed.

May I ring you tomorrow night? I typed the words into my mobile, not sure if I should hit send. *Do American girls like to chat on the phone? Do they only like to text?* I wanted to hear her voice, not just read her texts. Send.

Sure, she replied.

Ring you tomorrow. Good night. Send.

'Night :) she replied.

Well, that went pretty well, I decided. She didn't reject me outright, and I had plans to ring her tomorrow evening.

Overall, this was one of the best days of my life. Maybe this was the best day of my life. I'd literally—and figuratively—met the girl of my dreams. We apparently had some type of connection that was like an electric shock.

It might be wonky for most, but for a bloke who was possibly the reincarnation of a World War I Tommy, it seemed par for the course. It would be ace if Charlie was the reincarnation of the girl from my dreams. *Maybe I'll ask her...* I thought, *or maybe not.*

I pulled out my duffel bag and repacked most of the stuff I'd unpacked only days before. Tossing the duffel bag near the door and pulling a T-shirt over my head, I opened my door—leaving it slightly ajar so my key wasn't necessary—and walked to Andrew's room.

I tapped lightly on his door.

"Enter," he called.

Andrew glanced up and gestured for me to give him a moment as he finished typing.

"What's up, Wills?" Andrew asked while shutting down the laptop.

I glanced around the room and chuckled. Andrew's room was a disaster. His strategy for settling in had been to dump all his stuff in the middle of the floor and then shove as much as possible under the futon.

Andrew has been a bit off, but I need his assistance keeping Charlie safe, I told myself.

I'm not sure why I felt Andrew needed to watch out for Charlie, but the feeling was real and compelling.

"I thought you'd be shagging the American," Andrew said with a laugh. "Were you just quick? Or did she reject your best efforts? I'd take a lot more time with that one."

Punching Andrew in the face seemed like a bloody brilliant idea. He'd insulted Charlie, and he'd insulted me. Of course, that was Andrew. He thought with his knob and applied his one-dimensional thinking to the world around him.

"Andrew, I'm trying to remember you're my best mate," I said. "I really like Charlie, and she's not just a one-night stand. I'd appreciate you thinking with your brain, if you think about Charlie. Actually, I would prefer you not think about her, period."

"I'm just messing with you, old chap," Andrew said, and laughed again. "I'll bet you want me to keep an eye on Charlie when you're on holiday with your French businessmen. I like the Americans. And Charlie is a fit bird. It won't be a problem keeping my eye on her."

Once again, I had a feeling that trusting Andrew was a bad idea. *I've trusted him for most of my life,* I thought. *I hate thinking I can't trust him now.*

"Thanks, old chap," I said as I shook Andrew's outstretched hand.

I returned to my room and thought about the day. *I think I fell in love at first sight,* I told myself. *Is that even possible?*

Taking off my trousers and jumper, I tossed them in the corner. Grabbing the blankets and pillow from the closet, I prepared my futon for bed. I lay down and hoped to fall right to sleep.

Closing my eyes, I pictured Charlie. I could go to sleep with the picture of her in my mind every night.

Did the angel ask me my name? I'm pretty certain she asked, "Are you William James Harrington?"

I guess beautiful angels question you at the pearly gates, not Saint Peter. I would have preferred the kiss.

"Are you William James Harrington?" the angel asked again.

"Yes," I replied. "I'm William James Harrington. Where's Saint Peter?" Then I grabbed her hand. "Don't go get him. I'd really prefer you to stay."

She laughed again. "Pay attention, soldier—this isn't heaven; this is Base Hospital Twenty-One. And I'm not an angel"—a bit more laughter—"You can ask anyone. I'm definitely not an angel. I am, however, your nurse, and I'm very glad you are alive."

Much to my surprise, my body reacted physically to her light touch. How embarrassing. I tried to adjust my position so she wouldn't notice. I groaned as I shifted positions.

"Oh, my goodness," she said, "you're in pain. My father—I mean, Dr. Rawlings—doesn't like the staff to administer large doses of morphine. It's too easy to become addicted. Is the pain tolerable?" she asked as she adjusted the bandage covering my eye and forehead.

"It's quite tolerable," I replied.

"All right then, Lieutenant." Her smile was incredible. Her blue, blue eyes sparkled. It was like looking into the sky around twilight, when the blue of the day is changing into the black of night.

That was rather poetic. I really must be quite ill, *I thought.*

"I'll see you in the morning." she said.

My angel was leaving, and I didn't know her name. "Nurse," I called.

She was back in an instant with a look of concern. "What do you need, soldier?" Once again she placed her hand on my forehead to ensure the bandage was properly secured.

I had an incredible urge to grab her hand and pull her next to me on the cot. Luckily, I realized it was very bad idea prior to initiating the plan.

"We've not been properly introduced," I replied. "As we have no one present to make the introductions, I hope you won't consider me too forward if I ask your name."

Her smile was quite radiant.

"Charlotte—Charlotte Rawlings," she replied. "It's a pleasure to meet you, Lieutenant Harrington. Your mother will be quite pleased."

"Sleep well, soldier," she said as she walked away. She was gone before I could ask her to explain the comment about my mum.

Closing my eyes, I hoped sleep would come. I knew I wouldn't have nightmares about the battle. I was quite sure I'd have very pleasant dreams about an angel named Charlotte.

CHARLIE — WEEK ONE

"Au revoir," I called down to Ryan and Mike as we climbed up the stairs to our rooms. We decided we'd only speak French to each other for our first three weeks of intense language training. Our first week in Rouen had flown by.

One more day of school, and then we were going to see Monet's house and gardens in Giverny. Katie was so excited she could speak of nothing else.

As a result of Katie's excitement and our commitment to only speak French, I had an extensive working knowledge of artistic expressions.

French was a beautiful language. I was surprised we were learning the language so quickly. *Well, I shouldn't be surprised,* I thought. *It is an immersion program.*

I glanced at the clock. It was 11:00 p.m.; I waited impatiently for William's call.

I sat down at my desk determined to write in my journal. Tapping my pen against the table I considered what to write…I still dreamt in English...had a fun dinner with the group and Andrew...the key phrases I learned in French class that will assist me at the Office de tourisme Rouen...last night's dream.

Last night's dream had clearly been influenced by my conversations with William. In my dreams, William was a World War I soldier and I was a nurse.

Is that odd? I wondered. Maybe it wasn't so odd.

Let's see...last night's dream:

"Charlotte, are you visiting your lieutenant this evening?" Lilly sounded worried.

I wasn't ready to confide my feelings about William. I was so confused. Was I interested in William because he was everything I'd hoped to find in man? Was I interested in William because he was my first patient? Was I interested in William because I'd carried his photo with me, in hopes of finding him for his mother?

I was interested in William in a way I'd never been interested in another man. I liked being with him. It was pretty simple, really.

"He's not my lieutenant. He's just a lieutenant," I replied. "I promised him a game of chess. I'm not one to break a promise."

Lilly gently grasped my arm. "Be careful," she warned. "He's a soldier, and he's going back to the front. He's a junior officer. The death rate of junior officers is the highest in the British armed service. Don't fall in love with a man who faces a death sentence."

"I'm not falling in love with William." *As the words passed my lips, I realized they were absolutely correct—I wasn't falling in love with William; I was in love with William.*

Lilly shook her head. "Be careful, Charlotte. Protect your heart."

I walked across the field to the tents housing our patients. William had secured a chess set so he could challenge me to a game.

It was so peaceful. It was hard to believe there was a war on.

Soul Mates ~ Liz Morrison

My father was talking to William as I entered the tent.

"Hello, Dr. Rawlings, how's the patient this evening?"

"The lieutenant is healing quite nicely. He should be fit for service in approximately two weeks," my father said. Was there a warning in his voice?

"Don't beat him too soundly, daughter," my father said as he noticed the chess board. "You don't want to injure his pride, along with his head." My father shook William's hand, then walked to the next patient.

William's bandage was gone. A small scar marred his perfect features. Both of his grey eyes focused on me.

"Though I try to act the gentleman, I'm never one to let the ladies win," William smiled. His eyes seemed to drink me in. I felt uncomfortably warm. I'm sure I was blushing.

"Let the ladies win?" I rejoined, "There's absolutely no need to let this lady win."

"Charlotte," he said, as I was setting up my pieces, "what did you mean when you said my mum would be quite pleased?"

"I met your mother while in London. She requested I look for you. She was worried because they'd not received a letter in weeks. She'd be pleased I found you, and that you are well."

I remembered the rest of her request and blushed. Embracing William would be more exciting than a motherly squeeze. I felt my face heating up.

"Why are you blushing?" William asked. "What did my mum say?"

"Nothing, really," I stammered. "She requested I embrace you for her, as she was unable to, as you didn't tell her your plans regarding your enlistment." I replied in a rush.

"Hmm," William responded with a glint in his grey eyes, "I think I'd enjoy your embrace much more than my mum's."

My blush deepened.

William chuckled, "My mum said the same thing, I'll wager."

I nodded, not looking up from the chess board.

I recalled the conversation with William's mother and smiled. She certainly knew her son.

Another bit of our conversation tried to surface in my brain. I remembered. Today was June twenty-first. Today was William's eighteenth birthday.

"Happy birthday," I said, looking up from the chess board. "I may let you win after all."

My phone rang, jolting me from my journal-writing. It was William.

"Hi! I was just thinking about you," I said, before I thought better of it. What would he think if I told him I was thinking of him as a soldier from the very distant past? *Not going there, that's for sure.*

"That's a very good state of affairs," he replied, "as I was obviously thinking about you, too."

I moved to the futon and got comfortable for a long conversation. Last night, we'd talked for a couple hours. It seemed like we had so much to learn about each other.

"Tonight I shall ask you questions," he said.

I love his accent and I love his voice, I thought.

"What would you like to know?" I asked.

"Do you play chess?"

"Yes," I replied. "I started playing in elementary school. We had a chess club, and my dad likes to play. Do you?"

What a coincidence that he asked me about chess, considering the dream I had last night, I marveled.

"Of course," William replied. "Not many girls of my acquaintance play chess. When I toured with the Frenchmen today, I made a mental list of things we can do together. I wondered if chess would be part of the list."

"Can I ask something a little more personal?" he continued.

"You can ask, but I won't guarantee a response," I replied.

"Sounds fair," William said. "Have you had many boyfriends?"

How do I answer this? Well, in most cases, honesty is the best policy, I considered. *This seems like one of those cases.*

"No," I said, "I've actually never had a boyfriend. I've gone out with guys, but I never really liked them like that."

"Like what?" he persisted.

"You know," I said. "I just don't like them like that. Okay, I'm not romantically interested in them," I continued. "They kiss me and, well—nothing. I think you should feel something when you're kissing someone. Right? What about you, William?"

"It's my turn to ask you questions, remember?" William replied. "I've snogged my share of girls, but it was nothing. It seems like we have something else in common."

He'd answered my question, after all.

"Andrew gives the impression you're a real player," I said. "So, do you pick up girls at clubs or wherever, and then toss them aside?"

Like I think he's really going to answer that question, I told myself.

"William?" I said. "Wills, are you there?"

"Andrew said I'm a player?" William asked quietly.

"Yes, he told Ryan you wanted to shag me—though I'm not sure what that means—is it the same as snogging? Ryan was really pissed, but Katie said you don't seem like a player. She thinks Andrew is the player."

I asked softly, "Player, or not a player?"

Before William had time to reply I said, "I don't think you're a player."

"Charlie," William said, "I'm not a player. I've never really entered the game. Shagging and snogging are totally different. Ryan should be pissed, if that were my intention. Snogging is making out, and shagging is the same as—well—having sex."

"Charlie," William said, "I've never done the latter and have minimal experience with the former. I never met a girl that made me feel that way, until you. I know it might be rather soon in our relationship, but I can't help the way I feel."

William continued, "Okay, this is too deep for tonight's conversation. My intent is to find out about you. I have a list of questions and I'd like your response."

Not a smooth transition from a deep conversation about sex, but it works for me, I thought.

"Are you serious?" I replied. "You have a list?"

"Yes, I do," William said. "Did you hear that?"

"It sounds like paper rustling," I said.

"That's the list. Question number one: what's your favorite color?"

I could hear the smile in his voice. I wished he was sitting next to me on the futon, holding my hand with the lovely, warm current flowing between us as he asked his let's-learn-about-Charlie questions.

I'm not interesting, I worried. *I hope he's not bored.*

"You want to know my favorite color?" I repeated.

"Quite," William replied.

"Okay," I replied, laughing a little uncomfortably. "My favorite color is navy blue. I also like gray. And you?"

I thought of his gray eyes. *Not going there.*

"Hey, this isn't about me," William said. "But, since you asked, my favorite color is stormy-sky blue—similar to the color of your eyes—probably the exact color of your eyes."

So, he went there. I decided the best answer was no answer.

"Yes—contrary to popular belief, flattery will get you everywhere," I laughed. "I'm ready for the next question. Bring it on, question boy."

Let the games begin.

Chapter Nine

William—Week Two

Today was my final checkup with the doctor. I was sure my arm—and the rest of me—had healed quite nicely.

Dr. Rawlings wanted to give me one last look-see, to ensure I was ready to return to the front.

I'd been at the base hospital for three weeks. It's ironic, really; the past three weeks had been the best in my life. It was all because of Charlotte. I'd heard of blokes becoming attached to their nurses. I was attached to my nurse, but I don't think it had anything to do with her actually nursing me. She was kind, funny, competent, fair-minded, and stunningly beautiful—the most beautiful girl I'd ever seen.

I was going to ask Dr. Rawlings permission to court Charlotte.

He might not give me his permission, *I silently considered.* Who'd likely support a suitor who might be dead in a week? On the other hand, he might find the possibility quite appealing. It's just been him and Charlotte for almost all of her life. I'm not sure he'd appreciate a bloke attempting to woo his daughter.

"Hello, Doctor," I said as I entered the tent. "I think today will be my last inspection, sir."

"Hello, Lieutenant," Dr. Rawlings replied. "Let's look at the bumps and bruises and send you on your way."

I sat on the examining table and waited for Dr. Rawlings to complete the examination.

"Well, son," he said, "you've healed to perfection. It's a shame to send you back in harm's way. But I know you wouldn't have it any other way."

He extended his hand and I shook it gingerly. "Good luck, Lieutenant."

"Sir," I said.

It's now or never, *I thought.*

"I'd like your permission to write to Charlotte when I return to the front. And, when I'm able, I'd also like your permission to court your daughter.

"I know three weeks is a short time to determine one's feelings. Honestly, sir, I don't know if you believe in love at first sight—I know I didn't believe in it. Frankly, I thought one girl would be quite as good as the next when it came time to select a wife.

"I know there's a war on, and my chances of making it back aren't as promising as one would like, but if I come back, I'd like it to be to Charlotte. Your daughter is kind, funny, and smart. She's the girl I've been waiting for; I didn't even know I was waiting."

The silence was intimidating. I wanted to say more, but I thought I might have said too much already.

I considered myself an honorable bloke.

However, if Charlotte's father doesn't give me permission, it's quite likely I'll pursue her anyway—to hell with the consequences, I decided.

I could see Dr. Rawlings was considering my request.

Damn, *I thought.* I shouldn't have asked permission. If Charlotte was like any other nurse, her father wouldn't be here, and I would've proceeded without consideration of her parent. Since he is here, and according to Charlotte, the only reason she was able to join the unit from Washington University was because her father was in the group, I needed to proceed in the proper fashion.

"Well, Lieutenant," Dr. Rawlings finally responded, "my first response was no. You are correct, son. The life expectancy of a young man of your rank in His Majesty's service is approximately six weeks."

I noticed he used the past tense in his first response. Hope reigned eternal.

"However, Charlotte likes you. I like you. Maintaining a correspondence with Charlotte while you're at the front poses no threat to my daughter. I seems an inopportune time for you to be courting anyone. You have my permission to correspond with Charlotte. If your path crosses Charlotte's again, we can discuss the possibility of a courtship."

He grasped my extended hand securely, "Thank you, sir."

"Good luck, son," he responded.

Charlotte waited for me near the officers' mess, per our pre-arranged agreement.

I heard her laughter. The sound of it was like a punch in the gut. I hoped to hear it forever. As I took the corner, I located Charlotte, seated with a few nurses in chairs outside the mess. I loved the way she moved and the way sun reflected off her hair.

Charlotte glanced up and caught my gaze.

Breathe, old fellow, *I reminded myself.* You remember how, don't you?

Then she smiled. "Well, hello, William—I gave up all hope you were going to join me. You remember Lilly, don't you?"

"It's a pleasure," *I replied, and nodded to Lilly.*

"Charlotte, may I have a few moments of your time?"

She grasped my hand as I gently pulled her to her feet. "You most certainly may have a moment of my time, Lieutenant."

She placed her hand in the crook of my arm as we walked away from the mess hall. We strolled across the infield of the racecourse in companionable silence, with no real destination in mind.

"I spoke to your father a short while ago. He says I'm fit for battle."

Charlotte remained silent.

"I'll be returning to my unit tomorrow," I continued. "I'm not sure exactly where I'll find my unit, but my orders are drawn."

She abruptly stopped walking and turned to face me. "Well," *she said softly.* "I wish you well."

"Charlotte," I said, closing the space between us so our bodies were almost touching, yet with enough space to ensure propriety was observed.

I inhaled and absorbed her fragrance, hoping I could burn the memory into my senses. "I'd like to continue our friendship when I return to the front. May I write to you? Will you write to me? I requested permission from your father, and he gave me his support."

Charlotte didn't attempt to move away. Her body swayed toward mine.

"Charlotte?" *I whispered softly as I waited for her reply.*

The sound of my mobile ringing jolted me back to the present. It took me a moment to gather my wits and locate my mobile.

"Hello."

"Hey, Wills," Charlie was on the mobile.

My evening was complete.

"Hey, Charlie," I responded eloquently, as always.

"Sorry I'm calling so late," Charlie said, "we were at the café, speaking French for our exam tomorrow, and I didn't realize the time. I probably shouldn't have called, but I just wanted to hear your voice."

How could a bloke take offense? I glanced at the clock and realized it was past two in the morning. It was late.

"No worries," I assured her. "I missed hearing your voice, as well." *No need to tell her I was in the middle of a conversation with her early twentieth-century self,* I decided.

"We can practice speaking French, if you like," I said. "I'm getting very good at translating between French and English."

Soul Mates ~ Liz Morrison

Charlie laughed. I loved the sound of her laughter.

"Mademoiselle Charlie," I continued "*Je t'adore. Le son de ton rire est une joie à mes oreilles. Tu es très beau. Vous faites ma chaleur monter en flèche.*"

"Let's see," she began. "Apparently, you adore me. The sound of my laughter brings joy to your ears—I'll need to share that with Katie and Ryan; the sound of my laughter makes them laugh harder.

"I'm very beautiful—considering you've seen me once—I improved over great distances. And I make your heart soar. That's really sweet.

"You know, Wills," she said, "I really didn't think you were a player, but now I'm not entirely confident in my conclusion. I'll bet you say that to all the mademoiselles who come seeking your assistance."

I laughed.

"I missed being at home for the Fourth of July. Don't be mad at me, being that you're British and all. But it's really my favorite holiday." Charlie's voice was wistful.

"That's your Independence Day, right? Silly American girl," I replied. "We've been allies for over a century."

"I know, right," Charlie replied.

"So, I started researching information on World War I for my work assignment," she went on. "I think I'm a little depressed tonight. Thinking about all of those guys who died…it's just sad. I think being sad after the research reminded me I miss home."

I tried to connect the Fourth of July, missing home, and research on World War I. I got nothing.

"Did you know some guys lied about their age to join in the war? One kid was fourteen years old, but he looked old for his age. A lot of parents didn't know whether their sons were alive or dead, because they'd enlisted under false names. That would be horrible for the parents," Charlie continued. "It's just so sad," she concluded with a catch in her voice.

"Charlie, are you all right?" I asked.

"I don't know what's wrong with me," she said. "I shouldn't have called."

"If two people are going to begin a relationship, it's important that they really know the other person. We're building our relationship over the mobile," I said. "So, what else happened today? You did research for your job, you spoke a multitude of French, and you missed me." I concluded.

"Aren't you the confident one?" she retorted. "Yes, I missed you. I decided it's weird, because I hardly know you. But I feel like I've known you forever. Then I listen to Andrew discuss your conquests while speaking French, and it's just as depressing when he says it in French as when he says it in English. I don't believe him, but Ryan does. I find Andrew rather perplexing," Charlie said with a sigh.

I need to ring Andrew, I resolved.

"Thank you for not believing Andrew. I'll ring him tomorrow," I said.

"Why is it that young men are so eager to go to war?" Charlie abruptly turned the conversation back to her research on World War I. "If a war lasts long enough, their time will come. I think women should register for the draft. It doesn't seem fair only men can be drafted. What do they do in the UK regarding the draft? Do you have a draft?"

"Is the draft the same as conscription?" I asked. "We had conscription during World War I and World War II, but we don't have it today." *Charlie is interesting, as well as beautiful* I thought. *I like the way she moves back and forth between topics.*

"I had a dream on the flight from the States to France about meeting a woman whose son enlisted early," she told me. "It was so sad. But at least her son enlisted under his own name. Oh—here's something weird about me: I dream about World War I pretty much every night. Sometimes the dreams are so real. It's like I'm remembering, not dreaming."

Soul Mates ~ Liz Morrison

She sighed deeply. "Now you think I'm cray cray or something. I really shouldn't have called, but I wanted to hear your voice, and now I'm doing all the talking. Sorry."

"Charlie, I don't think you're cray cray. We don't say cray cray much in the UK. We have several other words that mean you've taken crazy to a whole new level, like nutter, stark-raving mad, bonkers, a few sandwiches short of a picnic, completely mental, mad as a hatter, loony, barmy, dippy, away with the fairies. I don't think you're any of those, either." I replied.

"You like my voice," I went on. "Well, I like your voice, too. I especially like it when you say 'Hi, Wills'. It's so American."

I followed Charlie's lead as I abruptly changed the conversation back to young men and war. "I think young men join the war effort because they want to be part of something bigger than themselves," I told her. "They believe in God and country and protecting their homeland. Young blokes don't really think they're going to die. They know death is a possibility, but not in their reality when they enlist. After they get to the front, the glory of the battle is probably lost in the reality of the battle. Look at all the guys who play *Call of Duty*. They get to be heroes, without the reality of the actual pain and suffering that accompanies a wound in battle. Anyway, that's what I think."

"Interesting," Charlie replied. "I don't understand the whole war-games thing. I like to read the letters from soldiers. It's interesting to read their thinking about the war. It's ironic so many of them want to go and fight and their letters are all about missing home. We won't have the same type of legacy from the recent wars. Most of the troops communicate with e-mail. I think getting letters is nice. Maybe I should write a letter to my mom and dad. They probably would like a letter, in addition to e-mail."

"I send handwritten thank-you notes. Does that count?" I asked.

Charlie laughed, "Hmmm, thank-you notes the same as a letter? I don't think so."

"I have a bloody brilliant idea," I said. "I'll write to you."

"Why yes, Sir William, that is bloody brilliant." Charlie said with a quite horrible British accent. "Okay, I'll write a letter to you, too."

"After we hang up, text me the address of your hotel," she directed. "Oh, send me the address for next week's hotel. I want to make sure the one letter I write to you in your entire life finds you in the right place."

"I'm super tired," Charlie yawned into the phone. "I hate saying goodbye."

"No worries," I said. "I'll ring you tomorrow. I think I may stay up and pen you a letter."

"'Night, Wills," Charlie said, in a sexy, sleepy voice.

"Good night, Charlie—dream of me."

"Always," she said, and the line went dead.

I dug around in my pack, trying to find my travel itinerary. After locating the hotel information for the next week, I picked up my mobile and sent Charlie a text with the address.

Writing a letter required the right materials. I had a pen, but I needed paper. *Hotels should have paper and envelopes,* I thought. I dug through the drawers—mission accomplished. I located writing paper and an envelope.

I stared at the blank paper. *Didn't I ask Charlotte if she'd correspond with me?* I considered. *It seems a little too coincidental that my past life and my present life are running a parallel course.*

Maybe my dreams are guiding my present actions. Or maybe my actions are guiding dreams. I don't know, I told myself. *I do know I promised Charlie I'd write her a letter. I need to get cracking.*

Dear Charlie...

Chapter Ten

Charlie—Week Three

"See you tomorrow, girls," I called to Katie, Holly, and Libby as I closed the door to my room.

Sitting down at my desk, I turned on my iPad and reviewed the events for the upcoming week on my desk calendar. I drew a heart on Thursday, because Wills would be back in Rouen.

Today the audio tour of the Rouen Town Centre had been awesome. Ryan was so excited as he tweeted about every site. For once, his tweets were probably worth reading.

Andrew, as always, was totally hilarious. I hoped Wills wasn't annoyed with my color commentary from each site. Really, how could anyone be annoyed with pictures of the Notre Dame Cathedral, Quartier Saint Maclou, and the necropolis of the Aître Saint Maclou?

The necropolis had definitely been the most macabre part of our day, as the courtyard was formerly an ossuary, where the bones of plague victims from the 1300s were buried, and victims from the 1500s bones were stacked. The building had carvings of skulls, bones, and gravedigger's tools. It was pretty interesting, in a disturbing way; Wills would have loved it. I hoped Snap Chat was almost as good as being there.

Wills would join us for the Monet tour next weekend, but Andrew would be in London with his tour group.

I'd planned a field trip for Wills and me to all of the World War I sites I wanted to visit. They weren't actually tourist attractions, but maybe with my work starting in a couple of weeks, I could propel them into worthy tourist-attraction sites. It was hard to compete with Notre Dame Cathedral.

"Hey, Wills," I said into my cell.

"Hey, Charlie," Wills replied, imitating the way I usually said hello.

"I'm uploading all my photos from our Tour de Rouen to Facebook. The only thing missing from the day is you."

"You sure know how to make a guy feel special," he replied. "I miss you, too. I enjoyed the commentary on each site. I really felt like I was with you."

"Oh, too much?" I asked. "I felt so bad you couldn't be with us."

"No, I'm sincere," Wills replied. "I really liked it. It was good."

"Speaking of good," Wills continued, "I received your letter today. It smells good. It smells like I remember you smelling."

"I'm smelly?" I asked, laughing at the same time. I'd sprayed a hint of my perfume on the letter, thinking it was romantic. Now it was kind of embarrassing.

"Okay," I said, "are you ready for William and Charlie's Excellent Adventure? I totally planned our World War I not-quite-ready-for-Office-de-tourisme-de-la-communauté-Rouen tour. Of course, the timing all depends on your work at the school. The benefit is, no matter what the timing, it'll fit in with the work I'm doing for the office of tourism.

"What are you doing right now?" I asked.

"I'm stretching out on the bed and assuming a comfortable position," he said. "I'm also picturing you lying on the futon in your flat, with your head on a pillow and your feet propped up on the backrest. Did I mention you're starkers?"

"Starkers?" I repeated.

"Starkers is British for 'naked'," William replied.

"William," I laughed. "You are so not-funny. Now, picture me with clothes on, because we have serious business to discuss."

"Right, then," William replied with a loud sigh. "Mmm, not working—you're still starkers."

I ignored him.

"Anyway...first, we're going to locate Base Hospital Twenty-One. After we explore that, we're going to St. Sever Cemetery. I think all of the Americans who were buried in the cemetery were shipped back to the States, but the British soldiers and other allied troops who were interred still remain," I explained.

"We also need to take a weekend trip to Ypres-Passchendaele. I want to go to the site of the Battle of Messines Ridge. I can convince Ryan and Katie to join us. What do you think?"

I checked out the information on my iPad while I talked. "Do you want me to send you the links?"

There was a long pause. "Wills," I said, "are you there?"

"What made you select these locations?" Wills asked quietly.

"I don't know, really," I replied. "I guess they're all connected to Base Hospital Twenty-One," I replied. "We can go to more places, if you want. I just really want to go to these."

"Charlie," Wills said with a question in his voice, "do you believe in reincarnation?"

"Wow, that was a real switch in the conversation," I replied. "Reincarnation? Well, I don't think it's impossible. So, I guess that means it's possible. It makes sense for people to come back to live another life if they didn't get it done right the first time. What do you think?"

"I think it's possible," William replied. "I read a book about a little kid who believes he is reincarnated from a World War II fighter pilot. The name of the book is *Soul Survivor*."

"'Sole' as in 'single,' or 'soul,' as in a person's spirit?" I asked.

"Soul, as in a person's spirit," Wills said. "Sorry I got off track. I think the destinations you selected are great. Interestingly, those would've been the same ones I selected."

"Are you sure?" I asked. "I can make any additions you want."

Wills laughed, "Additions, but no deletions. I got it. When we go to Ypres-Passchendaele, we can stay at Talbot House. It was actually used by British soldiers during World War I. What do you think?" William asked.

He went on, "We should also go to the Tommy Café in Pozières. It's about one and a half hours by car from Rouen. I tried to locate the Tommy Café website, but couldn't find it, so I used Google Images and found some great pictures. It's ace."

"Ace," I repeated. "That's British for 'awesome'? Okay, I just found the photos in Google. The Tommy Café is ace. I think the life-size trench will be wicked awesome to explore. The front of the café looks like a nice-yet-boring place to dine, but the back of the place is a museum. That'll be a great addition to our trip."

"Charlie, what'll make it ace is going with you," Wills said. "I'm looking forward to seeing you in a few days."

"Me, too," I replied.

"William," I said softly. "I hate saying good-bye to you." I glanced at my clock—it was almost 1:30 a.m.

"I never understood the hang-up-the-mobile conversations my mates had with their girlfriends. I get it now," Wills said. "Do you want to hang up on the count of three?" he asked.

I laughed.

"Right, then…dumb idea."

"It's sweet," I replied. "Good night, Wills. Dream of me."

"I always do," he replied. "Sweet dreams, Charlie."

The alarm was set for 6:30 a.m. I closed my eyes and thought of William.

Soul Mates ~ Liz Morrison

My Dearest Charlotte,

Yesterday I was playing chess with one of my mates and thought of you. I beat him quite soundly. After numerous games with numerous chaps, I've come to the conclusion that on the entire Western Front, you're my only worthy competition. I've put my chess board away and am determined not to challenge another to a game until my challenger is you.

Charlotte, God is probably confused by my prayers of late. First, I pray I'm not injured, so I may see you again. Then I pray I am injured—not seriously, of course—so I may see you again.

In your last letter, you asked me to describe my typical day, so I shall. Daily life at the front is really quite dull. A typical day in the trenches starts with a stand-to-arms, called a stand-to by the boys. Following the stand-to, we shoot into the air to ward off early-morning attacks from the Huns. The men call this time of shooting into the air the morning hate. It's ironic; Fritz also employs a stand-to and morning hate. Both sides stand and shoot at nothing simultaneously while each thinks the other side may attack. Maybe it should be called the morning hallo.

After the stand-to, we clean our weapons and wait for breakfast to be served. Following breakfast, we work around the trench, including repair work on the sandbags. During the remainder of the day we write letters, play chess, and turn shell casings and other non-reusable items into art. One of the chaps is assisting me in creating a gift for you from shell casings.

When we're not fighting, we suffer from excruciating boredom. I relive my boredom by thinking of you, writing to you, and making you gifts. If not for my injury, I wouldn't have the memory of you to fill my long days and even longer nights. So I also thank God that I was injured at the right place and right time to make your acquaintance.

A chap who returned to the front from Base Hospital Twenty-One said the camp was attacked by German bombers. I hope you and your father are well. I received your letter yesterday, so I concluded *you are hale and hearty and waiting eagerly for my return. Your letters are greatly valued, and I am ever grateful that you continue our correspondence.*

No more news at present, but will write again soon. From yours affectionately,

William

I read the letter a final time and placed it in the small bundle of correspondence I'd received from William thus far. The delivery of the mail was surprisingly reliable, and I received a letter from William every three to four days. I was afraid this would change with my assignment to the casualty clearing station at Ypres-Passchendaele.

Gathering my meager belongings and the letter to William, I left the hut. As a postscript, I included where I was going to be stationed. I planned to post the letter prior to our departure.

"Safe journey, Charlotte," Lilly said as I walked toward our waiting transportation.

"Time to move out, sister," a soldier shouted.

After several months, I was still uncomfortable being called 'sister.' As a Catholic, the reference to 'sister' made me think of nuns. I was certainly not a nun. Oh, well.

I waved a final time to Lilly. Joining the group waiting to depart our base hospital for the casualty clearing station at the front, I hoped I was ready for the task ahead. I also hoped, by some quirk of fate, I'd cross paths with William.

Chapter Eleven

WILLIAM—WEEK THREE

I glanced at the clock sitting on the table next to the bed. It was the perfect time to ring home. Grabbing my mobile, I assumed a comfortable position on the bed, dialed, and waited for a reply.

"Cheers, Mum, it's your favorite son, William."

"My only son," she replied. "We've been waiting for you to ring. How are your travels?"

"Well, my travels are ace," I said.

I needed to tell my mum and dad about Charlie.

"Well, England is just as I remember it. Do you see the irony here, Mum? I go to Rouen, and end up in London," I said with a loud sigh.

"I'm sorry, Wills," she said. "You still have months left of your trip to search for information on the other William Harrington. Were you able to dig through the satchel?"

Hmm, I forgot about the satchel, I thought. "No Mum, I haven't had time."

She laughed. "Okay, Wills, maybe the trip to Rouen is helping you get past the past and the entire William-Harrington-reincarnated-as-my-William-Harrington."

I took a deep breath. "Mum," I said, "can you get Dad to the mobile and put it on speaker?"

She paused and I heard her call Dad.

"Hey, William," he said jovially. "Are you enjoying your working holiday?"

"Well, Dad, I met Charlotte. Her name is Charlie, and she's from the United States. She's smart, funny, and gorgeous."

"THE Charlotte?" Dad sounded incredulous.

"Yes," I said, "THE Charlotte. I've been recording all of my dreams, or memories—whatever they are—in a journal. Trying to put it all together is kind of crazy, but I feel less crazy."

"Does she remember, too?" Mum asked.

"Yes, but she doesn't know it's a memory," I replied. "Her dreams are about me in a World War I setting. She thinks it's because she's fascinated with World War I and smitten by me," I said.

"Smitten, is she?" Father joked.

"William," Mum said softly, "are you sure her dreams aren't exactly what she thinks they are?"

"Mum," I replied, "I don't know. I do know when I met her, I knew her. She's Charlotte from my dreams—only more. I know it sounds impossible, but when we touched, it was electric."

I chuckled. "Seriously, it was an electric shock, like you get from static electricity. She felt it, too."

"So, have you discussed this with her?" Mum asked.

"No. I plan to when I see her in Rouen," I said. "I'm not exactly sure how I'm going to bring up the subject. I'm sure the right words will come."

"William," Dad joined the discussion, "what's next?"

I sat quietly for a minute. I looked up at the ceiling of my hotel room—hoping for an answer, I reckoned.

"Well, Dad," I finally replied, "I don't know. I just don't know. There must be a point to all of this, right? I hope there is a point to all of this."

"Whatever the past," I continued, "I'm totally enamored of her. Charlie is an incredible girl. I just hope enlightening Charlie of our possible—I think, quite probable—relationship doesn't have her running back to the USA."

"How's Andrew?" Mum asked, changing the conversation.

"Andrew's Andrew; for some reason he decided to tell Charlie's American friends that I'm a real player. Charlie doesn't believe him, but one of her friends does."

"A player?" Dad asked.

"Womanizer," Mum filled in. "Why would Andrew imply you were a player?"

"I don't know," I replied. "I haven't talked to him in over three weeks. I think he likes Charlie. I haven't told him Charlie is my dream girl."

Dad chuckled over my unintended pun.

"I probably shouldn't have told him about the reincarnation stuff. He's been acting a little odd."

"Andrew will come 'round," Mum continued.

My mobile clicked, indicating someone was trying to ring me.

"Hate to ring and run, but Charlie's giving me a ring. Cheers," I said, and clicked over to my other call.

"Hey, Wills," Charlie said as I answered.

"Cheers, Charlie. I was hoping you'd ring me."

"I'm super excited to see you," she continued. "I probably shouldn't tell you. It makes me sound eager."

"Are you eager?" I asked. "I'm equally eager to see you, too. What did you do today?"

I hated mundane conversations, but I enjoyed listening to Charlie describe the events in Rouen. I settled back on the narrow bed. *A long chat with Charlie is the perfect way to spend my last night in London*, I thought.

"Today—hmm," she replied. "Nothing too exciting; just the usual. Katie, Ryan, Mike, Holly, Libby, Andrew, and I went out to dinner and then to a café. Andrew's getting ready to take his group of French businessmen on a tour of Great Britain, which you probably already know. Umm, Katie starts her internship next week. Oh yeah, and I missed you. Nothing new there."

"We did have kind of a deep conversation on fate and destiny. We were debating the idea of soul mates, too. What do you think?" she asked.

My hands started to sweat. Leaning my head back on the pillows, I contemplated what to say. I wanted to blurt it out, "Hey Charlie, I loved you a hundred years ago, how about we pick up where we left off?"

That might be a bit forward, and she might think I'd gone mad, I decided.

"What do you think?" I asked.

Charlie's laughter made my chest constrict. I loved this girl. Whoa, I knew it, yet I didn't know it.

This must be love, even though it's totally insane, I thought. *It's too soon to come to that bold decision. We haven't even kissed. It just felt like what I reckoned love should feel like.*

"What do I think?" Charlie replied, with laughter in her voice. "You need to answer first."

"Why?"

"Umm, because you're the boy," she replied promptly.

Now I laughed. "That makes absolutely no sense. Etiquette, even in the backward United States of America, indicates it's always ladies before gentlemen."

"Did you just insult my country?" Charlie replied, still laughing. "I'm going to ignore the insult, because I want you to respond to the question. Fate or destiny? Soul mates or just mates? To be or not to be? Okay, you don't need to respond to the last one, but I'm waiting for your reply to questions one and two."

Soul Mates ~ Liz Morrison

As Charlie talked, I found a definition of fate and destiny. "According to dictionary.com, fate is defined as 'something that unavoidably befalls a person; fortune; lot'. It also includes death, destruction, or ruin as a possible definition—not very cheery."

"Wills," Charlie responded, "you're taking all the fun out of this conversation. Seriously, you're quoting dictionary.com."

She paused and then asked, "What's the definition for destiny?"

"Well Charlie, destiny, according to dictionary.com, is something that is to happen, or has happened to a particular person or thing; lot or fortune. This one includes a mention of a goddess. Well, since I think you are a goddess, I believe in destiny."

"Seriously, Wills, what do you think?" Charlie asked. "Do you believe in destiny?"

"I think meeting you was inevitable," I replied. "So, do I believe in destiny? Yes, I do. Now, on to the topic of soul mates. Charlie do you believe there's only one person who's your perfect match?"

There was a long pause. I hoped I was still connected. One of the many disadvantages of the mobile was the inability to see Charlie. It would be easier to have had some of our conversations if we were looking at each other.

"Well," Charlie said, "until recently, I hadn't thought about it at all. There's a twenty-question online survey to determine whether you've found your soul mate. The site says, 'some connections feel deeper than others, like they've been there forever.' It continues with, 'Sometimes it's just as if you click, and other times it's like you've known one another your entire lives, but the feeling is as eerie as it is cool.' Then it concludes with, 'Have you known each other before?'

"Anyway, it just made me think of meeting you at the café and the connection. We really haven't talked about the electricity thing—talk about eerie and cool."

I didn't know how to reply. I continued to stare at the ceiling, hoping the correct words would form and I'd know exactly what to say.

"The other thing," Charlie continued, "are the dreams. Seriously, I dream about you every night. Not the now-you, but you-from-a-hundred-years-ago, who apparently is embedded in my dreams of World War I. The feeling is eerie and it's cool."

"Charlie," I finally replied, "I have dreams about you, too. And, ironically, they're also you-from-a-hundred-years-ago. It's eerie and it's cool. I feel like I've known you my whole life...or longer."

A pause followed. "It's really crazy. I know we can figure this out," Charlie said with a sigh. "Shoot—hang on, Wills."

In the background, I heard her talking to someone. "Hey, Wills, I'm so sorry—I promised Katie I'd look over her portfolio before her presentation tomorrow. I don't want to hang up, and I don't want to end this conversation."

"No worries, Charlie," I replied. "I'm looking forward to seeing you tomorrow."

"Bye, Wills."

I wanted to bang my head in frustration. However, it was probably best to continue the conversation in person.

Resuming my online search for soul mates, I found the quiz Charlie referenced. The first question was, 'when you first met, was it as if you already knew each other?' The second question caused me to pause and remember: 'Did you become very close, very quickly, like within a matter of days, without a crisis situation to bond you?'

The heavy rains continued, turning the Ypres lowlands into a swamp. Our bombardment of the German lines destroyed the drainage system in the area, making matters even worse. The heavy mud challenged the infantry and made the use of tanks impossible. The newest shell holes were flooded to the brim.

Taking inventory of the men under my command, I saw that every man was soaked through, and each was attempting to keep his rifle at the ready.

Soul Mates ~ Liz Morrison

    The living conditions in the camp were disgusting. This morning, the cook had tried to supply bacon for breakfast to accompany the sodden biscuits and cold stew. The troops declared the bacon smelled like dead men...so much for the cook's attempt to provide a more appetizing option. The lack of healthy food was making the men sick.

    Many of the men looked ill. Their faces were gray, dirty, and unshaven, as we'd no clean water. I saw the habitual shrugging of the shoulders, indicating their clothing was full of lice. We hadn't been able to change our clothes for weeks. I was certain I looked as miserable as the rest of the men, and I knew my clothes were just as infested.

    As I trudged through the mud, I thought of Charlotte. Thoughts of her lightened my mood and gave me the will to fight. I hoped to receive a letter from her today. It was rather ironic that, amidst this hell-on-earth, the post always arrived on time.

    "Harrington, looks like another letter from your battlefield angel. Some blokes have all the luck. I've not met another who got himself injured and then wins the sister as a prize. As homely as you are, it's quite shocking, really."

    "Thanks, Sergeant," I replied, as I accepted the letter. "Send my regards to the missus."

    I examined the envelope. My name and rank were proclaimed in Charlotte's elegant handwriting. I gingerly sniffed the envelope and smiled as Charlotte's fresh, clean scent wafted from the note. I carefully sliced the envelope and unfolded the letter.

    My Dearest William,

    I was enormously relieved to receive your last later. It is quite selfish that I believe I should hear from you every three to four days, when other young women only hear from their loved ones once or twice a month—maybe even less. I decided not to let it bother me, as those other young women had the pleasure of knowing their young man before the war was on. I determined, since we met after the war began and only had a few weeks to build our friendship, that it is perfectly acceptable for me to be selfish in this way. How else, dear William, shall we get to know one other, if not in our letters?

Conditions at the front sound quite brutal. I'm confident, however, in your ability to keep both you and your men safe while defeating Fritz. I believe I'll see you again soon, but I don't wish for you to be injured so we can keep company. I'm sure you'll have a leave soon and will have the opportunity to visit Base Hospital Twenty-One.

You mentioned you enjoy hearing about my day. Therefore, I shall enjoy sharing it with you. Close your eyes and picture the hospital grounds, and it'll be like we're together.

My morning begins with a quick, refreshing bath and a light breakfast. After dining, we begin our rounds. During rounds, we check on patients and pray for their complete recovery.

The injured come to us during the night. Each time they arrive, I pray you're not among them. I also pray you'll be among those who arrive—with a very minor injury I can treat and keep you by my side in the relative safety of the base hospital.

'Relative safety' is a statement I wish was less true. A few days past, a bomb exploded in the hospital compound. We were in a state of shock in the aftermath of the explosion. Two orderlies were killed and several people were injured. It certainly brought the war home.

My dearest William, I think of you often and remember our last conversation with great clarity. I look forward to your letters, and hope to hear from you soon.

With Great Affection,

Charlotte

PS: I am being sent to the casualty clearing station at Ypres-Passchendaele. Please send your next correspondence to my new location. I will probably be at the station one or two weeks.

I read the postscript carefully.

Charlotte was coming to Ypres.

Chapter Twelve

CHARLIE

Ryan stood in the narrow hallway separating my room from Katie's, pacing impatiently as he tried to get us to move faster.

"Come on, ladies, we don't have forever. It's karaoke night, and I have my game face on," Ryan called for, like, the one-hundredth time.

"Ryan, seriously," Katie said from behind her closed door. "Chill, will ya? The karaoke machine won't disappear if we don't arrive at the exact moment you can start singing. I'm sure the ladies of Rouen are waiting patiently for you, like you're waiting patiently for us."

Silence from the hallway—good or bad? Good, if Ryan decided to give in gracefully, or bad, if he left us to find our own way to the karaoke place.

Ryan finally replied, "God, Charlie, I thought I could count on you to be unfashionably ready. You're really letting me down, girl."

"Two seconds," I responded.

"Great," Ryan said.

I opened the door with some trepidation. I hoped I looked pretty, but not like I was trying to look pretty.

"I'm ready." I turned the key to lock my room.

Ryan stared at me in what I would describe as stunned disbelief.

Well, shoot. I must look overdone, I winced. *Now I'll have to change. Darn it.*

"Well, crap. I look that bad—I'll go change," I said to the suddenly silent chatterbox Ryan.

"Charlie, don't change. You are smokin'." Ryan said.

Katie walked out of her room just as Ryan finished his compliment. "Wow, Charlie. I've never seen you look so put-together. You always look great, but seriously, you'll bring your British boy to his knees."

Ryan glanced from Katie to me. "British boy," he said, "is this whole outrageously gorgeous thing for William?"

"Outrageously gorgeous," mimicked Katie. "That's putting it on pretty thick."

Ryan looked at Katie. "I'd think you were getting all hot for the English boys, too, if you didn't always look all hot."

Katie looked at Ryan with a perplexed expression. "Ryan, I think you just gave me an incredibly nice compliment. Thanks."

Once again, Ryan glanced from me to Katie. "Girls!" he said, obviously exasperated.

"What's the name of the place with the finest karaoke in Rouen?" asked Katie.

"La Boîte à Bières. The Brits found it doing a Google search. Sounds like jolly good fun," Ryan said in his finest imitation of a British accent.

"Let's see," Ryan said. "What's the best way to travel to thirty-five rue Cauchoise?"

"How should I know?" Katie replied with a hint of irritation. "Oh, you're talking to your phone."

We walked down the steps into the lobby. Holly, Libby, and Mike were waiting for us.

Soul Mates ~ Liz Morrison

I didn't see William or Andrew.

"The Brits are meeting us at the bar," Mike explained. "They had to finish up some work at the school for their class tomorrow. I guess it's better to get it done tonight." "It's about a twenty-five minute walk to La Boîte à Bières. Looking at your shoes, ladies, we probably need to hail a cab," Ryan said.

Mike asked Peter about hiring a cab. We'd been in Rouen for almost a month, and we'd either walked or used public transportation. Getting a cab would be really quite a luxury.

"Peter called one of his friends who knew a guy who drove a cab. He should be here any minute; we just need to wait outside," Mike explained.

"Six in a cab," Holly said. "Well, that should be rather cozy."

Ryan told the driver the address to La Boîte à Bières and we cruised through the streets of Rouen. Mike and our cab driver had a lively conversation *en Français*. It was amazing how well we could speak French. After four weeks of intense French, we rarely spoke English.

I had a nervous feeling in my stomach. William had arrived in Rouen this afternoon while I was in class. When I finished class, he'd been engaged in a conversation with the head of the school regarding his work for the past several weeks with the French businessmen.

Our phone conversations had been amazing. It was crazy that we'd built a relationship over the phone and on Skype. I kind of felt like I'd bared my soul and he did, too; I hoped it wouldn't be awkward.

"We're here!"

We arrived at La Boîte à Bières. Mike paid our cab driver and we tumbled out of the cab.

La Boîte à Bières is a *maison à colombage*—half-timbered and half-plastered.

"This is the perfect corner bar," Libby exclaimed.

The building was four stories high. Many of the windows on the ground floor were adorned with fleur-de-lis. The pillar on the corner of the building seemed to bear the weight of the building and was slightly crumbling; it just added to the ambiance. It was perfect.

I leaned over and whispered to Katie, "My heart is pounding—in anticipation or anxiety. I have a sick feeling in my stomach, too. How can I be into a guy I've known for less than a month, spent a few hours with at a café, and then bonded with over the phone and texting?"

Katie whispered back, "He's totally hot, remember?"

Oh yeah, I remember, I thought. I dreamed about his hotness every night; though in my dreams he was a World War I soldier. When I saw him again, it would probably be a huge disappointment…or maybe the strange jolt of electricity would still be present. I figured I'd find out soon enough.

"Oh, wow!" Holly exclaimed. "This place is totally cool. Let's find a seat close to karaoke, so Ryan will have avid fans for his performance."

"Great idea, Holly," Ryan replied. "I know you ladies will want front-row seats."

Weaving through the crowd, we tried to locate a seat. Holly was right—the place was totally cool. The walls in some parts of the bar were the same half-timber as the outside. One room had a pool table with chairs positioned around the wall. A room on an upper level had a foosball table—referred to as table football—and the infamous karaoke corner.

"Charlie," Katie whispered directly into my ear, "It's going to be fine. And by the way, look to your left."

And there he was.

"Hey, you Yanks," Andrew yelled across the bar. "We've got ourselves a lovely table right near the karaoke machine, per Ryan's specific request. We moved a table here, a chair there, and Bob's your uncle."

Soul Mates ~ Liz Morrison

"'And Bob's your uncle'—I'm sure that's some British phrase that makes absolutely no sense to us Yanks," Katie replied. "Regardless, thanks for getting the table. This place is packed."

"Hey, William," Mike said, "good to see you. Tonight is destined to be the best night we've had so far. Ryan's been dying to get to the karaoke machine. I think he and Andrew put together a plan requiring us all to man up."

"You mean sing on the bloody machine?" Wills asked. He looked at me and smiled.

Can you still live when your heart stops beating? I wondered. The answer must have been yes, because I swear my heart missed several beats.

"I'm in," William said to Mike.

Wills moved around the others at our table, jostled a few people we didn't know, and ended up standing directly in front of me. I was so nervous.

I thought he might be nervous, too. He looked into my eyes and grabbed my hands. It was electric. Looking in to his eyes wasn't awkward—it was perfect.

"Hi," I said, "it's really great to see you."

"It's really great to see you," Wills replied. "And you—wow—you're so gorgeous. Good thing we're smashed into this corner. I can block you from other blokes in the room."

William turned me around, moving me into a corner, blocking my body with his body. I could feel the heat generating from his skin and my temperature went up by at least ten degrees.

"Charlie, I missed your touch." Bringing our entwined hands to his lips, he flipped over my hand and kissed the inside of my wrist. The jolt of his lips on my skin was more intense than when we linked hands.

I really thought I'd imagined our strange, physical connection, I considered. *However, it hasn't diminished; it intensified.*

"Hey, Wills!" Mike shouted. "Let Charlie go and come join our all-boy band, bringing the UK and the US together for an awesome vocal alliance."

William winked at me and let go of my hands. He grabbed my shoulders—electric—and kissed my forehead—bolt of lightning. Grabbing his arm, Mike pulled him to the karaoke machine.

I felt...I don't know...complete, now that he was here.

I joined Katie, Holly, and Libby at our table. I'm not sure how Ryan finagled it, but the UK-US Connection was going first.

The music started. "Oh, my God!" Katie laughed, "They're doing a song by One Direction."

"It's *What Makes You Beautiful,*" I said to the girls as I selected the video feature on my phone. *This is going to be great,* I told myself

Mike took the lead, and Ryan sang the next verse.

The other guys joined in for the chorus.

It was epic. The crowd was cheering them on. Tons of people had their phones up—probably recording, too. The guys rocked.

Andrew sang the next solo. The girls closest to the karaoke machine were totally into it. It was like the guys were really One Direction.

William took the mic—he was so damn sexy—and he walked to me, kneeling at my feet. I was going to die, he was singing just to me, and the boy could sing.

Standing up, he kissed my hand—jolt of lightning—and walked back to the corner.

The guys picked up the next lines as Wills moved back to the group.

The rest of the song was a blur. I was glad I'd recorded it, because I wanted to remember it forever.

William sang the rest of the song to me. I'm usually not confident about things like that, but he took two fingers and pointed them at his eyes and then pointed them at me; he didn't take his eyes off me for the rest of the song.

A month earlier, I would have totally freaked. Tonight, it seemed perfectly rational that the guy of my dreams—really; I dreamt about him all the time; the present him when I was awake, and the past him when I was asleep—would be singing to me in a bar in Rouen.

The crowd went crazy. The guys did the fist-pump-in-the-air thing.

Epic. They finished the song and the crowd went wild.

Ryan, Andrew, and Mike were in their element. William passed on the mic and returned to me.

Katie, Holly, and Libby all talked at once.

"Oh my God, you guys totally rocked."

"That was so awesome."

"I had no idea any of you guys could sing."

"I'm going to post it on YouTube."

Wills grabbed my hand. Electricity shot up my arm. He looked at me, lifted up our clasped hands, looked at our locked hands, and grinned.

He whispered in my ear, "It's nice to be home."

I thought he meant "home," as in his hand in my hand was home, or being with me was like coming home. Whatever it was, I nodded in agreement.

Ryan sat down and pulled out his phone. "I've got to tweet about this," he muttered as he started texting. He didn't notice the group of girls surrounding his chair.

"Ryan," Libby said, "upload the recording. Your followers will love it. You guys were amazing. I had no idea you could sing."

Ryan glanced up, looking at me. "Hey, beautiful, what did you think?"

"Epic, Ryan, totally epic," I said. "Best karaoke performance ever." I gave him a hug.

Mike, Andrew, and Wills were surrounded by girls.

"Charlie," Holly said, "it looks like you have some competition." As Holly described my competition, Wills walked to my side.

"Groupies?" I asked.

"I need one groupie," William said. "Are you interested in the position? The pay's not fantastic, but the company is."

Rather than responding, I was struck dumb. I saw him in a soldier's uniform, saying something similar. Call it Throwback Thursday.

I wanted to wrap my arms around him and bury my face in his neck…just like in my dream.

Wills stared back. *It should be awkward, but it isn't,* I thought.

"Do you want to take a wander?" Wills asked.

I must have look perplexed. "You know," he continued, "a walk around the bar."

"Oh, sure," I replied. "Girls, I'm going with Wills. We're taking a wander."

"A wander?" Katie repeated. "We'll save your spot. The guys are enjoying their five minutes of fame. We're going to spend many Thursday nights at this table. Maybe we should get a Reserved sign or something."

Ryan, Andrew, and Mike were encircled by their new fans. It was probably the greatest moment in Ryan's life. He'd definitely be back on the mic tonight.

William took my hand and electricity flowed. "I love that," he whispered in my ear as he tugged me off the barstool. His breath was so close to my ear, it made my skin tingle.

"Wow—it's totally packed," I said, and turned around toward William.

As I turned, I was knocked into him. Talk about an electric current—we were pressed together from chest to thigh. William's free hand rested protectively in the hollow of my back. He looked stunned. I was stunned.

"Oh God, Charlie," he responded, pressing me closer to him. He wrapped both his arms around me, pulling me closer.

"Hey, mates!" a guy caring several mugs of beer called, breaking our connection. "Can you take it outside? You're right in the middle of the walkway."

"Sorry," Wills said, but he didn't move.

"Sorry," I replied as I broke Wills' embrace and grabbed his hand.

He steered me toward our table, but stopped abruptly near the front door. "Charlie, can we leave?" he asked. "Will you leave with me now?"

I didn't hesitate. "Yes, I'll text Katie."

I pulled out my phone and asked, "Any particular destination?"

"We'll just head toward the flat," William said.

I finished the text and dropped my phone back in my bag. William led me to the door, pulling me through the dense crowd.

When we reached the street corner, Wills pulled out his phone to get directions back to the flat. "It's about a thirty-minute walk," he said. "Would you like to walk, or shall I hail a cab?"

It was a beautiful night, and we were in my favorite section of Rouen. "Let's walk," I said.

I looked at William. I couldn't believe this incredible guy was interested in me.

I had a horrible thought: *What if he wants to leave so he can tell me he isn't really interested in me?*

After all, with all the tales of William's conquests Andrew had shared over the past several weeks, I was the last person he'd be interested in dating. *Well, there goes the perfect night,* I told myself.

"Charlie," Wills asked, "what's wrong? Wait—don't tell me. If you're going to say you don't want to be with me, or this is too fast, or you realized you prefer Andrew, Ryan, Mike, or some other lucky bloke, then don't say anything."

"Are you crazy?" I replied. "I'm worried you want to give me the we-should-be-friends speech."

"You have that speech in the States?" he asked.

Stopping in the middle of the sidewalk, he said, "I want to be friends with you, but I want to be friends as in your boyfriend, not as in a boy who is a friend," he said. "Will that work for you?"

"Are you asking me to be your girlfriend?" I asked.

Rather than answering my question, William gently pulled me into an alcove of a store that was closed for the night. Cornering me, he placed both his hands on each side of my face. I stared into his eyes and waited. Wills was going to kiss me.

Leaning down, he rested his chin on top of my head. "Charlie, you're incredible. You're beautiful, smart, funny, and so damn sexy. I'm going to kiss you, Charlie. I'm a little worried. Neither of us have had much success with snogging."

Removing one hand from the window near my head, he tilted my face upward.

WILLIAM

This was it; the moment of truth. *I just need to lean down and press my lips to hers, and the agony of waiting will be over,* I told myself.

She smelled so good. Everything about her was addictive. I tilted her face upward and leaned down to press my lips against hers.

The kiss got hot and I went out-of-my mind crazy. Charlie wrapped her arms around my neck and I somehow wedged her into the corner of the entry way pressing my body against hers. She tangled her hands in my hair, bringing our bodies closer together.

The pull, the electricity—whatever it was—it connected us. As the kiss got hotter, the pull got stronger. Somehow Charlie's leg was wrapped around my thigh.

I wanted her right now, right here, in an alcove on a back street in Rouen. I wanted to do it more than I wanted to live.

But I wanted Charlie for—well—forever. I'd waited for her my whole life. *This isn't the time or the place,* I told myself.

I thought I deserved a medal or something for preserving Charlie's virtue. Do people say virtue today? Somehow it seemed appropriate.

I started to break the kiss, and Charlie pulled slightly away. "Oh my God, that was so not nothing," she murmured as she rubbed my shoulders, my arms, my back.

Slowly she unwrapped her leg from my body. I was in physical pain and in mental anguish. *Was it as incredible for her as it was for me?* I wondered. *Or was she disappointed? No way could she be disappointed.*

I reached out and took her hand. "Come on, Charlie, let's keep walking."

We continued silently through the streets of Rouen. I clasped Charlie's hand and sort of pulled her along. *No way am I going to discuss the kiss,* I decided. *I need to recover. A long, cold shower might work.* I glanced at Charlie—*probably not.* She looked dazed and confused; similar to how I felt.

"Ouch. Hang on, Wills, I need to take off these heels and put on my flip-flops."

Charlie took her flip-flops out of her bag and leaned on me to change shoes. Putting her shoes in her bag, she smiled up at me. "Much better."

I couldn't stop myself. I cupped her face and kissed her again.

I was prepared for the combustion. When my lips touched hers, it was like a lit match to dry kindling. Her body naturally curved into mine and once again I fell into the vortex. *Not prepared,* I thought. *Not even close.* I gently pulled away, breathing rather hard.

Charlie was breathing hard, too. "Wow." She laid her head against my shoulder.

"'Wow' sums it up rather nicely," I replied. I clasped her hand and we strolled toward our flat.

"Did you enjoy yourself tonight?"

"Which part?" She blushed and continued. "You guys were amazing. I'm sure Andrew, Mike, and Ryan are still basking in the glory of the moment. Do you want to see the recording?"

"I'd rather not," I replied with a laugh. "I'm glad you liked it, because it was great fun singing to you."

"You were singing to me," Charlie replied, with a hint of disbelief in her voice. "I thought you might be. It was so awesome. You were awesome."

Charlie continued, "Hey, there's our building. Thanks for walking me home."

She seemed a little aloof. I needed to make sure I was crystal clear on the path I foresaw for our relationship.

"Charlie, you did agree to be my girlfriend, correct?" I asked as we entered the lobby of our flat.

"Yes—yes, I did," she said.

"Are you good taking the stairs?" I asked. I preferred stairs over elevators.

"I totally prefer the stairs," she said. "I have a strange phobia of elevators. I'm afraid the door will close and I won't be able to get out."

"I'll escort you to the top of the stairs and make sure you get into your room with no troubles, okay?" I said.

"Great," she took the lead and tugged me along.

We reached the top of the stairs. Charlie was one step above me. We were face to face, and her lips were a few centimeters from mine. All thoughts of conversation vanished; it was a perfect opportunity to kiss her again. I was definitely prepared for the potential fireworks.

I looked into Charlie's eyes. I wrapped my arms around her and leaned in.

Our lips met—fireworks exploded. I took several deep breaths and rested my chin against her forehead.

"I'd better go," Charlie whispered. She didn't move.

"Right," I replied, "I should let you go."

I didn't move...she didn't move.

She kissed my cheek. *Not good enough.* I grabbed her chin and kissed her soundly on the mouth. Then I kissed her cheek, her neck, under her chin...

We were spiraling out of control. I kissed my way back to her lips and held her head between my hands to keep her solidly in place. I wasn't sure where I thought she might go, as her arms were securely wrapped around my waist.

Once again we were breathless. Unlocking her arms from my waist, she took a step back.

"I'm going now, really," she said.

THE KISS ACCORDING TO CHARLIE

Tonight was the best night of my life, I thought.

I slowly walked down the hall, away from Wills. The pull to run back into his arms was almost too strong to resist.

I don't know Wills well enough to make the kind of commitment my body appears to crave, I told myself. I blamed it on hormones and the romantic city of Rouen.

I walked down the hall and I knew Wills watched my retreating back.

I glanced over my shoulder; he stood by the railing at the top of the stairs. Exactly as I'd left him after our final kiss.

I smiled. He shook his head and mouthed, "Go to bed."

God, I wanted to kiss him again. I mouthed, "Sweet dreams."

After years, literally years, of kissing guys and being thoroughly disappointed, kissing Wills was totally different.

The problem was, I wanted more than a kiss. I really didn't think it was hormones or the romantic city of Rouen. I thought Wills was the one; THE one. The problem was, I was seventeen and Wills was eighteen, and we were way too young to find the one. I was back to hormones and the romantic city of Rouen.

The room was empty; our friends wouldn't be back till dawn. It required willpower not to call Wills. I laughed, thinking of calling Wills for a booty call. I wondered if guys from England knew what that was.

I hoped he wouldn't call me, either—I'd be a willing participant, and that would be bad.

Instead of calling Wills, I plugged my phone into the charger, hoping it would ring, and then hoping it wouldn't.

How desperate is that? I thought.

The phone rang as I washed my face. I stubbed my toe and tripped over my bag as I rushed to grab my cell.

It was Wills. My stomach totally knotted up. "Hey, Wills! I know—you miss me already."

I heard his disgruntled laugh. "Actually, Charlie, I do miss you already."

"Wills," I replied. *Does the boy have any idea how much I want to pick up where we left off?* I wondered. Hearing his voice made me want to throw away all my moral values.

"Charlie, I need to know something," Wills said softly. His accent was even hotter as a sexy whisper.

"It's about the kiss," he said. "Was it different from the other ones?"

Oh great, I thought. *Maybe the kiss was different for me. Maybe he felt the same way he did with all the other girls—nothing. Oh, shoot. Better to find out now if this was a me thing, and not a we thing.*

"Charlie?" Wills repeated. "Any thoughts on the answer?"

"Okay, I'm taking a risk, and if you don't feel the same way, that's cool. Just let me know," I said. "On a scale from one to ten, our kiss was a twelve. Actually, it's not scalable. Frankly, Wills, I wanted to rip your clothes off and make love to you in the hallway.

"The most I usually feel after—and sometimes during—a kiss is the urge to brush my teeth. Oh, and I don't plan on having sex except with the man I plan to marry. It was a pretty good kiss." I waited quietly for the bomb to drop.

"Bloody hell, a girl doesn't tell a bloke she wishes to rip his bloody clothes off—in the hallway no less—and expect the same bloke to go to bed alone." There was a pause, "But you do, don't you, love?"

Wills called me 'love.' How did I feel about that? Hmmm, I felt okay. Actually, I felt amazing. I felt amazing but anxious, because he still didn't tell me about the kiss and him.

"Wills, what about you?" *Please don't let the anvil fall,* I prayed.

Another long pause; it seemed super long.

I waited. *Please feel the same way.*

"Charlie," Wills said, "I'm trying to get this right. I'd prefer to say it to you in person, rather than on the mobile."

The sick feeling in my stomach spread.

"Charlie, kissing you centered my world. I feel complete. You complete me. And when you're ready to rip the clothes from my body in the hallway...in my room...on the bloody street corner...I'm your man. Good night, Charlie. Sweet dreams."

I completed him. I completed William James Harrington. Well, whatever was between us was a we thing, not just a me thing.

I finished washing my face and climbed between the covers, knowing any dream I dreamed wouldn't be as sweet as being with Wills. *Okay, now I'm downright mushy,* I told myself.

Turning off the bedside lamp, I closed my eyes and sent a quick thank you to God. "Thank you for leading me to Wills. He completed me, too."

I snuggled into my pillow.

The casualty clearing station was much closer to the fighting lines than Base Hospital Twenty-One. Glancing at the tent I now called home, I longed for the hut at the base hospital.

So much had changed in the past three months. I was certainly not the wide-eyed, innocent young girl who'd set sail from New York a few short months ago.

Shoving the hair from my face, I pictured horrific scenes of man's inhumanity to man.

Huns bombarded our campsite by the light of the moon. To provide protection during the attacks, the men helped us dig holes in the ground in which we slept. The holes were like a shallow grave; each grave was two by six, by eighteen inches deep. When exploding shells fell around us, we dove into our graves and pulled sheet iron over our bodies. Sleeping in a hole covered by metal was a regular event for us nurses at the station.

Treating the wounded at the clearing station was an around-the-clock job. So many boys came in with a leg blown off, or hastily amputated at the front line. I was an expert at holding down the stump so it wouldn't bump on the stretcher.

Gazing into the woods bordering our station, I tried not to recall the work of a few hours ago. A young soldier had lost both legs. The pain he'd suffered was frightful, and we'd had nothing to give him for the pain. Aspirin was not good enough, and morphine was reserved for the most severe cases. It was a crazy world when losing two legs in battle was not severe enough for morphine.

I wondered if William was here, somewhere, fighting at the front. The Western Front of the Great War extended hundreds of miles. Logically, I knew William wasn't likely anywhere near this location, but my heart wished he was.

"Sister! Charlotte!" a voice called. I turned toward the voice and moved from the relative calm of the forest to the chaos of the clearing station.

"Yes, sister," I replied, as I approached Helen, one of the nurses who was part of our team at Ypres. She turned to me with a brilliant smile, which was really quite out of place and out of character. I responded in kind. "Good news is it? Are we heading back to the base hospital?" I asked.

Helen laughed. "Now, that would be lovely. However, as far as I know, we're here for quite a stretch."

She looked me over in a peculiar manner, "Charlotte, wash up and meet me here in five minutes. Put on a fresh apron and take a moment with your hair."

Are we having an inspection? I mused. Do they actually inspect clearing stations? I looked at the mudholes surrounding each operating tent. "It seems like a waste of everyone's time to actually inspect this outfit."

"Charlotte," Helen continued in a slightly irritated tone, "go freshen up and meet me here in five minutes."

"All right, I'm moving," I replied. "I promise I'll look spit-spot and do the old place proud."

Luckily, one of the doctors had commandeered a vehicle and returned this morning with fresh uniforms. We'd left the base hospital with only two, unprepared for an extended stay. When the doctor arrived with a fresh supply of uniforms, we were ecstatic.

Rushing to the tent, I nearly plowed over a British officer standing near the entrance to my tent.

"Charlotte?"

I looked directly into the incredible gray eyes of William Harrington.

"William!" I exclaimed, throwing my arms around his neck. He folded me into his embrace. I couldn't believe William was standing at my tent.

My exuberant welcome was of a lover, rather than a friend. I reluctantly stepped back from the embrace.

William didn't release me. I looked up at him questioningly. Tipping his head toward mine I knew, without a doubt, he meant to kiss me. As he leaned toward me, thousands of thoughts rushed through my mind, including This will be my first kiss. I don't know how it's done.

William pressed his lips to mine. It was incredible. He pulled me tighter and we were once again connected from knee to chest. Our lips met; I never wanted the moment to end. He gently broke the kiss moving his lips down my chin to the curve of my neck.

"Charlotte," he whispered, "I dreamed of kissing you since we were last together."

A cough interrupted our kiss. A throat clearing followed the cough. I broke the kiss. I was too embarrassed to look at the witness to my wanton behavior.

"Charlotte," Sister Helen said, "I see you found your visitor."

"Sister Helen," I said, with as much calm as I could muster, considering the current state of affairs, "May I present Second Lieutenant William Harrington.

"I had the pleasure of meeting Sister Helen a few moments ago," William said. "It was upon her advice I waited for you by the tent."

"No need to woolgather here," Helen replied. "Charlotte, your lieutenant received a twenty-four hour pass in order to find you. The lieutenant has approximately twelve hours before he must return to the front. You, too, have a twelve-hour leave. Please be careful, as snipers seem to be a fixture in the landscape."

"Thank you, Helen," I replied, giving her an impulsive hug.

Much to my surprise, she hugged me back and whispered, "Have fun."

"Stop by the mess tent. I think cook will give you a few rations to take a picnic," Sister Helen continued.

William smiled at Sister Helen. "What a perfectly splendid idea."

William grasped my hand and pulled me toward the mess tent.

The cook provided a variety of items for a picnic. Grabbing a blanket from my tent, we walked away from the station and away from the battle line.

William held my hand securely as we walked in companionable silence.

"I hate to be out in such an open area," he said. "We make an easy target for a sniper's bullet." He glanced around the field. "We'll picnic near the trees on the opposite side of the field. We'll have protection in the rear and visibility."

I'm glad he was worried for our safety. I certainly wasn't. I wanted to forget there was a war on and pretend we were strolling in Forest Park. Of course, if we'd been taking a stroll in St. Louis, my father would have tagged along, ensuring no kissing would occur. I smiled at the image.

"Why are you smiling?" he asked.

"Well, I was thinking it would be lovely if we were in St. Louis and strolling in Forest Park. It's a park near Washington University's School of Medicine, near my home. It was the home of the 1904 World's Fair. It's the most beautiful place on earth."

"Charlotte," he replied, "wherever you are is the most beautiful place on earth."

I blushed. It was the nicest compliment I've ever received. How does one respond? Maybe one doesn't respond. I believe that's the option I'll follow, *I decided.* No response is the best response.

I wanted William to kiss me again, so I continued, "But that's not why I'm smiling. I realized if we were in St. Louis, a chaperone would accompany us; I'm smiling because I'm very glad we have no chaperone."

William's face turned red, "Charlotte, I don't intend to compromise you."

"Don't you realize there's a war on, soldier?" I grasped his face in both of my hands, stood on tiptoe, and pulled him toward me for a kiss. Now I knew what to expect and what I wanted.

Our lips merged and the incredible, overwhelming, hot feeling infused my body. Groaning, William pulled me tighter. His tongue played against the seam of my lips, first gently and then with more insistence. I parted my lips. I lost track of time and place. It was William and me and our kiss.

Soul Mates ~ Liz Morrison

William kissed my cheek and then my forehead. Gently he pushed my head against his shoulder.

"Charlotte, you're going to kill me," he declared. His hand caressed my back.

"Shall we set up our picnic area?" I asked.

I didn't want to let go, nor did I want to stop kissing. Stepping back, I glanced at William. He must have seen something in my eyes, because he gently pushed me away and said, "Oh, no you don't."

Laughing, I moved out his embrace and grasped his hand. "Aye, aye, Lieutenant, sir! A picnic it is!"

It was a beautiful day—no rain, and the sun was shining brightly. The picnic area William had selected was next to a small group of trees, creating a small alcove to lay the blanket and feel somewhat safe. It was a lovely spot to spend the few hours before returning to the reality of war.

"I missed you," I said at the exact same time William said, "I missed you."

We looked at each other and laughed. Laughing felt good, too.

He wasn't going to kiss me again—at least not yet. I was determined that he'd kiss me again, or, I'd have to kiss William Harrington. After all, there's a war on, *I told myself.*

Relaxing on the blanket, I examined William through half-closed eyes. I enjoyed sitting by him in companionable silence. Not an awkward silence, but the silence of two people who are content to be.

"You look good," I said. "Healthy. You've healed very well." Now I was blushing. That didn't come out quite the way I'd anticipated, *I thought.*

William looked at me and smiled. His gray eyes were warm and the deep cleft in his chin devastating. Suddenly, he pushed me down and leaned over me. I was not afraid. I was curious about where this was going.

I looked into his face. The sun was bright and his head was wreathed in a halo from the sun. He's so beautiful, I thought. Can a boy be beautiful?

Giving me a quick kiss on the lips, he popped back into a seated position.

"Charlotte, being here alone with you is testing my boundaries as a gentleman. I want to test myself farther—in for a penny, in for a pound," William inhaled deeply.

"I know this is forward," he continued. "Will you take down your hair?"

He didn't look at me as he made the request.

"I've dreamt about your hair many a night. I've never seen it. When I regained consciousness at the hospital and some of your hair was loose, I thought you were an angel."

Removing my cap, I let down my hair. It was incredibly intimate. I was sure my hair was a disheveled mess, so I ran my fingers through it, attempting to put it in some semblance of order.

William was mesmerized by my hair. I gave him a questioning look.

"You are gorgeous." *He ran his fingers through my hair. It was totally romantic. Then, much to our surprise, his fingers got caught in the tangles. My eyes met his and we laughed.*

Leaning over, he kissed me again. It was a heart-stopping kiss; once again, I never wanted it to end.

We were both breathing hard when William broke the kiss. Giving him a quick kiss on the cheek, I said, "Okay, Lieutenant, let's see the delicious treats, courtesy of Cook."

Laying out the items Cook had provided, I giggled at the less-than-inviting assortment.

William, however, looked at the spread, smiling in real delight. I guessed the food at the front was not as tasty as the food we had at the clearing station.

"Well, Lieutenant," I announced, "this looks almost as good as the tea and cakes I had with your mother."

William hesitated, indicating I should make the first selection. I selected an apple. "Please enjoy the meal," I said, gesturing toward the food on the blanket.

William ate while I plaited my hair into a loose braid.

"Charlotte, that may have been the best meal I've had in months."

Giving me a look reminding me of a child on Christmas, William presented me with a handkerchief. "I have a present for you," he said with a grin.

Opening the handkerchief, I found a beautiful letter opener—apparently made of a bullet—and an incredible bracelet crafted from coins.

"I made the letter opener myself, but a chum of mine made the bracelet for me for you." William gently took the bracelet from my hand and pointed out the miniatures. "Notice this piece," he said. "It's the queen. And this one," he continued, "is the king."

"They're lovely," I said. "I'll treasure them always."

William took the bracelet and placed it on my arm while kissing the inside of my wrist.

"I believe," William said, stretching his muscular arms over his head, "I shall commemorate the most wonderful day of my miserable existence by carving our names into a tree. It will be a tribute to the enchanting Charlotte of St. Louis, Missouri, of the United States of America, from her ever-faithful and besotted beau, William of the BEF."

William pulled his pocket knife from his trousers. He carefully examined the copse of trees, "This one?"

Pretending to examine the tree in great detail, I moved my head in an exaggerated slow motion, first up the tree, and then down. "Yes," I agreed in a solemn voice, "it's the perfect tree to inscribe the commemoration."

Tossing off his uniform jacket, William began carving the tree with his pocket knife. I admired his broad shoulders and incredibly muscular arms.

The sun was beating down and warming me with its rays. Closing my eyes, I enjoyed the moment.

"Charlotte? Charlotte," William's voice jolted me awake.

"Oh no," I exclaimed, "I slept the entire day away."

The sun was beginning to set. I'd wasted my day with William. Tears started building up behind my eyes.

"Charlotte, please don't cry." William pulled me into an embrace. "I sat by your side and fell asleep, too. The most restful sleep I've had in months."

Looking into his eyes, I knew with certainty I'd found my future. I don't know what he saw in my eyes. Taking my face between his hands, he kissed me. Wrapping my arms around his neck, I intended never to let go.

"You're going to kill me," he said again, resting his chin on the top of my head. "But I shall die a happy man.

"You need to admire my handiwork," he told me. "After you exclaim over the fine workmanship, we need to return to camp. Sister Helen may send out the troops."

Grasping my hand, he pulled me to my feet. Covering my eyes, he guided me to the tree.

It was incredible. Our initials were intertwined in a heart. The year 1917 was etched under the design. "William," I said in awe, "that's really beautiful."

Taking a step back, I really looked at our surroundings, focusing on our copse of trees.

"What are you admiring?" he asked.

"I'm not admiring. I'm memorizing," I said. "I want to remember this moment...this place...forever."

He rested his eyes on me. "Charlotte," he began, as he grasped both of my hands...

Soul Mates ~ Liz Morrison

"Charlie! Charlie!" a voice seemed to come from a great distance.

The voice was accompanied by tapping; the tapping brought me back to the present.

The persistent knocking continued. "Charlie, it's me, Ryan." Ryan loudly whispered. It was more of a soft yell than a loud whisper.

"I'm coming," I loudly whispered back.

I glanced at the clock. It was 5:30 in the morning.

"Geez, Ryan," I said as I unlocked the door. "This had better be important."

Ryan was still in his clubbing clothes.

"Hey, did you guys just get in?" I asked. "That must've been some wild evening."

Ryan peered into my room. "Are you alone?"

"Yes, I'm alone, you loser. Did you just knock to make sure I wasn't with Wills?" I said with a laugh, waving him into my room.

Ryan walked in and shoved some papers into my hand. "Charlie, we need to talk. Your friend from Britain is a real piece of work."

Chapter Fourteen

THE KISS ACCORDING TO WILLIAM

*B*loody hell!

Charlie walked away from me. *Past, present, future—that was incredible,* I thought. *She was incredible. So, if she turns around, it means she felt it too.*

I loved the way she walked, the way her hair flowed down her back, the sway of her hips…she was so gorgeous.

She turned; just a glance over her shoulder. A glance accompanied by a smile.

Charlie's smile was a promise; a promise of more nights like tonight. The smile of a woman who knows she has her bloody man. And I knew for damn sure that I was her man.

"Go to bed," I mouthed.

She silently replied, "Sweet dreams." She opened the door and walked into her room.

I slowly walked down the stairs to my flat. Katie, Ryan, Andrew, and the rest of the group were still at the club. It would be so easy to knock on Charlie's door. *It would be too hard if she's not interested,* I decided. *Rejection over the mobile is easier to deal with than face-to-face rejection.*

One ring, two rings, three rings…*come on, Charlie, answer the damn mobile.*

"Hi, Will. I know—you miss me already."

Soul Mates ~ Liz Morrison

I love her American accent, I thought. *It's so bloody sexy.*

"Actually, Charlie," I said, "I do miss you already.

"Charlie, I need to know something" I said softly. "It's about the kiss, or kisses—was it different from the other ones?"

Not one sound from her end of the line.

"Charlie?" I waited. "Any thoughts on the answer?"

Her incredible, sexy voice came across the mobile, "Okay, Wills, here's my story. I'm taking a risk, and if you don't feel the same way, that's cool. Just let me know. On a scale from one to ten, our kiss was a twelve. Actually, it's not scalable.

"Frankly, Wills, I wanted to rip your clothes off and make love to you in the hallway. Considering the most I usually feel after, and sometimes during a kiss, is the urge to brush my teeth. Oh—I don't plan on having sex, except with the man I plan to marry. It was a pretty good kiss."

I believe I heard Charlie say she wants to shag, I told myself. *Did she say I was the man she wants to marry?* This chat was ace.

"A girl doesn't tell a bloke she wishes to rip his bloody clothes off—in the hallway, no less—and expect the same bloke to go to bed alone."

I wanted to run back up the stairs to her room and make it come true, but Charlie wasn't that kind of girl.

"But you do, don't you love?" I said, after a pause.

"Wills, what about you?" she asked.

What about me? I repeated to myself. *The damn enticing Yank wants to know about me.*

"I'm trying to get this right," I began. "I'd prefer to say it to you in person, rather than on the mobile."

How do you say the right thing to the girl you'd waited your entire life to meet? *My speech for Fourth of June received numerous accolades and now,* I considered, *possibly the most important speech of my life, I'm afraid to speak.*

How did I feel? Not an easy task, because I didn't know exactly how I felt.

"Charlie, kissing you centered my world," I said. "I feel complete. You complete me. And when you're ready to rip the clothes from my body in the hallway…in my room…on the bloody street corner…I'm the right bloke. Good night, Charlie. Sweet dreams."

I ended the conversation.

Possibly I was a coward. Probably I was afraid Charlie wanted to see me. Seeing Charlie right now would be a bad choice. We apparently had no self-control when it came to each other.

My futon beckoned, but I wasn't tired. Regardless, I climbed into bed, closed my eyes, and prepared to dream of Charlie.

Staring at the ceiling, my mind wandered to another place, another time, another life. The memories rushed back with incredible clarity.

Charlotte was near. It was unbelievable that, in the midst of this hellhole, I was going to see her.

I looked around the trench, determined to find my commanding officer. A twenty-four hour pass…I just required a twenty-four hour pass.

"Captain," I said, "do you remember the young lady I told you about—the one from the base hospital?"

"Certainly, Harrington," the captain replied with a chuckle. "I believe every man in the company has heard of your battlefield angel. Did you receive another letter from your girl?"

"Actually, sir," I replied, "Charlotte is now serving at the casualty clearing station behind our lines. I'm here to request a twenty-four hour pass."

The captain stared at me for a moment. Pulling a cigarette case from his pocket, he offered me a smoke. Accepting the cigarette, I waited patiently for his reply.

Lighting his cigarette, he took a long drag. "When was your last leave, son?"

"Well, sir, I've not been at rest since returning from the base hospital. I'm probably not due a leave for months." I inhaled deeply from my cigarette. I might have lied, but I just couldn't do it. If a man lost his integrity, he didn't have much left to lose.

"Lieutenant, make sure you stop by the delousing station. Don't share the lice with your young lady. Now, let's see about getting you that pass."

I wanted to shout for joy. "Thank you, sir."

The captain clasped my outstretched hand. "Good luck, son."

I grabbed a few meager items, including two gifts for Charlotte.

The captain handed me my pass. If all went well, I could make it to the clearing station by mid-morning.

After explaining the purpose of my twenty-four hour leave to the officer in charge of the delousing station, he commandeered a louse-free uniform.

One of the chaps from the station directed me toward the medical unit. I was slightly disheartened to learn there were several such stations in the vicinity.

Approaching the casualty clearing station, I was determined and confident I'd find Charlotte. Convincing the commanding medical officer to let her spend the day in my company would be the greater challenge.

Faith, dear boy, faith, I said to myself as I approached the first tent.

The condition of the camp was rather frightful. The operating station seemed to be composed of haphazardly placed tents. A large indentation amidst the maze of tents appeared to be a bomb crater.

That couldn't be, I told myself. The rules of war dictate a Red Cross hospital station isn't a target.

"Sister," I said to a nurse passing me at a brisk pace. "Hello. Is a Sister Charlotte from Base Hospital Twenty-One part of your team?"

The nurse stared at me for a moment. Hesitating slightly, she said, "Yes, Sister Charlotte is part of our team. Who's interested in knowing that bit of information?"

"I am, Miss. My name is William Harrington. I'm a friend of Charlotte's."

"William Harrington. How did you learn Charlotte would be at the clearing station?"

"I received a letter indicating her location. It's my great fortune that I, too, am serving in the Ypres-Passchendaele."

How odd that sounded. No one felt fortunate to be serving in the mudhole that was Ypres-Passchendaele.

I laughed at myself and continued, "No one would consider themselves fortunate serving here, but I'm fortunate Charlotte is here, as well. I'm hoping she'll be granted a few hours of leave."

The sister extended her hand. "I'm Helen. I'm pleased to say I have the authority to grant Charlotte a leave. Let me take you to her tent," *she continued.* "I'll locate Charlotte and send her directly."

Sister Helen escorted me, guiding me around several tents and other structures serving as operating stations, recovery areas, and sleeping quarters.

The station appeared to be a target in the battle zone. The feeling increased tenfold as I stumbled in another crater.

"Watch your step, Lieutenant," *Sister Helen called over her shoulder.* "We have several shell holes around the station. The night bombings certainly make it challenging to maintain a sense of order."

Sister Helen stopped in front of one of the larger tents. "Charlotte's quarters. Stay here while I attempt to locate her." *She abruptly turned and walked away.*

As I stood by the tent, I suffered from an attack of nerves. What if she doesn't want to see me? *I fretted.* What if I'm just another Tommy she humors with her letters?

I waited impatiently for a sound indicating Charlotte was approaching. Life in the trenches teaches one a lot about patience. Trench warfare is one long waiting game. Then, when you believe you'll die of boredom, the alarm sounds and we're in the thick of it. Waiting for Charlotte was similar to waiting for the signal to go over the top. We knew it was coming, yet we still didn't know what to expect. Uncertain of the outcome, we headed into the fray, hoping we'd live to fight another day.

The wait was intolerable. I wanted to search for Sister Helen. I didn't want to leave my position, in case I inadvertently missed Charlotte.

I decided patience was a virtue.

A moment later, I was nearly plowed over by...

"Charlotte?"

She turned and I looked into the face of my battlefield angel.

"William!" Much to my surprise and delight, Charlotte wrapped her arms around my neck.

I must be dreaming, I thought as I folded her into my embrace.

I had to kiss her. I slowly lowered my head, providing her ample opportunity to walk away. She stood steadfast. I gently pressed my lips to hers, not knowing what to expect...

My head was full of memories; Charlotte in the past and Charlie in the present. The entire concept of having a past life was bonkers. However, I was quite certain of several things, and certainty equals sanity.

First, Charlotte and Charlie were the same soul. Second, Charlie was remembering our past life. Third, I loved Charlie; past, present, and future.

Staring at the ceiling, more memories of my day with Charlotte filled my mind with startling clarity. I remembered giving her two gifts; a bracelet and a letter opener. Maybe Charlie would dream about the gifts and we'd find them together. It would be brilliant to find evidence of our past life, but quite unlikely.

Charlie wanted to travel to Ypres-Passchendaele. What were the chances of locating the tree in which I'd carved our initials? Charlotte's smile when I unveiled the carving had been breathtaking.

I cannot imagine Charlie's reaction if we actually located the copse of trees with the carving. After one hundred years, the tree was probably someone's house, but a bloke can dream.

Dreaming was good; the reality of kissing Charlie was so much better. I remembered Charlotte's sweet kisses, but kissing Charlie was sweet and—well, hot.

I supposed I felt guilty kissing Charlotte. In 1917, a young man wouldn't be alone with a young woman for an extended period of time. There was a war on; many of the traditional boundaries of society had been blurred.

Memories of that day flood my mind. I remembered Charlotte kissing me soundly, and I remembered the kiss changed from sweet to hot, just like tonight with Charlie. That kiss, in France, was my first French kiss…pun intended.

Closing my eyes, I remembered.

Charlotte was just so damn beautiful. I wanted to pull her hair from its top knot and watch it tumble over her shoulders. I gently pushed her down so she was lying on her back, looking up into my face. I caged her under my body without actually touching her.

Giving her a quick kiss on the lips, I returned to a seated position. Charlotte remained on her back, glancing at me curiously.

"Charlotte, being here alone with you is testing all of my limits as a gentleman," I took a deep breath.

"I know this is forward of me," I continued. "Will you take down your hair?"

I didn't look at her. "I've dreamt about your hair many a night, and I've never seen it. I remember when I regained consciousness at the hospital and some of your hair was loose. I thought you were an angel."

Gazing off into the distance, I heard a soft rustling. I glanced over at Charlotte and was mesmerized.

I leaned over and kissed her again. I needed to end the kiss, or we'd end up in a position one shouldn't find oneself until one was married. I wouldn't dishonor Charlotte by anticipating our wedding night. With incredible fortitude, I broke the kiss.

Remembering Charlotte's face as I presented her with small tokens of my affection was a moment worth remembering.

"They're lovely." she said. "I'll treasure them always."

Taking the bracelet, I placed it on her wrist. I kissed the inside of her wrist near the bracelet.

"I shall commemorate the most wonderful day of my miserable existence by carving our names into a tree. It'll be a tribute to the enchanting Charlotte of St. Louis, Missouri, of the United States of America, from her ever-faithful and besotted beau, William of the BEF," I said.

"Besotted, are you?" she replied with a grin. "You shall commemorate, and I shall watch you."

She rolled to her back and clasped her hands behind her head. I tried not to notice how inviting she looked, lounging on the blanket.

I selected a tree and Charlotte pretended to examine it most thoughtfully.

As I carved the tree, Charlotte fell asleep. I successfully carved our initials into the tree. I admired my handiwork and was quite impressed with my craftsmanship.

Charlotte looked like Sleeping Beauty. I decided to lie beside her, rather than wake her up. I gave a quick prayer, asking Him to keep stray Huns away if I, too, fell asleep. I stretched out beside Charlotte, gently pulled her into my embrace, and closed my eyes.

Chapter Fifteen

Charlie

"Ryan," I said with a laugh as I closed the door behind him, "a piece of work? Who says that?" I asked as I tossed the papers Ryan handed me on the counter in the kitchenette.

I looked around the room—I really needed to do a better job of putting my clothes away. Every outfit I'd tried on prior to our night out was in colorful chaos.

As Ryan looked for a place to sit down, I picked up clothes and placed them on hangers.

"Wow, this place is a disaster," Ryan looked around in dismay. "I didn't know you were such a slob." Pushing his glasses up his nose, he shook his head in what I interpreted as disgust.

"Give me a sec," I said. "I couldn't decide what to wear last night. They're all clean, just in a bit of disarray."

"Disarray?" Ryan responded. "That's the understatement of the century. This place looks like a bomb exploded."

A flash of my latest dream popped into my mind. "Actually," I said, "I don't think this looks like a bomb explosion at all."

In my mind I saw bloody bodies and body parts and heard young men screaming in agony. My messy clothes looked nothing like an explosion.

"Charlie, I really need you to focus, girl." Ryan's stressed-voice cut through my happy recollections.

"Ryan, give me a minute to wake up, buddy. So far you've dissed my boyfriend, my cleaning skills, and my ability to focus. If I wasn't in such a wicked awesome mood, I might hit you." I assumed the stance of a boxer.

Ryan wasn't smiling.

"Hey, Ry, seriously—what's wrong? Last time I saw you were the hit of La Boîte à Bières."

"Did you say 'boyfriend?' You think that British ass is your boyfriend? Seriously, Charlie, I thought you were smarter than that. Well, at least you didn't sleep with him. That would've been just great," Ryan said with cutting sarcasm.

I was totally confused. "What's your deal? Wills is a great guy and he's a gentleman. And yes, he is my boyfriend."

"Listen," Ryan said, "that dude is so not what you think he is. I know you think Andrew makes this shit up, but I have proof that your boyfriend is a real dipshit. He is totally taking advantage of you, Charlie, and he kisses and tells. And, no matter how you might be acting in France, you're not that girl."

I took a deep, calming breath. "Okay, who are you and what have you done with my best friend?" I demanded. "Where's Katie? Maybe she can bring some clarity to the situation. You're attempting to ruin the most romantic night in my entire life. Why are you doing this?"

"Listen, Charlie," Ryan implored as he placed his hands on my shoulders, "I know you think William is all that and Andrew is a liar. But William is the liar."

"All these hints and innuendos are starting to worry me," I said. "So, what's the latest story Andrew is spreading about William?"

Ryan pushed his fingers through his already disheveled hair. He was pretty cute; no wonder all the ladies at the club were after him. And the guy could sing.

"Ryan, you were totally amazing," I went on. "I can't believe you came back here alone. I thought for sure you'd bring home a beautiful French groupie."

"Charlie," Ryan said, pulling me into a hug, "you know you're the only groupie I need." I pulled away and gave him a quick hug.

I hugged my pillow against my chest and curled up next to Ryan. "Okay, buddy, tell me the horrible story about Wills."

"Hey, where did you put the papers I gave you when I walked in?" Ryan asked. "I need you to read them."

"Oh," I said, "I tossed the papers on the counter in the kitchenette."

Ryan glanced at me and shook his head. He walked the two steps or so to the kitchenette and picked up the papers. He handed them to me as he sat next to me.

"Remember, don't shoot the messenger," he cautioned.

I leaned against Ryan's shoulder and began reading the papers. It looked like a term paper. The upper left-hand corner included the text *The Chronicle* with Andrew's name and the date underneath.

I looked at Ryan, who was staring at me. "So, you brought me Andrew's term paper. That's interesting."

"What do the letters after Andrew's name mean?" I asked.

"I don't know, Charlie," Ryan said in an exasperated voice. "Just read the damn article."

"Okay, I'm reading, I'm reading," I replied. In my best newswoman voice I began to read the article out loud.

Andrew Graham (TEJN) and William Harrington (TEJN) share their adventure in Rouen with *The Chronicle*.

SO GUYS, TELL ME ABOUT YOUR TRIP. WHY ROUEN?

A: Many Etonians go to Ibiza, Thailand, and South America. We thought we'd do something different: live and work in Rouen, France.

"Skip down," Ryan said impatiently. "Get to the part about the Americans. Most particularly, you need to read about the American girls."

HOW DID YOU COME UP WITH THE IDEA?

A: William's always been interested in World War I. His ancestor, also named William Harrington and an Etonian, was killed in Rouen a month prior to the end of the war. For a guy interested in World War I, Rouen is a great place to live and learn.

WHAT DO YOU HOPE TO DO MORE ON THE TRIP, LIVING OR LEARNING?

A: Well, I think we're learning and learning to live it up. For example, Wills learned to use his interest in World War I to chat up girls. He also learned girls really like guys who say they think they have some kind of deep connection. Who knew that our Wills was such a master of the female mind?

W: Yes, it's really quite a skill.

WHAT CONNECTIONS HAVE YOU GUYS MADE IN ROUEN?

W: To be honest, we've made most of our connections with a group of students from the States.

HOW DO THE CONNECTIONS WITH THE AMERICANS SUPPORT LIVING AND LEARNING IN ROUEN?

A: The Americans are a lot of fun. And just like the British Empire during World War I, William formed an alliance with an American. This American is of the female variety, and she, too, is interested in World War I. She's also interested in William. William convinced her they were together in a past life and they had a unique metaphysical connection, and the rest, as they say, is history.

W: What happens in Rouen stays in Rouen.

"William is an absolute ass," Ryan *was really mad*. "Who pretends they have a connection with someone? That's just wrong."

"Ryan," I said, "I don't believe this. Andrew is such an ass. He's William's best friend, yet he continually does things indicating he's not a friend at all." I shook my head and handed the papers back to Ryan.

"Charlie," Ryan said, "you need to think without your emotions getting involved. Andrew had no intention for me or any of us to see this article. I picked it up by mistake when I picked up my jacket from the table in Andrew's flat. Think, girl! Why would he put this stuff in an article that we were never meant to see unless it's the truth? We're not the audience for this article. All the guys at their school are the intended audience. Charlie, did you look at the byline? The article is being submitted by both Andrew and William."

I read the byline again and quickly skimmed the article. I noticed the letter *A* and the letter *W* next to some of the statements.

Wow! I thought. *William knew about this, and he contributed to the story.*

I tried to process the information. It didn't make sense. Or maybe I didn't want it to make sense. I closed my eyes and hugged my legs to my chest.

In my mind, I pictured kissing William—kissing my World-War-I-William and kissing my today-William. I just couldn't reconcile that picture with a William who'd take advantage of me.

"Ryan, I don't want to deal with this right now," I said.

I don't want to deal with this ever, I silently added.

"I really appreciate you bringing the article—or whatever it is—to me, but I'm not going to do anything right now. I'm going to take a shower and put on something cute, if I can find anything to wear in this disaster area. Then I'm going to borrow a scooter and report to my job at the Rouen Visitor's Center. I hope my new job will keep this latest mystery off my mind."

Ryan pulled me into a tight embrace. "Charlie, I'm really sorry. I know you like this guy."

"Thanks, Ryan," I whispered.

I took several deep breaths that kept me from crying. Crying over some guy was not how I operated.

Soul Mates ~ Liz Morrison

Pulling myself together, I kissed Ryan's cheek and stepped out of the hug. "You're the best friend a girl could have," I told him. "I'll text you later, when I get this figured out. Oh, I'm still planning on the road trip on Saturday. You plan on coming? Yes?"

"I wouldn't miss it," he replied as he headed toward the door. "A road trip with you and Katie—it'll be wicked awesome."

Okay, I need to pull myself together, I told myself. *What an ass. I can't believe what I said on the phone last night. He and Andrew probably had a good laugh over that. Oh my God. I said I wanted to rip his clothes off or something like that. Idiot!*

Grabbing my towel, I climbed into the shower. I hit the blue tile with my fist. *Ouch! Dumb!* "Stupid girl," I mumbled to myself.

Tears started to fall. No boy is worth my tears. I decided I'd cry during my shower and then I'd be done—done with feeling bad, and done with Wills.

I don't want to be done with Wills, I thought. *I was a stupid, stupid girl.*

What to wear? What to wear? I fretted. I grabbed a black miniskirt, a bra, and a green top from the floor display of my clothing.

Shoes—where are my black wedges?

One of the wedges was under the futon. Then I saw the back of the wedge sticking out from behind the shelf. I grabbed the shoe and noticed a beat-up brown leather briefcase.

What's that? I wondered. *Oh yeah—Katie and Ryan brought it to me from their dumpster-diving experience. We've been so busy, I forgot about it. Well, now isn't the time to dig into the briefcase. It probably doesn't have anything interesting in it, anyway.*

I grabbed a sweater, shoved my feet into my wedges, and grabbed my backpack. I pulled my phone from the charger and glanced at the calls and text messages. William certainly wasn't wasting time. *He probably figured I was ready for sex,* I inwardly fumed. *So stupid!*

I wasn't thinking about Wills anymore. I turned all the incoming call alerts to silent and threw my cell into the zipper pocket on my backpack. I closed the door quickly, trying not to slam it, because I knew everyone else was still sleeping after their night out.

I walked swiftly to the stairs. I tried not to remember kissing Wills and looking back over my shoulder to see him watching me walk away.

I won't think about it, I silently insisted.

"Bonjour, Philippe," I said to the young man who was monitoring the desk.

"Bonjour, Mademoiselle Charlie. Tu es magnifique, comme toujours. Est-ce que je peux t'aider ce matin?" Phillipe asked.

What a flatterer, I thought. Well, it's nice to know Phillipe thinks I look pretty this morning. I hated to admit it but my ego needed a boost.

"Aujourd'hui, c'est mon premier jour au centre des visiteurs Rouen. Je voudrais louer un scooter pour la journee, s'il vous plait, " I replied.

"Oui," Philippe replied. "I can hook you up with a scooter."

Philippe liked practicing English as much as we enjoyed practicing French. At first he only spoke to us in French. It was how the school had the employees at the apartment complex support our learning. Now that we were almost fluent in French, Philippe enjoyed practicing his English. We enjoyed hearing him speak English, too—especially when he talked in slang; it was cute.

Philippe grabbed a key and a helmet, directing me to the scooters. He pointed to a little red scooter I'd be using for the day. The scooter would make moving through the maze of streets in Rouen super easy.

Before we traveled to Rouen, we'd verified that our driver's licenses would work for scooters. However, Ryan was driving the car tomorrow, because he was the only one who was eighteen.

Until this moment, I'd pictured Wills as the driver, I realized. *C'est la vie. After all, when we planned our trip to Rouen I never planned on Wills.*

I realized Philippe was speaking to me. "Desolée, mon esprit etait d'un million de miles de là. Merci pour votre aide." I appologized for not paying attention.

Philippe smiled. "No problem, Charlie. The English boy you like is back, yes. He occupies your mind."

Yes, he does, but not in the way Philippe imagines, I thought grimly. "Au revoir," I replied, rather than answering the question.

I secured my helmet, placed the key in the ignition, and turned on the scooter. I missed driving. I navigated the bike through the maze of cars on our street and drove to the Rouen Visitors Center.

Driving with the traffic was really grueling. *Didn't anyone in Rouen attend driving school?* I wondered. Well, the focus on my driving and other people's driving blocked out thoughts of Wills.

Damn, I chided myself. *Now I'm thinking about Wills. What I should be thinking about is the stupid article and what a tool he was. Why was I thinking about kissing him, talking to him, the electric current when we touched?*

That was the thing—all of it could be true. He could be a total jerk. But it didn't explain the electric current I'd felt when we touched. That's what didn't make sense.

Everything else, he could've made up, used it to get me to like him, I reasoned, *but not the electric current. That was real. It was real the first time we touched, and it was real last night.*

A car horn blared, interrupting my thoughts and saving me from driving into the car next to me. *No more thoughts of William. Drive, sister, drive.*

The Office of Tourism was beautiful. It had been established in 1959. I hadn't realized the building was from the Renaissance period. It was right in front of Notre Dame, surrounded by small shops and street vendors.

I actually get to work here, I thought. *This is amazing.*

I parked the scooter, removed my helmet, and walked to the Office of Tourism. Once again, I was overwhelmed with the impossibility of it all. I was in Rouen, France, ready to begin the first day of my internship at the visitors' bureau, in a building that was built around 1509...unbelievable.

Standing on the walk in front of the tourism office, I was in awe. I opened the door and walked into my next adventure. I pushed all thoughts of Wills to the corner of my mind, ready to get on with this new challenge.

I walked in the front door.

"Bonjour! Je m'appelle Charlie. Je suis ici pour un stage," I said to the woman standing at the entrance.

She had a questioning look on her face as I completed my introduction.

Maybe I said it wrong, I told myself.

"You are Charlie?" she asked with a smile. "We've been waiting for you. Let's see...according to our records, you're interested in the World Wars in Rouen, particularly World War I, *non*? This is good," she continued in English.

I was nervous. It was a relief she spoke English.

The door opened and a man entered. The woman—I wish I knew her name—turned and welcomed the gentleman to the visitors' center. The man seemed a little ill at ease. He asked, in halting French, about nearby World War I sites.

Is that good karma or what? I thought. I wondered how often people stop in Office of Tourism with inquiries regarding World War I sites.

Madame motioned me to join the conversation. I couldn't believe it. I extended my hand to the gentleman.

"Welcome to the Office de tourisme Rouen," I said. "It sounds like you have a few questions about World War I sites in the area."

Much to my relief, I remembered everything I'd studied about the World War I sites in the vicinity. I told the man about the cemetery, the base hospital, and other locations in the area.

I glanced at Madame and she was smiling—really smiling.

Soul Mates ~ Liz Morrison

Thanking us profusely, the man picked up a map and some other brochures and left the building.

"Congratulations, Charlie," Madame said with a smile, "that was, as you Americans say, awesome."

"I am Madame Chevalier. You will be here with us today and Monday. On Tuesday, you begin your work at St. Sever Cemetery. We are counting on you to compile an incredible World War I experience for visitors to Rouen, corresponding with the anniversary of the Great War. We shall begin with a tour, yes?"

"Yes," I replied with enthusiasm. *To hell with dumb boys.*

Chapter Sixteen

WILLIAM

What an incredible night, I thought. *Charlie's mine. Now we can work together to decipher the mystery of our past.*

I still wasn't certain how to talk to her about the whole reincarnation concept, but I knew she'd listen and not judge.

I placed my hands behind my head and stared at the ceiling—my thinking position.

I rang Charlie. "Hey, beautiful! Good luck at the Visitor's Center. You'll be brilliant."

So, what to text? I pondered. Hmm, "you are my soul mate, and I can't wait to spend eternity with you." *That might be a bit much. I'll just leave the voicemail.*

Have I ever been this happy? I asked myself. I thought not.

Getting up and getting dressed seemed like a good idea. I probably needed to shower. Also, I needed to map out the trip for tomorrow, check on the car with Philippe, and talk to Ryan and Katie about the time we wanted to leave for Ypres-Passchendaele; it was ace that they'd agreed to change the destination for tomorrow.

Too bad Andrew was on his expedition with the French businessmen; he would have had a great time, and added quite a bit of levity to the entire excursion.

Rather than getting up and reviewing my notes, I did a mental checklist. *Okay, so I took care of reservations at Talbot House. I reserved two rooms, one for the girls and one for the guys.* I had a better idea, but I didn't think Charlie would go for it.

Charlie wanted to go to Base Hospital Twenty-One and the cemetery first, but the Talbot House didn't have reservations available later in the month. So, we were off on a grand adventure tomorrow.

What were the odds of finding the tree? One hundred to one, I'd wager. *Did Charlie dream about the tree last night?* I wondered. The memory was so similar to our actual kiss, maybe it would trigger her memories of Charlotte and William.

A loud banging on my door brought me from my pleasant contemplation. *What the bloody hell?*

I had on my vest and my boxers; not the correct attire for visitors. I pulled on my trousers and stumbled toward the door.

The banging continued. "Give me a bloody minute," I mumbled.

Ryan was standing at my door. Pulling back his arm, his fist flew toward my face. Luckily, adrenaline kicked in and I grabbed Ryan's fist before it made contact.

I quickly trussed his arm behind his back and pressed his face into the wall.

"Are you bonkers?" I yelled. "What the hell do you think you're doing?"

"What the hell do I think I'm doing?" Ryan said, struggling to break my grip. "What the hell do you think you're doing, you shithead? Charlie is beautiful inside and out, and she doesn't need a posh ass like you ruining her life."

Ryan called me a shithead and a posh ass? "What in the hell are you talking about?" I demanded. I didn't break my hold, just in case he decided to swing at me again. "Let me know when I can let go."

He took a deep breath, "You can let go, I'm cool," he said.

I loosened my grip on his arm and eased back.

He turned and sent an elbow into my stomach. Whoa, he knocked the wind out of me.

I grabbed him before he did more damage. "What is going on?" I asked. "I wouldn't do anything to ruin Charlie's life."

"Right," Ryan said. "Like writing the article with your good friend Andrew for your school newspaper wouldn't hurt Charlie. It might not ruin her life in the eyes of your school chums, but it made Charlie feel bad. I knew you were bad news, but Charlie liked you. You make me sick."

"Ryan, seriously, I don't know what you're talking about. What article? What school chums?"

"Listen, you don't need to lie about this. I found the article you and Andrew wrote for *The Chronicle*. I showed it to Charlie. She knows all about you and your metaphysical connections, or whatever you're calling it today."

"Okay, dude, you can let go of me. I'm not going to try to punch you, or elbow you again…not that I wouldn't like to," Ryan said with sincerity. He was still really angry, but I didn't think he was going to take another swing.

"Here you go," Ryan said, shoving papers into my hand. "Let's hear your explanation for this one. I'm sure it'll be good."

I took the papers from Ryan. It was an article for *The Chronicle*. The byline named Andrew and me.

I looked at Ryan, without reading anything else, "I didn't contribute to this article. I've never seen it before—I swear it."

"You know, I didn't think even you would try to deny the obvious. Seriously, dude, you think I'm going to believe you didn't contribute to this, while your name's in the byline and the *W* for William is all over the article? I'm American, not stupid."

"Ryan, I didn't contribute to this article," I said again, wondering why my name was included. "Where did you find it?"

"I found it in Andrew's room last night. I accidently picked it up when I grabbed my coat off the table in his flat. After I read it, I took it to Charlie. She'll never forgive you," he concluded.

I forced myself to read the article. *How bad could it be?* I silently asked.

The first part was pretty inconsequential, as Andrew and the mysterious *W* described life in Rouen. Then I read the part that hurt Charlie. Andrew had reduced the incredible connection between Charlie and me to a strategy to chat up girls.

Ryan was correct; Charlie would never forgive me.

It was a disaster. Charlie needed to know I hadn't written the bloody article.

"Ryan, I know this looks really bad," I said. "I didn't contribute to this article, and I didn't say any of this to Andrew. I don't know how to right this wrong. I didn't do this."

Ryan stared at me for what seemed an eternity, but was probably less than a minute. "I don't believe you," he stated with conviction. "It doesn't make any sense. If you didn't contribute, then Andrew made up a totally fake article to hurt Charlie. The article makes you look bad, and you guys are best friends. It doesn't make sense."

I sat down and rubbed my forehead. *This doesn't make sense*, I silently agreed. Why would Andrew write an article that looked like it was co-written by me, to submit to *The Chronicle*? Why would the article focus on me and my relationship with Charlie? Or really, why would it focus on making my relationship with Charlie a bit of a joke? I continued to rub my head. *This is just wrong.*

"Ryan," I said, "I know this looks bad, but I really didn't write, or co-write, or contribute anything to the article. I can't imagine why Andrew would write it and put my name on it."

"I don't know, dude," Ryan said. "If Andrew wrote this without your consent or contributions, he's seriously messed up. He certainly isn't your friend."

It appeared Ryan might be open to the idea that I didn't contribute to the article.

"Do you believe in reincarnation?" I asked.

"Oh, come on. The reincarnation thing may have sucked Charlie in, but it won't work for me. I almost believed you." He shook his head in disgust.

"I need you to listen," I said. "What I'm going to tell you, I've told one other person outside of my family." Ryan was thinking I was going to say Charlie. "Andrew was the other person.

"You may think I'm crazy; I want you to at least consider I had nothing to do with this article."

I continued, "Right, then; my family believes I am reincarnated from my great-great uncle who died in World War I."

Ryan looked at me like I lost my bloody mind, but he said nothing.

"When I was four years old, I was diagnosed with post-traumatic stress syndrome similar to what the soldiers returning from the first Gulf War experienced. The doctor couldn't explain why a four year old had symptoms similar to a war veteran."

I stopped talking and waited for a response.

Ryan said nothing.

"My grandmum found an old photo album. In it was a photograph of William James Harrington, a relative who died in Rouen, France in November of 1918. After my parents showed me the picture of my great-great-uncle, I stopped having nightmares. I haven't experienced those kind of nightmares in over twelve years. The nightmares resumed a few months ago."

"A few months ago?" asked Ryan.

"The dreams started about month before I decided to go to Rouen," I said. "The dreams are vivid, like playing *Call of Duty* in high def. And there's the girl. She's a nurse and her name is Charlotte. When I wake up, it feels like a memory, not a dream. I knew the dreams were connected to Rouen. I'm bloody sure the dreams are connected to Charlie."

Ryan was listening, but said nothing.

CHARLIE

I glanced at my cell, amazed that it was almost 7:00 p.m. It had been a great day. I'd learned so much in a very short period of time. The best part of the day was being assigned the task of sorting artifacts from the Great War that had been donated to the Bureau of Tourism.

According to Madam Chevalier, the donations had been made years ago, but were just recently found in the attic, in boxes labeled World War I. The boxes include journals, letters, and other mementos of the war. I wanted to stay all night.

Of course, that might be because I don't want to return to the apartment complex, knowing Wills will be there, I considered, *but he won't be there for me.*

"Charlie," Madame Chevalier called from the first floor, "time to close up shop. The items will still be here on Monday."

"Yes, Madame," I responded from my nook on the third floor of the building. Taking a final glance at the super-cool old stuff, I walked down the stairs.

"Thank you so much," I said to Madame Chevalier. "It was quite an incredible day."

Madame Chevalier unexpectedly hugged me, rather than giving me the more traditional peck on the cheek. "Charlie, you are great. I look forward to seeing you on Monday."

"Au revoir," I replied.

I took a final glance at the Bureau of Tourism. It was so cool.

I located the scooter, relieved it was in the same location. The traffic was even more congested that evening than it had been in the morning. Focusing on my driving, I maneuvered around several large vehicles, a few cars, and followed another scooter. Even though the traffic was worse, my driving was much better.

The apartment complex came into view all too soon. My stomach hurt. I didn't want to see Wills, but I did want to see Wills. I really hated this. *Why couldn't he be the guy I thought he was?* I wondered.

I steered the scooter into the parking spot. The sun was setting and lights were turned on in the lobby.

Glancing through the window, I saw a small group of people that included Ryan and Katie. The third person in the group wasn't visible.

The tightness in my chest increased. I didn't want to talk about the article or William.

Katie and Ryan would be supportive; I didn't want to talk about it. One of the strange, yet interesting, aspects of my relationship—short-lived as it was—with Wills was my inability to share it with Ryan and Katie.

Maybe I'd had a premonition it wouldn't last. *Why waste everyone's time?* If I was honest with myself, I just didn't want to spoil the new relationship by sharing it. Somehow, sharing with my two friends felt like a breach of trust with William.

So much for breaking trust. The guy basically told the entire world he was a player with a successful strategy for hitting on stupid American girls. *Shake it off!* I commanded myself. *Put on a smile and pretend you're good.*

Taking a deep breath, I opened the door and walked into the lobby. I wished the sick feeling would go away.

"Hi!" I said forcing a cheerful voice. "Why are you hanging in the lobby?"

Katie and Ryan turned toward me. *What the hell?* I wondered. *Why are Katie and Ryan with William?*

Ryan looked really guilty and Katie looked…well, disgruntled.

Don't puke, don't cry, be normal, I commanded myself. *We'll call it the new normal; the sadder-but-wiser normal.*

William stood up and stepped toward me.

"Don't touch me," I said in a low, mean voice.

Well, so much for being cool.

"Charlie, please let me explain," he began.

Soul Mates ~ Liz Morrison

"Ryan," I said, ignoring William, "would you like to explain why you and Katie are hanging in the lobby with William? Nope, never mind. I'm going to my room. When you're done here, I'll see you there."

I turned toward stairs. *Could it get worse than this?* I wondered. *How long does it take to recover from a broken heart. A day? A month? Never?*

A hand grabbed my arm. The electric charge made my knees buckle. Without looking at the person to whom the arm was connected, I said, through gritted teeth, "What part of 'don't touch me' did you not understand?"

"Charlie, please," Wills insisted. "I didn't write that article, contribute to that article, or discuss you with Andrew, except to tell him to watch out for you while I was gone. Please listen to me."

"William, let go of my arm," I snapped. "I'm going to continue to my room, where I will delete you from my phone, defriend you on Facebook, and pretend we never met." I waited patiently for him to let go.

"No," he replied after a long pause.

I turned—huge mistake. I looked into his eyes and couldn't look away. He gently took my other hand. The current flowed between us. I couldn't break his grip or eye contact.

"Charlie," William said my name in a voice that was simultaneously pleading and inviting, "please come back to the table. I convinced Ryan and Katie I had nothing to do with the article. Please let me convince you."

My eyes filled with tears. I remembered someone's advice that if you roll your eyes up you can't cry. I rolled my eyes toward the ceiling. *Don't cry. Don't cry*, I commanded myself.

"Charlie," William said softly. I looked at him again—big mistake. The tears slowly trickled down my cheeks.

"God, Charlie, I'm so sorry," he whispered.

William pulled me into his arms and wrapped me in a tight embrace. I started to cry in earnest.

Great...just great, I thought. *I was really successful with the entire not-crying-keeping-my-cool strategy.*

As I tried to regain my composure, I heard William say, "Please, love...I'm so sorry; please don't cry. I can explain all of this...please."

I inhaled deeply and let out a sigh. Mumbling into Will's shirt, "I don't know how you can possibly explain."

Wills stroked my back; the inexplicable current followed wherever he touched me. I wanted to melt into him. Instead, I tried pushing away. I moved my hands between our bodies and pushed against his chest.

William gasped from the shock of the contact and pulled me tighter. My hands felt fused to his body. It was incredibly weird.

"Charlie," William whispered, "I'm going to step back, but you need to take my hand, okay? I have a feeling if I break our physical connection, I'm going to pass out."

"Right," I replied sarcastically, "is this a new strategy to pick up women? Dumb American girls only fall for that one once," I said, struggling to break free.

"Look at me, please, Charlie." I looked up at William.

William was staring intently at me when I finally looked up. "God, you're even beautiful after you cry."

That was it, I decided. *This guy just didn't quit.* "Let go of me!" I enunciated each word.

"Charlie, I need you to understand, I'm not letting go, and I'll never let you go. I know you feel the connection. Seriously—I know if it's broken right now, I'll be out."

He seemed serious. I moved my hand to clasp his. "Okay, are you good?" I asked.

Our bodies were still touching, but now we were joined together by our clasped hands. "Yes, I'm good," he replied.

William gently turned me toward Katie and Ryan. Ryan was ready to attack William and Katie had a restraining arm on Ryan.

Soul Mates ~ Liz Morrison

"Charlie, are you okay?" Ryan asked quietly.

"Hmm," I replied. "Am I okay? Well, why did you turn into a William supporter?"

Surprisingly, Ryan looked at William before he responded. William and Ryan appeared to have had a male-bonding experience.

"Charlie, you know I'd prefer to believe that William is a jerk. But, for some reason which I cannot explain, Andrew set the whole thing up. Andrew's not here to explain, so we don't know the purpose. But being that I consider myself an observer of human nature, I came up with a plausible reason."

"Right," I replied. My hand was still clasped in William's and he was gently rubbing my palm. I knew I should pull away; I just couldn't.

"Here's what I think. I discussed my idea with Katie, and she agreed." Ryan glanced at Katie and she nodded in response.

"Wow, I was at my internship all day and you guys were talking about me. I'm surprised my ears weren't buzzing or something," I said. I was kind of pissed.

"So," Ryan continued, "Katie, who is a great judge of character, believes old British boy here is legit. When I visited William this morning—to beat him to a pulp, I might add—"

Wills sort of laughed.

Hmm; must be another story, I thought.

Ryan went on, "I heard Katie's voice in my head, telling me Andrew is the player, not William. Even when Katie read the evidence, she thought something was wrong with the entire premise."

"With Katie's conviction, William's total confusion, and my incredible power of deductive reasoning, I determined the following scenario," Ryan paused for a breath.

I glanced around the lobby and noticed it was getting quite crowded. "Do you guys mind if I sit down?" I asked.

Wills pulled out a chair for me. Katie, Ryan, and William sat down. It was a little awkward, considering Wills wouldn't let go of my hand.

The tightness in my chest started to ease. *Maybe today is going to end better than it began*, I thought.

"The theory is as follows: First, I thought Andrew wanted Charlie. Make your friend look bad so you can get the girl. Then, I thought, that doesn't make sense, because the article made Andrew look as bad as William. So, it wouldn't make sense if the goal was to win Charlie. It hit me: Andrew didn't want Charlie...he wants William."

Katie, William, and I all gave Ryan a questioning look.

"Not like that," Ryan shook his head like we were crazy. "He wanted William back as his wingman. After reading the article, it was obvious Andrew missed his friend. He had no intention of William seeing the article or getting the article published. Charlie would see the article, because yours truly, true to form, would make sure she saw the article. And, true to form, I did.

As planned, Charlie dropped William like a hot potato. Andrew didn't consider William might actually convince us he didn't contribute to the article. He also failed to consider William and Charlie both feel the connection. The physical connection is pretty hard to deny or ignore. So, Charlie, as much as it kills me to say this, Katie and I believe you should believe William."

I looked at my two best friends. I looked at the guy who in the last forty-eight hours had been the man of my dreams and the villain of my nightmares.

The connection was real, I reminded myself. *Last night was the single most incredible night of my life. Did I think William was capable of that type of duplicity?*

My heart said no way, and surprisingly, my mind agreed.

"Okay," I said softly.

William grasped my chin and turned my face toward his. "Okay what?"

Soul Mates ~ Liz Morrison

"Okay, I don't think you are the biggest jerk on the planet, you didn't write the article with Andrew, and you don't flirt with girls by saying you have some kind of metaphysical connection...except me," I said.

William leaned over and kissed me. I was not one for public displays of affection, but this one time seemed pretty appropriate.

Ryan interrupted, "Enough of that, please."

I broke the kiss. "Sorry, Ryan."

I reached across the table and gave Ryan a one-arm hug. "You guys are really the best friends a girl could have."

Katie laughed the kind of laugh you laugh when something totally uncomfortable occurred and it's finally over, "Well, that certainly was the most intense twenty-four hours," she said. "Since you and Wills are back together, we have the best plan for tomorrow. We were counting on you believing in him and our good judgment and, as expected, you did."

My head swam; I decided to just go with it.

"We're going to one of your World War I dream sites for the weekend," she went on. "We were going to do the whole Monet thing, but Wills was able to get rooms for us at a place we know you'll love. And I'll get inundated with Monet when I start my internship on Monday. You guys will be able to come to the museum when I can be your fabulous guide."

"Which site?" I asked.

"We're going to sites around Ypres–Passchendaele," Ryan said, looking pointedly at William.

I felt like I was missing something. Apparently, Wills and Ryan had an intense male-bonding experience.

"No way! That's the place I dreamt about last night!" I exclaimed.

Katie and Ryan looked at me strangely; I'd never talked about World War I dreams in front of anyone but them. Since we'd been in Rouen, I hadn't shared them at all.

"I told Wills a little bit about my dreams," I added. "He has them too; weird, right?"

"Well, this has been the worst day and the best day," I announced. "It's still early. Do you guys want to get something to eat? We can go to the grocery store, grab some random items, and have a picnic in my room. Wait—my room is a disaster."

"We can use my flat," Wills said. "It's in perfect picnic condition."

Chapter Seventeen

WILLIAM

We were meeting in the lobby at 7:00 a.m. It would have been ace to travel with just Charlie, though going with Katie and Ryan was good. They believed me, and traveling together would build trust and friendship.

I watched the stairs. Charlie would walk down any moment. My chest tightened in anticipation.

I almost lost her, I thought.

Andrew—what was he thinking? I wondered. *Would it be wrong to knock him on his ass?* Not a very charitable thought.

The experience was certainly turning out differently than I'd envisioned; different and better, with the exception of Andrew.

"Hey, Wills."

Charlie walked slowly toward me, carrying a backpack. "Katie and Ryan will be down in a couple of minutes."

Stopping in front of me, she clasped my hand. The electric current was strong, but not as shocking as the day before.

She reached up and placed her free hand in the crook of my neck. "Kiss me, Wills," she whispered.

Quite right—no need to be asked twice, I told myself. I leaned down and pressed my lips to hers. The touch was electric.

We shouldn't do this often, I decided; *I'd lose my firm resolve to protect Charlie from me.*

I slowly broke the kiss and smiled into Charlie's eyes.

"We won't be able to kiss with Ryan and Katie around—it would be rude," Charlie said. "I thought we should have one really great kiss before we hit the road."

"One really great kiss," I said. I pulled her tightly into my body and pressed my lips to hers.

Everything faded away as we got lost in the kiss. The feeling of Charlie's soft skin brought me to my senses. I realized my hand was on her waist under her jumper. *Bloody hell,* I thought.

"Wow—one great kiss," Charlie said with a sigh.

As if on cue, the elevator opened and Katie and Ryan emerged, both with relatively sparsely packed backpacks.

"Are you ready to roll?" Charlie asked. Her excitement was contagious.

"Ryan," Katie said "you weren't kidding when you said the car was small. It's small and cute."

"It's perfect," Charlie announced. "Katie and I can sit in the back to start with and then we can rotate, if needed. Wills and Ryan can start up front."

I opened the boot and we threw in our bags. "Good thing you ladies followed our instructions," Ryan said as he slid into the front seat.

I looked in the rearview mirror at Charlie and caught her eye. She smiled at me and I had to catch my breath. Love was impacting my equilibrium.

Chest hurts, hard to breathe…maybe I'm having a heart attack, I told myself. *It certainly seems that way.*

Maneuvering the car down the streets of Rouen was relatively easy on Saturday morning.

"Did you remember your passports?" I asked.

"Always," Ryan replied. He looked in his backpack, just to be sure.

Soul Mates ~ Liz Morrison

"Okay, so where are we going?" Katie asked.

"We're going to stay at the Talbot House in Poperinge, Belgium. We're going to travel to Zonnebeke and visit the Memorial Museum Passchendaele and the Tyne Cot Cemetery. Charlie's interested in nursing, so I added the Lijssenthoek Military Cemetery. The Lijssenthoek Cemetery is located near a casualty clearing station."

"What's a casualty clearing station?" Ryan asked.

Charlie, who was staring out the window, replied absentmindedly, "It's a military hospital close to the front line. I swear I had a dream about a casualty clearing station." She paused and seemed to ponder how she knew about casualty clearing stations.

If Charlie's dream-memory of the casualty clearing station were the same as mine, she was thinking about snogging with my World War I self. By the standards of 1917, the events of the day had been hot.

Once again, I caught her eye in the rearview mirror and gave her a slow wink. She blushed and sort of shook her head.

"The Lijssenthoek Cemetery is close to the front line," I continued. "I reckon we can explore the area and possibly locate the site of the casualty clearing station for Charlie.

"On our return to Rouen, we're going to visit the Tommy Café, located in Pozières."

"Look it up on your phone, Ryan," Charlie added from the back seat. "It really looks amazing."

"Why's it so amazing?" Katie asked.

"Well," Charlie said, "it's a café, but it's also a World War I museum dedicated to British soldiers."

"Referred to as Tommies," I chimed in.

"Right—Tommies," Charlie said.

"Our guys were called Doughboys during World War I," Ryan replied.

155

"Oh—so the name for the café comes from the British name for their soldiers. You know," Katie continued, "I hope I don't start having dreams about World War I...even if the dreams are about hot guys; or, as Charlie says, hot dead guys."

"Charlie," I asked, "you dream about hot dead guys?"

Charlie jabbed my shoulder, shocking me. "That's not what I meant. Katie's just messing with you. I dream about hot guys from World War I, but they're all dead—meaning not living now, and probably didn't live long then. Got it?"

"Yes," I replied. "You dream about hot guys from World War I."

"Actually," Charlie replied, "I probably shouldn't admit this in front of this group, but I dream about you as a World War I soldier, and you weren't dead."

"So, I wasn't dead, but I was hot?" I asked. It still surprised me I could chat up Charlie. I really enjoyed this banter with her.

"Totally," Charlie replied with a hint of sarcasm. I caught her eye, and she smiled her incredible smile which, conveyed to me she really did think I was hot, and the sarcasm was for the benefit of her friends.

Ryan was studying his phone. "Hey, we should go to the Pool of Peace, as long as we're staying in Poperinge."

"What's the connection?" Katie asked.

"Well, it's the crater from the Battle of Messines Ridge. According to the website, the Pool of Peace was created by an explosion. Hmm...apparently nineteen mines exploded, and the sound could be heard all the way to Downing Street. Isn't that where your Prime Minister lives?"

"The Prime Minister? Right, then—yes, he lives on Downing Street," I replied.

Ryan continued, "This war stuff is really kind of interesting. Listen to this: all nineteen mines were blown at three ten a.m. The Spanbroekmolen mine actually went up fifteen seconds late. It killed infantry who'd already started the advance. Talk about friendly fire."

Soul Mates ~ Liz Morrison

The smoke was heavy and the sound of men screaming in agony filled the air. We began our advance, the ground shook, another explosion occurred. I landed on the ground and lay stunned. My ears were ringing. I pushed myself to my feet and struggled to see through the haze, chaos reigned. On my left and my right, I could see several of my men were severely injured or dead. One of the mines must have exploded late. We killed our own damn men.

"Wills...pay attention, dude; you almost drove off the road."

"Sorry," I said again. "The Pool of Peace sounds like an interesting addition to the trip."

A jolt of electricity surged up my arm. Charlie was touching me. *Does she remember how we met?* I wondered. *Not at the café in Rouen, but at a base hospital after the Battle of Messines Ridge.*

I glanced at her again. She was waiting for it. She smiled and continued to gently rub my arm.

Charlie

The drive from Rouen to Poperinghe passed quickly. Staring out the window, I read the road signs for Boulogne-sur-Mer, Calais, Dunkirk...sometimes this life seemed surreal. This morning we'd been in France, and a few hours later we were in Belgium.

"How much longer till we get there?" Katie asked Wills and Ryan.

Ryan glanced at his phone. "We should arrive at the Talbot House in about fifteen minutes."

Poperinge was different from Rouen. It was more modern. Well, modern was probably not the correct word. Many of the buildings looked like they'd been built in the twentieth century.

William navigated the narrow streets like a pro. "The Talbot House is on Gathuisstraat," he said.

"Keep your eyes open," Ryan said, "I think it's going to be on the right."

"There it is!" Katie exclaimed.

"Right, then," Wills said as he pulled into a parking spot.

The Talbot House looked just like the picture from the website. The exterior was painted a light gray with white shutters framing the window. The windows were covered with white sheer drapery. The double front door had an intricate design of white-painted iron. Above the double door was the sign "Talbot House 1915—? Every Man's Club."

"Grab the bags and let's see if we can check in," Ryan said.

William opened the trunk and handed everyone their bags. "Charlie, may I carry your tote?" he asked. He was such a gentleman.

"Thanks," I replied, "I've got it."

He grabbed my hand and smiled. "I don't want you to get lost. Your friends tell me you have a horrible sense of direction."

Ryan noticed our clasped hands, "I think even Charlie could find the place—it's, like, two steps away," he observed. "Hey, we're right across the street from a bakery. I'll bet Belgium has great baked goods."

Katie and I looked at each other and laughed. Ryan loved dessert.

The Talbot House was three stories tall. It didn't look like a typical hotel.

Katie studied the exterior. "Well, it's not the Ritz," she remarked. "But it certainly has character. I wonder if it has ghosts."

William opened the door and we walked into the foyer. It was like entering another era. The chandelier basked the entrance with a warm, inviting glow. Armchairs lined the foyer, offering a comfy place to sit and rest.

A strong sense of nostalgia flooded my senses. It was like I'd been here before, but not exactly here; in the time period, but not in this exact place; not in the Talbot House. It was really hard to explain how I felt; I knew I'd never felt exactly like this before.

William placed his arm around my shoulders. He was breathing hard.

"Hey, are you okay?" I asked him softly.

William looked into my eyes. His eyes were sad and serious. "I'm fine," he said.

I gave him a questioning look. "Really, quite fine," he insisted.

I wished I could read William's mind. I also wished I had the confidence to tell him how this place made me feel. I thought we might be feeling the same way.

William kept his arm around my shoulder, "Okay, love," he whispered. "Let's do this." Then he propelled me down the hall toward Katie and Ryan.

Do this? Do what? I wondered.

"Well," Ryan said, giving me a disgruntled look, cocking an eyebrow at the casual manner in which William had me in his embrace, "we have two rooms in the Garden House. Katie and Charlie are in room one and Wills and I are in room two."

"I also asked about ghosts," Ryan continued.

"Seriously?" I asked. "What did you find out?"

"There have been rumors of ghosts," he said. "Some guy named Richard Heijster wrote a book, *mysterie 14-18*. In his book, witnesses reported sighting ghost soldiers and also ghosts of doctors and nurses. According to the receptionist, the ghosts aren't threatening. The Talbot House, after all, was a peaceful place amidst the horrors of war."

"Friendly ghosts," Katie said. "Well, this experience is certainly something to tweet about."

Ryan was texting again. He looked up from his phone. "What?" he said with a grin.

I felt the tension subside from Wills' body. Whatever was bugging him seemed to be resolved under the onslaught of Katie and Ryan's cluelessness.

My stomach was still in knots. *Is it being here? Being here with Wills?* I just didn't know.

We planned to tour the house and grounds, visit the Passchendaele 1917 museum, travel to the Tyne Cot Cemetery, and end the day with a visit to the Spanbroekmolen Mine Crater Memorial. Tomorrow, we were going to the cemetery, located near the casualty clearing station, and we'd stop at the Tommy Café on our way back to Rouen.

Keys in hand, we walked out of the Talbot House and into the garden. The garden was amazing. The Talbot House was attached to two other homes; we'd have never guessed that a huge garden was hidden behind the house.

"Splendid," William said as he glanced around.

"It really is quite splendid," I replied.

We entered the Garden House. The accommodations weren't luxurious, but they were historic. "It'll beat sleeping on the futon," Katie stated as we entered the narrow room that was furnished with twin beds and a few other pieces of furniture.

"Actually," I said, "I think it's pretty perfect." Then I grinned at Katie and gave her a hug. "Thanks for being part of this adventure. It's like my dreams are coming true."

Katie glanced around our sparsely furnished room and laughed, "You're certainly easy to please."

We left our bags in the room and joined the guys in the garden.

The day flew by. Why is it when we want something to last a long time, it seems like it goes by so quickly, and when we want something to fly by quickly, like algebra class, it seems like it takes forever?

"Hey, I see the exit for Spanbroekmolen Mine Crater Memorial. This was not easy to locate, even with all of the technology. William," Ryan continued, "are you okay, dude? You look kind of sick."

"Sorry," William said. "Trying not to get us lost in the middle of Belgium."

Something in William's voice was off. He sounded—I'm not sure of the right word—well, agitated...or maybe nervous. I reached over and placed my hand on his shoulder. The jolt of electricity wasn't as intense. It seemed the more we were in each other's company, the connection was more...well, warm and less...well, shocking.

He reached up and grasped my hand.

"I think we can park past the crater site," Ryan said. "It's not a designated parking spot, but there's room for a few cars."

Wills located the spot and pulled over. Only one other car was parked in the area. It was kind of late, yet it was still light out.

We were surprised other visitors weren't at the mine. *On the other hand*, I thought, *this is a pretty obscure memorial.*

I was thinking dinner would be a good idea. We'd skipped lunch. After visiting the Tyne Cot Cemetery, we'd been too depressed to eat. So many dead—it made me feel sick.

We got out of the car and walked toward the entrance gate. William grasped my hand and pulled me tightly against his side. He whispered in my ear, "Do you have any idea how much I need to kiss you?"

I was a little startled. I had no idea he was thinking about kissing. "Need" versus "want"—his word choice stood out in my mind.

Katie and Ryan were ahead of us. I turned in to William, wrapped my arms around his neck, and kissed him. I quickly lost all sense of time and place.

"Charlie! Charlie!" I heard Katie calling. I abruptly pushed William away and felt my face get hot."

"I can't turn around," I whispered to William. I didn't look up at him because I just couldn't. He tilted my chin up, smiled, and said loudly to Katie and Ryan, "Sorry...I know Charlie abhors public displays of affection; that public kiss was entirely my fault."

I looked at my feet and grinned.

"Come on, you guys," Katie said. "This looks really interesting, but I'm getting hungry. You know I'm not pleasant when I'm hungry."

I looked at Wills. "She really isn't," I affirmed.

"Isn't what?" Wills asked. He was staring at the entrance gate.

I tugged on his arm. "Come on," I said, "let's get this over with." *Okay, interesting choice of words,* I thought. *We wanted to be here; why would it be something we needed to get over?*

We caught up with Ryan and Katie at the granite pillar by the entrance gate. Katie read the inscription out loud. The inscription repeated the story Ryan had read to us in the car about the Battle of Messines Ridge and the explosion of the Spanbroekmolen mine.

We took the path to the Pool of Peace. William's breathing was hard.

"Are you okay, William?" Ryan asked.

William shook his head and sat down. He placed his head between his knees and took several deep breaths.

"Charlotte! Charlotte! You need to wake up. Our first casualties have arrived."

Lilly was trying to wake me. Suddenly, I was wide awake. I had a job to do.

We quickly donned our clothes. I asked, "Where did they come from?"

Lilly took a moment to answer, "Somewhere in Belgium; a place called Messines Ridge."

The memory popped into my head. It must be from one of my dreams. *I wish I had my journal,* I lamented. *I could've compared this to the notes.*

It was strange that a dream would pop into my mind right now. It was even stranger that it felt like a memory. *Must have been a super-vivid dream,* I thought.

I sat next to William and wrapped my arms around him. "Car sick?" I asked.

"Car sick?" he glanced up, giving me a peculiar look. "Not exactly."

William stood up and pulled me with him. "Let's walk."

Katie and Ryan led the way. It was very beautiful. Water lilies floated on the surface of the pool, which was surrounded by trees and other shrubbery. It was hard to believe a large explosion had created the pool.

William seemed to be a million miles away. I held his hand as we walked around the pool.

"Charlotte, it was quite a horrific experience," William stated. *"When the first explosion didn't ignite, we had to move forward as if it had. When it finally exploded, my men were directly in the line of fire. I knew many of them were lost. They were good men, Charlotte; men with wives and children. How do you tell the families their father, husband, brother, or son died bravely for their county, and the weapon that killed them was one of our own? Not a good story to tell."*

*Whoa, another one...*I realized. *World War I Wills and I discussing Messines Ridge. Weird.*

William looked...well, shell-shocked, as we continued our walk around the pool.

"Time to go," I said. Katie and Ryan nodded in agreement.

We walked toward the entrance. "Let's take a picture," Katie said as we return to the granite stone at the front gate.

Katie approached the other couple visiting the site. "Would you mind taking our picture?"

Katie and Ryan stood on one side of the monument and Wills and I stood on the other. William wrapped his arm around my waist and pulled me close. We smiled for the camera; it seemed slightly odd, considering the location of our visit.

As I looked at the camera and smiled, I recognized the man taking our picture. He was the gentleman from the first day of my internship, the one who'd requested information on World War I sites.

Chapter Eighteen

WILLIAM

The visit to Messines Ridge was very intense. I felt shell-shocked. I was relieved Ryan and Charlie stopped questioning me about my distress. Ryan knew more about my issues than Charlie. I was thankful he didn't pursue his thoughts about my behavior.

As we returned to the Talbot House, I wondered when the time would be the right to share my past with Charlie. I really wanted to talk about our past.

As I sat by the crater, my thoughts were about my men, but they were also about Charlotte. If I hadn't suffered injuries at that battle site, I would never have been sent to Base Hospital Twenty-One. I would never have met Charlotte. *I want to pull Charlie into my arms and tell her it was worth it,* I thought. *The injury, the memories of battle—everything; she's worth everything to me.*

I glanced back in the rearview mirror and watched Charlie talking to Katie. She was so beautiful...on the inside as well as the outside. Sometimes, like now, when I looked at her, it was hard to breathe.

She glanced up and caught my eye in the mirror. She gave me a slow, sexy wink. I smiled and returned my gaze to the road.

"What a day!" Katie exclaimed, getting out of the car at the Talbot House. "I'm starving. Let's freshen up and then eat. I hope we can walk. Ryan, why don't you ask the lady you talked to earlier? You seem to have a way with women of a certain age."

"What exactly are you implying?" Ryan asked in mock seriousness.

"Ryan," Charlie explained, "has a way with older women. He convinced our French teacher to pretty much leave us alone in Rouen, he convinced the airline ticket agent to upgrade said teacher, and he convinced my mom and Katie's mom to say yes to innumerable adventures that, if we'd asked, the answer would've been no."

"What can I say?" Ryan laughed. "It's a talent."

Katie and Charlie left Ryan and me in the garden as they raced to the Garden House to freshen up.

"Are you okay?" Ryan asked. "You looked pretty shaken up at the Pool of Peace."

"My great-great-uncle was wounded at Messines Ridge. He was in the first group—the group that moved forward before the explosion. I remembered."

Ryan awkwardly patted my back. Two days ago, he'd hated my guts. Now he had…I guess…empathy.

I had to ask, "Why are you being so kind? I'm surprised you don't act as if I am one slice of bread short of a sandwich."

Ryan kind of snickered. "Well, dude, you might be one slice shy, but I believe you. I honestly don't know why." He paused for a moment. "My brother served in Iraq. When he came home, certain things, certain places made him…I don't know…take shelter in his mind. Anyway, seeing you on the ground on the path by the pool reminded me of my brother."

"Okay, enough of this male bonding," Ryan said. "Let's find the lady of the manor and determine a good place for dinner."

We strode across the garden to the information desk, passing the couple who'd taken our photograph earlier in the day.

"Hello," Ryan called. Americans really do speak to everyone.

We entered the building and walked to the desk. The proprietress was on her mobile, speaking in rapid French.

Soul Mates ~ Liz Morrison

I couldn't help but listen. I noticed Ryan was, too. Apparently the Talbot House had a legend connected to a small treasure. The proprietress was upset because a couple checked in to the Talbot House hoping for information on the treasure. She was clearly exasperated by the couple.

When she noticed Ryan and me waiting patiently for her to ring off, she said a quick goodbye and promptly ended her conversation.

"How may I assist you?" she asked with a smile. "Did you enjoy your adventure in our region?"

Ryan smiled and asked for a recommendation for a restaurant within walking distance of the house. She paused then replied, "I have the perfect place for you and your friends to dine this evening, just down the road at the Café de la Paix, located in the Hotel de la Paix. It has beautiful outdoor seating—perfect for this lovely evening."

"Can you tell us about the Talbot House treasure? We aren't seeking a treasure; it just sounds like a really great story," Ryan asked.

The lady sighed and smiled. "It's a romantic story you can share with your girlfriends. Girls like a romantic story; it will be a perfect conversation for your dinner this evening.

"During the war, soldiers serving at Passchendaele had family members send special items to them in care of the Talbot House. According to the story, a British soldier, a lieutenant of wealthy birth fell in love with a battlefield nurse. In some versions of the story, he married her and requested the family jewels to present to her as a wedding gift. In another version of the story, he requested the jewelry so he could properly propose."

She took a deep breath, resulting in a dramatic pause. "During the Great War, our clerks at the Talbot House kept a ledger recording the anticipated package, the date the package was received, and the date the package was collected. In the case of the Talbot House treasure, our records indicate the anticipated package and the date the package was received at the Talbot House. The clerk who took the original request jotted a note stating the young man was waiting for an engagement gift, but the words engagement gift were struck through and the letters w.g. noted. We decided the w.g. indicated wedding gift."

The proprietress had a dreamy smile. "It sounds quite romantic. There's no indication the package was claimed. So, maybe it was quite tragic, not romantic. Our speculation is the young man died prior to retrieving the gift for his beloved."

"The Talbot House treasure is the belief that the gift of some undetermined value is hidden somewhere in the house. As you know, the house was occupied by the Germans during World War II. If a treasure was to be found, I'm sure the Germans found the treasure. But it still makes for a romantic, if not tragic, story of World War I."

"Sir," I said to my commanding officer, "would it be possible to obtain a pass to go to the Talbot House? I'm not requesting a leave, just a quick trip. I'd like to make a special request at the Talbot House. As you know, sir, on my last leave, I married the American nurse."

I paused for a moment; just thinking of Charlotte made it hard for me to breathe. "I have another three-day leave approaching in October. I'd like to present her with a wedding band and a few gifts from my family."

The officer grinned at me. "So, you want to have the goods delivered to the Talbot House? All right then. You have my permission."

"Thank you, sir," I replied.

I grabbed the counter and took a couple of deep breaths. Luckily Ryan was still engaged in conversation.

I was in shock, or something like it. *The Talbot House treasure had been for Charlotte. Did I die before I was able to collect it?* I wondered. *I mean, did the other William die before he was able to collect it? It would seem he did,* I thought. *I've never had this memory before.*

"Hey, William," Ryan said, "You don't look good."

I just looked at him for a second, and said, "Ask her the name of the soldier."

Ryan cocked his eyebrow and turned back to the counter, "Just out of curiosity, what was the name of the soldier?"

She smiled at Ryan. My heart was beating so hard it might explode.

"No one ever asks for the name of the soldier," she said. "They are most interested in searching every nook and cranny to find the treasure. His name, I am afraid, eludes me. For you, my guest from America, I will find the soldier's name. Stop in before you leave tomorrow."

I took a deep breath. It was a reprieve. I'm not sure what it would mean if the name of the soldier was William Harrington, but it certainly would mean something.

"I need to ring my mum," I said to Ryan. "I'll meet you and the girls in the garden in ten minutes."

"Sure," he replied. "You're sure you're okay?"

"I'm good," I replied. But I wasn't good at all.

Ryan walked toward the Garden House and I moved into the garden. I quickly dialed my mobile and waited for my mum to answer. Instead of my mum, I got her answering machine.

"Hey Mum, it's Wills," I said. "Can you have Dad contact Grandmum and ask if there's any record of William Harrington requesting some of the family jewelry? Thanks, Mum."

Charlie came out of the Garden House. "Hey, gorgeous," I said. She walked into my waiting arms. The electric current was intense—not painful, just compelling.

"Did you miss me?" she asked as she twined her fingers in my hair. I didn't answer. I leaned down and kissed her. Every kiss was better than the last. This time I'd control myself. As long as Charlie didn't move, we were good.

Then she slid her hand along my jaw. *Damn, I'm losing control,* I thought.

"Hey, get a room," Katie said with a laugh.

I pulled away from Charlie. "Sorry," Charlie said to Katie, giving me a quick kiss. "I think a room is a great idea," she murmured softly as she walked away. I knew she was teasing, but I really would like to get a room. *Oh well, not tonight, and probably not for a very long time,* I told myself.

I heard Charlie say to Katie, "I don't know—there's just something about him that—I don't know—makes me a little crazy. It's not just the accent, seriously." Then they laughed.

I loved it when Charlie laughed.

CHARLIE

I couldn't sleep.

Katie was sound asleep. *I guess she won't meet any ghosts wandering around the Talbot House tonight,* I told myself. *Maybe I'll tell her I saw a few ghosts, to cause paranormal envy.*

I can't stand it, I finally decided.

I threw off the blankets, shoved my feet into my flip flops, and walked toward the garden. *Maybe sitting outside for a while will help me fall asleep.*

A shadow shifted in the far corner of the garden. My heart was pounding. *Maybe ghosts really do haunt the Talbot House,* I thought.

I moved into the shadows, hoping the ghost didn't notice me. Then I realized it wasn't a ghost, but another guest. And it wasn't just any old guest; it was William.

"Wills," I whispered loudly. "Wills," I said again.

"Charlie," he responded as he walked toward me across the dark and eerie garden. "What are you doing out here?"

"I couldn't sleep," I replied. Suddenly I was incredibly self-conscious. Wills looked incredibly sexy in pajama pants and a plain white T-shirt. I, on the other hand, was a mess. My hair was in a messy bun and I was wearing boxers and a T-shirt.

"You know," he said as he closed the distance between us, "every time I see you I say to myself, *can this girl be any more attractive?* And the next time I see you, you're more beautiful than the last."

"Wills," I asked. "Do you wear glasses? You apparently didn't put them on this evening."

William grasped my hands—electric—and kissed my knuckles.

"Do you want to walk or sit down?" he asked.

"Sit," I said. "Are you okay? You seemed a little off today."

Wills stared at our clasped hands, but didn't speak. He raised his head and looked into my eyes. My breath quickened and my chest tightened. I thought, *I love this man.*

"Charlie, please don't look at me like that. I obviously have a hard time controlling myself around you. And when you look at me like you want to kiss me, I can't think."

"Maybe you shouldn't think," I replied.

"Come have a chat," Wills tugged on my hand and pulled me to a bench. He sat down and placed me on his lap. "I know I probably should have you sit on an entirely different bench, but I want to hold you."

"Okay," I said as I snuggled into his chest.

"Charlie, I need to tell you something, and I need you to promise to listen with an open mind," Wills said softly.

"I'm all ears," I replied. I was so comfortable lying on Wills. It was the best feeling ever.

"Remember when we met at the café in Rouen?" Wills asked. "Tell me what our meeting felt like."

Hmm, what did that feel like to me? "Oh…well, it felt like we already knew each other. And…well, there was that whole shock thing." I smiled. "That was really kind of strange, but cool.

"I don't know, I feel comfortable with you. And I like the shock thing, especially when it's more of current than a jolt."

"Oh," I continued, "and then you started invading my dreams; my dreams in the present, and my World War I dreams. You know what's kind of strange? Some of my World War I night dreams have started becoming day dreams. Like today, for instance, when we were at the Pool of Peace, I had this really weird daydream.

"Anyway, that's not what we were talking about. So, I love talking to you, and you're the first guy I've kissed that I really enjoyed kissing. Wait—but you asked me about the first night we met. I felt connected to you."

Wills grasped my chin and tilted my face toward his, and then he bent down and kissed me. It was a perfect kiss. "I've been looking for you my whole life," Wills whispered against my lips and kissed me again.

"When I walked into the café in Rouen, you asked me what took me so long. I know the question was for Ryan. But it really was for me…you just didn't know it," Wills whispered.

I thought about his comment and replied, "Actually, I was waiting for you; or the possibility of you."

"Maybe we were lovers from a past life or something," Wills said.

"Are you trying to get me into bed?" I asked as I slugged his arm.

Wills laughed. "You're the one who mentioned ripping someone's clothes off, if I recall correctly.

"Seriously, Charlie," Wills continued, "do you think it's possible we fell in love in another lifetime, and have been searching for each other?"

"Wow," I replied, "that's pretty deep. Well, it would certainly explain why you're interested in me."

"What do you mean?" Wills asked. "You're beautiful, smart, funny, intense, charming. Did I mention a great kisser and totally hot? You are quite a fit bird, Charlie," he said as he stroked my hair. "That's English for 'hot,' in case you're wondering."

I looked up at him. He leaned down and kissed me again.

"Will you do me a favor?" Wills asked. "Can you think about everything that has happened since we met—maybe even before we met? Then, entertain the possibility we knew each other in a previous life; a life connected to World War I and to the places we're both drawn to in France and Belgium."

I inhaled deeply, but I didn't respond. I didn't know how to respond. Wills held me close and stroked my hair. It was comforting and comfortable. *I've never considered the possibility of having a past life, though I was obsessed with the past,* I thought.

I slowly drifted off to sleep. I heard Wills whisper, "Remember, Charlotte, try to remember."

I read the letter from William for the tenth time. The letter had wonderful news. William was scheduled for a leave, and he was coming to Rouen. He'd arrive any day, and with any luck, he'd be here for the banquet and circus celebrating the work of our team in France. The nurses were performing a Maypole dance and the dress I was wearing was pretty. I'd love William to see me in a pretty dress, though I wasn't sure I wanted him to watch my Maypole dance.

I carefully folded the letter, placing it with the others from William. I secured our correspondence with a pink ribbon. I tied a bow to secure the letter opener—a gift from William—to the bundle.

The last time we'd seen each other was at the casualty clearing station, over nine months ago. I wondered if our tree was still standing. When the war was over, we could travel to Passchendaele and look for it.

I knew I'd see him again. This time, he'd ask my father's permission to court me. It was hard to imagine people still courted during these turbulent times. Though it probably wasn't respectable, I thought about kissing William. I wondered if his kisses would still be magical.

"Charlie...hey, beautiful, wake up."

I struggled to make sense of my surroundings. I was in a garden and I was sprawled across William. I scooted to a sitting position, threw my leg over his thigh, pulled his lips to mine, and we kissed. It was magical.

Chapter Nineteen

WILLIAM

The sun was coming up.

Charlie slept in my arms. I know I slept, but I tried not to sleep. Her soft, warm body pressed against mine was perfect. *The last few nights have been the best nights of my entire life,* I thought. I adored her.

The conversation about a potential past life went better than I'd anticipated. *She may change her mind this morning and determine I was mental,* I cautioned myself. *She must remember. I need her to remember.* I wasn't sure what that would actually mean, but I knew our reconciliation was inevitable.

I gently caressed her hair. She murmured something and snuggled deeper.

"Charlie," I whispered. "Hey, beautiful, wake up."

Charlie struggled to wake up. She pushed herself into a seated position. She turned so her legs were straddling mine. She reached up and tugged my head down. Then she kissed me.

All the self-control I'd mustered throughout the night was lost the moment her lips touched mine. I wasn't prepared; I was consumed.

Time seemed to stand still. A loud bang, possibly a door slamming, jolted me back to reality. My hands were inside Charlie's T-shirt. Her hands were inside my T-shirt. We were breathing hard.

Soul Mates ~ Liz Morrison

I slowly slid my hands out from under her shirt. "Wow," she whispered.

I grinned at her. "Wow—quite right."

I leaned down and kissed her again...a quick kiss; the kiss that sealed her destiny.

She's destined to be with me, I decided.

"We were out here all night?" Charlie asked. "Obviously," she said with a laugh. "I need to get back inside; Katie will totally freak out."

She stood up, then leaned down, and gave me a quick kiss.

Charlie waved as she entered the Garden House.

I rubbed my hands against my face; I definitely needed a shave. Exhaling deeply, I stood up from the bench.

Today would be interesting. *First, we're going to have breakfast,* I told myself. *Then I'm going to find out if William Harrington had jewelry for Charlotte sent to the Talbot House.*

Finding out on a full stomach was a good idea.

We'd then travel to the cemetery near the casualty clearing station. *If we find the tree with the carving, Charlie will remember,* I thought. *I know.*

I wondered how she'd react. Seriously, she was a smart girl. She must have considered the possibility. On the other hand, I probably wouldn't have considered the possibility if I hadn't known about it my entire life.

Quietly I entered the room. I didn't want to wake Ryan. Grabbing my jumper, trousers, and toiletries, I used the communal facilities to shower. *A fellow should look presentable when confronting a girl from his past, especially when he plans on the girl being his future,* I told myself.

"Ryan," I said as I entered the room, "Ryan, old man—time to wake up."

"Shut up, dude," Ryan replied as he rolled to his stomach and pulled the blanket over his head. "I'm not moving."

A soft tap on the door. I stopped trying to wake Ryan and opened the door. Charlie and Katie were at the door, ready to leave.

I opened the door wide, "Well ladies, if you can get his lazy arse out of bed, we can be on our way."

"It's even sexy when he swears," Katie whispered loudly to Charlie.

Charlie laughed as she and Katie entered the room. Glancing at each other, they made a short dash to jump on Ryan. They landed on him with oomph. Ryan tried to push them off, with no success.

"Get up, Ryan," the girls said in unison. "We're ready for breakfast."

Ryan popped up from his position under the covers. "Breakfast," he said. "Breakfast is definitely a reason to get out of bed."

"Come on, Charlie, Sleeping Beauty will get ready faster if we wait outside. Let's go sit in the garden and admire the beautiful surroundings."

I touched Charlie before she left the room. It was electric. "It still works," I said with a smile.

"Always," she replied. It was painful to let go of her hand.

"I'll join you in the garden as soon as I pack my things," I said.

Ryan rolled out of bed. "I'll be ready in ten minutes, tops."

"No problem," I replied. I grabbed my bag and walked out of the Garden House and into the garden.

I joined Charlie and Katie on a bench. Sitting next to Charlie, I could feel the current of electricity that flowed between us. I knew she felt it, too. Her smile caused a heat rush. Luckily, Katie was sitting right next to Charlie. If Charlie and I had been alone, it would have gotten a lot hotter.

Katie glanced toward the Garden House, "Hey Ryan—it's about time, you lazy bum."

"Lazy bum?" Ryan questioned. "You guys got up at oh-dark-hundred. I'm not lazy; you guys are totally crazy. But now that I am awake, I'm starving. Didn't someone mention breakfast?"

I stood up, grabbed Charlie's hand, and walked across the garden. "We need to settle the bill, and then we can get something to eat."

Charlie and I will return to this place someday, I told myself.

We entered the foyer. The feeling of nostalgia was very strong. "I'll settle up," I told the group. Letting go of Charlie's hand, I approached the counter.

This morning, a gentleman was working the counter. *Today won't be the day I find out if World War I William is connected to the Talbot House treasure,* I told myself.

We completed the transaction quickly. "William Harrington," the gentleman said as he looked at the signed credit slip. "I have an envelope for you." He reached under the counter and presented me with a plain, white envelope.

I took the envelope and stuffed it in the pocket of my trousers, "Thank you," I said as I turned to the group.

"We'll divide the expenses when we get back to Rouen," Ryan said as we left the Talbot House.

"Let's go to the bakery." Katie pointed to the bakery across the street. "I hope they have cappuccino."

The bakery smelled of fresh-baked bread. We placed our orders and found a spot at one of the café's tables.

The envelope was burning a hole in my pocket; I needed to find out whether the Talbot House treasure was connected to William Harrington. If it was, it would be the first memory to be verified with evidence.

I wanted to open the envelope, but I didn't want to open it in front of everyone. I stood up. "Does anyone want jam for their croissant?" Everyone shook their head in the negative.

As I walked to the counter, I pulled the envelope from my pocket and opened it. I took the note out of the envelope.

The soldier's name was William J. Harrington.

Whoa. I grabbed the counter so I wouldn't fall down.

Taking a deep breath, I turned back toward the table. Charlie smiled at me as I approached. "Are you okay?" she asked.

We'd asked each other 'Are you okay?' a lot on this trip. I guess the stress of discovering a past life causes one to not be okay.

"You know the story we told you about the Talbot House treasure?" I asked. Both Katie and Charlie nodded their heads, "Well, the chap who requested the jewels was none other than my great-great-uncle, William James Harrington."

"No way!" Katie exclaimed. "That's awesome. Not just awesome…it's wicked awesome. Is your family missing any jewels? A long-lost treasure trove; we could go on a treasure hunt. Now that would be something to tweet about."

"I'll call my mum later," I replied. "I don't recall a missing family treasure."

Charlie was really quiet. I wondered what she was thinking.

She reached over and took my hand. I squeezed her fingers, trying to communicate something. She squeezed back.

"Are you guys ready to go?" Charlie asked. "We have so much to accomplish today."

"You know, Wills," she said as we walked toward the car, "it's kind of exciting to have a mystery to solve. I'll help you any way I can."

I looked down into her deep-blue eyes. I was lost.

Looking into her deep-blue eyes, I was lost. "Charlotte," I said, "will you make me the happiest man alive and consent to be my wife?"

A moment of silence followed. Then Charlotte threw her arms around my neck.

"Yes," she said. "Yes, William, I would be honored to be your wife."

I stood up, still holding her hand in mine, leaned down, and kissed her.

"Wills...Wills," Charlie said, "Hey, Wills."

I couldn't help it...I leaned down and I kissed her. It was a short kiss...satisfying, but not satisfying enough.

"Sorry," I said. Charlie shook her head; she obviously understood I wasn't sorry.

I laughed as I opened the car door to assist her inside. She was shaking her head the whole time. My heart contracted. It was hard to breathe *I love this girl,* I thought.

The Lijssenthoek Military Cemetery was approximately a ten-minute drive from the Talbot House. I maneuvered the car down the road, away from the Talbot House and toward our next stop on memory lane.

I wondered whether Charlie would recognize the area. The location of the cemetery was relatively close to the location of Charlotte and William's picnic lunch. If the tree was there, she'd remember. I wasn't sure how she'd react, but I knew she'd remember.

"Let's see," Ryan said, scrutinizing his mobile, "the cemetery is the resting place of over 10,755 causalities of the First World War, and it's the second-largest British and Commonwealth cemetery in Belgium. William, you mentioned the cemetery is interesting because of the casualty clearing station. According to this site, all the soldiers buried here died while being treated at the medical facility. Well, all of them except forty-one."

"Wow, 10,714 died while being treated at the medical facility. It seems you'd be better off not going to the clearing station," Katie responded.

I looked in the rearview mirror. Charlie was staring out the window, apparently not listening to the conversation, and she seemed a little out of it. *She's probably tired from sleeping on the bench,* I thought. *Well, actually, sleeping on me on the bench.*

"I don't know," Charlie whispered. "The number of men who came to the tents was overwhelming. With only three surgeons on staff, it was nearly impossible to keep up with wounded. The soldiers came in with shattered heads and disfigured faces. Some would be gasping for breath and spitting out blood; others were riddled with bullets, and others came in with stumps and torn-off limbs. I think the surgeons did the best they could, under the conditions. But everyone felt like they could have done more."

Ryan and Katie were staring at Charlie like she'd gone mad. It was comical, the way Ryan turned in the seat so he actually faced Charlie.

Charlie, on the other hand, was staring out the window, apparently unaware of the upheaval she'd caused in the wake of her declaration. It wasn't what she said; it was how she said it. She wasn't repeating something she'd read; she was telling about an event she'd experienced.

I don't think she realized she was talking, I realized.

"Look," I said, breaking the unnatural silence, "I can see the entrance to the cemetery."

"Charlie," Katie said. "Charlie, look at me."

I watched the exchange in the rearview mirror. Charlie smiled at Katie. "What?" she asked.

"What are you thinking about?" Katie asked.

Charlie looked perplexed for a second. "Nothing, really," she replied.

Ryan glanced at me and I shook my head. I could see his concern for Charlie.

Charlie was remembering.

CHARLIE

The entrance to the Lissenthoek Military Cemetery was white granite and red brick. It was definitely a monument constructed to honor the dead.

I placed my hand against the car window, as if to touch the entrance. This site was oppressive with the feeling of grief and despair.

Soul Mates ~ Liz Morrison

As Wills parked the car, I took a deep breath in preparation for the ordeal ahead.

Interesting choice of words...Why did I think this would be an ordeal? I wondered. The Tyne Cot cemetery had been larger than Lissenthoek. More men are interred at Tyne Cot. *When we visited Tyne Cot yesterday, it wasn't an ordeal.*

Katie's remark about the casualty clearing station...I don't know...hurt my feelings. Which made absolutely no sense, but everything I'd read about the surgeons and sisters who served at the casualty clearing station indicated they'd worked miracles with limited resources and a never-ending supply of soldiers to tend.

"Let's go," Katie tugged my arm. "I think reading grave stones is pretty interesting."

"Come on, Charlotte," Nellie called as we trudged through the mud leading to the cemetery. I'd met Nellie the previous day, when she'd come to our clearing station for additional supplies.

Nellie served as a nurse for the forty-fourth casualty clearing station, and had been there almost three weeks. Nellie was determined to visit the graves at Lijssenthoek cemetery, and I'd volunteered to accompany her.

The cemetery was a little beyond the location of the picnic lunch I'd enjoyed with William. I hoped to see the tree with our entwined initials. Two weeks had passed since I'd seen William. I'd not received a note in over a week. As we approached the cemetery, I could see rows and rows of wooden crosses standing at attention.

I prayed William was not among the field of the dead.

"Come on, Charlie," Katie called. "This cemetery is pretty amazing. You know what I noticed? So many of the men were second lieutenants. I wonder why? Maybe they just had lots of them."

Katie grabbed my hand and pulled me along. "Look at this." She pointed to a row of headstones. "Seven second lieutenants. Maybe they put all of the same rank in the same row."

Then she moved to a different row, I guess to check her theory. "Nope," she called. "Here's another one."

"Did the cemetery always look like this?" I asked, to no one in particular.

I glanced around the cemetery. Wills was engaged in a conversation with a couple. I think it was the couple we'd crossed paths with yesterday. It was pretty intriguing that they were following our same schedule. I know I'd given the man the information about World War I sites in and around Rouen, but I didn't think this cemetery had been included in the list. *Maybe it was,* I thought.

I studied the surroundings. It felt like I was missing something. *But as I've never been here before, how could I be missing something?* I wondered.

I noticed the farm at the northern edge of the cemetery.

The name Corfu Farm popped into my head. I wondered whether that was the name of the farm. I gazed at the farm; I felt like I'd stood in this exact spot before and noticed the same sights.

I'd had enough of grave stones. I wanted to locate the visitors' center. This cemetery gave me a strange feeling of déjà vu I hadn't experienced at Tyne Cot. It was unsettling. I wanted William.

Wanting William seemed like a good plan. "Katie," I said, "I'm going to get Wills. I think he's speaking to the same people who took our photo yesterday. It's a little strange that they keep ending up where we are."

Katie was reading the sign near the Stone of Remembrance. She nodded her head, but I could tell she wasn't really listening. Ryan, I noticed, was at the southern edge of the cemetery, opposite from Katie and me.

I walked toward William, who was near the arch of the main entrance, still talking to the couple from yesterday.

I heard him say, "Yes, it is rather a coincidence. Cheers."

He turned and almost knocked me over. I waved at the couple and grabbed his hand. As always, the current passed between us. It was expected, and strangely comforting.

"What a coincidence," I said. "They're at the same locations as us, and it's kind of creepy."

"Actually, the gentleman mentioned the coincidence that the Talbot House treasure is connected to a chap with the same name as me. I didn't tell him the chap was my great-great-uncle. For some reason, he rubs me the wrong way."

Wills looked at our clasped hands and smiled. "You, on the other hand, rub me the right way. Have you noticed," he continued, "our connection seems to hum when we visit the sites?"

"The lovely current," I replied, attempting to imitate his English accent.

"You are lovely," he said in reply.

"Charlotte, you are so lovely it hurts," William murmured as he buried his head in the crook of my neck.

The entire evening had been lovely. It was more than lovely; it was life-changing.

"I love you, William," I said.

William lifted his head and cupped my face in his hands, "I will love you forever, Charlotte," he said reverently, and sealed his vow with a kiss.

"Charlie," Wills said. "Charlie, you're a million miles away. What are you thinking?"

I wondered what Wills would say if I told him I was remembering the first time we made love. *Only it's not us; it's my World War I Charlotte and William,* I thought. *It's also kind of disturbing a cemetery made me imagine that; doesn't seem like the two events should be connected. Either way, it would probably freak him out, because we haven't done more than kiss.*

I glanced around the cemetery. "Is your great-great-uncle buried here?"

"No, but I'd think many of his mates were buried here," Wills said. "He was quite lucky to live through the Battle of Passchendaele."

Wills scanned the nearby graves. "This bloke, for example," Wills said, pointing to a grave to his left, "Corporal George Bartlett, died of wounds he received on August 26, 1917. That was the same timeframe my great-great-uncle was in the battle."

"Wills," I said, leading him away from the grave, "I really want to leave. For some reason, this cemetery is super-unsettling. I can't explain it, but it feels like I'm missing something, or I forgot something; just unsettling."

Then I glanced toward the road. "Isn't there supposed to be a railroad track around here?" I asked.

"I don't think so, Charlie," Wills replied. Then he looked around. "Hmm, maybe you're right. I don't remember seeing it on the map."

Ryan walked toward us from the visitors' center. "Okay, here's something interesting. This is a photograph of the tombstone of the only British nurse buried here. Look—Nellie Spindler."

I swayed; William grabbed hold of me. "Charlie, what's wrong?"

"I'm good," I replied. "I'm ready to go; I think the Tommy Café sounds like a good plan. I'm a little tired of graveyards."

"Tired of graveyards," Ryan replied. "That's not good; your internship starts at a graveyard next week."

I ignored Ryan's comment. "What's the date on that tombstone?" I asked Ryan as we walked through arch leading out of the cemetery.

"Let's see," Ryan said while studying the photograph. "It looks like August 21, 1917."

We got in the car and drove away from the cemetery.

The late-night conversation I had with Wills last evening was stressing me out. I seemed to be having flashbacks to my dreams. I didn't think dreams should be so vivid and memorable. Now my dreams included real people. Maybe it was coincidental that I'd had a memory of nurse named Nellie one moment and then, not even an hour later, Ryan had found the grave of a nurse named Nellie.

As we passed a grove of trees, I remembered what was missing: a grove of trees. The grove of trees and the railroad tracks.

The dream about the picnic...there'd been a grove of trees, and definitely railroad tracks. A missing grove of trees was easily explained—a new house here, a highway there—but the missing railroad tracks...not so much.

We sat in silence as we continued to our next destination. We were lost in our own thoughts. It was hard to be upbeat after visiting a cemetery.

They'd died over one hundred years ago, but it was still so sad; all the lost potential of those who died; all the people who lost dads, brothers, husbands, sons...and sisters and daughters, too.

"So," I said, "I had this dream. The cemetery reminded me of the dream. I had the dream after I met William. Anyway, I dreamed I was on a picnic with a soldier during World War I. Oh, I was a nurse—now that's a surprise," I said with a hint of sarcasm.

"Anyway, in the dream, my soldier—who, coincidently, looked a lot like Wills," I caught Wills' gaze in the rearview mirror and winked, "—carved our names in a tree. You know, now that I think about it, his name was William Harrington. That makes sense, I guess, as I'd already met Wills, and we were both interested in World War I. Actually, I believe we actually discussed World War I.

"Anyway, the picnic in my dream took place by a cemetery, by a farm, near a casualty clearing station that was on a railroad." I continued my story.

"I want you guys to know I actually considered the possibility I was reincarnated from a World War I nurse. I know—totally crazy. The lack of the railroad convinced me I'm just twenty-first century Charlie."

I took a breath, "I just wanted to share that with you guys. I said it out loud, and it sounds crazy. I'm not crazy...maybe a little obsessed, but not crazy."

Everyone remained silent. This time the silence was awkward. *Maybe I am crazy,* I thought.

"Hey, Charlie," Ryan said, "not to freak you out or anything, but the cemetery used to be located next to a railroad. They got rid of the railroad and put in the highway."

Chapter Twenty

WILLIAM

Charlie looked like she was going to be sick. Ryan and Katie looked…I'm not sure…confused, at best.

I'd known it was going to be rocky, but it was also a relief. Charlie was remembering Charlotte's life, which means she was remembering me—or us. By the look on her face, this was not a good thing.

Katie broke the silence and said in a firm voice, "Charlotte, you've been fascinated by World War I for a long time. Being here, visiting the sites from your dreams, is making all of your reading, your dreams, your wonderings come together."

She continued, "It's just a coincidence you knew that stuff about the cemetery. You probably read about it and just don't remember reading about it."

Did Katie call Charlie 'Charlotte,' or, did I just imagine that? I wondered. *Whoa, Charlie is probably short for Charlotte. I can't believe I didn't ask Charlie about her name. Who names a girl Charlie, anyway?*

"Charlie," I asked, "is 'Charlie' short for 'Charlotte?'"

Ryan glanced at me as if I were crazy. "You totally hook up with my girl Charlie and you don't even know her name? That's totally shady. Maybe the whole player thing Andrew convinced us of is actually true. I think I'm going to tweet about it."

"Ryan," Katie and Charlie said in unison. Ryan's stupid comments alleviated the tension. I could see why he was Charlie's best mate.

Charlie's mobile played "Mama Mia."

"Hey Mom," Charlie said into her mobile. "No, I'm fine." Charlie listened to her mom. "Oh, you just had mother's intuition that something was wrong? Nothing's wrong, Mom...I promise." Another pause, "Katie and Ryan are right here."

"Hi, Mrs. Longley," Ryan and Katie said in unison.

"Mom, I can't talk about him right now," Charlie sort of whispered into the mobile. "Yes, he's driving."

It's possible to decipher an entire conversation when hearing only one side. Charlie's mom had asked about me.

"You want to say hello? Mom, seriously, that's just weird. I'm not giving him the phone." Another pause. "I'll tell him you said hello." Pause. "Right now? Wills, my mom says hi."

Charlie caught my eye in the rearview mirror and gave me what appeared to be a resigned smile.

"Tell your mum hello," I replied with a grin.

"Yes, Mom, his accent is totally hot." Another pause, "I love you, too. I promise I'll call if I need anything. Say hi to Daddy."

"Well, that was awkward," Charlie said.

"Do you have songs for everyone on your mobile?" I asked. I really wanted to know if she had a special song for me.

"Look," Ryan said, "there's the sign indicating our destination is quickly approaching. I'm starving."

"Me too! What does the Tommy Café serve? Not that the menu matters. I'm willing to eat anything," Katie exclaimed.

Ryan studied his phone. "It looks like they serve fish and chips and other 'traditional' English fare. What's traditional English fare?"

"We're here," Charlie said. Her interruption refocused Ryan's attention.

Ryan was carefully studying the exterior of Le Tommy Café. "Well, it's not pretentious."

Charlie laughed "Definitely not pretentious."

The exterior of the Tommy Café resembled a diner. It was a one-story building with a tan brick exterior. Blue plastic chairs flanked the outside of the building, while two World War I-era statues guarded the front door.

We entered the café and were surrounded by artifacts from World War I. Ryan quickly found a table. We decided we'd order our lunch before looking at artifacts.

"Let's take a look around," Katie said as she pushed her chair back from the table.

We walked to the door leading to the outdoor museum. The interior of the café was certainly well done. The bar appeared to be constructed from sand bags, and the walls displayed numerous artifacts from the Great War.

Outside, behind the café, was a trench scene modeled after the warfare of World War I. If the interior was well done, the exterior was amazing. Unlike the cemetery and the Pool of Peace, however, the scene behind the café didn't make me melancholy.

Charlie didn't appear distressed by the display, either. Grabbing my hand, she tugged me toward the structure for a photograph.

I placed my arm around her shoulder and posed for a picture in a recreated trench. It was certainly cleaner than the trenches I remembered. *I guess the tourists wouldn't be enamored by rats the size of cats*, I thought.

Charlie looked up at me just as I looked down at her. I leaned down and kissed her. It was electric.

"Hey, I got a picture of that, too," Katie said. "You know what they say—what happens in Pozières stays in Pozières, unless you look on Facebook, YouTube, and Twitter."

Charlie looked like I felt—dazed and ready to continue the kiss. Now wasn't the time or place, though it certainly felt like the right time.

"Hey, beautiful, are you ready to dine on fish and chips?" I asked.

"I was born ready," she said. "Let's get one more pic by the other trench with Ryan and Katie."

Charlie glanced around at the people visiting the museum. "Look, it's the same people from the cemetery," she said. "Very coincidental, wouldn't you say?"

It was definitely odd.

Charlie asked a gentleman to take our photo. Katie, Ryan, Charlie, and I posed for a photograph in front of a trench next to a mannequin dressed as a Tommy. We were a handsome group. I was sure the photograph would be stellar.

I held Charlie's hand as we returned to the café. It's interesting how natural it was to hold her hand. The electricity seemed to become less...I don't know...shocking...after we'd been together for a few hours.

We returned to our table and, as expected, the fish and chips were waiting there. I pulled out a chair for Charlie and we sat down.

We sat in companionable silence, enjoying the food. Charlie placed her hand on my thigh; I nearly jumped out of my chair. She looked at me and giggled, then continued to eat her fish and chips with a single hand. She liked being connected to me as much I enjoyed being connected to her.

"This is so good," Charlie exclaimed.

"I know, right," Katie agreed. "I know I wasn't actually starving, but it certainly felt like it."

Ryan continued to eat without joining the conversation. He didn't speak until he ate his entire plate, and some of Katie's and Charlie's.

"That was great," Ryan said. "Now that I'm fed, I'm ready for a nice, long nap. Too bad we have to get to Rouen tonight."

Ryan leaned back in his chair with a contented sigh. Katie glanced at Ryan. Then she sort of punched him in the arm.

"What?" Ryan asked.

Katie gestured with her eyes to a point behind my head.

"Charlie," Katie asked, "you know in your dream, you mentioned something about a tree carving?"

"Yes," Charlie tentatively replied, "why do you ask?" It sounded like Charlie thought Katie was going to tease her.

"Um, what did it look like?" Katie continued.

"You seriously want me to describe a carving from a dream?" Charlie asked.

"Yes, I do," Katie replied.

"Let's see, well, it had the initials WH and C something. I don't think it was CL. That's weird. Anyway, they were carved in really nice, kind-of-fancy cursive. Oh...and I don't want to forget...they were inside an intricate heart. 'Intricate' being flowers and ivy in the heart design."

Charlie closed her eyes, as if she was trying to visualize the carving. "The year 1917 was carved below the heart."

"Charlie, please don't freak out," Katie said. "Turn around and look up."

Turning simultaneously, Charlie and I looked up. On the wall behind us, enclosed in a glass case, was a slice of bark from a tree. On the bark was an intricately carved heart with WH and CR within the heart, and 1917 carved below.

It was the heart I'd carved for Charlotte.

Charlie looked at the tree carving. She looked at me. Then she fainted.

Chaos erupted and Charlie remained unconscious.

"Charlie...Charlie," I said gently. "Come on, baby, come on back."

"Ryan, settle the bill," I directed. "We need to get her out of here."

I lifted her and carried her to the car. Opening the back door, I slid into the seat with Charlie in my arms.

"Ryan, drive. I think Charlie's in shock."

"You should have told her, dude," Ryan said as he climbed into the driver's seat.

"Told her what?" Katie asked as she sat in the passenger seat

CHARLIE

The Tommy Café was incredible. My stomach wasn't upset, the way it had been at the cemetery. Though the Tommy Café was rich in World War I history, it was a museum. Le Tommy Café was perfect for taking photos. It was fun, informative, and less intense; nothing wrong with that.

Sitting in companionable silence, we devoured our fish and chips. Actually, Ryan devoured his and the rest of us ate ours.

Katie seemed to be staring off into space. She broke the silence with a question about the tree carving from my dream. I gave her a look that must have said, "Really?" "Um, what did it look like?" Katie continued.

I closed my eyes, trying to visualize the carving. "Charlie, please don't freak out," Katie said. "Turn around and look up."

Turning simultaneously, William and I looked up. On the wall behind us was a glass case containing tree bark with a heart. It was the heart from my dream.

I looked at Wills, only I wasn't looking at Wills in his polo shirt and khakis. I was seeing William in his World War I uniform.

The world tilted. I felt like I was falling.

As I fell, scenes of my life flashed across my mind. I felt like I was sitting in a movie theater with two shows playing at the same time on the same screen. The movie on the left was from the early 1900s; the movie on the right was from today. The name of both movies was, *Hey, Charlotte! This is Your Life.*

The movies were playing incredibly fast, like Fast Forward on the remote.

On the left, a little girl with blonde hair, dressed in button-up boots, a dress that hit above the knees, and huge bow in her hair, pushed a bike in a park; on the right, a little girl with blonde hair in pigtails, wearing a Mini Mouse T-shirt, rode a hot-pink tricycle down a driveway.

Then, the girl on the left had her hair pulled back in an enormous bow. She wore a white blouse and dark skirt as she talked to her father in a science lab. I don't know how I knew the man was her father; I just did. The girl on the right had her streaky blonde hair pulled back in a ponytail; she wore a red St. Louis Cardinals T-shirt and sat at a kitchen table in a heated discussion with her mom and dad.

The movie played faster. The girl on the left boarded a ship; the girl on the right boarded a plane. The girl on the left lived in a hut; the girl on the right lived in a dorm room. The girl on the left cared for soldiers in a tent; the girl on the right hung out in a café. The girl on the left attended a picnic; the girl on the right danced at a club. The girl on the left smiled at a handsome soldier; the girl on the right smiled at a hot guy in a polo shirt and khakis.

A tree appeared on both screens. I watched as invisible hands carved a heart into the trees. The trees were being carved simultaneously. The heart was finished. Inside the heart on the left were the initials WH and CR; inside the heart on the right were the initials WH and CL. The trees moved faster and faster and then stopped.

The two scenes became one. The girl on the left and the girl on the right merged into one girl. The soldier on the left and the young man on the right merged into one guy. I stared at the screen. I was the girl. I was the two-in-one girl. William was the boy. Wills was the two-in-one boy.

Memories flooded my mind; memories of the girl from the past and memories of the girl from the present. I knew without a doubt all of the memories were mine.

Last night, as I drifted to sleep, I'd heard Wills whisper, "Remember, Charlotte, try to remember."

With sudden clarity, I knew that William knew. Maybe, subconsciously, I'd known, too…from the moment we met at the café. The electric current, it must be our past selves trying to connect, trying to get our present selves to recognize our…I guess…soul mate.

From a distance, I heard voices calling my name. I wasn't sure I wanted to answer. I felt safe, but really cold.

The numbness was fading and the voices sounded closer, "Charlie. Come on, baby, come back," Wills whispered in my ear.

"Maybe we should go to a hospital. I think she's in shock," Katie said.

"Dude, you should've told her your theory about reincarnation. Even if she thought you were a nut case, at least she would've been prepared." Ryan's voice was laced with concern.

"Reincarnation," Katie replied, "Charlie said she actually considered the idea. Oh my God, she's a reincarnated World War I nurse. Oh my God, William is the soldier. Oh my God, you guys must've been looking for each other. Oh my God." Katie was losing it.

"Oh my God, the carving…the carving must have triggered the memories from her past life. Oh my God, she may never recover." Katie was clearly distressed. I needed to respond, but I wasn't ready. I felt so cold.

"Stop saying 'Oh my God,'" Ryan said. "You're starting to freak me out, and I'm not easily freaked."

Katie hit Ryan and exclaimed, "Oh my God, we need to find the treasure. We need to find out about your past lives. We need to find out what happened to you and to Charlie. We need to find out why here and why now for your reunion. Seriously. Oh my God."

"Katie," I said in a whisper. "All of the 'oh my Gods' are freaking me out."

"Oh my God, you're conscious."

"I'm so cold," I said.

"Oh God, Charlie," Wills said. "Thank God." Then he whispered, "Thank you, God," over and over again into my hair.

I slowly opened my eyes. I stared into the warm, gray eyes of William Harrington. *I know this man*; the thought flooded my mind and my senses.

My head rested in William's lap and my feet were elevated on the door's armrest. William's arms were wrapped protectively around me, securing me in place against his thighs.

"You remembered?" Wills asked quietly.

"I remembered," I replied.

"Can you sit up?" Wills asked. "You're so cold. If you sit up, I can warm you up with my body heat."

I liked the idea of his body heat warming me up. I edged my legs off the armrest to the floor. I didn't feel lightheaded. I just felt cold.

I might be in shock. Being cold is a sign of shock. I didn't, however, need to go to a hospital. I snuggled into Wills, pushing his shirt up and putting my arms inside his clothes, against his warm skin.

"Devilishly chilly," he said, pulling me tighter.

My face was smashed into William's chest. I knew Ryan and Katie wanted to talk about past Charlotte and present Charlie. I didn't—not yet. I wanted to sleep.

"Hey, guys," I said softly, "I don't want to talk about this right now. I just want to sleep and get my head together. When we get to Rouen, we can talk about it then."

I paused. "I'm sure Wills has stuff he wants to talk about, too. I'm just not ready right now, okay?"

Ryan and Katie replied together, "Okay, Charlie."

Wills slowly rubbed my back, warming me up. "No problem love. Enjoy your kip."

Kip, I thought, *Hmm, 'kip' must mean 'nap.'* I closed my eyes, praying for a dreamless sleep.

Chapter Twenty-One

WILLIAM

Charlie slept the entire ride. That was good, because I wasn't sure how this situation would be resolved.

Katie wanted to talk about the entire situation, but Ryan was able to hold her off. He said he could only stomach the story one more time. Ryan wasn't keen on the whole Charlie-and-Wills scenario. I really thought he believed he was in love with Charlie.

He's a pretty good chap, all in all, I thought. *Unlike Andrew, who's supposed to be my best mate, he did nothing to sabotage my relationship with Charlie, except when he was trying to protect her. I respect that kind of friendship.*

"Hey, we're almost back to the apartment," Ryan said. "It might be time to wake Sleeping Beauty...I guess that's two Sleeping Beauties." Katie was asleep, too.

"I hate to wake them up," I said. "It's like the calm before the storm."

"You've got that right," Ryan replied. "I'm not sure how Charlie's going to react, once she's awake and the shock wears off. Does the shock ever wear off?"

He deftly maneuvered the car into a parking spot near our flat. The spot he found was next to a dumpster.

Ryan shook his head.

"What?" I asked.

"You know, it seems like a year since we arrived in Rouen. It's hard to believe it's only been a couple of months. The dumpster reminds me of our first day in Rouen. That day—our first day in Rouen—was certainly less complex than right now. On that day, if anyone would've said, 'Hey Ryan, in a couple of months you're going to find out Charlie has a past life...as in reincarnated,' I would've thought the person was crazy. Now, I think we all might be crazy."

I paused before replying. "My life has always been complicated," I said. "Now, it feels like there may actually be resolution. I just wish I knew the point. Was finding Charlie the point? Is there more? Does the Talbot House treasure fit into the story? It seems every answer leads to more questions."

Ryan and I shook our heads. This was pretty complex stuff.

"Charlie," I said as I gently prodded her shoulders. Her body temperature was normal, if not a little hot. Or maybe her position was making me hot. "Charlie...wake up, love."

"I don't want to wake up," she replied against my chest. Her warm breath against my skin made it hard for me to breathe.

"Come on, love—time to wake up. We're in Rouen."

"Katie," Ryan said loudly. "Katie we're home. It's time to wake up."

"Home," Katie replied groggily, glancing at the complex. She came alert relatively quickly. "How's Charlie?"

"I'm fine, Katie," Charlie replied, still speaking into my chest. "As fine as I can be. I just don't want to move. It's comfortable and...well...tidy in the car. My room is still a total disaster, and will probably remain that way for several days."

Charlie sounded remarkably normal.

She slowly unwrapped her arms from my back. Her palms caressed me as she moved them from my back to my chest. I thought it might have been an accident until I glanced down. Charlie was looking at me with a mischievous smile. She totally knew what she was doing. I shook my head and smiled.

She pushed off my chest. "Oh, I'm so stiff," she complained. "I must've stayed in the same position the entire car ride."

"Out you go," I said as I assisted Charlie from the car.

I opened the boot and we retrieved our bags. I grabbed Charlie's, too.

"Thanks," she said.

I knew she wasn't herself right now. Any other time, she would've grabbed the bag and rolled her eyes.

It was 9:00 p.m.—still early by our Rouen standards.

"I know we need to talk about this and determine what it all means, or at least come up with a plan to determine what it all means," Charlie said. "Can we do it tomorrow? I know I slept the entire drive; I just need a little more sleep."

Katie hugged Charlie. "No problem," she said. "We all need to get up early for our internships. We can meet tomorrow evening and try to decipher all of this. I love you, Charlie." Katie gave Charlie another hug.

Charlie looked at Ryan. He reached for her and pulled her into a bear hug. Jealousy, pure and simple, was the emotion coursing through my veins as Ryan held Charlie.

"I love you, Charlie," he said. "This is going to be okay. Have a great time at the museum tomorrow, and we'll talk about all of this tomorrow night." He stepped back and gave Charlie a kiss on the cheek.

Charlie pulled Katie in and the three of them stood in a hug circle. I got an empty feeling in my chest. *What if I found Charlotte, but she didn't want to be found?* I worried. *What if finding Charlie wasn't World War I William's purpose?*

The hug circle broke. Charlie stepped back and walked to me. She grabbed my hand and wrapped my arm around her waist. He message was clear; her friends were important, but I was more important.

Ryan and Katie stepped into the elevator, but Charlie didn't move. "I want to take the stairs. Are you okay with that?" she asked me. I nodded in reply. "Good luck, you guys," Charlie called as the elevator doors closed. "See you tomorrow night."

Charlie turned around so we were chest-to-chest. She reached up and pulled my head down for a kiss. It was a kiss of remembrance and longing. It felt like coming home.

She stepped back.

"Wills, do you keep a journal?" she asked as we walked up the stairs.

"A journal?" I repeated.

"A journal," Charlie replied. "It's a book you write your private thoughts in…but that's not important right now."

"Did you just misquote from the movie *Airplane?*" I asked in disbelief. "*Airplane* is one of my favorite films of all time. The quirky American humor is brilliant."

Charlie cracked a smile. "Why, yes…yes, I did. I love the movie *Airplane*. We quote and misquote it on every family vacation."

"Seriously," she continued, "do you keep a journal? I've been tracking all of my World War I dreams in a journal. I was thinking we could swap journals and compare what we remember. By the way, for right now, I've determined the best way to handle this is like a scientific experiment. I'm sort of acting as a third party…like an observer or something."

We reached the third floor, but I continued with Charlie up the stairs to the fourth floor.

"Yes, I keep a journal," I confirmed. "I think swapping the journals is a good idea. I'd kind of like to be together when we read them. Would that be all right with you?"

Charlie stopped in front of her door and turned to reply. "Yeah, I think that would be perfect."

She opened the door with her key and turned the knob. She pressed her head against the door and sighed.

Soul Mates ~ Liz Morrison

"Charlie, love, I know this is difficult," I acknowledged. *What an idiot,* I chided myself. *Difficult? Traumatic? Life-changing? Shocking? And I came up with difficult.*

She turned around and looked at me with an expression that I couldn't read. "Wills, what is hard—almost impossible—is walking into my room and not having you come in with me. I can't bear being separated from you tonight. Will you stay?" Charlie asked softly.

Putting a finger under her chin, I tilted her head so we were looking into each other's eyes. I knew what she was asking; she wanted my comfort and my support. I wanted her any way she wanted me.

"Charlie, love," I replied, "of course I'll stay."

"Good," she said as she pushed on the door to her flat.

I glanced into her flat and laughed. "So this is the mess you were referring to? I'll give you a hand in putting your wardrobe back in your closet."

"Hey," she play hit my chest, "I had to find the perfect outfit for the night out. Wow, that seems like years ago. I can't believe it was just three nights ago."

Charlie closed the door and turned the lock. I'm sure it wasn't okay for her to have a man in her room, per her school rules. However, we had no rules for gap year, and the language school didn't have rules restricting male and female visitors. Unless her teacher arrived before 0730 tomorrow, we should be ace.

"I can't sleep in this mess," Charlie exclaimed as she began to place the clothes back in her closet. "You can grab my journal if you like," she continued as she placed her shoes on the floor of the closet.

"The first part is about my journey to Rouen. That would be something you don't know much about."

I picked up the journal from her desk.

"Just sit there," Charlie said, gesturing toward a chair at the table near the kitchenette. "I'll clean around you as you read."

I opened the journal. The first entry was titled, "Atlanta to Rouen." I began to read, and was quickly engrossed in Charlotte's story.

"Wills," Charlie interrupted my reading, "you need to admire my beautiful, clean flat."

I glanced up from the journal and admired Charlie. She was wearing pajama pants and a white vest. Her hair was damp, indicating she'd taken a shower while I was engrossed in her journal. I looked directly at Charlie and then gave her a slow, full-body appraisal. I grinned at her and said, "Yes…beautiful and clean."

"Speaking of clean," she responded with a smile, "do you want to take a shower? Do you have something to sleep in?"

I got up from the chair, placed the journal on the table, and pulled Charlie in my arms for a long kiss. I'm not sure how long the kiss lasted. When I finally gained some sense of balance, I had Charlie pressed against the table, her arms wrapped around my shoulders and her ankle wrapped around my calf. It was going to be a long night.

"I have toiletries in my overnight bag that accompanied me this weekend," I said. "I'll take a quick shower, and then we need to go to sleep."

Sleep. *Now sleep would be the last thing on my mind, lying with Charlie,* I told myself. *The quick shower needs to be a cold one.*

My quick shower took a few minutes. Then I brushed my teeth and brushed my hair. I walked out of the water closet into Charlie's dimly lit flat.

"I'm on the futon," a soft voice called from the center of the living space.

I slid under the covers on the futon. Charlie rolled into my arms, "Thanks for staying with me," she said in a whisper-soft voice.

"The pleasure's all mine," I replied.

I softly stroked Charlie's hair, lulling her to sleep. Her breathing changed to slow regular intervals, indicating she was sound asleep. I closed my eyes and a feeling of...I don't know...rightness...spread through my body.

"I love you," I whispered into her hair.

CHARLIE

I tried not to think. Trying not to think is pretty challenging. Maybe it's more accurate to say I was trying to avoid thinking about the *R* word...reincarnation. Glancing at Wills, sleeping soundly on the futon, made the idea seem plausible; no way would a guy be sleeping in my room. After one night, I knew he belonged here. *My mom would kill me*, I thought. Then I decided, *I'll worry about it later.*

Silently rolling off the futon, I grabbed an outfit from my now-organized closet to wear to the visitor's center and then possibly to the cemetery. Regardless of the latest twist to the adventure, the chance to create a tour of World War I sites for the visitors' center was amazing. What other seventeen-year-old girl could have such an amazing opportunity?

Finding the grave of William Harrington should be easy because Wills knew his great-great-uncle was buried at St. Sever. Charlotte R. was a mystery.

I liked thinking William and Charlotte were totally separate from Wills and me. Tonight we were going try to figure out what it all meant. Maybe the only purpose was to bring Wills and me together. That, in itself, was pretty incredible.

My black pants, red top, and red pumps were a pretty stylish outfit. One thing about working in France—I didn't want to look like a typical American teenager. Styling my hair into a side-braid ponytail, I quickly completed the look and was ready to go.

Wills was stretched out on his back, taking up all of the space on the makeshift bed. I wanted to kiss him goodbye, but I didn't want to wake him.

I leaned over Wills to kiss him on the cheek. As I leaned down, Wills opened his eyes. A slow smile crossed his face and I bent down and kissed him full on the lips.

Wills tried to pull me down next to him as I tried to stand up.

"Hey," I said, "I have to get the visitors' center. Don't you have somewhere you have to be?"

He grasped my hands and asked, "Are you okay?"

"Yeah," I replied. "I decided to think of William and Charlotte as our ancestors, and we're here to discover the mysteries of their past."

Wills looked at me intently. "You're sure you're okay?" he asked again.

I kissed him again, this time with more intensity. "I'm okay, really," I said, somewhere in the vicinity of his left ear. "I'll see you tonight."

"Be safe," Wills said as I walked out the door.

I quickly ran down the four flights of stairs and almost knocked over Philippe, who was back on the job at the main entrance.

"Sorry," I apologized.

"Bonjour, Charlie. The keys are on the front desk," Philippe called out.

"Merci," I replied as I grabbed the keys from the desk and walked to the same scooter I'd borrowed on Friday.

My cell phone started to vibrate. I noticed the number was local. *That's odd*, I thought. "Bonjour," I said.

"Charlie, this is Madame Chevalier. We had a robbery at the Office de Tourisme," Madame explained. "Do not come to work today. You'll begin your work at St. Sever tomorrow. I'm so sad to say the criminal took several of our World War I artifacts."

"Are you sure you can't use my help?" I asked.

"Non, non," she said. "The police are here. They wish no interference. Au revoir; I'll see you on Friday."

Madame hung up before I had time to reply. Who would steal the artifacts? As far as we knew, they weren't valuable from a collectors standpoint, but from an exhibit standpoint, they were invaluable.

I turned back to the reception desk. "That was my boss," I said to Philippe as I handed him the keys to the scooter. "Apparently there was a break-in at the Office of Tourism. It just seems so odd, because Rouen has a low crime rate, and the Office of Tourism doesn't seem like a likely target."

I waved at Philippe as I pulled out my cell and started to climb the stairs. Wills answered the phone on the third ring. "Hey, Wills," I greeted him.

"Hello, Charlie," he replied. His voice made me feel all tingly.

"Do you happen to be where I left you a few moments ago?" I asked, in what I hoped was a nonchalant manner.

"I am exactly where you left me," Wills replied.

"I'm on my way up," I told him. "Madame Chevalier called to let me know the Office of Tourism was robbed. The only items removed were several boxes of World War I artifacts. Weird, right?"

I reached the door, unlocked it, and entered my room. Wills was exactly where I'd left him, looking super sexy in an early-morning-disheveled sort of way. Just seeing him lying on the futon made my heart race.

It was a beautiful morning. William gave me a sleepy smile as he pulled me back into his embrace. "Good Morning, Mrs. Harrington," he whispered into my hair, close to my temple.

It was true; I was a married woman.

"I love you, Charlotte," he proclaimed. "I'll always love you."

Whoa—this memory-or-dream thing was really unsettling.

"The Office de tourisme had a break-in?" Wills asked. I nodded.

"Well, then," he said, "what do you say about locating Base Hospital Twenty-One? I don't have to instruct a class today, and you don't have to work."

"Great idea," I replied "Get up and let's get going."

Chapter Twenty-Two

WILLIAM

Standing in the lobby, I stared out the window. Charlie would be down any minute. Her idea of pretending we were researching our ancestors was bloody brilliant.

I wish I could find the satchel with William Harrington's personal effects, I thought. *The satchel might have some clues to the Talbot House treasure.*

"Hey, Wills," Charlie called.

I turned. Looking at her made my chest constrict. *I love this girl,* I thought. *I'll always love this girl.*

"What?" she asked, taking my hand. The electric current almost knocked me on my arse.

"Good God, I thought it would've been…well…less shocking after spending the night together," I said with a laugh, not letting go of her hand.

"It's funny how the voltage changes," Charlie replied as she tugged me toward the desk. "Let's get scooters. Did you figure out how to locate champ de courses? Should we stop at the bakery and get food for a picnic?"

I shook my head and thanked Philippe for the keys to the scooters. I pulled Charlie out the front door.

We mounted our scooters and rode through the city streets, heading toward the champ de courses home of Base Hospital Twenty-One; the place where William and Charlotte had met over one hundred years ago. The place where Charlie and I would...I don't know...we'd do something. I had no idea what that might be.

I glanced back at Charlie. She was seriously concentrating on maneuvering her scooter in the traffic. *We should have shared a ride,* I thought. *On our next adventure, we're definitely riding double.*

Concentrating on the directions was rather challenging. I kept thinking of the last couple of days and nights with Charlie. She completed me. I wondered whether William had felt Charlotte completed him...or did Charlie complete me because Charlotte had completed William? This was really confusing. I'd wager Charlie was even more confused.

I noticed the turn leading to the champ de courses. I turned on to the dirt road and continued toward the racetrack. It was an old track surrounding a field of grass.

Charlie removed her helmet and glanced around.

"What are you thinking?" I asked.

"Well," she said softly as she stepped away from the scooter and walked toward the dirt track. "It looks just like the pictures on the website, but nothing like I remember." She paused. "Or dreamed about."

I reached for her hand. The current was like thick, molten lava ebbing and flowing between our entwined fingers and the palms of our hands. I pulled her hand to my lips and kissed her fingers. She looked into my eyes and smiled.

"It's different, but it's good," she said. "Come on; let's walk around the track and discuss what we remember."

I was confused. "I know," she continued, "I'm embracing the past."

"It really has been over one hundred years," Charlie whispered. "It's hard to believe it still has a track."

"So, in my dreams...or memories...or whatever, all of the components of the racetrack were still in operation, just not being utilized for their original purpose. The pavilions, paddocks, and café were used for administrative purposes. There was a Post de Police used as the laboratory, and the hospital office was in the racetrack office. The turf was free of buildings, like it is now, when we first arrived. Later, it was used for medical purposes."

Charlie didn't notice her use of first person in describing the base hospital from one hundred years ago. I decided not to mention it.

We completed our walk around the track in companionable silence. I pulled Charlie into the center of the turf and tugged her down to the ground. I lay down, and she laid her head on my chest. Our hands remained linked.

"Wills," she asked in a quiet voice, "do you remember when you proposed?"

"Sorry?" I replied.

"Do you remember when William proposed to Charlotte?" Charlie asked again.

I paused for a moment, "Yes, I remember when I proposed."

I paused for a moment. *What the hell,* I thought. *Here goes nothing.*

"Yes, I remember when I proposed," I said. "It was June 11, 1918...a few weeks shy of my nineteenth birthday, and almost a year since we first met when I was a patient at Base Hospital Twenty-One."

I didn't look, but I knew Charlie was smiling. She remembered, too.

"The base hospital appeared to be decorated for a celebration. I asked one of the orderlies what was happening and he explained the celebration was in commemoration of the Yanks' first year at the hospital. He said there would be a grand dinner for the medical personnel, a circus for all to enjoy, and the much anticipated Maypole dance, performed by the nurses.

"I asked if Sister Charlotte was participating in the Maypole dance, and the orderly replied that he was unsure."

I paused in the retelling. "You know, Charlie, sometimes these memories are more real than memories from a few years ago."

She squeezed my hand in response.

Charlie continued, "I remember the tables for the banquet were arranged to spell USA. We gathered in the grandstand to view them. It was incredibly exciting and strange. It was exciting, because it was a celebration. It was strange, because we were celebrating amidst the wounded and dying.

"Despite my reservations regarding the appropriateness of the celebration, I was involved in the Maypole dance. I loved my dress. It was made of white gauze from the Red Cross and had flowing sleeves and a gathered skirt that was exactly twelve inches off the ground. It revealed an ankle and a little more. It was a beautiful dress."

I smiled. "I remember you in the dress, and acknowledging I didn't want any other blokes to admire you in it."

Charlie giggled. "You were so jealous. I remember that, too."

"We were practicing the dance," Charlie continued, "and I felt someone watching me. It was an electric feeling, and I knew without a doubt who'd be staring at me when I turned around. I spun so fast, I almost fell."

"You spun so fast you knocked Lilly on her arse."

Ignoring my last remark, Charlie pushed off my chest and placed her head on the ground right next to mine. I stared into the eyes that had haunted my dreams for the past eighteen years.

"And then I saw you," she continued. "I forgot about Lilly, I forgot about the Maypole dance, I forgot about the celebration. My heart was racing. I wanted to run across the field and throw myself into your arms, but I didn't know how you'd respond. So I calmly walked across the field, away from the dancers and toward you." I picked up the narrative. "I watched you walking toward me and my heart was about to burst," I told her. "I wanted to do a proper proposal and ask your father for your hand in marriage, but he wasn't at the hospital. For one hour, as I walked through the complex trying to find you, I'd considered not asking you to be my wife. I'd convinced myself it was the right path to follow. But then I saw you in your gauze dress and I knew, without a doubt, that we needed to be married as quickly as possible."

"Then I was standing in front of you," Charlie continued.

I went on. "I grasped your hand and dropped down on one knee, right in the middle of the field, in front of all the dancers and in front of all the soldiers who were waiting patiently in the grandstand for the show to begin." I paused, remembering the moment.

"I said, 'Will you make me the happiest man alive and consent to be my wife?' A moment of silence followed, and you said nothing. And then you threw your arms around my neck and said, 'Yes.' I stood up, holding your hand in mine, and kissed you. I forgot about the crowd of soldiers waiting in the stands for the performance until I heard the thunderous applause. It took me a moment to realize the applause was for our public demonstration of affection."

"I should've been mortified," Charlie added, "but I didn't care."

"You missed your big Maypole debut, if I recall," I continued.

"Yes," she said. "We decided to get married instead."

"I reckon we did," I replied.

I couldn't help myself. I rolled over, pinning Charlie beneath me, bracing most of my weight on my arms. The kiss was all-consuming...the past and the present crashing together. Remembering the proposal brought back memories of our wedding, our wedding night, and the five incredible days and nights following.

I looked into Charlie's eyes. "I love you," I said.

Charlie reached up and cupped my face in her hands. "This is so confusing," she said. "The one thing, however, I know for sure is...well...I'm just going to say it: I love you, too."

"Ace," I replied. *Bloody brilliant.* I leaned down and kissed her again.

Charlie

I looked into William's eyes and I knew we'd be okay. Well, I wasn't actually sure. After all, I was seventeen years old, a senior in high school, and heading home to St. Louis before Thanksgiving.

Well, we found each other after one hundred years or so, I reasoned. *Maybe this won't be a problem.*

"I found you," he said, staring deeply into my eyes. It was like Wills was trying to see into my soul. Well, if he could, he'd see I'd found him, too.

"You do realize we're lying in the middle of a field? A field which is in the middle of a racetrack, surrounded by homes and people, and it's the middle of the day? Not that I mind what we're doing, but I'm a little concerned about where it might be leading. And I'm just saying this might not be the right location." I smiled at him and playfully pushed him to the side.

Pushing myself into a seated position, I noticed we were not alone.

"Hey, Wills," I said, "look over by our scooters. Isn't that the man and woman who were on the same trip to World War I sites we were on this weekend?"

Wills looked over at the scooters, shielding his eyes from the sun. I sort of grabbed his arm. "I was hoping for something a little more discreet than the hand-over-the-eyes and pointing directly at them," I protested.

Laughing, he shook his head. "Come on, Charlie," Wills said, and pulled me to my feet. "Rather than speculating on another chance encounter, let's go say hello. Besides, I'm starving. We did pick up some scrummy snacks from the bakery."

I brushed the grass off my body and brushed some off Wills, too. When I started brushing his back, the molten-lava feeling entered my hands, distracting me from the job at hand and focusing me on where I wanted my hands to travel...under his shirt, along his shoulders, down his arms. I leaned my head against his back between his shoulder blades.

"Charlie, Charlie," Wills said in a kind of strangled voice, "I can't move when you touch me like that."

"Sorry," I said as slid my hands down his back again. I really wasn't sorry.

Wills grabbed my hand. We walked toward our scooters and the couple who were standing near them.

"Cheers," William called when we are about ten feet away.

"Cheers," the man replied "What a coincidence. If you weren't here first, I would think you might be following us."

"Hello," I said. *Funny,* I thought, *I was thinking the same thing only about them.*

"I've been following your advice and visiting the World War I sites in the area," the man said. "Today we're visiting the old base hospital." He glanced around the area. "Pity; it appears nothing of the hospital remains."

"I was thinking the same thing," I replied. "One of my goals as an intern at the Office de tourisme Rouen is to get a display of images at this location."

"Such a shame about the break-in at the Office de tourisme Rouen," the man replied. "I hope nothing of value was stolen."

"Artifacts are interesting when it comes to assessed value," I explained. "What makes them valuable is sometimes determined by the desire of the collector to possess them. So, what was taken may be valuable to some, and not valuable to others. It just depends on the focus of their collection."

"So nothing stolen was of value?" the man asked.

"Well, it was valuable to the Office de tourisme Rouen," I replied.

I edged closer to Wills. Something about this guy gave me the creeps.

"It was a pleasure seeing you again," Wills said politely. "Have a pleasant day."

"I'm sure we'll see you again," the woman replied as she and the man walked toward the open field.

"Those two give me the creeps," I said to William. "They stare at us like we have the answer to some deep, dark question. Are we going to St. Sever today? I can say hello to my new boss and we can find your grave."

William sort of choked.

"Okay...well, that didn't come out right, did it?" I added. "I'm trying to take this whole reincarnation thing in stride. Maybe I'm a little too nonchalant. 'Let's go find your grave.'—Wow."

I was leaning on my scooter, contemplating what an idiot I was. Then Wills spun me around and kissed me.

"I love you," he said when he broke the kiss. "What the hell? Let's go find my grave." He started to laugh and I did, too. I laughed so hard tears rolled down my face.

Wills looked at me and said solemnly,

Ah, yes! You dig upon my grave...

Why flashed it not to me.

That one true heart was left behind!

What feeling do we ever find

to equal among human kind,

a dog's fidelity!

"Thomas Harding—English poet," he explained.

"What the heck?" Laughing so hard I could barely speak, I said, "Did you just quote a poem about a dog digging up a grave? Oh my God. I think we've finally lost it."

William grasped my shoulders. I knew he was going to distract me with a kiss. *Hey, good idea.* I was still laughing as he kissed me. Surprisingly—or maybe not surprisingly—I stopped laughing.

I rested my head against his chest. His arms were secure around my waist. I shook my head and whispered, "A dog digging up a grave...seriously?"

He whispered back, "The love of my life asking to find my grave...seriously?"

Soul Mates ~ Liz Morrison

What could I say? Really, it was crazy.

"Have a croissant." I reached into my backpack, digging up the treats we'd bought at the bakery.

"What else do we have in the bag?" he asked as he tugged the backpack out my hands with a grin.

Chapter Twenty-Three

WILLIAM

"Charlie," I said as we were parking our scooters in the area designated for such at the entrance to the cemetery, "I have the plot location for William Harrington's grave."

I was speaking as I was digging through my pockets—first the pockets in my backpack, and then the pockets in my trousers. "I recall putting it in my backpack."

"Not to worry," Charlie replied. "I'm sure the cemetery office will have a data base of the graves. Come on—let's go find the final resting place of William Harrington. Maybe it'll give us some clues about the mysterious nurse Charlotte."

I clasped Charlie's hand. "It is a tad bit ghoulish, your incredible fascination regarding the location of the grave."

Charlie stopped and turned toward me. "I don't know what happened. We know that William Harrington and Charlotte met, fell in love, and got married. We also know they spent an incredible honeymoon, predominately in bed. We know that William had family jewels sent to the Talbot House. We know William is buried in Rouen. We don't know what any of this means. Maybe they had a baby. Maybe William was killed before he reached Rouen. Maybe he was coming to bring Charlotte her wedding gift. We have so many questions to answer, and I can't figure out why neither one of us has dreamed about it. So, I'm hoping we can start putting some of the pieces together when we visit the grave of William Harrington."

She paused. "Wills…Wills, are you listening?" she asked.

"Charlie, you remembered our honeymoon?" I asked as I looked into her blue, blue eyes.

She blushed from the roots of her hair to the V-neck in her jumper.

"I remember, too," I said. "We definitely need to share journal entries on that one."

She asked, "Wills, do you remember anything I said beyond the honeymoon part?"

I thought for a moment, trying to replay her words. "Baby...we might have made a baby. We could have great-great-great grandchildren. We don't know what happened before William died. And we don't know what any of it means. Yes, I remember all of your explanation regarding your morbid fascination for locating my grave."

She gave me a disgruntled look. "What if we had a baby? That would be so crazy. We could have great-great-great-grandchildren. Maybe we came back to save our family...you know, like that one movie. That's a little too dramatic. I'm thinking no baby."

I stared out in the distance, remembering our honeymoon. For five days and five nights, we'd hibernated in a guest house near the café. We left the room to get food. We certainly could've made a baby.

What happened next was inevitable. I kissed Charlie at the entrance of the St. Sever cemetery. How could I resist the temptation of her lips right then, with the memories of her past kisses so crystal clear?

I gently caressed her cheek. If we didn't make a baby in our past lifetime, we would in this one.

Bloody hell! What am I thinking? I wondered.

"Come on," I said, rather abruptly. "Let's go."

The cemetery was surrounded by a wall made from stone and concrete. White-painted iron gates guarded the entrance. The entrance gate was attached to two stone-and-concrete buildings.

The buildings were two stories high. One looked like a house, with its window boxes overflowing with flowers. The other looked like a guard tower, with small windows that appeared to have no purpose.

Charlie was staring at the entrance to the cemetery. "So many young men," she said. "I didn't like how close the base hospital was to the cemetery. It was just so convenient. It shouldn't be convenient. 'Sorry, we can't save you, but we can roll you down the street to the conveniently located cemetery. No problem boys; Base Hospital Twenty-One is your one-stop shop, from injured to interred."

I studied Charlie. That was definitely Charlotte's opinion regarding the location of the hospital and the cemetery. Charlotte had felt the same way at the casualty clearing station.

"Oh my gosh," Charlie exclaimed. "That was the unsettling feeling at the cemetery. It was right by the casualty clearing station. I know we didn't locate the station, but I know it was near Corfu Farms. I hated knowing the young men knew we were so conveniently located."

"Charlie," I said, "the young men didn't know a cemetery was so closely located to cours de champs. I had no idea, and I was one of those young men."

"I know it happened a long time ago, but it feels like it happened yesterday," she complained. "It feels like it's happening right now. I treated hundreds of young men who ended up here."

What does a bloke say to that? "Charlotte was an incredible nurse; she made every young man she treated more comfortable, whatever the situation," I reminded her. "In times of war, that's the best a guy could hope for, truly."

She continued to stare at the entrance. "Thanks," she whispered.

"Charlie, I adore you." I pulled our clasped hands to my lips and kissed her knuckles. I had no idea I could be so free with my affection.

Two police officers approached the gate from the inside as we were about to enter the cemetery. In rapid French, they explained that a grave had been desecrated, and the cemetery was closed for the remainder of the day.

Charlie looked at me in stunned disbelief. We were so close to finding a piece to our puzzle.

"Whose grave?" I called to the police officers.

The officer looked at me and replied in English, "An English soldier. Come back tomorrow."

"Do you want to climb the wall?" Charlie asked.

I grinned. "That's a brilliant idea, but I don't fancy spending the evening in a French police station."

We stood, staring at the closed gates.

"Well, I guess we should head back to the dorm," she said. "Katie and Ryan are probably waiting for us. It's surprising they haven't called. After all of the excitement from yesterday, I'm surprised we had a moment of silence."

"They believe you're at your internship," I replied.

"Oh, right—I can't believe I forgot about the break-in," Charlie said.

We got back on the scooters. Charlie secured her helmet. "You know, Wills, next time we go on one of these trips, I think we should share a bike. Would that be okay?"

"Sure, Charlie, that would be ace," I agreed. *Maybe she can read my mind. Mind reading,* I mused. *Almost as exciting as being reunited lovers from World War I.*

Actually, it wasn't even close.

CHARLIE

What an interesting day. Some of it was incredible, but overall it was…well, interesting.

I picked up my journal and flipped through the pages. I wondered how similar our journals would be.

Will's proposal story was exactly as I remembered. *I'm trying not to think about the fact that my memories occurred over one hundred years ago,* I told myself.

A soft tap on my door pulled me out of my reverie. I opened the door to Katie and Ryan.

"Hey, how was your day?" I asked as I pulled them into my room. "All the details, please—no holding back."

"It was awesome," Katie exclaimed. "I died and went to future art majors' heaven. It was incredible. I felt like I was one with Monet. I'm so excited for the next two months."

My heart dropped. *Is that possible?* I wondered. *Only two more months in Rouen; how is that possible? I won't be able to leave Wills. Okay, one more thing I'm not going to worry about right now.*

"Ryan…hello…are you tweeting?" I asked.

"Put down your phone and spill to your live audience," Katie added.

"I have one thing to say," Ryan paused. "It rocked. This is going to look so good on my resumé. They love me, I love them, and one of the girls at the office was at La Boite à Bières. She loved me. Is this a perfect day, or what?"

"How was your day?" Katie asked.

"It was interesting," I replied. "Do you guys want to grab something from the grocery store for dinner? I'm thinking we could do some bread, cheese, maybe some grapes?"

"Perfect," Katie replied. "Is that good for you, Ryan?"

Ryan was texting away. "Why, yes, you beautiful young things," Katie said in a mock Ryan voice, "that sounds wonderful." Ryan rolled his eyes and continued to text.

My phone started playing Paramore's "Still Into You."

"Sounds like you have a call from Wills," Katie said with a laugh.

"Hi, Wills," I said. "Would you like to join Katie, Ryan, and me for a delicious dinner of bread, cheese, and grapes? We're going to walk to the grocery store in a few minutes."

"Hello, gorgeous," Wills said. "Bread, cheese, and grapes sounds ace. I'll meet you by the stairs."

"See you in a few minutes." I clicked off my cell.

"Let's go," I said. "Wills is coming, too."

Ryan stopped texting and said sarcastically, "Imagine that."

Grabbing my purse, I walked to the door. "We really had quite the adventure today, and I'm dying to tell you guys about it, but I want Wills to be part of the discussion. After all he's like my...I don't know...forever boyfriend."

"Forever boyfriend; great," mumbled Ryan.

"Cheer up, Ryan," Katie replied, "Charlie won't be able to bring him home."

"Well, there is that," Ryan agreed.

Now I was not going to think about the *R* word or the *H* word. *Reincarnation...that's just freaky* I shivered. *Home...that's just coming way too quickly.*

Wills was waiting in the corridor when we reached his floor. He waved and walked toward us as he talked on his cell.

"Yes, Mum," he said, "she's right here. No, I'm not going to give her my mobile so you can have a little chat. Maybe you and Dad could come to Rouen for a weekend? Right. Cheers."

He kissed my cheek. The jolt of recognition caused me to pause and take a breath.

It's nice to know he feels the same way I do, I thought. *No wonder we didn't leave the room for five days. Okay, I can't start thinking about that right now.*

We entered the store and made our selections. Wills and Ryan added some meat to the menu. Katie and I added cookies. Macaroons are the best.

"Let's go to my room," I said. "We can grab two chairs from Katie's room."

For a few moments, I forgot the reincarnation thing and that I was going home in less than two months. Well, I guess I didn't forget them, but they were overshadowed by the fun we were having.

"Okay, you guys," I said to Katie and Ryan, bringing the reincarnation deal to the forefront of the discussion. "It's time to discuss the possibility of Wills and me having a past-life connection."

"Past-life connection" sounded much less intimidating than "reincarnation."

Wills grabbed my hand, tugging me close. I relaxed into his side. The hot-lava feeling was back. I melted into him. Wills sighed; I guess he felt it, too.

"So," I continued, "we're going to treat this like a research project. Our project is to research the life and death of William Harrington, Will's great-great-uncle, and to find information about a nurse named Charlotte."

Wills continued the explanation. "Here's what we know in a nutshell: William Harrington was buried at St. Sever cemetery in early-November of 1918. It appears he was killed the day before the armistice."

"We also know," Ryan continued, "that William Harrington had a gift sent to the Talbot House sometime in summer or fall of 1918. We don't know whether he retrieved the gift. But we do know the gift is no longer at the Talbot House."

"In addition," Katie said, "we have Charlie and William's journals, which may have clues in the information that neither Charlie nor Wills have noticed."

"We have two goals, maybe three: The first goal is to figure out what happened to William and Charlotte. The second is to discover the Talbot House treasure. And the third goal is to figure out what all of this means," I concluded.

"Today," William explained, "we went to Base Hospital Twenty-One and attempted to go to St. Sever Cemetery."

"Wait," Katie interjected, "I thought you had to work."

"I did," I replied. "But the Office of Tourism was robbed, so it was closed for the day."

"Robbed?" Ryan said "What could the office have that would be of interest to anyone who's not into World War I or other historical stuff?"

"Well, that's the thing; the robber took the two boxes of World War I artifacts I was sorting," I said. "According to Madame, that was it. Obviously, someone was looking for something."

Wills chimed in, "When we got to St. Sever, a grave had been desecrated. I'm not sure if the two issues are connected, but it was certainly coincidental. Anyway, the police didn't know the name of the person whose grave was vandalized."

"Oh, the couple that kept showing up this weekend at all of the historic sites also showed up at Base Hospital Twenty-One. Most likely, it was a result of Charlie giving them the list of her favorite World War I locations, but it was kind of strange."

We sat in silence for a few moments. "It's not a lot of information," Katie stated, filling the silence.

Wills shoved his hand through his hair. "I had a satchel of William Harrington's effects my mum gave to me prior to the trip," he said. "I haven't seen the satchel since arriving in Rouen. It's not like our flats are so large that you could actually lose something…unless you turn your room into a disaster area upon occasion." He looked at me and grinned.

"What did the satchel look like?" Katie asked. "We could run down to the front desk to see if anyone turned it in. I think they have a lost-and-found area. Don't most places?"

"It's a brown leather satchel. I checked with Philippe a couple of weeks ago; nothing," Wills explained.

"Is a satchel like a tote bag or a briefcase?"

"Oh, the American and British language gap," Wills said with a smile. "You'd call it a briefcase."

"An old, beat-up, brown leather briefcase?" Katie asked.

"Yes, it was definitely old, and possibly beat-up," Wills replied.

"Dumpster dive!" Katie exclaimed. "Charlie, you have a beat-up, brown leather satchel," Katie emphasized the word "satchel" and said it with a British accent.

"I do?" I asked. "Yes, I do. It's in here somewhere."

I stood up from the table and scanned the room. "I remember seeing it when I was looking for a shoe Thursday night…or maybe it was Friday morning." I closed my eyes, trying to concentrate.

"Ah-hah!" I stumbled toward the futon and plopped down on the floor—very graceful. I lay on the floor and crawled under the futon. It was here…a beat-up, brown leather briefcase, or "satchel," as Wills would say.

"Is this it?" I asked Wills, holding up the briefcase like it was an amazing prize.

"I think so," Wills replied. He reached over, plucking the briefcase out of my hands. "How did you get this?" he asked as he examined the case.

"Dumpster diving," Katie and Ryan said simultaneously. The three of us started to laugh.

Ryan was the first to regain control. "The first day in Rouen, Katie and I found the briefcase in the dumpster. We salvaged it for Charlie, because she likes old stuff. Hey, Charles, I'm a little hurt that you shoved our gift behind a chair. After all we went through to retrieve it for you."

"Obviously there's more to the story then you're telling," Wills said as he carefully unlatched the briefcase. "How did it end up in the dumpster?" He asked the question to himself, not to us.

"Andrew—the bloody bastard," William muttered.

"Charlie, come here," Wills said softly.

"You know what, Charlie?" Katie said. "Ryan and I are going to hang out in my room. Call me when you want us to come back. Better yet, why don't we plan on meeting tomorrow night, okay?"

Soul Mates ~ Liz Morrison

"Thanks—same time tomorrow night." I gave Katie a quick hug.

I turned away from the door and walked to Wills. I reached for his hand as he reached for mine. The shock was as electric as the first time we touched.

"Bloody hell, there must be something of great importance in this satchel," William said.

Chapter Twenty-Four

WILLIAM

Charlie was secure in my arms. The brown satchel was unlatched, but not opened.

"Wills, think of it as a search for artifacts. We—you and me—are looking into our ancestors' past." Charlie rubbed my arm as she soothed me with her words.

What am I afraid of? I wondered. And I was afraid.

I dropped the satchel on the floor and drew Charlie across my lap. She took charge of the situation and placed her hands on either side of my face. She leaned up to kiss me. Right before her lips met mine she whispered, "I love you, Wills…always."

Our lips merged and I slid my hands under her jumper. She pressed her arms down, stopping their upward climb.

"We need to look inside the briefcase, Wills." She didn't move away or attempt to remove my hands from her person. She smiled, and I knew she knew I was avoiding the inevitable in a way I knew would distract both of us.

"I love you, Charlie," I said as I reached for the discarded satchel.

"I know," she replied with a laugh. "Nice maneuver, by the way."

"Your defensive action was quite impressive," I responded.

I opened the satchel and pulled out the items secured inside. A bundle of letters and several official-looking documents, including a telegraph, an envelope of photographs, several medals, a diary, and a Bible were all revealed.

My fingers tingled when I touched the letters, the photographs, the diary, and the Bible.

"Where shall we start?" Charlie asked.

"Hmm, photographs?" I suggested.

"Photos it is," Charlie said as she picked up the envelope from the pile. "You're sure you want to start here?"

I nodded slowly.

Charlie slid to the floor, pulling me with her. She carefully removed four photographs and laid them in a row.

Two of the photographs captured William as a young boy and as a scholar at Eton. "Wills, can you grab my journal from the table?" she directed me. "Umm…and then flip to the stuff at the beginning. It's the dream I had on the flight."

"Just so you know," she continued, "I think I might pass out." She was taking deep breaths.

"The picture of William in his uniform—that's the picture his mother gave me when I was in London. It's how I knew you. Remember, when I knew your name and you thought I was an angel? I carried that picture of you with me."

My breathing was shallow, too. Thinking I was reincarnated was one thing; actually having proof was another.

"Charlie, I think we're looking at our wedding picture," I gasped.

Charlie and I stared at a picture of us that wasn't exactly us. Anyone looking at the picture, however, would think it was Charlie and me wearing period costumes.

Charlie—well, Charlotte—was wearing the white gauze dress from the Maypole dance. I—or rather, William the first—was in my…his…uniform. Charlotte clasped William's arm at the elbow with one hand and held a bouquet of flowers in the other hand.

I flipped over the photograph. *Lieutenant and Mrs. William Harrington, 11 June 1918* was written on the back of the photo.

We were both taking deep breaths.

"I don't know if I can do this," Charlie said.

"I know you can," I replied as I put the picture down and picked up the diary. "I'll read the diary and you read the letters, okay?"

Charlie nodded as she picked up the stack of letters and stood up. "Let's sit on the futon."

I sat down and Charlie lay down with her head in my lap. "It's my reading position," she explained as she made herself comfortable.

We read the diary and the letters.

"Charlie," I said, "it's almost midnight. We've been at it for hours."

She looked up at me, startled by the interruption.

"What are you thinking?" I asked.

Charlie stared at me. Then she reached up, placed a hand behind my neck, and pulled me down for a kiss. I loved kissing Charlie, but each kiss made me long for more.

"I'm thinking people in the 1900s knew how to write really great letters," she said. "The letters keep the reader informed about the war effort, while sharing bits and pieces of the soldier's private life. Also, they're a great chronology of William and Charlotte's love story. It really was a love story," Charlie said with a smile. "So, what about the diary?"

"Well," I said, "it's very interesting. I think we could put my journal next to the diary, and one would think it was the same document."

"Read this letter," Charlie said as she handed me a letter. "It's about sending jewelry so William could present Charlotte with a wedding ring and bride gift. The letter is dated 20 June 1918."

"That makes sense," I replied, "William was back at the front, a happily married man."

Charlie sort of laughed a kind of shy, embarrassed laugh. We both knew why William was happy.

"That really doesn't provide us with more information," I continued. "We knew the parcel ended up at the Talbot House. We don't know what happened to it."

Charlie handed me another letter. "Read this one," she urged.

I quickly perused the letter. It was a thank-you note dated 14 July 1918.

"Hmmm, apparently the parcel was delivered to the Talbot House, and William was waiting until he had a short leave to retrieve the items and deliver them to Charlotte," I announced.

"When's the last letter?"

"It appears the last letter from William to his family was dated 6 November 1918. William expressed his concern that he hadn't heard from Charlotte in almost a month. The last letter he received was on October 15. He was a little concerned, and planned to travel to Rouen to ensure her health and safety." Charlie paused. "Hey, you know what? My birthday is October 12."

I looked at the documents on the floor. "Look, Charlie." I pointed to the stack of official-looking documents. "The telegraph said William was killed by enemy fire on 10 November 1918. That was the day before armistice. I knew he died close to the end of the war, but I just realized it was the day before the war ended—rotten luck."

"Wow," Charlie said, pulling another document from the pile. "This one is from the Keeper of the Privy Purse, expressing the regret of the King and Queen of England to William's mother over his death."

"Charlie," I said, "I don't want to look at this anymore tonight. I think we have a pretty good timeline of events for William, but no clues regarding Charlotte."

Charlie laid the letters on the floor. "Are you staying?"

Charlie

William placed a ring on the fourth finger of my left hand; a man's signet ring with a crest carved on the face. Holding it there, he said in a clear, strong voice, "Charlotte Alexandria Rawlings, I give you this ring as a sign of our marriage. With my body I honor you; all that I am, I give to you; and all that I have, I share with you, within the love of God—Father, Son, and Holy Spirit."

Our hands were clasped and I repeated the words of the exchange of rings in the marriage vows. "William James Harrington, I receive this ring as a sign of our marriage. With my body I honor you; all that I am, I give to you; and all that I have, I share with you, within the love of God—Father, Son, and Holy Spirit."

The ceremony finished with the minister joining our right hands and saying, "Those whom God has joined together, let no one put asunder."

William looked at me and smiled; he lifted my hand and kissed my fingers below the ring he'd so recently placed on my hand. Still clasping my hand, William turned to shake the minister's hand. "Thank you for making this lovely woman my bride," he said.

The minister replied, "In times of war, I don't often have the opportunity to officiate happy events. This might be the only happy event I've officiated in three years. Mrs. Harrington, I hope you were happy with the wedding vows of the Church of England."

"Mrs. Harrington," I repeated. "Father, did you hear that? Mrs. Harrington," I said as I raised a brow.

My father clasped William's hand and pulled me into a bear hug. "I love you," I whispered.

My father looked tired and rather sad. I looked into his blue eyes, so similar to mine, and wondered what he was thinking. Belatedly, I realized the significance of my marriage to his life. The father who'd dedicated the last seventeen years of his life to me would be returning to America alone. Unless, of course, I could convince William he desired a life in the States.

"I love you too, daughter," my father replied, "and even though you're now a married woman, you remain my daughter."

SOUL MATES ~ LIZ MORRISON

"Interesting ring," my father said to William as he examined the signet ring adorning my left hand.

"The ring was created by a bloke in the trench. I sketched out my family's crest, and he created a ring with material found in the trenches," William smiled. "He thought the ring was for me, hence, the man's ring. I've contacted my mum to send the family engagement ring. Dr. Rawlings, I promise your daughter will have a ring worthy of her."

I squeezed William's hand. "This is the perfect ring," I insisted. "I, Charlotte Alexandria Rawlings, accepted this ring. I'll treasure it always."

Charlotte Alexandria Rawlings—the *R* engraved on the tree—Rawlings.

I touched the side of William's face and slowly rolled from under his arm. I hated to leave the warmth of his arms, but I had an idea. We knew that William Harrington was killed on November 10. We had no idea what happened to Charlotte. We hadn't known her last name. Even in the correspondence from William to his parents, he hadn't included her last name—but I'd now remembered. I remembered her name—or my name. *It's easier to go with her name*, I decided; *keeps it a research project*.

Searching the net would be a great way to start a research project. I quietly turned on my laptop.

One of the letters had included information on the base hospital. Sifting through the letters, I found the one I was looking for—the letter describing Base Hospital Twenty-One, where William had been treated for his battle wounds of June 1917, and where William had met Charlotte.

Charlotte Alexandria Rawlings had been a nurse with Washington University. I wasn't surprised Charlotte was with the medical group I located that had inspired my trip to Rouen. It made perfect sense; of course, Charlotte was searching for William.

I searched the web. Charlotte Rawlings, Charlotte Rawlings World War I, World War I Nurse Charlotte Rawlings, Great War

229

Charlotte Rawlings, Base Hospital Twenty-One Charlotte Rawlings, Charlotte Alexandria Rawlings World War I, and nothing.

It shouldn't be this hard, I thought.

"Hey, Charlie," Wills whispered from across the room. "What are you doing?"

"I know the *R* on the tree," I replied. "Rawlings. Charlotte's last name was Rawlings. I'm trying to find her on the Internet. I've found nothing."

Glancing at Wills, I waited for his response.

"What are you doing, love?" William asked softly.

"Just writing in my diary," I replied as I scrutinized the handsome man lying on the bed. He was my husband, and he was going back to the front line tomorrow. His chest was bare and his arms were clasped behind his head. He was so handsome.

"You look quite smashing in my jumper," William said with a smile as he admired me in his shirt. I knew he liked what he saw.

Quelling my innate modesty, I stood up, and slowly slipped his shirt off my shoulders. From William's sharply indrawn breath and the smile on his face, I was certain he appreciated my effort. He held out his hand and I walked toward him.

"Charlie," Wills said, interrupting the memories of Charlotte's wedding week, "what about contacting Washington University's historical society and requesting information regarding the medical team, including Charlotte?"

Did Wills see my blush? I wondered. I felt hot from the top of my head to the soles of my feet.

"That's a great idea," I replied as I started searching for the Washington University site.

"I found it!" I exclaimed. "The Bernard Becker Medical Library at Washington University; let's see...here's the e-mail address.

"What do I say? I've got it—I'll explain I'm working on a project on Base Hospital Twenty-One in Rouen, and I'll ask if they have any record of Charlotte Alexandria Rawlings." I examined the e-mail one last time and hit Send.

"I wonder what we'll discover?" I asked as I shut down the laptop.

Once again, Wills didn't reply immediately. "I don't know, Charlie," he finally said. "I wish I could force the dreams or memories to come, but they seem to happen...well...when they want. For example, just a moment ago, I remembered Charlotte sitting at a desk, writing in her diary."

Wills didn't complete the memory. I'm not sure whether that was all he remembered, or whether it was all he wanted to reveal. Then he sort of blushed and said, "It was a really splendid memory."

I stretched out next to him on the futon. "I located William's burial plot information while searching for Charlotte Rawlings," I informed him. "At least I accomplished something," I said as I clasped his hand, triggering the lava-flowing feeling. "I'll see what I can find out tomorrow while I'm at St. Sever."

Wills pulled me closer and tossed the blanket over both of us. He rolled over and kissed me goodnight. The kiss turned hot. Memories of Charlotte and William blended with the memories of Charlie and Wills, making it incredibly hard to stop.

Wills kissed my cheek, my forehead, and my hair. "Charlie, it's so hard to stop."

"I know," I replied, "especially if your memory was the same as my memory."

I gave him a quick kiss and rested my head on his shoulder. "'Night, Wills."

"Good night, Charlie," Wills replied. "You're killing me. At this rate, I'll be dead by morning."

Chapter Twenty-Five

WILLIAM

Sleeping with Charlie was heaven and hell. Heaven, because I couldn't imagine being anywhere except by her side. Hell, because we just slept—or attempted to sleep—though we were in bed together.

Tomorrow—or rather, today—Charlie would visit William Harrington's grave at St. Sever. With any luck, I'd be able to join her.

I can't believe it's already 0700, I mused. *Charlie and I need to get up and get moving. Frankly, moving is a bloody challenge, as I don't want to move. I love Charlie's head resting on my shoulder as she sleeps.*

I loved watching Charlotte sleep. I should have closed my eyes for a kip, but I didn't want to miss a moment with my new wife.

I glanced at my watch. It was already 0700. Our honeymoon was almost over. Ending the honeymoon was different if the marriage was beginning. Our marriage would be on hold while I returned to the front and Charlotte returned to her duties at the base hospital. Maybe the war would end soon.

"Charlotte, love, it's time to get moving," I whispered into her ear. "Come on, love, I need to report for duty by 1700 hours."

She snuggled deeper into the covers, wrapping her arms securely around my waist and burrowing her head into my neck.

"I've decided we're not reporting for duty...ever," she announced.

Soul Mates ~ Liz Morrison

"Charlotte, you're killing me," I said as she kissed my neck while exploring my chest with her hands.

"I reckon another hour will allow me time to escort you to the base hospital and report for duty."

Charlotte rolled on top of me and captured my hands above my head while draping her glorious hair around my face, blocking out everything but her beautiful countenance. Her eyes sparkled with laughter and desire. "I love you, Lieutenant William Harrington. I'll love you always." She leaned down and pressed her lips to mine.

Seriously, I thought, *these honeymoon dreams needed to end.* I need a cold shower.

Carefully, I slid out from under Charlie's arm. If I kissed her now, we wouldn't stop. Even though we knew our past selves had consummated their relationship, we were still twenty-first century Charlie and William.

Charlie's not ready to take our relationship to the next level, I thought. *I want the next level to be her commitment to spend her life with me. I'm not sure she's willing—or maybe more correctly—able to make that type of commitment. She's going back to the States in mid-November; that gives us about two months to solve the mystery and determine how we can move our relationship forward. It's bloody awful being so in love; when it's not bloody wonderful.*

Charlie looked so cozy, lying under the covers. I wanted to crawl back between the covers and stay with her there forever. It must have been bloody painful for William to leave Charlotte and return to the front line, knowing death was a real possibility.

It was bloody painful for me to leave Charlie when neither one of us would face a life-or-death situation. I couldn't imagine leaving this room…leaving Charlie…knowing death was an imminent possibility.

I kissed Charlie on the forehead. I sent her a text detailing my whereabouts for the morning. I also told her I'd meet her at St. Sever after 1300 hours so we could go to the grave together. *That sounded kind of strange*, I silently remarked.

At my flat, I logged into the computer. The language instructor who was also my boss was contacting me via e-mail with my work assignment.

I read the assignment as sort of good news and bad news. The good news was, the assignment started tomorrow. The bad news was, I'd be gone for at least a week.

I sent a text to Charlie:

I'll meet you downstairs in thirty minutes. I love you.

My mobile vibrated and I glanced at my text messages:

Okay. I love you, too.

I noticed several messages from Andrew. *He can go to bloody hell,* I thought. The bastard had attempted to thwart my investigation into the past life of William Harrington. He'd pitched the bloody satchel. He'd attempted to sabotage my relationship with Charlie with the damn article. *If I ever speak with him again, it would be interesting to hear his explanation,* I thought.

After a quick shower, I joined Charlie in the lobby.

She was chatting animatedly with Philippe.

"Hi, Wills," she said, reaching for my hand. "Philippe secured two scooters for our use. I was going get one for us to share, but I thought you might get bored, stuck at the cemetery all day. I wanted you to have options."

I didn't think I'd be bored, but Charlie needed to concentrate on her job. "Smashing," I replied.

"Merci," we said to Philippe in unison.

We hopped on the scooters and maneuvered around the traffic to St. Sever Cemetery. Charlie's control of the scooter was questionable at best. She almost tipped it.

She waved, letting me know she was fine.

The gates to the cemetery were open. Apparently the mishap that had occurred yesterday had been resolved.

Charlie parked her scooter and removed her helmet. "I know," she said. "That was really bad driving. I was thinking about everything we discovered last night, and wasn't focusing on the road. The curve brought me back into focus." She smiled at me.

"Seriously, Charlie, if something happened to you, I'd die." I grasped her shoulders and looked into her eyes. "You're my reason for being." I kissed her until we were breathless. "Be careful."

"Yes, sir." She gave me a mock salute. She started walking toward the cemetery gates, pulling me in her wake. "Just so you know, I feel the same way about you," she informed me.

"Quite right," I replied. "Since this is your first day on the job, I was thinking I should locate William's grave while you're getting acquainted with your boss. I'll take a few photos, but we can go back to the grave later. I'll be an inconspicuous visitor at the caretaker's office and start looking for information on William Harrington in the archives."

"Sounds like a plan," Charlie replied, "as long as we can return to the grave together. Maybe being at the grave site will trigger some memories. Charlotte's memory of burying her beloved would be strong. I don't know how she was able to go on."

Charlie seemed unable to fathom how Charlotte could live without William. *I know the feeling,* I thought.

"Be careful," Charlie said as I walked toward the sign illustrating the layout of the cemetery.

The cemetery was quite beautiful. Tall, narrow trees standing side by side formed a natural barrier separating the cemetery from the surrounding town. The grave stones were organized in pairs, with many separated by low-growing shrubbery.

Looking at the map, I realized the manner in which St. Sever was organized was conducive to locating loved ones. Tommies who died after 1916 were buried in the cemetery extensions. The extensions were additional burial sites added to the cemetery as casualties from World War I continued to grow. Row upon row of gravestones stood at attention, much like the soldiers themselves would have stood during roll call. William Harrington's grave would stand among those who died in the final days of the war.

Walking slowly through the cemetery, I admired the monuments. Like all cemeteries monitored by the Commonwealth War Graves Commission, St. Sever included the Cross of Sacrifice and the Stone of Remembrance. The Stone of Remembrance rested on the three required steps and included the inscription, "Their Name Liveth for Evermore." I was looking for the chapel.

Plot S, where Harrington was buried, was near the chapel. Locating the chapel was easy; locating William's resting place among the 8,000 graves was more of a challenge.

I slowly walked down the row of graves, reading each headstone as I passed. Many of the headstones included personal inscriptions, presumably added by relatives. Inscriptions like, How We Miss Him; We Who Loved Him, and Greater Love Hath No Man Than This; That a Man Lay Down His Life for His Friends.

Gazing over the plot where William Harrington was laid to rest, I noticed a tilted headstone surrounded by freshly turned soil. *That must be the grave vandalized yesterday*, I realized.

I walked cautiously toward the damaged grave and read the inscription: "Second Lieut. William James Harrington, 10 November 1918, Age 19, Never Forgotten Shalt Thou Be."

The ground shifted. I sat down near the tombstone. My breathing was shallow and my heart pounded in my chest.

My mobile vibrated; it was Charlie.

"Hey," she said. "Are you okay?"

"Charlie," I replied, "I found the grave."

"And?"

"I don't know," I replied. "I feel rather lightheaded. It's the grave that was vandalized."

I waited for Charlie to reply. I could hear her breathing.

"Charlie?"

Soul Mates ~ Liz Morrison

"Don't move," she said, which was rather funny, because I apparently was incapable of rising from my current position.

"I'll meet you at your grave. Okay—well, that sounds weird. See you in a few minutes."

Time stood still as I examined my emotions, trying to ascertain how I felt: confused and, frankly, nothing.

"Well, old boy," I said to the headstone, "bloody brilliant. Now I'm talking to headstones. It seemed appropriate. What is it you want from me?"

I examined the headstone carefully. "Bloody hell—you earned the Victoria Cross. You must've been one hell of a soldier."

I heard the sound of footsteps and lifted my head from my arms. It was Charlie, running toward me. I placed my hand on the headstone and pulled myself to my feet.

Maybe the question was, "Whom do you want for me?" rather than "what do you want from me?"

Charlie wrapped her arms around my waist and read the inscription, whispering, "Never Forgotten Shalt Thou Be.' I forgot you, William, but I remember. I remember now."

Tears slowly rolled down Charlie's cheeks.

I had to kiss her. It was impossible not to, standing in the middle of St. Sever Cemetery by William Harrington's headstone.

I leaned down as she leaned up. It wasn't just electric, it was more. It was cataclysmic, in a bloody good way.

I had no idea how much time passed. When our lips parted, Charlie's arms were wrapped around my neck and mine held her pressed against me.

"I love you, Wills," she whispered, "but I know I—or Charlotte—have never been to this grave. I feel like…I don't really know how to explain this, but here it goes…like I just found out you died, but then found out you weren't dead. But I have no memory of this place, or mourning your death. Maybe that'll come; I don't know. What I do know is, we're here, we're alive, and I love you more than…well, anything."

Charlie

I pulled out my phone and took several pictures of the grave, never letting go of Wills' hand.

He seemed to be in shock, sort of like me after I saw our heart carved in the tree at Le Tommy Café.

Well, if he can't move, we can stay here all day, I decided.

"Wills," I said, "let's go to the caretaker's office. I have an idea."

I decided the best strategy at this point was to talk—a lot. "I don't know, but I think the man who I met on the first day at the Bureau of Tourism is responsible for this. He and his girlfriend seem to be where we were. I know I gave him the info, but it still seems strange. What are the odds that your grave—" Wills shook his head—"sorry," I replied. "What are the odds that the grave of your great-great-granduncle (I emphasized great-great-granduncle) would be vandalized at the exact time we were looking for the grave? It could be a coincidence, but I think it's more."

"The bloody bastard was probably after the Talbot House treasure. The bloke probably thought it was buried with me…I mean, Great-great-uncle Wills Harrington," Wills said ruefully.

"Charlie," Wills said, "slow down. I may appear to be in a state of shock, but I now have all of my wits about me."

I slowed my pace and looked into Wills' face. He gave me a slow smile. "Well, love," Wills said, "what's your incredibly brilliant idea?"

Staring into warm, gray eyes sparkling with…I don't know…adoration—something like that, I forgot we were standing in a cemetery on a quest for the couple who probably vandalized Harrington's grave. My mind emptied of all coherent thoughts except for one: *I love this guy.*

"Charlie. Charlie," Wills asked, "are you okay?"

"As crazy as this is, I can't think of a place in the world I'd rather be than here with you right now," I said. "I am so okay."

William took my hands, pulling them behind my back so I was pressed against his chest. I knew the kiss was coming; as always, I wasn't prepared for the incredible feeling of completeness that accompanied it.

"How very inappropriate," a distraught voice broke though the haze.

"Sorry," William said. "We were celebrating life." Letting go of my hands, he put his arm around my shoulder, steering me away from the woman who commented on our less-than-appropriate public display of affection.

"Good thing that wasn't my new boss," I said to Wills. "Now, keep your hands to yourself." I snuggled into his side and clasped the hand that was over my shoulder. "I think we should describe the couple to the caretaker and determine whether he saw them yesterday."

"What if," William continued, "I happen to have a photograph of the couple to share with the caretaker?"

"Bloody brilliant," I replied, teasing Wills with one of his favorite expressions.

"Charlie," Wills said, "ladies don't say 'bloody.'"

"Whatever," I replied with a smile. "Do you have a photograph? When did you take it?"

"No worries, Charlie," Wills said with a sly smile. "Introduce me to the caretaker and I'll take it from there."

I nodded, shrugging out from under William's arm with an apologetic smile. *I hate to break the connection,* I thought. *It's kind of painful. It might be bad to introduce my boyfriend to my boss. Introducing my friend who's searching for information on his great-great-grand-uncle—now that was perfect.*

"Monsieur," I called as we entered the office.

"Bonjour, monsieur," I said. "I'd like you to meet William Harrington. He is researching his great-great-grand-uncle, who's buried at St. Sever."

"Bonjour, monsieur," William said, extending his hand to the curate. "I'd appreciate your assistance in locating information on William James Harrington. I must say I was quite distressed when I located his grave a few moments ago and found it vandalized."

"Oui," monsieur replied. "It is quite distressing a gravesite of a fallen hero was desecrated. I have been the curate for over thirty years, and we have never experienced any vandalism. This is a disgrace. Please accept my heartfelt apology. Please assure your family that we will restore his final resting place to its previous beauty."

"Monsieur," William interrupted, "we may know who is responsible."

Wills handed his phone to Monsieur Dupree with the picture of the couple.

"Oui," Monsieur Dupree said with conviction. "The man and woman were here yesterday, researching William Harrington. Fascinating," he mumbled in French, "no one to visit the graves of the soldiers and then, in two days, voilà; one soldier has two visitors."

"Monsieur," William asked, "did the vandals remove anything from the grave?"

"None, non," Monsieur Dupree replied, "It didn't appear anything below ground was disturbed."

Monsieur Dupree looked at me. "Charlie, assist your friend in his research."

"Oui, monsieur," I replied, leading Wills to the corner of the building where the binders of information on those interred at St. Sever were stored. The binders were stored in several large, wooden bookcases protected by doors with glass windowpanes. The glass, the curator had explained to me earlier in the day, protected the books from the elements. Guests could view the binders through the glass and then only select the book pertinent to their research.

"Let's see," I said as I perused the dates labeled on the spines of the large, leather binders. The book with information on Second Lieutenant William Harrington should be relatively easy to locate, as the binders for the cemetery extension were organized by month and year.

"Let's see," Wills said. "I see September 1918, October 1918..." Then he paused. "That's odd—do you see November 1918?"

I studied the binders carefully, looking at the spine on each binder for a book that was out of sequence.

"Oh, there it is," I said as I opened the case protecting the books. "I guess someone shoved it back into an open spot, not worrying about order. Organizing binders will be a project to accomplish here at St. Sever."

Near the bookcase was a large, wooden table surrounded by several chairs—the research area at the cemetery.

Wills took the book from my hands and gently laid it on the table. "All right, then," he said, studying the layout of the book. "It looks like it's organized in numeric order by the date the soldier was buried in the cemetery. If that premise is correct, the record on William Harrington should be toward the beginning of the book. Or," he continued, more to himself than to me, "as 10 November was the day before armistice, it might be toward the back of the book."

I leaned over Wills' shoulder as he carefully turned each page. The process seemed to take forever; page after page recalling the death, and sometimes the life, of men who'd died during the final days of World War I. It was all sad, but it was somehow sadder that these men died the day before armistice.

"Bloody hell," Wills exclaimed. "Bloody hell, someone tore the page from the book."

"Oh no!" I said as I examined the book. A page had been carefully removed from the binder, but not carefully enough, if you were looking for a certain page.

"Damn, damn, damn," William cursed softly.

I wrapped my arms around Wills' shoulders, trying to provide comfort while struggling to make sense of the information. *Why would anyone else—like the couple who seemed to be following us—*

care about Second Lieutenant William Harrington? Maybe the Talbot House treasure was worth the trouble.

"Wills, do you remember what your parents...I mean...hell, this is so complicated. Do you remember what was in the treasure?"

Wills glanced around the room and then pulled me into his lap, "I can't remember a bloody thing. The last memory I have is the memory of you dropping my jumper and joining me in bed. I'm sorry, love; I just can't seem to get past that memory."

"Me too," I said into his neck.

"Okay," I went on, pushing myself away from Wills' shoulder. "Maybe we'll have other memories surface after you leave today. Give our brains time to clear the honeymoon memories, or something."

Wills looked at me with...I guess...desire in his eyes; I'd never noticed eyes could talk. At seventeen, I'd never looked for a guy to have desire in his eyes.

"Don't give me that look," I said as I stood up. Wills smiled his sexy, devilish smile.

"Seriously; you need to go back to your room and pack for your trip," I told him. "While you're gone, I'll dig through all the items in the valise and try to put some of the pieces together."

Wills opened the glass door and replaced the book on the shelf in the correct order. Shutting the door, he turned and grinned. "All right, love," he said. "We'll return to the flat and clear our heads."

I attempted to locate Monsieur Dupree. Monsieur was small and slender. Probably in his mid-seventies, he was very spry. He walked with a spring in his step and as he walked toward me, he seemed to bounce with vitality. "Monsieur," I said with a smile, "I'll be back tomorrow at nine o'clock. Is that the correct time?"

"Oui, Charlie," he replied with a crooked grin, revealing a smile with several gold-capped teeth. "Be careful on the scooter. I saw you approach the cemetery this morning. Practice make perfect, non?"

"Oui," I replied. I decided not tell Monsieur about the missing page. He'd delay our departure, and Wills needed to get back for his job. We needed to ensure our search for the past didn't mess up the present—or the future. I wasn't sure how prepared we were to deal with all of this.

I walked through the white iron gates guarding the entrance to the cemetery. Wills waited patiently by the scooters with my helmet in his hand. *Damn, that boy is fine,* I told myself.

"I didn't say anything to monsieur," I said as I placed the helmet on my head and straddled the scooter.

Wills pulled his scooter next to mine. "I know this is complicated, but we'll untangle it together," he assured me.

Chapter Twenty-Six

WILLIAM

Eight days without Charlie, I lamented. I needed to be clear with the Language Institute—I needed to stay in Rouen for the next two months. *I need to be near Charlie,* I told myself.

Now, back in Rouen, I was still waiting to see her. Charlie, Katie, and Ryan were at their current positions and would return to the flat later that afternoon. Andrew had apparently returned to Rouen. I was in absolutely no hurry to see or talk to him, though I was sure he'd have quite the story to tell.

From the conversations I'd had with Charlie, she'd made no progress in putting William and Charlotte's story together. She hadn't heard from Washington University—probably a dead end. However, she, Katie, and Ryan had categorized the information from the valise. The valise reminded me of my mum and dad.

Picking up my mobile, I dialed my mum.

"Cheers," I said.

"William Harrington," my mum replied, "your father and I have been quite worried. Do tell all."

Hearing my mum's voice rather normalized the abnormal. I should have contacted my parents, rather than leaving them in the dark.

I chuckled into the phone, "Tell all, eh, Mum? I'll just give you the highlights."

I chuckled again. What I considered the highlights weren't appropriate to share with my mum, so I'd share the highlights that were appropriate.

"Where to begin?" I pondered. "We started examining the items in the valise. It really was quite the treasure trove of World War I artifacts. We found a letter confirming some family jewelry was sent to William Harrington when he was serving at Ypres-Passchendaele."

"Right," Mum replied. "We couldn't find any record of family jewelry being sent to France. Your grandmum, however, has been scouring the attic, hoping to find items to help you in your quest. I have to say, she's having quite the grand time, feeling quite useful.

"How's your American friend?" she continued. "Do you still believe she's Charlotte from the Great War?"

"Mum," I replied, "she is Charlotte from the Great War, but honestly, more importantly, she's Charlie from right now. She's smart, funny, and quite the detective. I haven't seen her in over a week. Right now, I'm waiting in my flat for her to return from Office de tourisme Rouen."

"When does she return to the States?" Mum inquired.

"Middle of November," I replied.

"That's coming up rather quickly," she observed. "I hope all of your questions will be answered prior to her departure."

The thought of Charlie leaving made me physically ill. My mum, like Katie and Ryan, thought our romance would be over when Charlie returned to the States—destined for failure because of...well...the Atlantic Ocean.

"Wills," Mum said, "no need to worry about this today. I'm sure you and Charlie will figure it out when the time comes."

"You need to know," I said softly, "I can't live without her." That was the truth. We'd have to figure it out when the time comes.

"The trip with the American businessmen was quite an event," I continued on a lighter note. "I wonder if they thought it odd that a bloke from England was their French interpreter. We actually had two interpreters on the team; me and a French bloke who was really an incredible fellow. His knowledge of France and the French countryside is second to none. I sincerely hope he'll need my services in the future."

"How's Andrew?" Mum asked.

"Andrew is Andrew; I haven't seen him much lately," I replied. For some reason, I was uncomfortable telling my mum what a bastard Andrew had been during our gap-year experience.

"Mum, tell Dad I rang," I said. "Bye."

"Bye, Wills," Mum replied.

Glancing at the clock, I realized I had loads of time before Charlie returned...plenty of time for a kip. Kicking off my shoes, I lay back on the futon and closed my eyes.

Those of us still alive were exhausted; we'd fought at Ypres, Cortrai, Ooteghem, and Tieghem. Since the end of September, we'd regained much territory lost to the Germans. Many had been lost, but I lived for Charlotte.

No shells had been fired in the last several hours, no orders given to go over the top. Now was a good time to read the letter from Charlotte. I pulled the letter from pack to read it again. Holding it in my hand brought a smile to my lips and a glazed look to my eyes. If my mates glanced my way, they'd think I suffered from shell-shock because of my dazed, thousand-yard stare. I'd not seen Charlotte since June, but our correspondence was regular and our love undiminished.

Dearest Husband (I love calling you husband),

Every day I hope to receive a note from you, my beloved; when the letter arrives, I thank God you're alive. Yesterday I posted many letters of farewell found on young men who made it from the front to our base hospital, but will not make it home; I can only imagine the anguish of their loved ones when they receive the note or telegraph. The news we hear sheds a hopeful light that the end of the war is drawing near. Over the last few days, we heard British troops took Le Cateau, Rouvroy, and Sallaumin, while the French forced Fritz beyond Oise Canal, Champagne, and from part of the Chemin des Dames. The Argonne forest is clear of Germans. I question the arriving soldiers about their division. Based on my stalwart detective work, I believe you're in Flanders. If you're in Flanders, then, my darling, you're not so far away from me. Wherever you are, keep yourself safe; I know that's a tall order for an officer on the front line, but as an officer, you are quite good at carrying out orders. I rather like the idea of ordering you about. I hope that makes you smile.

Influenza invades the hospital again. This strain seems a more severe type. The three-day fever in the spring was a challenging time at the hospital, but the patients recovered after a few days. The new strain, however, leaves some victims dead within hours of their first symptoms. It's really quite horrid for the people suffering, as their lungs fill with fluid and they suffocate. I've been serving in the ward with the flu victims the past few days. Don't worry, my love, I had the same duty during the last outbreak, and it appears I am quite immune. I know the boys appreciate the comfort I can bring. Death in battle is tragic; it's ironic the flu is killing the boys faster than the Huns.

You are assuredly tired of reading gloom and doom. Amidst all of the suffering and loss I have joyful news to share. If you're standing up, you may want to sit down. However, having seen a trench, it may be better if you lean against a wall. I've thought of any number of ways to share the news, but here it is: we're having a baby. I wanted to be absolutely sure before sending you a letter. I hoped you'd appear at the base hospital, so I could wrap my arms around you and whisper, "We're having a baby."

I'm sure your commanding officer won't give you a leave at this time, as he so generously gave you five days in June. However, I'll remain hopeful. I'm feeling somewhat fatigued and have a slight headache, so I'll say good night and sweet dreams. I'll love you forever.

Your loving wife (and baby),

Charlotte and Baby H (for Harrington)

I need to get a short leave to check on Charlotte, *I realized.* *"What day is it, mate?" I asked a fellow soldier.*

"November 7," he replied.

I'd not received a letter in almost a month. Her last letter was dated 12 October. I could blame the mail system, but the post always arrived on time.

"Sir," I said to my commanding officer, "may I have a word?"

"Certainly, Lieutenant," he replied, clasping my soldier, "I was actually looking for you."

"Always at your service, sir," I replied.

"Lieutenant," he continued, "you were recommended for the Victoria Cross for your extreme devotion to duty in the presence of the enemy at Ypres. Your recommendation documented your actions in battle when all other officers in the conflict were dead. Taking command of the remaining soldiers, you led them forward under heavy fire; you and two comrades successfully cleared numerous enemy dugouts, taking machine guns, killing the enemy, and capturing prisoners."

I was speechless. The Victoria Cross was the highest decoration awarded to a British soldier. "I was just doing my duty, sir."

My commanding officer smiled and extended his hand. "Well done. Now, what did you want to ask me?"

I handed him the letter from Charlotte. He read the letter and cautiously said, "Congratulations."

"I'm sorry, sir," I replied with a grin, "I'm quite excited with the news. I'm just concerned. The letter is dated 12 October. I've not heard from Charlotte since. I hope you'll allow me a few days' leave; I believe a hospital train is leaving the area. If I catch the train, I can be back in three days."

"Three days, and back to the front," he agreed.

"Thank you, sir," I replied. "Thank you."

I grabbed my kit and ensured the items I'd collected from the Talbot House were within.

I was going to see Charlotte.

My mobile rang. Whoa, my head was spinning. *Charlotte had a baby, I thought.*

"Hi, Wills," Charlie said. "Are you in Rouen?"

"Hello, love, I'm at the flat." I needed to share my dream.

"I can't wait to see you," she said before I could begin. "I made an incredible discovery at the Office de Tourisme." I could hear her voice shaking with excitement. "I found Charlotte's letters to William."

"No bloody way," I replied.

"Yes, bloody way," Charlie said with a laugh. "So, I'm hoping you can come to work with me tomorrow and we can read through the letters. Are you in?"

"Ace," I replied. "Of course I'm in."

"I love you, Wills," she said softly. "I'll see you in a little."

Hearing her voice made me smile. *We've only been together for a few months, but I can't imagine life without her,* I told myself. *She can't leave me.*

CHARLIE

Madame Chevalier waved as she locked the door to the Office de Tourisme.

Madame and I were now friends. When I found the letters, I'd shared the story of William and Charlotte with Madame. Well, I'd shared the part about William's quest for his great-great-grand-uncle; not the reincarnation part. I also told Madame about the Talbot House Treasure and the grave being vandalized. She was quite intrigued with the entire story.

That day, we locked the letters in the safe for extra security. The thief who'd broken into the Office de Tourisme had obviously been looking for World War I artifacts. Madame and I took every precaution to guard our new treasure.

As I mounted my scooter, I thought about finding the letters. The storage area, located in what I considered the attic of the building, was littered with boxes donated in preparation for the hundredth anniversary of the Great War.

Part of our task was determining what to send to museums or other historic sites, what remained at the Office de Tourisme, and what to sell at public auction. Some of the items might be trash.

I moved into traffic, driving toward the apartment. I needed to focus on maneuvering the scooter, not on the latest and greatest find at the museum.

My mind returned to the museum and discovering the letters.

I was overwhelmed by the number of boxes. I sat down by the nearest pile and started to review the contents.

Whoa, that car went by me super close, I thought. *I need to focus.*

Traffic zoomed around me, but my mind continued to wander.

I picked up a box and pulled out a soldier's knapsack. It was obviously from World War I. The knapsack included a copy of A Shropshire Lad, *a journal or diary, and a stack of letters. When I touched the letters, I felt the same jolt of electricity I felt when I touched Wills. It nearly knocked me over.*

I pulled the letters into the light and read the name on the envelope. Second Lieutenant William James Harrington, BEF. The return address read Charlotte A. Rawlings, Base Hospital Twenty-One, American EF.

I could barely breathe. I was holding in my hand a letter Charlotte had written to William.

I didn't open the envelope; I closed my eyes and remembered...

Dear William, My Dearest William, My Darling Husband

A horn honked, bringing me back to the present. I waved at the driver, indicating I was paying attention. From the corner of my eye, I saw a car speeding around the corner.

Swerving to the left, I avoided disaster.

I looked to my right; a car was heading straight for me. I swerved again; my wheel hit the curb, the scooter flipped, and I sailed through the air.

I moved in slow motion. Time seemed to slow down...to stop. *I need to protect my head*; I thought. I stuck out my hands to brace my fall.

I completed the letter to William and took it to post. It would have been wonderful to tell him our news in person. But there was a war on. The letter would have to do.

I giggled with the realization that the censor would be the first person to know I was pregnant with William's baby. There definitely was a war on. I hoped he wouldn't congratulate me when he saw me at breakfast. Lilly would beg for an explanation, and I'd have to come up with a plausible response.

Today was quiet, except for the onslaught of the patients with influenza. I walked toward the doctors' quarters, anxiously searching for my father. My headache was growing worse, and I was so tired I could barely walk. Even though I was a nurse, a married woman, and a mother-to-be, when I didn't feel well, I wanted my daddy. Luckily for me, he was somewhere in the vicinity.

"Hello," I said to an orderly. "Have you seen Dr. Rawlings?"

"Sure, Charlotte," he replied. "He was heading to his quarters a few moments ago."

"Thank you," I said as I continued to my father's lodgings. I was glad we were here together, but I missed spending actual time together. Maybe tonight he'd keep me company.

Knocking on the door to his quarters, I called, "Daddy, it's me, Charlotte."

The door opened and my father gave me a tight hug. "Charlotte, I was just thinking about you. Would you care to play a game of chess? Or we can practice cheating at cards," he said with a grin.

"I love you," I said. "I'm not sure I could concentrate on chess. I don't feel well, Daddy." I used my little-girl voice, a voice I hadn't used since before we'd left St. Louis for Rouen.

"What's wrong, sweetheart?" he asked.

"Well, I have a headache, and I'm so tired I can barely stand. And I feel hot."

My father looked at me with real concern. His tone sounded perfectly normal when he asked, "What duties have you been assigned lately?"

"Hmm," I replied, "I've been mostly working with the soldiers who are suffering from influenza...Oh my God, I've contracted the flu!" I looked at my father. "I need to go to the tent for flu patients immediately. I don't want to infect you."

I sort of staggered toward the door. I was so hot.

"Charlotte," my father said. He sounded far away. "Lie down on my bed, honey. I'll see what I can find to make you more comfortable. You're going to be just fine."

My father was a doctor— the best doctor in the whole world. If he said I was going to be fine, I'd be fine.

"I'm tired, Daddy," I whispered. "I'm going to take a nap."

I woke up and heard voices. I wanted to say something, but I couldn't form any words.

"Her skin is blue-tinged," the voice said. That was not good for the poor girl; blue-tinged skin indicated the patient was starting to suffocate. Soon foamy blood would exit from her nose and mouth. The poor thing was certainly a goner.

"I'm sorry, Dr. Rawlings," the voice continued.

"I'm sorry, Dr. Rawlings?" Oh no; I must be the goner!

It was so hard to breathe. I needed to open my eyes. I forced my eyes open and looked directly into my father's eyes. I'd forgotten how much his eyes looked like mine. It was like looking into a mirror...well, sort of; his eyes looked like a blue pond because he was crying. I gasped for breath and felt lightheaded from the lack of air. I really was a goner.

The benefit of knowing you're dying is that you get to say goodbye.

"Goodbye, Daddy; you're the best father a girl could ever have. Please tell William I'll love him forever. I love you, Daddy."

I couldn't speak anymore. As far as deathbed goodbyes go, it was the best I had to offer.

"Charlotte, can you hear me?" my father called, but he was too far away for me to respond.

"Ce que vous m'entendez? Ce que vous m'entendez?" Someone yelled at me in French. They were asking me if I could hear them.

I can't remember how to say yes in French, I fretted. *Why are they speaking French?*

Chapter Twenty-Seven

WILLIAM

Unbelievable, I thought. *Charlie found the letters Charlotte wrote to William. Maybe the letters will help us solve the mystery and find the Talbot House treasure.*

"Come in," I called when I heard a knock on the door.

The door opened and Andrew walked in.

"Don't punch me," he said. "I know you're angry. The article for the *Chronicle* was pretty low."

Almost to himself, he continued, "Though the execution itself was bloody brilliant. The American responded exactly as I predicted. I forgot about the weird shock you two share. If it wasn't for that strange connection, it would've been a grand success."

He was gloating. I quite despised him.

"Andrew," I interrupted his self-congratulatory speech. "We've been best mates for almost our entire lives. For that reason, and that reason alone, you have three minutes to explain why you don't want me to be with Charlie, and why you pitched the satchel." I glanced at my watch. "You now have two minutes and fifty-five seconds."

"Wills," Andrew said, "you're my best mate. I'm not going to stand by and watch you ruin your life thinking you're a reincarnated World War I bloke. You need some psychological help, and you don't need a girl from America holding you back. You're young, good-looking, and experiencing your gap year. You're obsessed by the past and by a girl that will be gone in November.

Soul Mates ~ Liz Morrison

"If I thought your plan was to shag her, I'd be all in. But for some reason, you want to commit. You're eighteen years old. Right now is the time girls across the globe want to shag. You need to live for the moment, not for the past or for the future. I did you a favor."

What an ass. I stood up, plowing my fist into his jaw. Andrew's head snapped back from the impact. My days playing rugby and the Wall Game had taught me how to throw a good punch. He grabbed his jaw, looking astonished.

"You tried to destroy my relationship with the girl of my dreams before it started, you slandered me, and you tossed away a piece of my family's heritage. I think I'll punch you again." I drew my arm back to throw another punch.

Philippe rushed into my flat, shouting in rapid French. *"Il y a eu un terrible accident. Charlie est à l'hôpital de l'université de Rouen. Katie et Ryan sont déjà à l'hôpital, et ils t'attendent. En plus, mon frère t'attend dans sa voiture maintenant. Il faut aller à toute vitesse."* It took a moment to translate. "Oh my God—Charlie's been in an accident and she's in the hospital. Katie and Ryan are at the hospital and your brother's going to drive me. How bad are her injuries?" I asked as we ran down the stairs to the car.

"I'm sorry, mate," Andrew said as he followed me down the steps.

"I'm so uninterested in you and your apology," I replied through gritted teeth.

Andrew ignored me and climbed into the back of Philippe's brother's car. I decided not to dissuade him. I had more important matters on my mind.

Charlie's ring tone played.

"Hello, love—you gave me quite a fright," I said when I answered.

"Umm, Wills, this is Katie. Ryan and I are at the hospital. Are you on your way?"

"Yes, we should be at the hospital in…" I glanced at Peter; he held up five fingers…"five minutes. How is she? What happened? Is she going to be okay?" My chest felt like it was being crushed; it was hard to breathe.

"She had an accident on the scooter. She's not great, but it could be worse," Katie replied. She sounded like she was trying not to cry.

"Go to the Charles Nicolle side, and then to the ground floor of the Pavilion Félix Dévé," she continued. "Look for the entrées aux urgences." Katie rang off.

"How is she?" Andrew asked.

"I don't know," I replied.

I took a deep breath; *She's going to be fine,* I assured myself. *I didn't wait a hundred years to find her again so she could die.*

At the entrée aux urgences, I quickly got out of the car and thanked Peter for the ride. Andrew followed me into the hospital.

"Je cherche Charlie Longley. Elle était dans un accident de scooter," I said to the receptionist.

She looked on her computer then directed me down the hall. "Andrew," I said, "I'm not actually sure why you're here, but please stay out of the way."

He nodded as I continued to her room.

Charlie was lying on the bed, her head wrapped in a bandage. Her arm was a in a sling. She was connected to numerous tubes and monitors. The room was white, the bedding was white…Charlie was a spot of color amidst the sea of whiteness.

Ryan looked at me, walked across the room, and punched me in the stomach. The punch propelled me into the wall, knocking the wind out of me.

"What the hell was that for?" I asked.

"You son of a bitch," Ryan said, unconcerned that Katie, Holly, Libby, Mike, Andrew, and members of the hospital staff were watching the altercation.

Katie grabbed Ryan's arm, pulling him away from me. "What Ryan wants to know—what the doctors need to know—is Charlie pregnant?" she asked.

"Charlie's not pregnant," I replied. "You guys know her better than anyone. She'd have to be shagging to get pregnant."

I pulled a chair to Charlie's bedside and clasped her hand. *No electric current...that's bad,* I told myself.

Ryan and Katie looked at me like I was lying.

"If I may be blunt, Charlie and I haven't had sex," I snapped.

Katie looked at Ryan. "Charlie hasn't regained consciousness, but she was talking about William and a baby. The doctors thought they should give her a pregnancy test. Ryan naturally thought you got her pregnant so she wouldn't go back home. Or, maybe his first impression of you was accurate; you're just a player who used Charlie and accidently knocked her up—his words, not mine."

Charlie remembered Charlotte was pregnant. *The doctors probably think she's pregnant,* I realized.

I walked into the hallway, attempting to find an attending physician.

"Katie," I asked, "did you call Charlie's parents?"

"No, we were waiting for you," she said. "We didn't want to tell Mr. and Mrs. Longley Charlie was pregnant."

"Where's Charlie's mobile?" I asked.

"I can't find it," Katie replied. "I had it when I called you, and then I set it down. Now it might be lost forever."

I pulled my mobile from my pocket and dialed Charlie's number.

Paramore's "Still Into You" started playing somewhere on the floor at the foot of Charlie's bed.

I looked at Charlie and whispered, "I'll always be into you."

A nurse entered Charlie's room, "Il y a un trop grand nombre d'entre vous dans la salle. Vous devez partir immédiatement. Quelqu'un parle français?"

It was too crowded in the room, she said, and we needed to leave. The nurse asked if anyone spoke French.

Katie, Ryan, Mike, Libby, Holly, Andrew, and I regarded the nurse with blank stares.

If the situation weren't tragic, it would be comical—the seven of us spoke fluent French, yet with one look, we convinced the nurse we had no idea what she was saying.

The nurse shook her head, mumbling under her breath as she left the room. "Je vais trouver le Dr. Rawlings. Il parle anglais. Il obtiendra ces enfants hors de la chambre du patient."

She was going to find a doctor who spoke English.

A young doctor entered a few minutes after the nurse left. "Hey," he said as he entered the room, "I'm Dr. Rawlings, your friend's doctor. Is one of you guys William?" Dr. Rawlings sounded like an American with a French accent.

I nodded my head.

"All right," he continued. "Everyone but William needs to leave the room. You guys can hang out in the waiting area. I'll let you know if there's a change in Charlotte's status."

Katie touched Charlie's hand and Ryan kissed her forehead below the bandage. Holly, Libby, and Mike gave an awkward wave. Andrew said nothing as he walked out the door,

I continued to hold Charlie's hand, willing her to come back to me.

"Well, William," Dr. Rawlings began his interrogation, "is Charlie pregnant?"

"No sir," I quickly replied, "Charlie and I haven't consummated our relationship."

Consummated our relationship; I sounded like a freak. "She's never been intimate with anyone," I continued.

"Okay, William," the doctor replied, "that's all I needed to know. You can join the others in the waiting room."

"I'm sorry, sir; I'm not leaving Charlie." I gripped her hand.

The doctor studied me carefully before he answered. "We have permission from Charlie's parents to perform a CAT scan to make sure there's no bleeding or bruising inside her head. Her other injuries are relatively minor," he said.

"Our major concern is the length of time she's been unconscious. You can wait for Charlie here, or you can wait for her with your friends in the waiting room."

"I'll wait here, sir," I said.

I gently stroked Charlie's hair. "Charlie? Charlie, can you hear me? I love you so much. I'll be right here, waiting for you."

An orderly came into the room, taking Charlie for the CAT scan. The waiting was intolerable, but I felt better waiting alone in her room, rather than waiting with our friends in the waiting room.

Staring out the window, I saw nothing. I tried to force the memories of my past life to the forefront of my mind; I needed to remember what happened to Charlotte. *Even thinking in terms of past life and not saying it out loud sounds bonkers,* I realized. *No wonder Andrew thinks I'm one sandwich short of picnic.*

The transport didn't go directly to Rouen. I made so many train changes, I was surprised I made it to Rouen. It was a cold, wet, rather miserable day. Knowing I'd see Charlotte soon kept me from dwelling on the condition of the base hospital and the deplorable weather. The damp air and continuous rainfall turned the old racetrack into a swamp that was challenging to navigate. Bad as it was, however, the poor conditions at the base hospital seemed like a luxury liner compared to the conditions in the trenches.

I negotiated my way around mud puddles as I walked across the field toward the nurses' quarters. I doubted Charlotte would be in her quarters, but I could leave my kit inside her tent and get it later. I thought the best course of action would be to send Charlotte to my family in England. I knew my mum would be quite pleased to entertain my wife.

I knocked on the door and waited impatiently for a response. No one responded, so I quietly opened the door. Hmm—the room was relatively bare, and the bed where Charlotte slept had all of the bedding—sheets, pillow, blanket—stored under a folded-over mattress. No personal items were anywhere to be seen. Could she be at a clearing station?

Taking one last glance around the semi-abandoned hut, I tossed my kit over my shoulder and walked briskly toward the surgical ward.

An orderly was walking in the same direction. "Hello," I called to the orderly. "Can you point me in the direction of Sister Charlotte Harrington?"

The orderly stared at me blankly. "Sorry," I corrected myself, "Sister Charlotte Rawlings—or Dr. Rawlings?"

"Dr. Rawlings is in his hut." He pointed in the general direction of the quarters used by the doctors at the base hospital.

I continued my brisk pace to the doctors' lodging. Dr. Rawlings appeared from nowhere.

"Dr. Rawlings," I called as I broke into a run.

He stopped, turned toward me, and waited for me to catch up.

"Hello, sir," I said, extending my hand. Dr. Rawlings looked terrible. I wondered if he was recovering from influenza.

He clasped my hand and didn't let go. By the look on his face, I knew something was wrong.

My stomach was in knots. The words stuck in my throat. I forced them past my lips.

"Where's Charlotte?"

"William," Dr. Rawlings said in a soft voice, "Didn't you receive my missive? I sent it several weeks ago."

The mail was the one certainty in this Godforsaken war. Yet, I had not received the note from Dr. Rawlings. "No sir," I replied. "I received a letter from Charlotte on October 15th."

"I'm sorry son," he said. "Charlotte is gone."

"Gone," I repeated. He meant "gone" as in "dead;" I knew lots of people who were gone...gone, as in forever...this was war, after all. But not Charlotte, I told myself. Charlotte cannot be gone.

"Gone, sir?" I said again.

"Charlotte passed away on October 12. She contracted influenza and died. I'm sorry, son."

I started to breathe quickly. My heart rate accelerated and I started to sweat. Charlotte is not dead, I insisted to myself. Charlotte is my wife. We're having a baby.

My world crashed around me.

"William...William!" Dr. Rawlings repeated.

"William. William!" Dr. Rawlings said as he tapped me on the shoulder.

Oh God, I can't turn around, I thought. *I can't bear for history to repeat itself.*

Tears rolled down my cheeks...tears for Charlotte; tears for our baby. If Charlie was dead, I'd be done.

I scrubbed my face with my hand and turned to face Charlie's doctor.

"How is Charlie?" I choked out the words, afraid to hear the response.

The doctor examined my face closely. He didn't look like a man who was about to tell me the love of my life, the love of all my lives, was gone.

"Charlie's great," he replied, patting me on the shoulder. "She regained consciousness during her scan. She knows who she is, where she is, and she has a vague recollection of the accident. Her mom gave me permission to keep you updated on her status. You may want to update her friends; they look pretty distraught. We're going to keep her in the hospital for a few nights to observe her. She took quite a crack on the head."

"Thank you, sir," I said, shaking his hand.

"Dr. Rawlings," I said as we walked toward the waiting room, "you sound like an American with a French accent."

"I went to Washington University's School of Medicine in St. Louis, Missouri," he said. "Charlie and her friends are from St. Louis. I recognized the area code when I called her folks. What a coincidence."

A coincidence? Charlotte's team had been from Washington University. Charlotte's last name was Rawlings—a coincidence or a connection?

Chapter Twenty-Eight

CHARLIE

Cautiously I opened my eyes. Wills was sound asleep in the chair next to my bed, his hand resting on my stomach. He looked totally uncomfortable. Wills had only left my room to shower and change, poor guy.

Tonight was my last night in the hospital. I was so ready to continue investigating Charlotte and William and planning the exhibit at the Office de tourisme.

"Charlie," Wills whispered, "are you awake?"

"Yeah," I replied. "I guess you are, too. Can you come lie with me?"

Wills stood up and stretched. "It actually looks quite comfortable," he said. "I don't want to pull your plugs out. Though I'd prefer to climb in bed with you, I should keep my distance."

He sighed and leaned over the bed. "How's your head?" he asked.

"Fine," I replied. Wills cupped my face. My heart rate accelerated. Warmth quickly spread from where his skin touched mine.

"You'd better watch it," I said with smile. "The nurse is going to come in because you make my heartbeat race and my blood pressure rise." I turned my head sideways and kissed his palm.

"Hey, Wills," I whispered, "While I was unconscious, I remembered the day Charlotte died. She'd been treating victims of the influenza epidemic and caught the flu. It was crazy; I died...I mean she died...within hours of her first symptoms. And you know what's even sadder? She was going to have a baby."

I started to cry. It was weird; it was like I was retelling a super sad story. But it also felt like I'd lost a baby...that Wills and I had lost a baby.

Wills climbed into the bed on the side opposite of the arm with all the tubes. He pulled me into his arms and held me close. He buried his face in my hair; he was crying too. Tears rolled down his cheeks like he didn't want to cry, but he couldn't help himself.

"I remember, too," he said. "I arrived—I mean William arrived—at the base hospital to find out you were—I mean Charlotte—was dead.

Wills took a deep breath. "Charlie, I'm never letting you go," he said. "We're destined to be together." He linked our fingers together and brought my hand to his heart. "I love you, Charlie."

"I love you too, Wills," I replied.

"You know what?" I asked.

"No, what?" he replied with a laugh.

"I know why I didn't remember your grave...I mean William's grave. Charlotte was never there. I died—this is so crazy—I mean Charlotte died—before William."

"We need to return to the cemetery and find Charlotte's grave," I told him.

Yawning, I snuggled into Wills' shoulder and wrapped the arm free of needles and tubes around his waist.

"Hey, Charlie," Wills whispered, "do you think there might be some connection between Charlotte Rawlings and Dr. Rawlings? It's awfully coincidental that Charlotte Rawlings was from Washington University and your Dr. Rawlings studied at Washington University."

"I don't know," I replied. "We can ask tomorrow."

"One more thing," Wills said softly. "Well, three or maybe four more things: Andrew's very sorry, but I haven't forgiven him. Katie and Ryan miss you. Your mom thinks I'm ace. Strangely, the couple who we seem to meet at various World War I sites stopped by the hospital. They seemed rather dodgy. That's it; now you can go to sleep."

I was already dozing off...

WILLIAM

Dr. Rawlings was calling my name. I didn't turn back.

Charlotte was dead. My beautiful, funny, compassionate, and loving Charlotte was dead.

Images of Charlotte flashed through my mind; the first time I saw her and I thought she was an angel...asking her for the privilege of continuing our correspondence before heading to the front...when she let down her hair on our picnic in Ypres...asking for hand in marriage in front of crowd at the base hospital celebration...repeating our wedding vows...when she dropped my jumper and came to me the last night of our honeymoon...looking at life through her eyes in her numerous letters.

I managed to arrive at St. Sever with no recollection of walking there. Row after row of wooden crosses stood like soldiers waiting for battle...only these soldiers would never see battle again.

My beautiful Charlotte was out there somewhere, amidst the newly interred. I should have asked Dr. Rawlings to take me to her grave. But I needed to say goodbye to my love—to my life—privately. However, if I can't find her resting place, I'll never be able to say goodbye, I told myself.

"William! Lieutenant! Lieutenant Harrington!" A voice called from a distance. I turned toward the voice; it was Dr. Rawlings.

"William," he said again as he finally caught up with me. "You won't find Charlotte here."

"Wills," Charlie said. "Wills, pay attention."

"Sorry," I replied. I glanced at Charlie and grinned. "We can't find Charlotte's grave at St. Sever because she wasn't buried here."

"What are you talking about?" Ryan asked. Ryan was diligently digging through the record books, looking for any information regarding the burial site of Charlotte Rawlings, or Charlotte Harrington, or Charlotte Rawlings Harrington.

We were spending another Saturday at St. Sever, trying to locate Charlotte's grave.

I remembered something. I hadn't had any dream memories since Charlie's accident a couple of weeks ago.

"I just had a memory flashback," I said to the group, "I remembered walking to St. Sever to say goodbye to Charlotte. Charlotte's dad followed me to St. Sever and told me, and I quote—or at least I'm attempting to quote something that was said a hundred years ago—'You won't find Charlotte here.'"

"Not helpful," Katie said as she closed the large book she'd been examining.

"It is rather helpful," Andrew replied. "At least we won't have to spend another bloody Saturday digging through moldy old journals."

"No one forced you to come, dude," Ryan said. Ryan was still mad at Andrew. It was easy to understand, because I was still angry. Andrew was trying to regain his status in the group, but Charlie's friends weren't buying what he was selling this go.

"You know," Charlie said, "maybe Charlotte's dad shipped her body to the States. Or maybe she's just buried in a different cemetery. She hated how the guys died and then were conveniently deposited in the nearby cemetery. Maybe her dad buried her somewhere else."

"Don't you think he would've wanted her nearby, so he could visit the grave?" Katie wondered.

I glanced at my watch. "It's time to take Charlie for her follow-up visit with Dr. Rawlings," I announced.

We carefully returned the books to the shelf and gathered our backpacks and phones.

"Do you guys want to go to La Boîte à Bières tonight?" Ryan suggested as he placed the last book on the shelf. "We haven't been in a while. I don't think they have karaoke on Saturday nights, but it'll be fun. We can get Mike, Libby, and Holly to come, too. I'll text them and see if they're up for it."

I ushered Charlie toward the door. "Right, then," I replied. "We'll meet you at La Boîte à Bières around eight p.m. Dr. Rawlings' office is about five minutes away from the bar," I explained.

Handing Charlie her helmet, we mounted the scooter. She wasn't keen on driving it—or riding one, for that matter. I quite enjoyed having her arms wrapped securely around my waist.

We sped through the streets of Rouen to Dr. Rawlings' office on rue Lecanuet. The building had both offices and flats. A pizza place was next to the building. "Maybe we can get a piece of pizza after your appointment," I said to Charlie as I assisted her from the scooter.

"Look, Wills," Charlie said, "let's check out the beautiful building and the cathedral." She glanced at me and took my hand—still electric—"after we get pizza, of course."

I leaned down to give her a quick kiss just as she tilted her head back. The sound of the bus brought me back to earth. I moved my mouth from hers and whispered, "Good thing we're in the middle of the sidewalk, or I wouldn't stop," I remarked.

She buried her face in my neck. "I thought the British were much more restrained concerning public displays of affection."

"Not this Brit," I said into the top of her head.

Charlie stepped out of my arms, shook her head at me, and smiled as she tugged me toward the doctor's office.

"I wonder if he lives here, too," Charlie said. "It's such an awesome location."

We entered the four-story brick building and climbed the stairs to the third floor. Dr. Rawlings' office was on the left. I knocked on the door prior to entering; it seemed more like a flat than an office.

"Entrez, s'il vous plaît!" a woman called.

Entering the office, I sat down and Charlie approached the receptionist to verify her appointment, "Salut! Je suis Charlotte Longley. J'ai rendez-vous avec le Dr Rawlings."

The young woman smiled and extended her hand, "Hello! I am so pleased Christophe invited you to our office, rather than having you return to the hospital. I'm Christophe's wife, Chloe. He loves St. Louis and is pleased—I'm not exactly sure pleased is the correct word—he was able to treat a young lady from the area. You must be William," she said as she glanced at me. "Christophe told me how you stayed by Charlie's side. Young love; it's so romantic."

Chloe was a very pretty, petite brunette with dark eyes and an open smile. She seemed quite nice.

"Bonjour," Dr. Rawlings said, as he entered the waiting area from an examining room. "Come on back, Charlie," he said. "This is Angelina; she's my nurse. Didn't you say you were interested in nursing?"

Charlie, Dr. Rawlings, and Angelina entered the examining room, leaving me with Chloe in the waiting room.

"Christophe mentioned your research on a relative killed in Rouen during World War I; Second Lieutenant William James Harrington and his bride, Charlotte Rawlings Harrington, who died of influenza in 1918. Christophe's interest was piqued when you mentioned Charlotte Rawlings and her father were in a unit from Washington University assigned to Base Hospital Twenty-One. His family has connections to Washington University dating back to the First World War."

Chloe paused, "Would you care for a glass of wine? Tea?"

"Nothing, thank you," I replied.

"We have some resources that might help you in your investigation, but we'll wait for Charlie and Christophe."

As if on cue, Charlie and Dr. Rawlings emerged from the office.

"Charlie looks great," Dr. Rawlings shared, "and everything is healing quite well."

"I didn't tell—well, at least not everything," Chloe said with a smile.

Charlie glanced at me; I could tell she was confused; I sort of shrugged in response.

Chloe pulled a box from under her desk. "This," she said with flourish, "belonged to Christopher Rawlings, a doctor with the American Expeditionary Force who came to Rouen in 1917 with his daughter as part of Washington University's medical team, assigned to Base Hospital Twenty-One. Dr. Christopher Rawlings was also Christophe's great-great-grandfather."

Charlie fell into a chair. Dr. Rawlings rushed to take her pulse. "I'm fine," she said. "I just need to breathe."

"So, what happened to Dr. Rawlings—the one who was your great-great-grandfather?" Charlie asked.

"William," Chloe said, "why don't you take a seat. Would you like a glass of wine?"

"Yes," Charlie and I said simultaneously. Then we looked at each other and laughed. Though our lives seemed to be one strange event connected to another even stranger event, we kept growing more connected.

"Bonne nuit," Angelina called as she left the office for the evening.

Chloe handed everyone a glass of wine. I had an incredible urge to down the entire glass, but I just took a small sip. Charlie grinned at me; I knew she was thinking the same.

Chloe sat down next to Christophe. "So, tell them the story. I think the Charlotte you're looking for is Christophe's great-great-aunt Charlotte. It's an amazing coincidence."

"So here's our family's story," began Dr. Rawlings. "In 1918 Christopher Rawlings buried his daughter, who'd died of influenza.

He selected Cimetière du Mont Gargan as her burial site and contracted with a local stonemason to carve her headstone. The stonemason's sister was a beautiful woman in her late twenties whose husband had died at Flanders. Dr. Rawlings and the stonemason's sister, Josette Noblet, became friends. After being discharged from the AEF he bought a home in Rouen, within walking distance of the cemetery, and started teaching at the local hospital. Two years later he married Josette, and they had five children, one of whom was my great-grandfather. My grandmother and my mother tended Charlotte's grave and the graves of many of the Rawlings family interred at Cimetière du Mont Gargan, including Dr. Christopher Rawlings and his wife Josette."

I glanced at Charlie; she looked stunned. *Is she thinking like Charlie or Charlotte?* I wondered. If she was thinking like Charlotte, she was rejoicing over her father's life.

"It sounds like the Charlotte you're looking for is our Charlotte," Chloe said. "Here's the box of memorabilia. Please go through it at your leisure. I'll pour more wine, yes?"

"Yes," Charlie and I said—at the same time again.

Charlie moved slowly toward the box, me, and Christophe. It would be better to open it together.

Chapter Twenty-Nine

CHARLIE

I felt sick. The box of memorabilia of Dr. Christopher Rawlings loomed before me. My stomach churned as I sat on the floor next to Wills and Christophe. Wills touched my hand. The warm, electric current was reassuring, but I still felt sick.

"Right, then." Wills opened the box and pulled out a scrapbook. The first page was a marriage license. I carefully read the. The marriage was between Dr. Christopher Rawlings and Susan Alexandria Longley; it was dated June 1898.

"According to my grandmother, Dr. Rawling's personal papers arrived in the early 1920s. They were organized in chronological order. The next document was the birth certificate of Charlotte Alexandria Rawlings, followed, sadly, by the death certificate of Susan Alexandria Longley. Oh—here's a picture of Dr. Rawlings and his daughter Charlotte."

Christophe's voice was coming from a great distance.

I'm going to faint, I thought. This fainting stuff really had to stop.

"Incredible," he observed. "You look a lot like Charlotte."

"Charlie...Charlie," Wills called, wrapping his arm around me, holding me up and trying to bring me back to the present.

"Sorry," I mumbled. Wills and I needed to get out of here, but we still needed more information. Taking several deep breaths, I pulled myself together.

Dr. Rawlings took my pulse. "I'm okay...really," I said.

"Would it be okay if we took pictures of the birth certificates and other stuff that pertains to Charlotte Rawlings?" I asked.

"Sure," Christophe replied. "Take pictures of whatever you like. I'd let you take the box, but my grandmother would shoot me."

He flipped through the first few pages. "These are some articles and awards connected to Dr. Rawlings and World War I. You might find them helpful."

"Where did you say Charlotte is buried?" I asked as I viewed her death certificate.

"Cimetière du Mont Gargan. It's quite nearby, actually," Chloe chimed in. "I bring her and other family members buried at Mont Gargan flowers upon occasion. All of Christophe's family was buried at Cimetière du Mont Gargan."

Chloe glanced at her watch. "The cimetière is closed for the day, but it opens again tomorrow. Christophe and I would take you to visit the grave, but we have an engagement. I will jot down instructions so you may find the grave, yes?"

"*Merci beaucoup*," Wills said to Chloe. "I have all the photos we need. We probably should be going. Thank you for sharing your story with us. It was ace. If we determine Charlotte is the Charlotte we're looking for, we'll let you know, if you'd like."

"*Oui*," Chloe and Christophe said, and laughed.

"If Charlotte is William's bride, we're family...very distant, but family nonetheless," Christophe said, clasping Wills' hand.

"Charlie," Christophe said, "take this picture of my great-great-grandfather and his daughter Charlotte. I am amazed by how much the two of you look alike; you could be sisters."

Christophe handed me the photo. "Thank you so much," I said. "I'll treasure it."

Chloe and Christophe stood in the door of the office as Wills and I walked down the hall.

"I remember when the photograph was taken," I said to Wills. "Do you?"

He grinned. "Our wedding day...or William and Charlotte's wedding day," he replied.

When we stepped outside the building, I pulled out my phone and started texting.

"I'm texting my mom," I told William. "I'm asking her to get on ancestry.com to find out if we have a Susan Alexandria Longley in our family who married Dr. Christopher Rawlings in 1898. That would actually make sense, right? If someone from my mom's family is connected to this story, that would make sense about why I...I mean Charlotte...would be reincarnated as me."

I glanced at Wills and gave him a smile. Then I kissed him, because he was so cute and this was so confusing

WILLIAM

"Come on, Charlie," I said as I pulled her through the door of La Boîte à Bières. "The text said they were in the dart room. We're playing boys against the girls."

Charlie laughed. "Prepare to have your ego crushed. I have wicked skills with a dart board."

I tugged Charlie into a corner, blocking her from the other patrons. "Wicked skills—ace. I like a girl with wicked skills."

I leaned down and kissed her. She grabbed my shoulders and pressed her body tightly against mine. *Wicked...quite wicked,* I decided.

She pushed me away. "Remember that when you're throwing darts," she taunted.

She scooted around me, grabbed my hand, and led me to the stairs. She stopped one step up and turned around so we were face to face. We could have been alone, because all I saw was her.

Charlie cupped my face in her hands and kissed me softly on the lips. "Let's go have some twenty-first century fun, Wills."

I didn't tell her the fun I had in mind. Normal fun sounded ace after all of our paranormal activity.

Charlie continued up the stairs and walked into the room with darts. "Hey," she said, "I hear it's boys against the girls. Game on!"

Andrew was with the group. I'd sort of forgiven him after Charlie's accident. All the petty nonsense seemed so unimportant.

"Are you ready, mate? The Yanks are counting on our skill to take down the girls," Andrew said, handing me the darts.

I glanced at my companions. It was easy to pretend I was hanging out with new friends from the States, and Charlie was a fit bird with whom I'd just recently fallen madly in love. *For tonight, that's what I want,* I told myself.

"Hey, love," I called to Charlie, "come here and distract me from hitting the target."

She laughed and gave Ryan a quick kiss on the cheek. Reaching me, she placed her hand in the small of my back. The current was electric, and I was definitely distracted. Throwing darts was fun; holding Charlie was bloody brilliant.

Charlie turned, smiling sweetly. "I totally suck at any game requiring decent eye-and-hand coordination," she admitted. "I told you I had wicked skills to distract you." She threw her dart into a wall, relatively near the dart board.

Placing my arm around her shoulder, I pulled her close. "I think you're pretty perfect, with or without wicked dart skills," I replied, giving her a quick kiss.

"Hey," Katie said, "I swear I saw the stalker couple outside the door. They seem to show up wherever we are. It's pretty creepy."

I squeezed Charlie's hand. I agreed with Katie—it was pretty creepy.

"How was your doctor's visit?" Ryan asked.

"It was fine. I'm fine," Charlie replied.

"You don't sound fine," Ryan studied Charlie with concern.

Charlie opened her purse, pulled out the photograph, and slid the photo to Ryan. He looked at the photo and back at Charlie. His face drained of all color. Ryan gave Charlie a questioning look.

Charlie shrugged. "I know, right?" she said.

"So, we know where Charlotte is buried," she whispered to Ryan. "We're going tomorrow. I hope you and Katie will come."

"I got your back," Ryan said with affection.

The table discussion returned to the present. Katie shared her adventures with Monet, Ryan's gig, and the work Lilly, Holly, and Mike were doing. Holding Charlie's hand, I didn't need to engage in the conversation to be part of the conversation.

As the conversation continued, I tried to remember.

"William, Charlotte isn't buried at St. Sever. She's interred at Cimetière du Mont Gargan, near the old section of Rouen. The cemetery has a beautiful view of the city, and it's situated amongst the old buildings she loved. I want her to have a headstone, not just a wooden cross. St. Sever couldn't accommodate my request, so I found a stonemason in Rouen who made a tombstone for Charlotte."

"Let's go back to the base hospital," he continued. *"I'll take you to Charlotte's grave tomorrow. The cemetery is already closed for the evening."*

A motor vehicle drove us back to the hospital. Dr. Rawlings directed me toward his hut. *"You can sleep in here tonight, and we can go to Charlotte's grave in the morning. I'm on duty for most of the night, and will sleep at the surgery."*

He bent over and pulled a small, metal box from under his bed. *"This belonged to Charlotte, and now it belongs to you,"* he said. *"The items you gave her are all in the box."*

Dr. Rawlings handed me the box as he left the hut.

I held the box for a few moments. I slowly opened the lid. Inside the box were the remains of Charlotte's life. All of my letters were secured with a pale-pink bow. I lifted the letters and discovered the bracelet, the letter opener, and her wedding band. I picked up the wedding band; memories of placing it on her finger overwhelmed me. I dropped the ring back in the box.

I opened my kit and removed the box I'd retrieved from the Talbot House. I knew the family engagement ring was inside the box. I couldn't bear to see the ring I'd never be able to place on her finger. I placed the box from my parents inside Charlotte's memory box and snapped the lid shut. The box, and all it contained, needed to be buried with Charlotte, my beloved, at her grave. It would be appropriate to rip out my heart and leave it there, too.

"Wills," Charlie asked, "are you okay? Are you ready to go? I've had a good time, but I think I'm ready to call it a night."

I looked at Charlie carefully; she looked tired. She hadn't fully recovered from her accident.

"Come on, love," I said. "I'm getting a cab."

"Sounds good," she replied, and laid her head on my shoulder.

"Hey, guys," she said, "we're going back to the apartment. Does anyone want to come?"

Charlie glanced at the group. Everyone shook their head in the negative. "Okay, then," she said. "Have fun."

I grabbed Charlie's hand. "Sorry," I said, as I bumped into a man on the steps.

It was the stalker man. I pretended I didn't recognize him and pulled Charlie past him.

"Isn't that stalker boy?" Charlie asked.

"Yes," I replied. "Let's get out of here, before he follows us home."

As soon as we reached the curb, I hailed a cab.

"Charlie," I said, "two items: one, can I sleep with you tonight? Two, I know where I put the Talbot House treasure. I buried it at your...I mean Charlotte's grave."

CHARLIE

Walking up the stairs to my room, I thought about Wills' memory of the Talbot House treasure. I wondered whether we'd find Charlotte's memory box at the grave.

"Tomorrow's going to be an interesting day. I'm kind of scared," I whispered. "Are you?"

Wills smiled. "You probably feel the same way I felt when I knew we found my...I mean William's grave. It's a very unusual feeling."

We walked into my room. I quickly checked my e-mail—still nothing from Washington University regarding the service of Charlotte Rawlings or Charlotte Rawlings-Harrington.

William stood near the door, waiting patiently for me to finish. I looked up to see him watching me intently.

"What?" I asked.

"I'm so bloody glad I found you," he replied reverently.

I held out my hand. Wills walked toward me and clasped my hand in his. The electric current shot up my arm. I looked into his eyes and knew, without a doubt, he'd forever and always be the only one for me. His lips touched mine...

Wills pulled me to the futon and wrapped me in his arms. "Good night, Charlie," he said in a sexy, sleepy voice.

I stared at the ceiling, thinking about life, death, and rebirth.

Is it possible a person could be born again? I wondered. *Is it possible some dreams are not dreams at all, but memories of a past life? Is it possible I, Charlotte Susan Longley of St. Louis, Missouri, could have a second life to finish unfinished business from a previous life? Is it possible my unfinished business is intertwined with William's unfinished business? If it is possible, then what was the probability our two lives would come together again? Could we pick up where they left off? Could we start over based on who we are today?*

The answer to all of the questions was yes. Yes, it was possible...probable...I was living my second life so William and I could finish our unfinished business; being together. It wasn't going to be easy, but we'd picked up where they left off, and we'd started over, based on who we were today.

I'd known my study abroad in Rouen would be life-changing.

In a few hours, the adventure would lead me to a cemetery; a cemetery where we'd search for a tombstone—a tombstone that was very likely mine.

Some questions should be unanswered. The questions I had, however, needed to be answered.

Eighteen seems so young, but in 1918, it was a good age to be married, I considered. *It was a good age to start a family. How do I explain this kind of love to my parents? How will I explain that Wills and I belong together? Will they understand William is my soul mate? Questions lead to more questions.*

I burrowed my head into Wills' shoulder and pulled up the cover. I wanted to enjoy this moment. I wanted to enjoy lying next to Will.

Wills sensed I was awake as he pulled me tighter into his embrace. "Don't leave me, Charlie; don't leave me."

"I won't leave you," I promised.

Chapter Thirty

WILLIAM

Charlie's hand was clasped in mine as we approached Cimetière du Mont Gargan. I glanced down, trying to determine how Charlie was feeling. She pulled out her phone, texting Katie and Ryan another reminder to meet us at the cemetery.

By the number of texts she's sending, I'd wager she's feeling nervous, I told myself.

"It's pretty," Charlie whispered.

I glanced around at our surroundings. The cemetery was surrounded by a grassy hill leading up to a moss-covered stone fence. A French flag flew at the entrance.

"Are you okay?" Charlie asked.

I stopped and turned to Charlie. I placed my hands on her shoulders and looked into her eyes.

"I remember losing you—I mean Charlotte—like it was happening right now," I said. "My stomach aches and it's really hard to breathe. I feel you, and I know you're here beside me; but I'm afraid something's going to happen and you'll be gone. I don't think I can live through it again.

"Charlie," I said, as I moved my hands from her shoulders and grabbed her hand so we could continue walking through the cemetery, "Charlotte didn't want to leave William; she loved him like you love me. She died. She left him."

"Look at me, Wills." She stopped walking and stared at me until I looked into her eyes. "I'm here; I won't leave you—I promise." She wrapped her arms around my waist and pressed her body to mine.

"Come on," I said gently. "Are you ready for this? Charlotte's grave is over there." I gestured to a row of graves near a grove of trees.

"Are you sure?" Charlie asked.

"It feels like I was here yesterday," I said.

We walked through the cemetery, getting closer to Charlotte's grave. The grave was quite a walk from the main entrance, but in a beautiful location. The tombstones at Mont Gargan were unique—like Charlie...like Charlotte.

"I'm texting Katie and Ryan," Charlie said. "Once again, I'm pretending this isn't real."

I stopped at the foot of a tombstone—Charlotte's tombstone. Her grave was surrounded by gravel, rather than dirt.

Charlie read the words on the grave. "Charlotte Rawlings–Harrington, Nurse, Base Hospital 21, ANC, Missouri, 12 October 1918."

I read the verse from Tennyson's poem Dr. Rawlings had inscribed in honor of his daughter. I believe the message was for me—or rather, for Lieutenant Harrington.

I hold it true, whate'er befall;

I feel it, when I sorrow most;

'Tis better to have loved and lost

Than never to have loved at all.

Charlie touched my hand; the electric current almost knocked me off my feet.

"Look," I said, and pulled her down to the headstone. I pointed out the words "Baby H" carved into the side of the stone, hidden from sight.

"I carved them, you know," I said, "to remember the baby."

Charlie's shoulders shook. She was crying, but not making a sound. I realized I was crying, too. I wrapped my arms around her, trying to come to grips with whatever this was, and what it meant to us now, and to us in the future.

"Well, this is quite the touching scene," a voice said.

I looked up into the barrel of a gun.

Holding the gun aimed at Charlie and me was the man who'd been stalking us for over a month.

I shoved Charlie behind me to separate her from the threat. "What do you want from us?" I demanded.

"You know what I want," he said. "The Talbot House treasure. Now, where is it? You 'and it over, and you won't 'ave more trouble from me."

"I don't know where it is," I said with conviction.

"You're a bloody liar," he sneered. "You and your bird from the States 'ave been 'unting for the treasure as long as I 'ave."

I tried to keep Charlie behind me, but she wouldn't stay put. She peeked her head out from behind me and focused her deep-blue eyes on our assailant. Her hair was slightly disheveled, her eyes were swimming with tears; she looked innocent and angry.

"What treasure?" she demanded. "We were visiting the grave of one of my ancestors, who died during World War I from Spanish Influenza, not treasure hunting."

"Don't give me that bloody bullshit," the man growled. "I've been lookin' for the treasure for years. I know it exists, and I know you two know where I can find it. I guess it's buried right 'ere, next to the grave of yer ancestor. Now start diggin'."

"We don't have shovels, sir," Charlie replied. "Don't you think we'd have shovels if we were going to dig up a treasure?"

"Use your hands, then—get diggin'," he snarled.

Charlie seemed relatively calm, considering we were being held at gunpoint. I knew where to dig, but I wasn't digging up my gifts—William's gifts—to Charlotte for this bloody bastard.

"Well, Wills," she said, "where do you think we should start digging?"

"Quit yer yappin'," our captor hollered. "I've spent me entire life lookin' for war treasures. This one is going to be me fortune; it's a real treasure. Keep diggin'."

The bloke sounded like a pirate. If we weren't being forced to dig at gunpoint, I probably would have laughed.

Charlie and I started digging. We easily dug through the gravel surrounding the grave, but without equipment, we couldn't go deeper.

I looked up. "We can't dig any deeper without the proper tools," I told him. "It's as solid as a rock—take a look."

Much to my surprise, he walked toward us.

Just a little closer, closer, I thought, willing him to get close enough for me to wrestle the gun from his hand.

"I'm not gettin' that close," he said, in apparent response to my thoughts.

"Look," I said. "It's rock-solid."

I heard a noise behind me. I prayed it was Ryan and Katie—not that I wanted them in danger, but I hoped I could use them to distract our captor.

I grasped a handful of gravel in my hand and threw it in the gunman's eyes. Before he had time to aim and shoot, a red-haired madman dove at him from behind a tree and knocked him to the ground.

The two men wrestled in earnest for control of the gun. Without thinking, I dove into the fray to assist Andrew in his assault.

"Look out!" Charlie shouted. I rolled away just as our captor's girlfriend tried to nail me in the head with a shovel. The woman tumbled down the slight incline after Charlie used a slide tackle to knock her off her feet.

Andrew and I continued to wrestle for the gun.

A loud bang cut through the air. The gun exploded. Andrew's anguished cry echoed through the cemetery.

I rolled away from the struggle, grabbed the shovel, and coshed the bloody bastard in the head.

I observed the chaos around me as if it were all occurring in slow motion.

Ryan, Katie, and two police officers rushed up the hill. One of them grabbed the girlfriend while the other secured our assailant.

Charlie's jumper was torn. She was applying a makeshift bandage to the wound in Andrew's shoulder. We needed to get Andrew to a hospital.

"Thanks, Andrew," I said. "I owe you one, mate."

"If you forgive me for being such an arrogant ass and lousy friend, we can call it even," Andrew said extending his good arm so we could shake on it.

"I think we're square," I replied.

Charlie glanced at me and Andrew. "I called Dr. Rawlings," she informed us. "Chloe said they can fix Andrew up at the office. The police can give us a ride, so we should be good. I think I might be in shock; that man had a gun pointed at us, and he was ready to use it. I'll faint later."

Katie and Ryan hugged Charlie. "I'm so glad you're okay," Katie said.

"You know," Ryan said, "before you met the British dude, you didn't get into accidents or have to fight off gun-wielding crazy people. Do you think it might be the company you keep?"

"Thanks for your words of support," Charlie replied.

I wrapped an arm around Charlie's waist as we walked behind the rest of the group out of the cemetery.

"Wills," Charlie whispered. "Do you think the treasure is buried at Charlotte's grave?"

"Charlie," I replied. "I know it is."

CHARLIE

Oh my God, I thought. *We were in a life-or-death struggle. This doesn't happen to me—or at least, it didn't use to happen to me.*

Luckily, the bullet had only grazed Andrew's shoulder. Dr. Rawlings cleaned and wrapped the injury. Andrew had picked the perfect location to get injured. Okay...that didn't sound right.

Katie and Chloe were discussing Monet and art in general. Ryan, Andrew, and Christophe were debating the merits of gun control. I rested my head on Wills' shoulder, taking it all in.

"The treasure's at the grave?" I asked.

Wills gave me a mischievous smile. "You want to go dig it up?"

I glanced out the window. "I don't think the cemetery is still open," I said.

"No worries," Wills said with a grin, "we can hop the fence."

He pulled me to my feet. "We'll be back in less than hour," he announced. "We have some unfinished business at the cemetery."

"Seriously, Charlie," Katie asked, "it's pitch black outside. You're going to a cemetery in the dark?"

"I'll be fine," I replied.

Wills and I left the office and rushed down the steps. Wills practically pulled me down the street toward the cemetery. "By the way," he said, "that was quite an amazing slide tackle."

"I play a lot of soccer," I replied. "Now you know not to mess with me."

"Shh," Wills whispered. "We're going to sneak past the officer on duty to get to the grave. The French patrol their cemeteries; probably to keep grave robbers—such as ourselves—out."

Soul Mates ~ Liz Morrison

We sneaked under the window of the guardhouse. I tried not to giggle. Wills gave me a disgruntled look as he shook his head in mock dismay.

"I hope it's not haunted," I whispered.

"It probably is," Wills replied, "but you're probably in good standing with the other ghosts."

"Thanks," I replied sarcastically.

"Right, then," Wills said as we reached the grave. "I tossed the shovel..." he glanced around, "right over there."

"Let's see," he said. "It's buried right here."

He carefully tapped the blade of the shovel in the ground next to the headstone until we heard the clink of metal on metal.

"Brilliant," he said, digging the shovel into the ground.

The cemetery was dark and there was a chill in the air. The hair on the back of my neck tingled. It was pretty creepy.

Wills held up the box.

Crack. Oh my God—a bullet whizzed past my head.

Wills held onto the box and my hand as we sprinted through the cemetery.

Wills grabbed me and pulled me into his embrace. He kissed me with so much passion I almost passed out.

"Charlie," he said, "William was killed by a sniper at your grave. I think that was a ghost, not a gunman."

Was it the kiss or the comment that left me speechless?

"Let's go back to the flat. I want to be alone with you when we open the box," he said.

I smiled and nodded as I sent a text to Ryan and Katie, informing them of our plans.

We found the bus stop and took a bus back to our apartment.

The trip took about ten minutes, but it felt like ten hours. When we arrived at the apartment, we rushed through the lobby and up the stairs.

I opened my door. We walked inside and sat down on the futon. Wills placed the metal memory box between us.

"The custom trench-art ring, letter opener, letters, and bracelet are in the box. Also, the package from the Talbot House; it remains unopened, inside the box," Wills said quietly.

I opened the box and pulled out the items, one at a time...the letters, the letter opener, the bracelet, and finally the ring. Wills picked up the ring and slid it on my finger. Then he kissed the knuckle below the ring.

He looked up as I looked down and we kissed. It was a different kind of kiss...sweet and passionate; full of longing and hope. It was a kiss shared with Wills and a kiss shared with William. It seemed the placement of the ring on my finger blurred the lines between past and present...real and unreal...Wills and William...Charlie and Charlotte.

"Does this mean we're married?" Wills asked against my lips.

I knew where he was going with this. *Boys will be boys*, I thought.

I gently pulled back and looked into his eyes. He looked happy and relaxed and in love with me—Charlie.

I carefully examined the ring on my finger. "I don't think Charlotte would've wanted a different ring," I declared. "This is amazing and special, and she received it when she spoke her vows."

"Well," Wills said, "let's take a look at what's inside the box known as the Talbot House treasure. After all, someone was willing to kill for the bloody box."

"That was surreal," I said. "Some guy holding us at gunpoint and telling us to dig. He sounded like a pirate from a bad movie. I know we were in a life-threatening situation, but I kept waiting for him to say 'argh' or something."

Wills laughed really hard. "Bloody hell—I thought the same thing."

"I love you so much," I said. "Argh, matie, let's open up this here box, and see what booty lies inside."

"Charlie," Wills said, still laughing, "that's a horrible imitation of a pirate. It was bloody awful."

"Okay," I said, "no more pirate accent." I tried to catch my breath, but it was too funny. "Really, I'm good—just don't look at me."

I handed Wills the box his mother—or rather William's mother, had sent him. I patiently waited for the big reveal.

"Charlie, I have a thought," Wills said solemnly, "let's not open the box until we become officially engaged to each other in this lifetime."

I looked into his gray eyes and listened.

"I see the ring on your finger as our promise to each other; the promise of a brilliant future…a future where we're husband and wife. I love you, Charlie; I'll love you forever. If I open this box, I'll ask you to marry me, and I'm afraid you won't say yes."

"William, I want to say yes," I told him. "I love you, too. If being engaged in high school wasn't unusual, I'd say yes if you asked me to marry you. Not only would I say yes, but I'd insist we get married right after I graduate. But just saying that—'get married after graduation,' is—well, weird."

I looked up at Wills, trying to gauge his response.

"So, what you're saying is if…and that's a big if…you can get past the timing, you'd say yes to a marriage proposal from me?" Wills asked.

I carefully examined his handsome face, a face that haunted my dreams and was my living fantasy. I slowly nodded in the affirmative.

"Yes," I whispered, as I reached up with both hands to draw him down for a kiss—a kiss confirming our love and commitment.

Wills lifted my hand and examined the ring. "I promise I'll always love you and wait for you to accept my formal proposal of marriage."

"Wait," I said, jumping up and grabbing my jewelry box. I pulled out my St. Louis Cardinals twist team necklace. "Now, don't laugh—when Charlotte and William got married, Charlotte didn't give William a ring. Anyway, I want you to promise to wear this," I held up the twist team necklace, "as an acceptance of my promise to you."

"What exactly am I promising to wear?" Wills asked with trepidation as he regarded the necklace.

"This is not only an incredibly cool promise necklace, it's a souvenir for you from the States—an authentic St. Louis Cardinals twist team necklace."

Wills gave me a blank stare. "They're a baseball team; you know—the great American pastime. When you come to the States, I'll take you to a game."

Wills looked startled.

"Well, we certainly can't get married if you never meet my parents," I pointed out.

"Ace," Wills said with a smile.

I sat back down. "Put your head down, so I can put your promise necklace—now don't think of it as a noose—around your neck," I said with a grin.

"I, Charlotte Susan Longley, promise to love you always. And I promise, when the time is right, I will accept your proposal of marriage."

Wills pulled me into his arms and we kissed.

"We aren't going to open the box?" I asked.

"No," Wills said leaning down to kiss me again.

A while later we came up for air.

Wills looked into my eyes, holding my face between his hands. "I love you, Charlotte Susan Longley."

Soul Mates ~ Liz Morrison

"For always, in all ways," I replied.

WILLIAM

I'd been staring at the wall for a while, contemplating our separation. Charlie was returning to the States in less than forty-eight hours.

How will I manage to live without her for the next seven months? I wondered.

I realized I was afraid to let her go. The last time I left Charlotte, she'd died from influenza; what if something happened to Charlie when we were apart?

The past week had been bloody crazy. Ms. Booth, Charlie's teacher, was in Rouen. *I should be with Charlie 24-7, and now we have a chaperone—bloody brilliant,* I grumbled inwardly. *Charlie's been busy getting ready for today. Odd...I've seen her less, but I know her more.*

Charlie's event was going to be ace.

I pulled my clothing from the garment bag, thinking, *I can't believe Charlie convinced me to wear a World War I uniform.*

Chapter Thirty-One

CHARLIE

"Charlie," Madame Chevalier called, "we'll open the doors at exactly eleven a.m. This is very exciting. Everything is perfect—oui?"

I slowly walked around the exhibit, examining each item in the showcases. The exhibit's theme was *Remembrance: Love, Loss, and Legacy,* and it was dedicated to soldiers, civilians, and medical personnel from around the world who lived, served, and made the ultimate sacrifice in Rouen during World War I.

The exhibit consisted of a series of letters from World War I, illustrating three different perspectives: soldier to his family, soldier to his sweetheart, and sweetheart to the soldier. The exhibit also included information linking people from the present to the events in the past, and to a variety of locations in and around the city of Rouen.

One entire display case was dedicated to the history of Dr. Rawlings from Washington University Base Hospital Twenty-One and his French family. All of the items in the display case were on loan to the exhibit from Christophe's family. The majority of the exhibit, however, was dedicated to First Lieutenant William Harrington and his sweetheart and bride, Charlotte Alexandria Rawlings.

The exhibit had interactive parts, allowing the visitors to hear several of the letters being read. It was wicked awesome, because Wills reads the soldier's letters and I read the letters from Charlotte. I recorded William's mom reading the letters from the family of William Harrington.

Soul Mates ~ Liz Morrison

I glanced at a picture of Charlotte. It really was quite uncanny how much we looked alike, especially today.

Reviewing the exhibit, I thought aloud, "Wow, this is amazing. I can't believe I was part of this really incredible exhibit."

The exhibit was truly a labor of love, I thought. *That sounds corny, but I'm feeling like that today.* Maybe this exhibit commemorating World War I—honoring the memories of those who sacrificed so much—was one reason Charlotte and William had been reunited. *Mostly, I think we were reunited because...well...we're soul mates,* I told myself. *That's corny, too, but I believe it. I really believe it.*

"Charlie," Madame Chevalier said, "it's perfect. And you, Charlie, you look perfect—so much like the Charlotte in the photograph. I cannot wait to see your friends. Especially your William—he's going to look so elegant."

Madame moved quickly from one topic to the next. "The collection is quite remarkable," she observed. "Not only will visitors be interested in the exhibit, they'll also want to visit all of the sites associated with the story. *C'est magnifique.*"

In a few minutes, it would be 11:00 a.m. We'd open the exhibit at the eleventh hour, on the eleventh day of the eleventh month. November 11th at 11:00 AM; the month, day and time the hostilities of World War I came to an end. It really was perfect.

"I'm afraid to look outside," I whispered to Madame Chevalier, though I'm not sure why I whispered.

I heard laughter and knew Wills and the rest of the group had arrived.

Suddenly I was so nervous. *What if my friends hate it?* I worried. *What if they hate their costumes? What if no one, except for my very small group of friends, comes to the exhibit?*

Katie, Holly, and Libby entered at the front of the group.

"Oh my God, you girls look amazing," I exclaimed as I admired them in their World War I outfits. Katie was wearing an Australian nurse's uniform, while Holly wore the uniform of a BEF nurse. Libby was a Hello Girl—one of the telephone operators of the war effort.

Katie looked at me and said, "You're rocking it, sister. I don't know what else to say, but you own that uniform!"

Katie continued, "Ryan, Wills, Mike, and Andrew look amazing, and it was brilliant to have Peter and Philippe dress as French soldiers."

I took a deep breath. It was time to see Wills.

I turned toward the voices in the hallway. Andrew, Ryan, and Mike looked great in their uniforms. Andrew represented the Royal Air Force, Mike the American Expeditionary Force, and Ryan the Australian Imperial Forces.

My eyes locked with William's. I froze; I was frozen in time. My heart may have stopped beating.

Wills crumpled and fell to the ground. My stupor was over as I raced across the floor to his side.

I placed my fingers on his pulse. The electric shot was like the first time we touched—almost painful. His pulse was strong, but his breathing was shallow.

"Wills...William," I said, "can you hear me? Come on, William, open your eyes."

Wills' head was cradled in my lap. He was probably out for a few seconds, or a minute at the most, but it felt like an eternity.

He opened his eyes and he looked at me. "Are you an angel?" he asked. Then he smiled and said, "I know who you are...you're my angel." Pulling my head down, he kissed me soundly on the lips.

Ryan and Andrew were laughing, "You fainted...you bloody well fainted. I've never seen the likes of it; a bloke fainting at the sight of a girl."

Wills stood up, pulling me with him. "Charlie has that effect on me," he said. "She sends electric shocks up my arm and causes me to faint with a glance. Actually, seeing Charlie was like seeing a ghost." He was laughing as he said it. I guess he didn't care.

He whispered in my ear, "I'm so glad you're not a ghost or an angel, but a real girl—my girl."

I grabbed William by the hand and tugged him toward the display case. I pointed to the picture of William and Charlotte. It was really quite amazing—unbelievable, but amazing.

"*Allez les enfants, il est temps de commencer notre ceremonie.* Let's get going," Madame exclaimed. "The big event is about to begin."

Madame opened the door and stepped to the podium positioned near the front door. I couldn't believe it. There were over a hundred people waiting to enter the Office de tourisme de la communaute de Rouen.

The Office de tourisme was too small to accommodate all of the people waiting to see the exhibit. Wills and I walked around the waiting spectators, answering questions and sharing stories. The audience thought we'd done a ton of research, but we just told tales from our past lives.

It was fun being Charlotte and William from 1918 for the day, knowing we'd be Charlie and Wills tomorrow.

We found Chloe and Christophe in the crowd with their entire family.

"Chloe, the display is amazing," I said, giving her a hug. "I'm so glad you're here. You know," I continued, "if I wasn't a horrible scooter driver, we never would've met. It makes you believe in fate, doesn't it?"

Christophe added, "*Ce qui semble à nous comme amer des épreuves est souvent des bénédictions dans le déguisement.*"

"What seems to us as bitter trials are often blessings in disguise," Wills translated the quote. "That's quite appropriate."

"Is this the rest of the family?" Wills asked.

"Oui," Christophe replied. "I tried to explain you're our family by marriage. It was rather lost in translation," he finished with a laugh.

Family! I pulled out my cell and called my mom and dad. "Hey, it's Charlie! I'm standing here with Wills among hundreds—really hundreds—of people. I wish you guys were here. Anyway, I love you and I'll see you on Saturday."

I looked at Wills and he looked at me. Our time together was so short. *I can't imagine leaving tomorrow,* I thought. It made me sick.

"Sorry about that," I said to Chloe and Christophe. "I forgot to call my parents. Anyway, I hope I'll see you again. It was truly a blessing to meet you." I hugged them before walking away.

"Love," Wills said, clasping my hand. We paused for a moment, imprinting the memory of the electricity in our minds. "It'll work out," he said. "We'll make it work. For now, let's enjoy the moment."

I nodded in agreement.

"By the way," Wills said, "I like you in the nurses' uniform, but I'd prefer to see you in my uniform jumper. Now that brings back memories that would bring a lesser man to his knees."

Pretending to ignore William's comment, I glanced around the crowd, looking for Wills' parents. He didn't know they were coming; I was so excited about the surprise.

I recognized Wills' mom from our Skype conversations and waved. She looked startled, and then smiled broadly.

Grabbing Wills' hand, I steered him toward his parents. "Did I tell you how incredibly hot you are in that uniform?" I asked with a smile. *That should distract him for a few minutes*, I thought.

"Bloody hell, Charlie," he replied, "you really shouldn't tease me; my ability to resist you has reached an all-time low."

Wills suddenly pulled me into his arms, replicating the photograph of a kiss a sailor planted on a nurse in Times Square on V-J Day. Wrong war, but the crowd went wild.

I pushed away from Wills, laughing at the spectacle we made, until I glanced up into the eyes of Wills' mom and dad. *Great.*

"Hey, Wills," I said hesitantly. "I have a little surprise for you."

WILLIAM

Charlie had a little surprise for me.

I should kiss her again, I told myself. *And she could definitely use another kiss—to hell with the audience. Besides, they loved it.*

I leaned down, closing the space between my lips and Charlie's.

"William," my mum's voice halted me in mid-maneuver.

Charlie gave me a look I believe I could correctly interpret as, "I am going to kill you."

"Mum, Dad," I said, as I tugged Charlie forward, "I'd like to present Charlie."

"Good thing it's Charlie, and not some other bird, or you truly would be the reprobate Andrew painted you to be," Dad said with a smile, extending his hand to Charlie.

"It's really nice to meet you in person, Mr. Harrington," Charlie replied. "I try to keep William in check, but sometimes he gets a little crazy."

My mum and dad exchanged a look. For eighteen years I hadn't done anything even slightly resembling crazy.

"It's really great to meet you, Mrs. Harrington," Charlie said, extending her hand to my mum. "Your voice was perfect for our letter-reader. It's a huge hit. Come on—we'll sneak you guys in through the back door. I'm so glad you could come."

"You look good, son," my dad said, examining me closely, "and it's not just the dapper uniform. You look happy."

"Dad," I said throwing my arm around his shoulder as we walked to the rear entrance, "I love this girl. Now, tomorrow I may not be so happy, but today I'm probably the happiest guy on the planet."

"Tomorrow?" my dad asked.

"Charlie goes back to the States tomorrow," I replied, trying to keep my voice neutral. "I want to ask her to marry me...I reckon I rather did ask her to marry me, but she's in her last year of school. She won't say yes right now, but she will say yes in a few months. I know everyone will say we're too young, but we aren't. I've been waiting for her my entire life. Hell, I've been waiting for her for a hundred years. I suppose I can wait a few more months."

My dad didn't respond. He walked with me toward the back entrance Office de tourisme in contemplative silence.

Charlie and my mum waited at the door. "Come on, Wills," Charlie said, "let's get your mom and dad inside. You can show them the items we used from the satchel. Also, they need to hear the letter readings; the technology is so cool."

"Charlie," my mum said, "that's quite an unusual ring. I believe it's the Harrington family crest." She lifted Charlie's hand and studied the ring carefully.

"Mum, that is the Harrington family crest. William Harrington had it made in the trenches as a wedding ring for Charlotte."

I'll let her ponder that bit of news, I decided.

"Come on—I'll show you the exhibit," I said. "Charlie needs to accept accolades for all of her hard work." Then, for good measure, I kissed Charlie again.

"Charlie...William," Madame Chevalier called, "many people would like to take your photograph by the exhibit. What a magnificent success—so beautiful to remember the soldiers, and also to bring visitors to Rouen."

"*Bonjour*," Madame continued, turning to my mum and dad. I knew she'd keep them entertained.

Charlie and I mingled. We had numerous pictures taken of us in our uniforms. Everyone remarked on our incredible resemblance to the nurse and the soldier in the photographs. Katie, Ryan, Mike, Libby, Andrew, Holly, Peter, and Philippe seemed to be having a good time.

Soul Mates ~ Liz Morrison

Ms. Booth arrived at some point during the day. She was quite impressed with Charlie's work. I hoped she was impressed enough to leave Charlie alone tonight—our last night in Rouen.

The time passed quickly. At 5:00 p.m., Madame Chevalier escorted the last guest to the door.

My mum and dad invited everyone out to dinner, including Madame Chevalier and Ms. Booth. If the success of the event wasn't enough to soften up Ms. Booth, maybe dinner with my parents would do the trick.

Dinner was quite a celebration. We celebrated the success of the exhibit, the success of all of our endeavors in Rouen, and our continued success.

Charlie was exceptionally quiet.

I held her hand in mine. The warm current was reassuring. The dread I'd successfully avoided all day caused my stomach to roil.

Only twelve more hours together, I thought. *I don't want to spend them with a group.*

"Mum and Dad," I said, "thank you for the incredible dinner. I reckon I'll see you tomorrow evening. Andrew and I plan to accompany Charlie and her friends to the airport. We should be back by eight p.m."

I pulled Charlie to her feet, tugging her around the table so I could give my mum a kiss on the cheek. Much to my surprise, my mum stood up and hugged Charlie, which was definitely out of character.

"Curfew is midnight," Ms. Booth declared. "We'll be leaving the hotel at eight a.m. to catch the train to the airport. Good night."

Charlie and I said goodbye all around and left the restaurant to walk back to the flat. "Wills," Charlie asked as we walked through the streets of Rouen, "how do you know you love me for who I am today, and not just because you loved me in the past?"

That was an interesting question. "Honestly," I replied, "I can't tell the difference. I just love you—whoever you are, whenever you are—you."

Charlie rested her head on my shoulder. "That's how I feel about you. I'm glad I found you."

We were almost to the flat. "Charlie, let's stop by my room," I said.

She raised an eyebrow.

I grinned. "I have a few gifts for you. I hope they'll help you remember me when you go home…alone…without me. Can't stand it," I mumbled. "I can't stand it. I don't want you to go."

Bloody idiot, I chided myself, I wasn't going to say any of that, but I wanted her to know this—her leaving—was killing me.

Charlie didn't speak as we walked into our building and up the three flights of stairs to my flat. At the top of the steps, she bowed her head and pressed her forehead into my chest.

"Wills, I have no idea how I'm going to get on the plane tomorrow," she said.

I didn't respond, because I didn't have an answer.

Opening the door to my flat, I followed Charlie inside. "Take a seat on the futon and close your eyes," I said.

"Wills," Charlie said as she glanced around my flat. "It's so clean in here. Were you expecting company?"

"I was hoping for company," I said with a wink. "Now sit down, woman."

"Yes, sir," Charlie replied. "I think you were really getting into the officer-boss-you-around role today. It was sad leaving the uniforms at the Office de tourisme."

"The other girls didn't like the uniform much; I thought it was quite the thing, you know." Charlie was remembering Charlotte's memory. I was getting used to it.

"Close your eyes and hold out your hands," I commanded.

Charlie obediently closed her eyes and held out her hands.

Soul Mates ~ Liz Morrison

"Keep them closed," I said in a menacing voice, but Charlie smiled. I guess it wasn't menacing. I carefully arranged my gifts on her outstretched hands.

"Now open your eyes," I said.

Charlie looked at her stack of goodies. "You're too much," she said. "So, tell me about all of these gifts."

"Okay, these are serious, life-changing gifts," I said, switching to my best *Golden Balls* game-show-host voice. "Your first gift is the cute and cuddly Buster the teddy bear, who is conveniently wearing the traditional Eton school dress—tail coat, trousers, waistcoat and shirt. Buster is your new bed mate."

"To continue the bear theme, your second gift is the ever-popular key ring bear, which happens to be sporting a fashionable white shirt with the college coat of arms. Next, we have the pewter schoolboy-wearing-school-dress pencil topper, with an unsharpened pencil included; this pewter schoolboy is a must-have for all American schoolgirls.

"Finally—and I'm sure this will be your favorite—a classic rugby shirt, used for playing field games."

Charlie dropped all of my gifts on the floor and threw herself into my arms. Then she kissed me.

In a flash, I had her pinned against the wall. "Charlie," I whispered, "you need to set a limit."

She wasn't listening. She continued to kiss my neck, my throat, pretty much any exposed piece of skin. I was losing control of the situation quickly.

I shifted positions so I could capture her lips with mine; I'm not sure what I was thinking.

"Charlie, listen to me, please," I said, with a little more conviction.

She looked up at me. Her eyes were midnight blue. "Bloody hell," I whispered. "Charlie, you need to set some boundaries for me; I promise I won't cross them."

"Boundaries?" she asked, in a confused voice.

"Boundaries...limits...I need to know when to stop, or we aren't going to stop," I said, more to the top of her head then to her face.

"Oh," she said into my shoulder. "Boundaries...good idea...right." She didn't sound like she liked the idea of limits. *A guy could hope.*

She peeked up at me and said, "Okay, nothing below the waist."

I placed my chin on top of her head. "All right, then."

Charlie pushed on my chest. "First, thank you for my presents," she kissed me on the cheek. "Now, take off your shirt, schoolboy."

Chapter Thirty-Two

CHARLIE

Wills was sound asleep on my futon. We left his room around 11:30 so I could finish packing and be back in my room if Ms. Booth decided to do a room check at midnight. I was going to hide Wills in the closet. Seemed like a good plan, but there was no room check, so hiding wasn't necessary.

The gifts from Wills were the last thing I put in my suitcase. I decided to wear his rugby shirt with leggings and my Uggs. I put my hair in a lose side braid so I wouldn't get a ponytail headache. I stuck Buster in my backpack; he could also be my seat mate for the plane ride.

I walked to the futon and pulled out my phone to take a picture of Wills. I had hundreds of pictures, but this one could be my phone background. I could feel tears prickling in my eyes.

It's November, I told myself. *We'll be together in June. That's seven months away; one of us could die tomorrow.*

I need to stop thinking morbid thoughts, I resolved. *People don't die of the flu anymore. Well, actually, they occasionally do. Wills isn't a soldier.*

I suddenly realized something—I wasn't worried about things we could control, like our feelings for each other, which was a good thing.

He's so handsome, I thought as I leaned down to kiss him awake.

In a flash, he had me underneath him, engaged in an incredibly hot kiss.

He pushed himself up on his elbows and gazed into my face. "I love you, Charlie, and I'll love you always, in all ways." He kissed me again.

Wills made a kind of growling noise in his throat, "You're going to kill me, love. I think I've said that every morning for the last several months."

He rolled off me and stood up. He looked down and examined my outfit.

"Stand up," he commanded. I slowly stood up and gave him a questioning look.

"I have died and gone to heaven," Wills said. "Looking at you in my jersey is the sexiest thing I've ever seen..." he paused, "...in this life. Well, actually, it's number two; last night, no shirt—that was definitely number one."

"Come on," I said. "At this rate, we won't leave this room."

Wills gave me a look. "and...?"

WILLIAM

I sent a text to my mum, reminding her I was taking the train with Charlie and her friends to the airport. Charlie's flight would depart for the States at 4:10 p.m.

My stomach was in knots. I knew we shouldn't be apart; we'd been apart for a century.

I don't know how to convince Charlie to stay, I fretted. *I know she needs to graduate from high school, and I can't come up with an idea for her to earn her diploma in England.*

The airport was less than thirty minutes away. I kissed Charlie on the head. She looked up and smiled at me. I looked down at our entwined hands. I lifted the hand with the ring and kissed it.

"I have Buster bear in my backpack...that's a lot of *b*'s," Charlie said. "Wills, if I talk, I'll cry, so I'm not talking. I love you. But I'm not talking." Tears trickled out of the corners of her eyes.

"I love you, too," I whispered.

The train stopped at Charles De Gaulle airport. Everyone grabbed their luggage and backpacks and left the train.

"Students," Ms. Booth called everyone to attention, "we're going to the ticket counter to check bags, and then we'll go through security. Charlie, your friends can accompany you to security. We have two hours till departure time." She glanced at her watch. "We're doing great on time."

Ms. Booth spoke too soon. The line to check bags took an hour. I walked Charlie to security, holding her hand tightly. My stomach was cramped. This was really happening.

Charlie was the last one in the queue, but the security agents were very efficient and they moved the group through quickly.

I pulled Charlie into my arms and kissed her. For me, it was a kiss I would not forget; I wanted it to be a kiss she'd remember.

Charlie was trying not to cry. I could feel tears welling up in my eyes, too. I gently cupped her chin and looked into her eyes. "I'll love you always."

"In all ways," she replied. "Okay, then, I'll Skype you tomorrow night. We'll figure out the time zone stuff," Charlie said.

The security guard had the get-your-arse-moving look; I pulled her into my arms and kissed her again.

Tears rolled down Charlie's cheeks as she handed her passport to security. She walked backward through the line. She mouthed, "I love you" and made a heart with her fingers and pointed at me.

That was it.

I leaned against a wall and tried to pull myself together.

"That's it?" Andrew said. "You're just going to let her get on a plane and fly home? I thought you were a better man."

"She can't stay here," I said. "She needs to graduate from high school. I get it; I just don't want her to go."

"For someone who's allegedly smart, you're pretty thick," he retorted. "Charlie can't stay here, but you can go to the States. Seriously; it's your gap year. You can go save the planet in St. Louis, Missouri—wherever the bloody hell that is."

"You're bloody brilliant," I replied. "I need to purchase a plane ticket." I looked in my phone. "Let's see…Air France Flight 8984."

We ran to the ticket counter. The queue was still an hour long. I joined the queue and Andrew tried to finagle an opportunity for me to move forward. I texted my mum and dad, telling them I was going to the States.

Andrew waved for me to join him. Andrew explained to the agent my one true love was on Air France Flight 8984, heading for St. Louis via Atlanta, Georgia.

The ticket agent couldn't resist a good love story. *If he'd known the entire story, he would have put me in first class,* I told myself.

As the agent processed my ticket, he asked me the name of my girl.

"Charlotte Longley," I replied.

"Let's see…you have your kit, your passport, your phone, and your credit cards. That's about all you need for now," Andrew said.

We sprinted toward security; the flight was departing in thirty-five minutes.

"Thanks," I said to Andrew.

"No trouble," Andrew replied. "I'm really glad you found her, you know. I'm also glad you told me about the whole reincarnation bit. It's going to work out. The only request I have is that I can be your best man. Oh, and that Charlie wears the Eton College jersey to every event we attend—she's smokin'."

I shook my head at Andrew. "Smokin'? When did you start talking like an American?"

I handed my passport to the security agent. "I'll ring you from the States," I said to Andrew, giving him a final wave.

I didn't look back; I was heading to my future.

The queue was long and slow. *I can't miss this flight*, I told myself.

CHARLIE

Boarding the plane to leave Paris was so different from boarding the plane taking us to Paris. When I'd walked onto the plane six months ago, my stomach had had butterflies of nervous excitement. Now, as I walked on the plane, my stomach had butterflies, but it wasn't nervous excitement—it was dread.

Leaving William is like leaving a piece of me, I thought.

"How are you doing?" Katie asked as we settled into our seats.

"Not good," I replied.

"You're going to see him again," Ryan said as he sat down in the aisle seat, "as much as I wish you weren't going to see him again."

"Ladies and gentlemen, this is your captain speaking. We have several passengers at security. They should be on board in the next few minutes. The winds are good tonight, so even with a delay, we should arrive a few minutes early."

I closed my eyes and remembered the last six months. All my thoughts were of Wills. *Oh my God, I'm leaving him in Rouen while I go back to the States? I don't think so. What's a GED, if not a viable alternative to high school diploma?*

I pulled out my cell to text my mom. What was I going to say? "Don't freak out, but I'm staying in France." Probably better to wait and call her when I figured this out. Instead, I texted Wills:

<u>Don't leave airport. I love you.</u>

"Ryan…Katie," I said softly, "you're my best friends. I love you guys, but I'm not going home with you. Maybe high school diplomas aren't that important in Europe."

Standing up, I pulled my backpack from the overhead. "Come on, Buster," I whispered to the bear in my backpack, "we're out of here."

"Charlie," Ms. Booth called out, "what are you doing?"

WILLIAM

The airport was huge. I wasn't going to get to the flight on time. I was going to be stuck in Paris while Charlie went back to the States; that wasn't going to happen.

"Final boarding call for Air France Flight 8984, non-stop service from Paris to Atlanta, Georgia. All passengers with tickets should be on board at this time."

I sprinted toward my gate; it was like an airport scene in a movie.

There are two ways for this to end; I thought. *I'm going to just miss her plane, or I'm going to arrive just in time.*

I could see the gate. *Please don't close the door*, I prayed, hoping for a miracle.

I jumped over an aisle of chairs and sprinted to the ticket counter to hand the agent my ticket. The door to the jetway was closed. The Air France Agent was not at the boarding door.

I dropped my ticket on the counter. *No, no, no!*

The door opened and two ticket agents walked into the terminal. The agent glanced my way and strolled to the counter. "Bonjour. Comment puis-je vous aider?"

I handed the agent my ticket.

The agent glanced at the clock and the scheduled departure time, and then looked back at me. My future was in his hands. What could I say to convince him to open the door?

"Sir," I said, "I met the girl of my dreams in France. She's on that plane. Please, can you help me?"

The agent didn't know I meant it literally; Charlie was and will always be the girl of my dreams.

CHARLIE

"Attention, ladies and gentlemen," the flight attendant's voice came over the PA system, "would Atlanta passenger Charlie Longley please report to the boarding door in the main cabin? Once again, passenger Charlie Longley, please report to the boarding door."

Ms. Booth stood up, intending to follow me to the boarding door. I glanced at Ryan and Katie and shrugged my shoulders. I tried to squeeze around people who were trying to find their seats.

I glanced over my shoulder; Ryan was standing in the middle of the aisle, blocking Ms. Booth from moving forward. I shook my head and smiled.

"Oh, I'm so sorry, Ms. Booth," Ryan said, "I need to get my headset out of my backpack; it's so rude to do that during the flight, don't you think?"

Finally I made it to the boarding door. *I don't know what the flight attendant wants, but it doesn't matter,* I thought. *I'm getting off the plane and finding Wills. I hope he received my text and is waiting.*

"*Bonjour,*" I said to the flight attendant, "I'm Charlie Longley."

She gave me a brilliant smile. *Odd,* I thought. *I'm not sure why she's so happy to see me.*

"This way, please, mademoiselle," she said.

The flight attendant directed me to a staircase. I gave her a questioning look—stairs on an airplane?

"It's a Boeing 747, it has an upper deck."

Okay, I didn't want to go to an upper deck; I wanted to go out the main door.

The flight attendant followed me. I reached the top of the short flight of stairs...nothing too exciting; just more seats, though the section was pretty empty.

"Miss," I said, "I'm sorry, but I need to get off the plane."

She laughed. "Oh, I think you'll want to stay." She knocked on the cockpit door. I'll admit, I was pretty curious.

The door opened. "Oh my God—William!" I cried.

Throwing myself at him, I said, "I was trying to get off the plane. I can't leave you! I love you. GEDs are a good thing." I sobbed into his shirt. "You're here, you're here!"

"Charlie," Wills said, "Look at me, love."

I looked into his eyes. I smiled stupidly, still crying.

He dropped down on his knee, clasped my hand, and said, "Charlie, will you make me the happiest man alive and consent to be my wife?"

I took a deep breath. We were young; it was complicated; we were going to have to tell my parents.

Hell, I thought, *I'm going to play soccer my senior year with an engagement ring.*

I knew, beyond a doubt, Wills and I were meant to be together forever, and forever might as well start right now.

I threw my arms around his neck, nearly flattening him. "Yes," I said. "Yes, William, I'd be honored to be your wife."

Wills stood up, still holding my hand in his. Leaning down, he kissed me.

"Ladies and gentlemen, this is your captain speaking. Please join me in congratulating William Harrington and Charlotte Longley on their engagement."

The airplane erupted in applause. I giggled. They were probably cheering because we were finally going to take off.

I'll bet Ms. Booth had a heart attack, I mused. *This is going to be hard to explain to our principal. Oh well—not my problem.*

"I have a gift for you," he said with flourish.

Wills took my hand and guided me to a row of empty seats. "We have seats together up here," Wills explained. "The agent who let me on the plane moved us together."

"Don't smash Buster," I said as Wills put my backpack in the overhead.

Wills sat down and secured his seatbelt. "It seems I have a history of proposing to you in very public settings."

"Like the June celebration in Rouen? Now that was quite the public declaration of your intentions," I agreed.

He took my hand—still the electric current. "Here's your gift."

The gift was wrapped in brown packing paper and addressed to Lieutenant William Harrington, British Expeditionary Force, Talbot House, Poperinge.

I carefully unwrapped the package. I glanced at Wills, who gave me a look. "Hey, the wrapping is historic; I think we should save it," I said.

I opened the box, glancing again at Wills, watching him watching me carefully open the lid.

I removed the packing paper and found three black-velvet boxes. I opened the first box and looked in, "Oh my God," I whispered.

Wills looked at the open case and then at me. "It doesn't compare with your eyes," he said with conviction, and then kissed me.

Epilogue

When we landed in the States, I sent a text to my mom.

<u>Hey Mom! I'm bringing home a souvenir. His name is William.</u>

About the Author

Liz Morrison is the author of *Soul Mates*, the first book in the *It's You Again* series, a compilation of contemporary/historical young adult fiction featuring "R and R"—Romance and Reincarnation. Morrison's work is classified as young adult fiction; however, her novels have universal appeal.

In addition to being a writer, she is a National Board Certified Social Studies Teacher, a NCSS National History Teacher of the Year, and a former flight attendant for Trans World Airlines. Morrison combines her passion for history and her world travels to create memorable characters and settings, both past and present. Her work also pays tribute to the sacrifices of the men and women in the armed forces by using military conflicts as part of the historical context.

Liz earned her B.S. from the University of Iowa and her M.A.Ed. from the University of Missouri-Columbia. She lives in St. Louis, Missouri with her husband and four children. She enjoys family vacations to beaches and historic sites, her career in education, and reading romance novels.

CPSIA information can be obtained
at www.ICGtesting.com
Printed in the USA
LVOW12s1708290916
506736LV00001B/273/P